THE PRESIDENT'S SON

THE PRESIDENT'S SON

a novel by Krandall Kraus

ALYSON PUBLICATIONS
LOS ANGELES

Copyright © 1986 by Krandall Kraus. All rights reserved.
Cover design by B. Zinda.
Model photo by Martin Ryter.
White House photo © 1996 PhotoDisc Inc.

Manufactured in the United States of America.
Printed on acid-free paper.

Published by Alyson Publications Inc.,
P.O. Box 4371, Los Angeles, California 90078.
First published in 1986 by Alyson Publications Inc.
as a trade paperback original.

First Alyson edition: May 1986
First AlyCat edition: March 1995
Second Alyson edition: March 1996

5 4 3 2 1

ISBN 1-55583-603-8
(previously published with ISBN 0-932870-83-X)

For Andy

THE PRESIDENT'S SON

Somewhere in the south of France

"Would you fuck with Parker?" Terry asked D.J.

They were lying head to head on a banquette in the hotel sauna. D.J. turned and opened one eye. It had been a long day at rehearsals and the dry heat was intoxicating, relaxing every muscle.

"I've never thought about it," D.J. said drowsily, matter-of-factly. "I have you."

"It could happen. A lot of people fall in love with their bodyguards." His voice was alert, perky, as usual. Almost annoyingly so for D.J., who was trying to unwind.

"This is a little different," D.J. said.

"Movie stars do it all the time," Terry persisted.

"You've been reading those cheap tabloids again. I'm going to buy you a book." D.J. was fully awake now.

"I have a book," Terry said. "Look at that black country-western singer. You know ... what's-her-name, who used to do disco when disco was popular."

"Oh, I know who you mean. Uh ... uh ... I can't think of her name," D.J. said, now sucked into the conversation. "The one who started out by breathing heavily on all her records."

"Yeah. She married her bodyguard. At least she fucked with him," Terry argued.

"He wasn't her bodyguard; he was a member of her band."

"Same thing."

"It's not the same thing and this is ridiculous. Would you fuck with Rodney?" D.J. teased.

"Not even at gunpoint," Terry said.

"Oh, come on. He's gorgeous."

"Rodney's nuts. Do you know what those little yellow pills are that he pops?" Terry asked.

"They're for high blood pressure. Parker told me."

"Bullshit."

"Parker wouldn't lie."

"Then Parker doesn't know. That's Thorazine and it's not for high blood pressure. It's for high psycho pressure."

"Are you sure?"

"Penny Cash back in Syosset used to take them. She was fine unless she hadn't taken her 'zines, and then watch out!"

"Well, I guess you ought to know."

"What does that mean?" Terry asked defensively.

"I mean you know all those drugs, you should know. That's all I meant."

"I hope so. You know I haven't done any drugs at all since we've been here. I've been completely straight except for the pot we smoke now and then. You know that, don't you?"

"I know, I didn't mean anything," D.J. said. "Come on, let's get cleaned up for dinner. I'm famished."

As they stood to leave, the door opened. Parker's six-foot-three-inch, 200-pound frame of solid muscle filled the doorway and the look on his face told them something was wrong.

"We're coming, settle down," Terry said.

"There's a call for you, D.J. I told them you were on your way back to the room. They're transferring it there."

"A call?" Terry's stomach knotted. There was only one person who knew where they were, only one person who would call them, and only one reason he would call while they were on a five-day tour with the repertory company. Terry looked at D.J. and couldn't hide the panic.

"We're coming," D.J. said to Parker. "It's okay, baby. Don't jump to conclusions."

They rode the elevator to the top floor in silence, Terry clutching the corner of D.J.'s towel all the way.

The White House

The huge helicopter touched its round black feet softly onto the south lawn and the rotor abruptly slowed, then cut to a complete halt with a loud pop. The crowd on the grass began to stir now as the door of the aircraft opened. President Donald Marshall emerged, smiling and waving to the applauding group. He was wearing his customary Stetson and carrying a large leather briefcase.

Unlike his return from the first trip to Camp David three years ago, when he wore blue jeans and his favorite plaid cowboy shirt, he stood now in Brooks Brothers khakis and a blue, button-down, oxford shirt. A black fountain pen bearing the presidential seal, which his wife, Claudia, had given him on Inauguration Day, was clipped to the shirt pocket.

"One pen in your pocket at a time, Donald," she had said, retrieving a second pen and a mechanical pencil from his shirt pocket as he was readying for a television debate one night in Flagstaff. That was when he was running for his first term as governor. "Only salesmen carry more than one pen in their pockets — and no one trusts a salesman."

She had kissed him on the cheek, picked a long blonde hair, which she assumed was her own, from the left shoulder of his jacket, and sent him onstage, where he trounced his opponent and gained six percentage points in the polls overnight. The press credited his victory to that single debate.

The First Lady watched as her husband made his way toward her. The March air was brisk, unlike the Arizona climate she was accustomed to, and she wore a pink cashmere sweater over her white silk blouse. She stood at the head of the small line that would greet the President and turned to make a casual, last-minute inspection of the rest of her party. She smiled at her best friend, Fran Altman, then reached and plucked a tiny dead leaf from her daughter-in-law Elaine's hair, looking up to see which tree had broken protocol in the early Washington spring. The culprit couldn't be found, but standing half-hidden behind a second-floor window, a large man took in the events below. Spotting him, a slight shiver ran up Claudia's arms and over her shoulders. The man appeared to nod at her. She didn't acknowledge that she had seen him, but she knew that he would assume she had. Very little went on around her that Claudia Marshall was unaware of. Suddenly, a large hand grasped her upper arm. Startled, she gasped and turned abruptly, the smile momentarily lost, her eyes wide with fear.

"Did you miss me?" the President asked, giving her a small kiss on the cheek.

Her smile returned broader than before as she let out an audible sigh. "Every minute," she answered. She clutched her husband's arm and walked close behind him as he greeted the rest of the welcoming party. Then they made their way toward the downstairs entry to the White House. The President turned and waved to his staff. Claudia smiled and waved too, forcing herself not to look up to the second-floor window, where the surreptitious observer's gaze fell heavily upon her. It was an uncomfortable, violated feeling that didn't abate until the tiny entourage had filed through the glass doors of the south corridor.

Lyon, France

Terry carefully turned the bolt one last quarter turn, slid it from the hole where it held the side railing to the iron headboard, removed the thin metal washer, and slipped it into his pocket. He replaced the bolt, watching as the ancient bed leaned slightly toward him with a creaking sound, then came to rest. Seeing that it was not going to topple over, he eased backward and stood up slowly. He pictured the bed crashing to the floor and the fat concierge below waddling up the rickety salmon-colored stairs, muttering a stream of French epithets.

As he stood there, inspecting the room to make sure he had taken the most appropriate memento — and one that wouldn't be missed — he realized he hadn't seen the place empty like this since he and D.J. walked into it nearly sixteen months before, when the two of them had arrived in France, ostensibly for D.J. to study acting.

He turned 180 degrees, continuing his inspection, but stopped when his eyes fell upon the six dark suitcases standing near the bedroom door. On top of one of the bags was a week-old *New York Times* with a headline he didn't read, but knew by heart: PRESIDENT SLIPPING IN POLLS; TUCKER ANNOUNCES CANDIDACY. A wave of anxiety coursed through his body and the knot, which had been in his stomach to some degree since the day they received the phone call to return, tightened.

Now he could hear D.J. standing up in the tub and the sound of water rushing through the drainpipe. He imagined the warm, soapy water moving through the rusty pipe under the floor, turning where it met the wall, and rushing with a loud *whoosh* just inches from the fat face of the sleeping concierge.

"Are you wearing Levi's?" D.J. asked, appearing in the doorway drying his hair with a white towel.

Terry nodded his head as D.J. lowered the towel to catch his response. D.J. stood for a moment, locked in the gaze of Terry's green eyes, then went back into the bathroom, shut the door, and leaned against it, sighing deeply, tears starting to burn his eyes.

They loaded the car in silence, climbed the stairs one last time, and slowly inspected the rooms. Blue light filtered through the windows, and in the distance, the train whistle called them through the sleepy silence of the morning. They closed the door and descended slowly down the dark, narrow stairway, D.J. going first, feeling for the hideous pink stairs as he went. Terry followed close behind, one hand on the wooden rail, the other pressed tightly against the washer in his pocket. Down he went, stepping lightly and with trepidation on the pink tongue of steps, down into the building's dark throat. He felt more like he was leaving home than going home, and he had the sinking feeling that the word "home" would never really apply to him again.

The White House

Billings reached up from the chair where he was sitting, directly in front of the President's desk, and took the cup of coffee the servant offered him, while he waited for the President.

Thaddeus Billings was the senior member of the White House staff. He had been with Marshall since the early days in Arizona and was the only survivor of the "Marshall Gang," the media's name for the group that met at the Marshall ranch the weekend Donald was persuaded to enter the race for governor. The only other member of the administration with seniority was Thad's brother-in-law, Carl Stone, whom Thad had recruited for intelligence work during Marshall's first term as governor. Thad had endured all and come out on top: White House chief of staff, with unprecedented power. He was the President's eyes and ears, and, along with Claudia, his most trusted and unerring political advisor.

Donald Marshall could persuade a group of voters to believe anything; it was Thaddeus Billings who told Marshall what they should believe. Billings translated the President's political philosophy into practical political action and strategies.

Before the Marshall Gang received its name from the press that weekend, Thad was just another close friend. He lived near Donald and Claudia in North Scottsdale, where their children grew up together. Rachael Billings and Claudia, along with the ubiquitous Fran Altman, spent their days shopping at favorite boutiques and lunching at chic restaurants in Phoenix and sometimes flying to Los Angeles for afternoon shopping on Rodeo Drive.

The children attended the same private schools and summered together at the Marshall ranch in Carefree. Billings, who commanded a chain of automobile dealerships throughout Phoenix and Tucson, would often show up at the Marshalls' with a new Cadillac or Mercedes for them to drive for a few months. He once gave Claudia a powder blue Rolls Royce Corniche convertible for her birthday to use for a year. But six months later, after Marshall decided to run for governor, Thad took it back to avoid the bad press. "Besides," he told Claudia the afternoon he called to say he was sending someone to pick up the car, "it won't be long before the government will be providing your transportation. Powder blue is fun, but you've always looked more elegant in basic black." It was the kind of endearing comment that made Claudia appreciate him in the early days. Perhaps the only thing she appreciated more than his wit was his political savvy.

Thad's public relations acumen demonstrated itself time and again during Marshall's political career. When D.J. announced he was leaving school to join the New York City Acting Ensemble, and it became clear that no amount of pleading or pressuring would prevent or postpone it, Billings delayed the announcement until he could arrange, through political, financial, and personal pressures, to have the group's name changed to the New York Actors' Troupe. As he explained to Donald and Claudia, "Asking a car salesman in Des Moines or a truck driver in Tulsa to say the word 'ensemble' is like asking him to turn off the Super Bowl and listen to Stravinsky."

D.J.'s leaving school created a chasm between him and his family that was never to be completely bridged. Even now, five years later, there were strong feelings about it. His father didn't speak to him for over a year, and it wasn't until after his inauguration that he would allow photos of them together to be published. Even at the nominating convention, D.J.'s only appearances were in the hotel room with the entire family gathered in front of the television and once on the stage after his father's acceptance speech.

But matters went from bad to worse when Billings informed Donald two months before the crucial New Hampshire primary that D.J. had been seen at a gay bar in Greenwich Village and that this would have to be stopped. Marshall refused even to discuss it with him. Thad had to go to Claudia. He flew to Philadelphia where she was campaigning.

"I'm not making any judgments about him, Claudia. Please understand that from the start. I'm sure there's plenty of this sort of thing all around us that we don't even know about. What I'm saying is that this could hurt us in the primaries. And if we lose the primaries, we'll obviously never have a chance at the general election."

"I understand that. I guess what I don't understand is what I did wrong. How could this happen? Where did he get it? What didn't I do?" She looked to him for an answer. Thaddeus always had the answers.

"That can be dealt with later, and it's not my place to analyze it. Right now, you have to slip into another mode. It's not a time to be mother, it's time to be the devoted wife and political trooper that I know you are. We have to nip this thing in the bud and fast."

"But how? A psychiatrist?" she asked, but immediately she began musing again. "I've never understood this ... I had a close friend in college at USC, we dated for a while..."

Billings went over and put his hands on her shoulders. "It's nothing you did or didn't do. It just happens and even the best doctors can't explain it. We certainly aren't going to be able to figure it out this afternoon; however, we *can* figure out what to do for Donald."

"You're right of course, but ... What *can* we do? We've come too far and fought too hard to lose it all now."

"I have a plan."

"A plan? What kind of plan can possibly change this?"

"Elaine."

"Elaine? You think you could get him interested in her?"

"Not interested. Married."

"Married?!" Claudia exclaimed.

"Our only hope of stopping this thing before it blooms into a front-page spread in the New York papers is to get him married."

"To Elaine? Why would he marry Elaine? Why would he marry *anyone* for that matter?"

"To save his father's career. To prevent his family's destruction, protect his own interests. He does love you both, you know. I think I can persuade him if you'll let me," Billings offered.

Claudia got up from the wing-backed chair she was sitting in and moved to the fireplace. She stared vacantly for a moment at the family photograph that traveled with her, which was resting on the mantle. In it, D.J. knelt on the grass in front of his father, whose right hand rested on his son's shoulder. They were all smiling. It was Easter Sunday at the ranch and D.J. had just turned eleven. She turned back to Thaddeus. "I'll have to think about this. I'll have to discuss it with Donald."

"I'm afraid you won't find Donald very receptive to talking about it. I tried yesterday in Manchester. He's very tired and irritable."

"I see," she said, moving now to the window.

She looked out over the Philadelphia skyline. She was there to address a national teachers' convention, but wished now that she were at the ranch. She always could think better there. In the next four months they would face the first seven primaries and none was more crucial than New Hampshire. Right now Donald was just about even with Jim Strong, the Texas congressman who was giving him his greatest challenge. Strong had five daughters, all married with children. She turned back to the photo on the mantle. She recalled the scent of bougainvillea, which surrounded the house. Elaine, Elaine, she thought. Elaine Goldman. "She's Jewish, isn't she?" Claudia asked.

"Her father is Jewish. Her mother is French Catholic. Since joining the acting company's public relations department she's been using the name Duprés, her mother's maiden name. It'll wash."

"But how? We have so little time."

"Will you let me handle it?" Thaddeus asked again.

Claudia bit her lower lip. "Yes, but you have to explain it to me and keep me informed. What's your plan?"

"It's relatively simple," Billings said. "Elaine and Donald have been keeping company for a long time. They met when she signed on as assistant publicist for the acting company and now have decided to tie the knot. They want a simple, private civil service and will be married in New York by Judge Margaret Simmons."

"No church wedding? Won't that offend a lot of people?"

"Which church? A synagogue? A cathedral? No, no questions about religious affiliations. These are two professionals who have to work and have no time to take out of their busy schedules for fancy weddings. They're doing this practically and because they want to get married, not because they want publicity. Quick and clean, cut and dry. It'll be over before anyone knows it. We'll announce it afterwards."

"But when?"

"Saturday."

"Saturday?!" Claudia exclaimed. "That's impossible."

"Trust me, Claudia. Do you trust me?"

She turned away from him to the window again. "I hardly think I need to answer that, Thaddeus," she said softly.

The following Saturday, Elaine and Donald Marshall, Jr., were married in Manhattan. The newlyweds went to the Plaza Hotel for tea afterwards, then he to rehearsals and she to a fund-raiser. There were no family in attendance, at the couple's request. And it was Billings again, two years after that, when Terry began making a spectacle of himself, who arranged for D.J. and his lover to spend a year in France.

Now the family was tense about the return, even though Billings had arranged for Terry to work with the New York City Transit Authority in the hope that the job would keep him busy during the day and too tired to carouse at night. His time with D.J. would be severely restricted until after the convention in June. Billings was considering what he would have to do if this plan failed to keep Terry occupied, when the President entered the Oval Office.

"Well, Thad," the President said, pouring himself a cup of coffee from the silver service at the sideboard and moving to his desk, "I think we accomplished a few things at Camp David this weekend. Out of ten judiciary appointments we were able to come up with two women, a black, and one Hispanic. I'll have the details to you on Monday and you can begin to see that it is leaked to the proper sources. Will you call Williamson at the NAACP?"

"No, we should let him find out through the ordinary channels. We don't want him to think we're patronizing him. I'll see he gets word before the press, but not directly from us. When he calls, I'll act miffed and say we wanted to tell him first."

"Good. What do we need to discuss?"

"I've made up a list and divided it into two categories," Billings said, adjusting the papers in his lap. The President picked up a pencil and waited for Billings to begin itemizing. He always preferred getting information orally, rather than on paper. He was a much better listener than reader.

Billings went on. "These are campaign constraints and they fall into two areas of concern: People and Issues. Under the category of People our primary concern is the media, specifically NBC. They've led off their network news with very negative items for over two months now, everything from the economy to problems within the White House staff. Lately, they've been focusing strongly on people and organizations who either aren't supporting you or have refused to endorse you yet — their latest celebrity being the next on my list — the Reverend Doctor Horace Dolan."

Marshall jotted the name on his tablet, dropped the pencil on the desk, and leaned back in his chair. "That self-righteous ass," he said, frowning. "What the hell are we going to do about him?"

"He's got a large following."

"Yes, I know. His 'flock.' The fat leading the blind. God, there's nothing I hate more than these pompous, religious hypocrites who want political power. When am I meeting with him?"

"I've tentatively set it up for the tenth, but we haven't contacted him, yet. Claudia's secretary is trying to arrange a luncheon for the wives of the American Morality League then. We'll shoot him in and out of here the same day and it won't look like you've invited him alone to meet with you. That way he won't get so much coverage with the press. We've really got to watch ourselves with the moderates."

"What's Dolan going to want?" the President asked, leaning forward again and picking up his pencil.

"A lot. For one thing, he's going to want integration quotas dropped for private schools that have shown what he calls 'good-faith attempts.'"

"Well, he can shove that, goddamn it," Marshall said in a rare show of anger. "The moderates aren't going to stand for it and neither will the blacks, Adam McCann, or..."

"I know, I know, but there are other concessions we can make," assured Billings.

"Like what?" Marshall asked, trying to regain his composure. Billings was the only person on his staff besides his wife with whom he felt comfortable enough to show a little temper now and then. He detested displays of emotion that were negative, even in private, and he worked hard at maintaining constant composure. It was part of his personal philosophy of self-determination and positive thinking.

"Sources tell me he's going to hit you with a request to name his right-hand man Claggett deputy secretary of education if you're elected."

This was more than Marshall could bear. He stood up now and went to the window behind his desk, his hands clasped tightly behind him, fingers interlaced. Billings sat in silence, watching the President's knuckles turn white as he squeezed his hands together. "How much of this are we going to tolerate?" the President asked slowly.

"As much as it takes to win, Mr. President."

After a few seconds, Marshall returned to his desk and picked up his pencil again. "Okay, so what are we going to give this holy man?"

"The irony is that he's playing right into our hands. If giving him the deputy secretary's position will assuage him — and I'm more than sure it will, especially if we act like it's more than we could possibly consider and then give in — we're home free. The entire department will be phased out by next January. Claggett won't even get his desk filled and he'll be packing up for North Carolina again."

The two men had a good laugh over that, then went on to the other names on Billings's list. First was Senator

Adam McCann, Marshall's chief Republican rival and the front runner for that party's nomination. He was also chairman of the powerful Senate Foreign Relations Committee.

Next was Senator Bif Tucker, a member of the President's own party, a moderate, and a very popular young man from California who was challenging the President for the Democratic nomination. Tucker was a former Olympic decathlon winner.

"How's that going, by the way?" the President asked, putting down his pencil again.

"Tucker is a tough one, sir. He's young and popular with a lot of people, especially young voters who remember him from the Olympics and the cereal ads he did on television before he began serving in the Senate."

"Who else?" the President asked, returning to the list.

"The only other one right now is Miles Cameron," Billings said.

"Cameron?" Marshall asked with a degree of astonishment. "You don't mean the guy in the Communications Office?"

"Yes, sir," Billings replied. "I'm not saying he's an outright enemy, but he's very aggressive. And he did work in Tucker's California office originally. I'm not so sure he isn't where some of these leaks to the press have been coming from. I think we ought to watch him."

"I can't believe it. He's such a hard worker. He was so dedicated during the campaign, especially in California,"

"He was also seen less than a week ago coming from Tucker's house on Capitol Hill."

"Are you sure?" the President asked, but immediately corrected himself. "Of course you're sure; you don't make mistakes like that."

"Neither does Gasher, and it was one of his men who spotted him," Billings said. Glenn Gasher was the FBI director appointed by Marshall early in his term.

"Do we need to fire him?" Marshall asked.

"No, not yet. We just need to watch him. It's not out of the question that he may end up being very useful to us," Billings commented wryly.

"All right," Marshall agreed. "Anyone else on this little black list?"

"No, not for now. The next category is Issues. These are items we need to address to see that the public is correctly informed about what they are and how they relate to us and to your administration in general. They're topics for 'public education,' as I see it."

"Shoot," Marshall said. "What's first?"

"First, but not necessarily most important, is the economy," Billings said. "The economy is an ever-present problem, but your position on it, and your current programs, are as much as needs to be actually done. More needs to be said, but that's just the regular run-of-the-mill campaign bullshit. No one has any better answers to the problems the economy faces, and the American public knows it. They want more income, more cash flow, and they're starting to get that. By the time the election rolls around, they will feel the effects of your tax cuts and they'll be seeing more take-home pay. That will count for a lot in November. Also, we plan to coerce two banks — one in New York and one in Chicago — to lower the prime rate another percentage point in mid-October. Everyone talks about the economy during an election year, but no one has anything concrete to offer. They never do, and the public doesn't understand the issues anyway. What they do understand is cash in hand, and they will have that by late September, early October at the latest, and that will buy votes in November. On top of that, there is the decreasing rate of inflation, which no one can dispute.

"I'm suggesting you give federal workers a 7.2 percent pay raise October first, and that will buy you at least half a million votes. We can't do better than that."

"I think you're right," the President said. He rang for more coffee and a bottle of brandy. It was brought almost immediately, and they poured themselves some and went back to work.

"Now," said Billings seriously, "we have a tough nut to crack, something much more crucial than the economy."

"APANS," the President said.

"APANS," Billings echoed.

The Airborne Protective and Neutralizing System was a fleet of sophisticated aircraft built by Fairbanks Aircraft of Seattle, Washington. It was the most advanced defense system available, capable of detecting enemy aircraft and missiles from incredible distances and launching counter-defense systems to destroy the incoming aircraft within six seconds of their detection.

The President had been negotiating to supply the Sudan with current APANS hardware that was being retired by the U.S. military to make way for a more sophisticated system. The new system was also being manufactured by Fairbanks — provided the current hardware could be sold. In exchange, the Sudanese government would allow the United States to establish a military base on the Egyptian-Sudanese border near the Red Sea. Fragile negotiations had been going on among the United States, the Sudan, several Mideast countries, and Israel, who felt threatened by the idea of more military hardware being placed in Muslim hands. The Sudanese wanted the aircraft to protect them-selves from the encroaching danger presented by the Soviet Union's stronghold in Afghanistan, Iraq, and Iran, all of which had come under direct Soviet control within the decade prior to Marshall's election to office.

The President was making a strong stand against the Communists and felt that it was only a matter of time before both Egypt and the Sudan fell to the Soviet Union. Marshall was putting his entire reputation on this legislation now before the Senate to approve APANS. But he was getting stiff opposition from the other side of the aisle, and from some members of his own party who disapproved of the terms of sale. The Sudanese would not allow American military personnel to man the aircraft after the initial train-ing period. This worried liberals and conservatives alike, since the Sudan had not only discovered rich oil reserves in the south, but had also recently struck upon great deposits of uranium near the Chad border.

"We're putting a lot of pressure on state leaders to talk up the need to secure the area militarily," Billings said. "To let the Sudan fall would be to write off the entire Middle East and perhaps all of Africa as well."

Party national headquarters had sent out a series of thirty-second television spots soliciting voters to write or wire their congressional representatives. It was a direct appeal, showing the situation as a threat to peace in the region and, by extension, peace at home. "We've included the Western Union telephone numbers in the TV spots to facilitate sending wires and mailgrams," Billings said.

The President was sitting back again, listening intently. "There's no question that this is the most crucial issue we've faced, Thaddeus. We could lose the whole Middle East if this isn't checked. The oil, the uranium, the Suez Canal — all of it could go down. And it will, if we don't get this damned bill through the Senate."

"I'm just as concerned about our leadership profile," Billings added. "This would be the first major issue we've lost to the Senate, and this is no time to be losing battles with the Hill. Another setback like the Marcus affair could give either McCann or Tucker just the edge he needs in the primaries."

Four weeks prior, one of Marshall's advisors, Gregory Marcus, had been forced to resign over allegations of a conflict of interest. A consulting firm he owned before joining the White House had been awarded a multimillion-dollar contract with HUD, and the *Washington Post* had charged that Marcus hadn't fully divested himself of the company. Marshall had held off asking Marcus for his res-ignation, but when it was revealed that the terms of sale for Marcus's firm called for payments stretching over a two-year period and were tied to profits during that two-year period, Marcus had to go.

The President got up and poured himself another glass of brandy and began walking around the Oval Office. "Well, I've had every son of a bitch on the Hill to breakfast. I've divulged classified information to some, threatened others with severe federal fund cutbacks in their states. I've made phone calls at all hours of the night. How many votes has that won us in the past six months?"

"So far we've gained six. That brings the tally to forty-one yes, fifty-two no, and seven uncommitted if they were voting today. So it's time to get tough. No vote, no money. We're going to have to hit them where it hurts."

"I'll make some phone calls this evening," Marshall said, the concern more than apparent both in his voice and on his face.

Billings refrained from sighing. Phone calls were not going to change votes. "There is another possibility," he tendered hesitantly, knowing the response he was about to get.

"What's that?" Marshall asked, eager for new strategies.

"A visit to the Hill..."

"Never," Marshall replied firmly before Billings could add anything.

"Now, wait a minute; hear me out first," Billings pleaded, holding up his hand, suggesting Marshall shouldn't dismiss it so quickly before hearing the entire proposal. "Jake Renfrow's seventieth birthday is two weeks from yesterday. The boys are planning a huge reception in the rotunda. I know they're going to ask you to speak and I also know they expect you to decline. I say you go. Not only do you go, but you go armed with a lot of good jokes as the smiling, affable, good-natured president everyone knows you are."

Billings paused, giving the President time to digest this.

"Go on," Marshall said.

Billings was convincing him. "After the luncheon you stick around and socialize. Mr. Nice Guy. No grudges, no petty hard feelings. All's fair in love and politics. You have a few drinks with the boys, then as they trail off back to their offices, you pay a few personal visits. Just you and the undecideds. Imagine, having the President of the United States in your office. Think of Hailey from Vermont, a junior member of the Senate, thirty-six years old, being visited by the President because his vote is so crucial to the defense of this country. Because the country needs him. Because his president needs his support in a dangerous hour and isn't too proud to ask for it."

"I think you're right," Marshall said, beginning to pace again, his spirits greatly lifted. He even stood straighter now, "Another brandy, Thad?" he asked, trying to show Billings his approval and appreciation.

"No thank you, sir. I have a couple of memos to write before I leave this evening and I'd better keep a clear head. Thanks just the same."

"Ah, Thaddeus," the President said, his arm around Billings's shoulder as he walked him to the door, "I think we just might pull this rabbit out of the hat yet."

"I'm sure you will. You always have," Billings said, shaking the President's hand. He sighed deeply as he headed back to his office. He hadn't had the heart or the energy to bring up the most sensitive issue of all — the President's son. That would have to wait. But it won't wait for long, he thought.

Somewhere over the Atlantic

D.J. sat facing Terry in the lounge of the 747. The entire upper area of the plane had been secured and posted off-limits to the rest of the passengers aboard the flight from Paris to New York. Only the two young men and two Secret Service agents occupied the large upper cabin. One agent sat near the circular stairway that led to the first-class cabin and galley; Parker, D.J.'s personal Secret Service bodyguard, reclined on the sofa near the rear of the lounge, allowing D.J. and Terry some privacy.

D.J. had met Terry Guidi seventeen months to the day after his father had taken the oath of office, and from the beginning it spelled trouble for the White House. D.J. and a friend had driven out to Long Island for the weekend, and on the way back Monday morning, D.J.'s sports car developed carburetor trouble. They pulled into a garage in Huntington, and Terry was the mechanic on duty. He looked under the hood, fooled around with a few things that looked intimidating to D.J., then announced that it was the carburetor and he could fix it, but it would take a couple of hours and he'd have to get the part from his wholesaler in Manhasset. D.J. said that would be all right so long as he could have it that day. He would wait for it.

D.J. and one Secret Service agent waited in the garage while the other agent drove D.J.'s friend back into Manhattan. D.J. studied Terry while he worked, watching his strong, calloused hands disassemble parts, plunge them into cleaning solution, light nonfiltered cigarettes, grasp his coffee mug without using the handle.

Terry was about five-feet-seven with light brown hair, a slight mustache, and a well-defined chest that was revealed from under his coveralls from time to time as he leaned to pick up tools or stretched to retrieve something from the shelf near his workbench. As he repaired the car, he bounced up and down to the country-western music that blasted from a radio D.J. couldn't locate. His eyes were an intense sea green.

He moved without grace, the way so many men do who perform physical labor, but he handled his tools with respect and put each one back when he was finished using it, wiping it carefully to remove any grease. He was manly without being overbearing, and he was a craftsman who took pride in his work.

As D.J. watched, he noticed that the zipper on Terry's coveralls was gradually working its way farther and farther down, until it was well below his navel. When he had finished repairing the carburetor, Terry told D.J. to come into the office and he'd total up the bill. D.J. and the agent followed him through the door that separated the garage from the office.

"This your shadow or something?" Terry asked jokingly, but discernibly perturbed that they were being followed around.

D.J. chuckled a little, thinking that only the families of presidents ever got used to constant companionship. He asked the agent to wait outside. The agent frowned, looked carefully around, and, deciding that there was no present danger to his charge, since no one there even knew who he was, went back into the garage and stood by the candy machine.

"That better?" D.J. asked, smiling.

Terry unabashedly looked him over and asked, "Where you live?" He rummaged around on the cluttered desk, found what he was looking for, and stuck it in one side of his mouth. It was a toothpick.

"In the city," D.J. answered. He hadn't seen anyone use a toothpick since his grandfather lived with them in Scottsdale and used to keep a shot glass full of them on the round oak dining room table. D.J. imagined the look on his mother's face if she could see this guy now, sucking on a used toothpick. He grinned widely at the thought.

"Any chance of you and me getting together?" Terry asked straight out, pushing a shock of hair back from his forehead with one greasy hand.

D.J. was stunned. A greasy auto mechanic on Long Island? But he liked his boldness and there was no denying the classic Italian beauty of the man. He laughed and felt his face flushing. "Maybe. Do you ever go into the city?" Now D.J. was enjoying not only the come-on, but the fact that Terry was completely in the dark as to who he was.

"Yeah, I get there once in a while. Got an address or a phone number you wanna give me? I could give you a call, maybe come over or meet you someplace," Terry said, reaching inside his coveralls to rearrange something that seemed to be giving him trouble between his legs, and in the process revealing even more of his lean, brown torso. The zipper slid farther down and D.J. could see that he had nothing on under the coveralls. Terry retrieved his hand, but didn't bother pulling up the zipper, which now rested where D.J. could see the beginning of a distinct tan line.

D.J. wrote his phone number on a piece of adding machine tape that Terry tore off for him.

"You got a last name?" Terry asked, looking at the tape, which had only a number and the initials "D.J." on it. "Aw, never mind. It don't matter. Not trying to be personal or anything." He winked at D.J. and looked him up and down once more. "Nice options," he said, folding the paper in half and sticking it in his pocket.

"Is this Saturday okay?" Terry asked. "I mean if I happen to be in the city?"

"Anytime," D.J. answered. "And if someone else answers, just ask for me and tell him you're a friend from Long Island. What's your name, anyway?"

"Terry. See?" he said, pointing to the red lettering that spelled his name on his grimy blue coveralls.

"Oh, I wasn't sure those were yours. They looked so big on you."

Terry looked down at his coveralls and smiled a little, showing that he had gotten the point. "Yeah, I need a lot of room in here," he teased. "You live in a group house or something?" Terry asked, rolling the toothpick from one corner of his mouth to the other, revealing a glint of exquisitely white, perfectly straight teeth.

"Well, not exactly, but there's usually a lot of people around my place."

"Well, that's okay. We can go someplace."

Terry came out from behind the desk and they headed for the door. As they neared it, Terry grabbed D.J.'s ass and squeezed it firmly. D.J. jumped a little and began laughing, causing the agent to turn and look inside. "Pay this man, will you, Donahue?" D.J. said. "I don't have my card with me."

Terry watched as D.J. revved the engine, waved, and peeled out of the drive, heading for the Long Island Expressway. D.J. could see Terry reflected in the rearview mirror. His coveralls were still unzipped to below his stomach, and his chest glistened with sweat in the hot afternoon sun. Even from this distance, he could tell by the way Terry's mouth crooked in a lopsided smile that he was still chewing on the toothpick. D.J. would remember this image for the rest of his life. It was what Terry was to him.

Now D.J. sat watching Terry, who had been staring silently out the window for nearly twenty minutes. The two of them hadn't exchanged more than a dozen words since taking off from Orly that morning. D.J. wanted to hold him, to stroke his head and reassure him that it would be all right when they got home, that things wouldn't be the way they were over a year ago when they were shipped off to France.

Their relationship had been at the breaking point then. Terry's access to D.J. had been so limited that he had resorted one night to climbing the fire escape to D.J. and Elaine's row house in the Village and banging on the living room window. The shot that Parker fired through the window actually tore a hole through the shoulder of Terry's jacket, and had D.J. not seen Terry and shouted his name, Parker probably would have killed him.

It was the last straw in a series of incidents that threatened to expose the relationship between the two men. D.J. was hauled off to Washington, where he, his mother, and Billings tried to work out a solution. Billings moderated what turned into a heated battle between D.J. and his mother. Claudia said that she wouldn't tolerate another incident and that he was going to have to end "whatever this childish relationship is that has developed between you and this grease monkey."

Her face was red with anger and she clenched her fists tightly on the arms of the Queen Anne chair in which she sat. It was the first time D.J. had seen his mother lose her composure in front of someone outside the family, especially Billings, who was her archrival for the President's time and attention. "I simply don't understand what hold this fellow has over you. How did he get control of you, Donald? Is he that important to you? More important than your father?"

"He has nothing to do with my father," D.J. said, slumping even farther into the red velvet cushions of the sofa.

"Unfortunately, he does," interjected Billings in a calm voice. "The kinds of things that have been occurring between the two of you in New York — some of them in public — are not going unnoticed, even by the press. And your father — any president — has certain political enemies who wouldn't hesitate to use something like this to bring him down. But you know all this, D.J. We've been through this before."

"Well, I won't give up Terry, so you can start from there. If we could see each other more often, or at least under more-normal circumstances..."

"Normal?" his mother sneered. "Now you're going to talk to me about what's normal?"

"Sure, why not? Let's talk about what's normal in this administration. Or the last one, or the one before that. Let's talk about Watergate, or John Mitchell, or Billy Dailey. At least I'm not going around setting hotels on fire, killing innocent people."

Billy Dailey was Billings's nephew and CIA Director Carl Stone's stepson. He had been arrested for arson and manslaughter when he set a Las Vegas hotel ablaze and four people lost their lives.

"I can see this is getting us nowhere," Claudia said, standing now and brushing her skirt. "I thought I could handle this, Donald, so you wouldn't have to face your father with it, but I can see I was wrong. I don't know how we've grown so far apart. There was a time when you and I were close, when we could communicate, but this ... this friendship you have with that mechanic..."

"I love him," D.J. said defiantly.

Claudia headed for the door, unable to control her anger or her tears. D.J. was crying now, too. "I love him!" he shouted after her. "Quit telling yourself he's a friend. He's my lover!"

But she was through the door that led to the outer hall. D.J. looked at Billings, who was staring at him with incredulity and concern. The situation was clearly out of hand.

"What the fuck are you staring at?" D.J. asked, wiping his eyes and turning away from Billings to face the fireplace.

"I'm sorry, D.J. I didn't mean to stare. It's just that I'm worried. For you and for your father. This could really hurt both of you. We have to find a solution. Will you help me?"

"Help you?! How can I help you when I can't even talk to my own mother without her calling me names? She thinks I'm sick, a threat to her royal station of First Lady. Well, I could tell her about a few of her friends if she wants to hear something threatening."

D.J. was highly agitated and Billings let him talk.

"Her dear bosom buddy, Franny Altman, for example. Does she know that the affluent Mrs. Altman was handing out quaaludes and coke on the way to the Capital Center on Inauguration night? Does she know that her trusted secretary, Martha, drowned her daughter's cat in the bathtub right in front of the kid? Let's talk about who's sick. Let's talk about who's a threat to this administration. You want to talk about who's gay...?" D.J. checked himself. He knew of two people on the White House staff who were homosexual, but he didn't believe in exposing people who didn't choose to reveal themselves. Besides, Billings would be the last person to whom he would want to tell something like that. Next to his father, Billings was probably the most powerful person in the country and D.J. didn't trust him.

"Well, then," Billings said, seeing that D.J. wasn't about to go on, "what are we going to do to cool this engine down?"

D.J. got up and walked to the window. The Washington Monument looked surreal against the cloudless sky. It reminded him of the three-dimensional slides he used to look at as a child. Some of them were so real, it seemed he could reach into the hand-held viewer and put his finger between the objects he was looking at. "You tell me," he said tiredly. "You're the mastermind around here."

That remark coming from someone else would have been taken as subversion, but D.J. was no threat to Billings now. Thaddeus had wedged himself so tightly between Donald Marshall and the rest of the world — with the exception of Claudia, with whom he remained cordial, but highly competitive, even jealous — that no one could sway the President's opinion in any direction Billings didn't want it to go. And while this didn't apply to D.J., Thaddeus had virtually cut off all direct communication between the President and his son.

"If you could do anything in the world you wanted to right now, what would it be?" Billings asked, beginning to doodle tiny cannons on the clipboard he was holding in his lap.

D.J. laughed. "As if that were possible," he said. "I'd like to be standing in line at the Washington Monument with Terry. I'd like us to be free to roam about and talk and buy a Popsicle from a vendor without anyone recognizing me, without reporters following me, without that fucking Parker watching me like a voyeur."

He turned to face Billings now, fully aware of the message he was about to send. "You know, I think Parker really gets off watching me. I've never had an agent like him before. Twice I've woken up and found him in the bedroom. Once when I was sleeping with Elaine and once by myself, after Terry had visited. He's strange, Thaddeus. The perfect pinscher — he never lets up on his guard."

Secret Service agents who watched the First Family had been dubbed "pinschers" by Elaine's best friend, Jessica, whose family raised Dobermans. The term, not necessarily an endearment, but one Parker seemed to enjoy nevertheless, had spread and was used now by nearly everyone on the White House staff.

"You want him taken off?" Billings asked.

"I didn't say that. I'm just making an observation. Do what you like."

Because of the "delicate and complex profile" of the President's son's personal security, Billings had assumed direct responsibility for the agents who were assigned to him. Rather than reporting to their regular chief in the Treasury Department, they all reported directly to Billings. He had the authority to select, direct, and remove these particular agents.

"Well, I can hardly give you the kind of freedom you want, but we might be able to give you a certain amount of anonymity," Billings said.

"How?" D.J. was interested. He knew that if it could be done, Billings was the one who could do it.

"Let me work on it. Would you be averse to going out of the country for a few months, even a year? Maybe take a leave of absence from the acting company and study abroad for a year?"

"That would be great ... as long as Terry could come with me."

"I think that might be arranged."

"And so long as it wasn't someplace like Iceland."

"Even I wouldn't go that far," Billings quipped, making sport of his reputation.

Three weeks later, D.J. and Terry were on their way to Lyon, France. And it was to be the best sixteen months of their relationship. Terry had D.J. all to himself, except for the five hours a day D.J. spent in classes. It was a fantasy come true for both of them.

They spent their weekends exploring small villages and driving through the countryside, Parker and his partner Rodney always less than half a kilo behind D.J.'s Alfa Spider, or discreetly bunked in twin beds in a room next to theirs in the little hotels and pensions where they stopped.

"What are you thinking about?" D.J. now asked Terry, who was still staring intently out the window of the 747.

Terry turned away from the glass porthole and looked at D.J. as though he had woken him suddenly from a trance. His green eyes were clear and sparkling.

"What?" he asked.

"What are you thinking about?" D.J. repeated. "You've been a million miles off for about half an hour."

"Nothing," Terry answered in a tone of voice that D.J. recognized. It meant "Ask me again, please."

"C'mon," D.J. pleaded softly.

"I was thinking about the first time we kissed."

Kennedy Airport

D.J. and Terry waited in the VIP lounge at Kennedy while their luggage was gathered by the chauffeur. They had been ushered into a tiny room that was painted bright red and was covered with red carpeting. Two chairs molded out of red plastic sat on either side of a mahogany table that held a single issue of *Time* magazine. Donald and

Claudia Marshall, both in cowboy hats, stared out from the cover. The feature story was titled "The Marshalls at Home on the Ranch." D.J. and Terry ignored it. Terry was leaning against one red wall, his hands in his pockets. A lone tear coursed its way down one cheek. D.J. felt helpless and miserable; this would be the last he would see of Terry for days, perhaps weeks, if Billings had his way.

They had just spent every day of the past sixteen months eating, playing, traveling, bathing, sleeping together. Now they were being separated, like prisoners going off to their separate cells to serve out their sentences.

D.J. didn't know exactly why he allowed himself to be victimized by his father's career. He felt somehow it was a power over him, a fate he was unable to avoid. The country, the White House, the FBI, the CIA, the Secret Service were all more than he could fight. He had to go along with it. He told himself there was always a choice, but not one that any reasonable person would make. His finiteness was no match for the workings of the American political system. He had become an unwitting part of the political process, and there was no civilized, acceptable way to extricate himself. If only Terry could see that and just bear with it until it was over. But Terry was a man of basic emotional needs, not one who analyzed and acted out of reason.

He crossed the room and leaned against the wall next to Terry. "Hey," D.J. said, nudging him gently with his elbow. Terry looked up, his eyes filled with tears. He looked like a child who had just been severely scolded for something he didn't do.

"I love you," D.J. said, feeling the tears coming now to his own eyes.

"I just want to be with you," Terry said, his voice barely audible. "I don't care about anything else. I don't care what you have to do, where you have to go, what you have to say. I just want to know that sooner or later you'll be coming home to me, to our place."

D.J. rested against the wall just inches from Terry. The tears were flowing freely now. The moment he had resisted thinking about since they were told they had to return had arrived and he was less prepared for it than he'd thought he would be.

Terry went on. "Do you know what it's like for me? Do you know what it's like to be alone, without you, not to know when I can see you or how long we'll be allowed to spend together? I watch TV, play the stereo, I smoke and try not to think about you. My whole fucking life is spent waiting. I'm afraid to go out, because while I'm gone they might call to tell me we can meet for a couple hours and I have fifteen minutes to get ready. Every time a phone rings somewhere, I wonder if mine is ringing too, if I'm missing our connection. It makes me crazy."

"I'll fix it this time. I'll tell Billings it has to be different now, that we have to have more time together. He'll arrange it so we can meet more often, maybe even go off on weekends together," D.J. said.

Terry smiled knowingly. "Billings," he said contemptuously. "He's got your life planned. We haven't got a chance. I'm going to lose you this time, D.J."

"Don't say that," D.J. shot back, almost yelling. "That's not true."

"They hate me. I'm big trouble for your father. Just mention my name and your folks see red flags. I'm scared, D.J. I admit it, I'm scared this time."

At that moment Parker entered the room and announced that he had the bags and they should leave immediately. A look of panic came over Terry's face and he grabbed D.J.'s arm. Parker took hold of D.J.'s other arm and led him through the door, Terry trailing behind the two of them, still holding on. As they entered the main lounge area, another agent removed Terry's hand and began escorting him in an opposite direction.

"Hey, wait a minute," D.J. said. "Where's he going? What's going on here?"

"He's going home," Parker said, moving into position behind D.J. and pressing him forward, his hand flat against D.J.'s back, urging him toward the car.

"Wait a minute," D.J. said, trying to keep his voice down and turning to look for Terry. Two agents were ushering him through a side door. Terry was struggling, and for a second their eyes met. "D.J.!" Terry cried out plaintively, and then he was gone.

Suddenly D.J. was surrounded by uniformed policemen and it seemed like only seconds before he was hurled into the rear of the waiting limousine and speeding toward Manhattan.

"We're home now, D.J.," Parker said as they headed for the Midtown Tunnel. D.J. felt as though he had been given some drug. His head was light; he felt dizzy. He looked down and saw Parker's hand resting on his knee. He looked up into Parker's face. Parker was grinning. "Things are different here ... sir," Parker said. He removed his hand and settled back into the seat next to D.J. The Manhattan skyline rose up from the highway before them, and with red and blue lights flashing all around them, they descended beneath the East River.

The White House

Thaddeus signed the last memo of the day, dropped it into his out box, and had just flicked his desk lamp off when the phone rang. He looked at it with disdain. The lighted button on the phone told him it was an inside line, which meant it could be the President. "Billings," he answered.

"Thaddeus?" It was the President. "Claudia and I were wondering if you might stop up for a minute on your way out. For a short cocktail. If you're not too pressed to get home."

"Sure. I'd love to," Thaddeus said, not sure of how he really felt. He wanted to be out of there, yet it might not be a bad idea to unwind with a drink before he got on the George Washington Parkway in the middle of heavy traffic.

Billings straightened his tie and went upstairs. When he arrived, the President and Claudia were in the living room. Neither Elaine nor her friend Jessica, who had come with her from New York, were there. Marshall was standing at the bar pouring drinks.

"Thaddeus, come in," the President said warmly. "I hope we didn't inconvenience you, but Claudia reminded me it's been so long since the three of us sat down and had a drink together, that we thought it would be nice to have a cocktail. By the way, you're more than welcome to join us for dinner."

"Oh, no thank you," Billings said, noticing Claudia's surprised look in response to Donald's invitation. "Rachael is waiting with dinner for me at home. I just spoke with her a few minutes ago. Thanks anyway."

The President crossed the room with Billings's usual, Scotch and water. "Well, then, we won't keep you long," he said, smiling. "Have a seat, Thad. You've put in quite a day."

Billings took a chair, and Marshall sat on the sofa next to Claudia, resting his hand casually on her lap. She lifted it to straighten her dress, then replaced it, her own hand on top of his. "Donald tells me you were an avalanche of ideas today," Claudia said, smiling thinly.

"Just suggestions, really," Billings said carefully, sensing from her tone of voice there was something on her mind and that this friendly little get-together was her idea.

"Come now, Thaddeus," Claudia said, reaching for her Manhattan on the table in front of the sofa. "You're being modest again. I know how indispensable you are to Donald." She sipped her drink and set it back on the table. As she replaced the glass, Billings noticed the Style section of the evening newspaper sitting on the table. It was folded in quarters to display a photograph.

"I hope you and Rachael can come with us to Camp David for a weekend soon," the President said. "Maybe we can squeeze some time in before the convention."

"That would be terrific," Billings said, "but we'd probably have to make it a working weekend. There's an awful lot to do before then, especially with the APANS vote coming."

It was obvious that Marshall was adding filler, killing time until one of them got to the point. It wasn't like him to make this kind of small talk. Claudia charged ahead.

"Speaking of the convention, Thaddeus," she said, looking at the newspaper on the table, then back to him, "what is the campaign strategy now?"

"Now?" Billings asked.

"Yes, now that D.J. is back."

Aha, Billings thought, there must have been an item in the evening paper about his returning from France. Billings had forgotten that today was the day. "Well," he said, measuring his words as he went and flashing momentarily on the afternoon the two of them had met with D.J. in that very room, "we're going to use him of course, but only in a limited way. We don't want to interfere any more than we have to with his work, but it will be helpful to have him accessible. There will be a few functions we'll want him and Elaine to attend. Just for ... well, to represent the administration."

"Have you made up a schedule for them?" Claudia asked, sure that he hadn't.

"No, not yet, but Carl and I have a few things in mind that we think would be appropriate. You know, dinners and such in New York. They won't have to travel far."

Carl Stone had taken a leave of absence as director of the CIA — a position Marshall had appointed him to — to manage the re-election campaign.

"I see," Claudia said, reaching for the newspaper.

"Let me freshen that, Thad," the President offered, getting up and holding out his hand for Billings's glass. He seemed nervous, but that wasn't unusual when the subject of D.J. came up.

"Have you seen this, Thad?" Claudia said, holding out the paper for him.

Billings took the paper from her. There was a photo of D.J. at Kennedy Airport in the passageway from the VIP lounge to the security entrance. He was looking over his shoulder with a pained expression while Parker was obviously pushing him forward.

"No, I haven't. Lucky photographer, I guess. Nothing was put out about his return," Billings said, starting to feel a little knot in his stomach. He could have sailed through this interview with the President alone, but dealing with Claudia was always unsettling, because she had a motive for everything she did and she loved to show Billings in a bad light. There was also the unavoidable handicap that once

Billings left a little confab like this, she had the President alone and it was clearly known that he listened carefully to every word of advice she gave him. He trusted her instincts when it came to politics. After all, wasn't it she who had brought everyone together at the ranch to discuss his running for governor?

The President was taking a lot longer to fix the second drink.

"Lucky for him, not so lucky for us," she said flatly, but without malice in her voice.

"How's that?" Billings asked just as flatly, handing the paper back.

"Donald doesn't look exactly thrilled to be home, does he?" she asked in a tone that could be taken as jocular except that she never joked.

"Oh, I don't know, it's just a candid shot of him leaving the airport. He's been flying for several hours. Jet lag."

"Perhaps," she said.

"Here you go," Marshall said, trying to inject some cheer into the conversation. "If that's too strong, I can water it down a bit."

Billings sipped the drink. "It's fine," he said.

The President returned to the sofa. "We were wondering how you plan to use D.J. and Elaine," he said, trying to take the ball away from Claudia. "I mean, specifically."

"Nothing special, as I said," Billings explained, wishing it were just himself and the President. "Carl and I are in touch daily, but we haven't discussed D.J. and Elaine in detail yet. Small functions mostly — dinners, receptions, things like that. No speeches, no travel." He knew that Claudia did not want any overnight travel that would allow Terry and D.J. to rendezvous. She still held out hope that D.J. could be "cured."

"He'll be here tomorrow, you know," Claudia said.

"We think it might be a good idea to have some sort of talk with him while he's here. To let him know precisely what he will and will not be doing until the convention," Claudia said and stared intently at Billings to make sure he caught her meaning.

"Yes, that's probably a very good idea," Billings responded.

There was silence.

"Would you like me to take care of that?" Billings offered.

Now Claudia turned charming, gracious, almost warm. "Would you do that for us, Thad? Would you just take him aside while he's here and have a little talk with him? Donald and I would appreciate it so much. He takes things like that better from you. He respects your position with the campaign and within the White House staff."

"We know tomorrow's a hectic day and they'll only be here a short time...," Marshall said, gratefully.

"'They'?" Claudia asked, the color vanishing from her face instantly.

"He and Elaine," the President said, slowly catching on to what she was thinking. "D.J. and Elaine, darling," he said in a near whisper. He patted her hand. Claudia quickly began to recover her color, but inwardly she rebuked herself for even this tiny slip in front of Billings.

"It's a hell of a busy day, but if you could find time, I'd be truly grateful. So would Claudia. We hate to talk politics with him when we're together. We have so little time to spend with him."

It was still difficult for Marshall to talk about his son's "delicate situation," but Billings knew that, next to Claudia, nothing was as important to him as D.J.

"I'd be glad to, sir. Consider it done," Billings said.

He downed the rest of his drink and stood up. They exchanged good-evenings and Claudia offered her cheek for Thaddeus to kiss. He gave her a little hug instead. "It was so nice to see you again, Claudia. I hope we'll be able to make that weekend trip before long. I know Rachael would love it."

In the elevator on his way downstairs, Thaddeus took out his handkerchief and wiped his cheek. That woman is a pro, he thought. Now she has even me doing her dirty work. I wonder who else around here she's charming?

New York City

D.J. closed the door, shutting out Parker and the rest of Manhattan. As he stood in the center of the room, he realized he couldn't remember the last time he had been by himself. He left his suitcase in the middle of the floor, stripped off his clothes, and took a long, hot shower. The hard jets of water tingled his skin and massaged his tired muscles, and the fresh scent of the soap seemed to rise with the steam and surround him. He stood for a long time letting the water pour over him before he began to feel his body relax.

He dried off and put on his favorite pair of baggy, ripped gym shorts and an old number-twenty football jersey, then went to the kitchen and fixed himself a tequila and bitter lemon. The black stove gleamed and he could see his reflection in the door of the black refrigerator. Either the cleaning woman had been in after Elaine left for Washington or Elaine had become a better housekeeper in his absence. A bouquet of white and yellow freesias sat in a teal blue pitcher on the counter.

He moved to the living room and climbed onto the wide sill of one of the four windows that overlooked the Hudson River and New Jersey beyond. The sky was unusually blue for New York and he was glad to see the city again. If only he and Terry could be together, they could call their friends and have a welcome-home party, drink and be loud and go out dancing and carousing, dress any way they liked, walk openly in the streets, call each other "honey" or "baby."

Instead, he was a prisoner. Every freedom guaranteed by the Constitution to the most socially and economically deprived citizen was denied him simply because he was the son of the man who was charged with maintaining those freedoms, those inalienable rights.

How ironic, he thought, pouring himself another drink. A society that extols truth, liberty, individualism, and romance would brand me an outlaw for exhibiting any of those traits. "To you, Dad," he said bitterly, toasting the empty room. "May you lose by a landslide."

No, he thought, plopping down on the sofa. I don't mean that. I love him; he's a good man and he's good for the country. I can make this sacrifice for him. It's not forever. He reached for the telephone and called Terry's number, but there was no answer. He called another number, pressing the buttons on the telephone deliberately as he felt the liquor taking its effect. He hadn't eaten all day and had drunk half a bottle of champagne on the plane.

"Second floor," a woman's voice said on the other end of the line.

"I'd like to speak with the President, please," he said.

"I'm sorry, you'll have to call downstairs. The President is in his office."

"Well, then let me speak to Mrs. Marshall."

"Mrs. Marshall is also in her office. I'm sorry, you'll have to call downstairs."

"Well, who is home?" D.J. asked, joking with the woman.

"Who is this please? Who's calling?" the woman asked.

"I don't hear anyone calling," D.J. teased.

"How did you get this number?" the woman demanded.

"I found it on a bathroom wall in Moscow," D.J. said, hearing the several clicks on the other end that meant the automatic tracer had been switched on. He hung up. No sense of humor, he thought.

He tried Terry again, but still no answer. He got up and went into his bedroom. There were dozens of jonquils on a stand near the bed and anemones on his desk. He sat down amid the brightly colored flowers, switched on the desk light, and found a pad of writing paper in the drawer.

Terry,
    You are right, of course, when you tell me they are against us, but I cannot bring myself to say it out loud. I will never admit that things between us can ever again be bad, because my love for you is so strong, so overwhelming, I will let nothing come between us. If I have to, I will rebel. I will break away somehow. I make this pledge to you: I will love you forever and

will fight to preserve this beautiful thing we have.
Wherever you are, whatever we are forced to endure,
I am with you and you with me. Please, don't ever
give up. They can imprison us, they can even kill us,
but they can never destroy our love for each other.

He signed it, then folded it and put it in an envelope and
addressed it to Terry. He would mail it in the morning on
his way to Washington.

He fell asleep on top of the covers and dreamed of a
puppy he had as a child, a brown-and-white cocker spaniel
named Corky that had only three legs. One of its front legs
had to be amputated after it was hit by a delivery truck. In
the dream, D.J. was curled up on a blanket in his closet,
holding the puppy and petting it, telling it over and over
that everything would be all right. In his dream, the pup had
all four of its legs.

New York City

D.J. stood in front of the narrow window with his drink.
Phil was busy in the kitchen trying to keep the chicken he
was baking from drying out before the corn on the cob was
done. Phil Kramer and Jessica Wood had been living together for nearly two years. They met when CBS assigned
Phil his first feature, a report on "farm art" that was showing
at the gallery where Jessica worked. It consisted mostly of
dyed chickens and goats with wire sculptures in their horns.

D.J. watched Rodney get out of the limousine that was
parked half on the sidewalk across the street from Phil's
apartment. Rodney leaned on the front fender and lit a
cigarette. Parker, of course, was stationed directly outside
the apartment door. Across the street was one of the last
empty lots in Manhattan, and through the branches of a tall
elm that occupied nearly the entire space, D.J. could see the
ivory moon, full and almost perceptibly rising before him.
He felt a hand on his shoulder. It was Phil. They stood for
a moment in silence.

"I guess it's kind of strange to be back after so long,"
Phil said.

"I don't know if I can do it this time, Phil," D.J. said, pouring out the thoughts he had been grappling with all afternoon. "I thought I loved Terry as much as I could love a person when we left here, but after so much time together, such a perfect time, such a fun time, just the two of us, not having to parcel out the hours, not having to rush through our lovemaking ... I love him a hundred times more now. I honestly don't know if I can be apart from him."

Phil squeezed D.J.'s shoulder and hugged him compassionately. Through Elaine and Jessica they had become close friends. Phil was the only straight male D.J. could talk with about his situation with Terry. Phil was not at all intimidated by homosexuality; neither was he suggestive or seductive in the presence of gay men, like so many straight men D.J. knew, sure that any gay man is racked with lust in the company of any other male.

"I wish there was something I could do," Phil said. "I wish I could help ease the pain and frustration in some way. It must be terrible to live under these conditions."

"Having a friend like you helps," he said.

"Come into the kitchen with me while I try to salvage our dinner," Phil said. D.J. followed him and stood in the kitchen doorway, playing with the ice in his drink.

"How's Terry holding up?" Phil asked, opening the oven door to check on the bird, which now appeared to be half its original size.

"Not too well, I'm afraid. We had a really bad scene at Kennedy. We were both crying. There was no time for any decent good-byes, and they swooped the both of us up and carried us off in separate cars. We weren't even allowed to ride into the city together."

"Jesus, that was nice of them," Phil commented, poking the corn with a fork. "These fuckers are never going to get done. How do you tell when corn on the cob is ready?"

"I don't know," D.J. answered. "Just don't let it get mushy." He peered into the pot. "It looks done to me. I like it crunchy anyway."

Phil served the dinner on a small oak table in a corner of the living room. An old-fashioned milk bottle holding a small bouquet of sweet williams sat in the center of the table. "These are Terry's favorite flowers," D.J. said, fingering one of them gently. "He says he likes them because it's one big flower made up of hundreds of little flowers. I like their deep, rich colors."

"Jessica brought those home yesterday before she and Elaine left for Washington. They brighten up the room a lot."

"Anyway," D.J. continued, "there was a lot of tension on the flight back and we really hadn't resolved anything before we got here. What makes it so bad is that I was trying to convince Terry it wouldn't be like it was before we left. I told him we'd be able to spend more time together. Then the airport scene happened."

"Sure you weren't trying to convince yourself?" Phil asked, leaning over the table and taking his first bite of chicken.

"I suppose I was."

"God, this chicken is awful. Just eat the salad and the corn," Phil said, grimacing and shoving his portion to the far side of his plate.

"It's not that bad," D.J. assured him, chewing the tough piece of chicken he had just put in his mouth. "Just a little dry."

"Dry! It tastes like an old carpet. I'm sorry, I really wanted to welcome you back with a nice dinner. Oh well, you'll have a real dinner tomorrow night at the White House. That's one place you don't have to worry about the food. Or the service." Phil laughed.

"I don't think we're staying in Washington tomorrow. I think we're coming back here right after the luncheon at the Kennedy Center. It's just a trip to see my folks and let the press see the family together. At the Kennedy Center, of course. The First Family got culture."

Phil put down his fork and reached for his wine. "You are bitter, aren't you?"

D.J. dropped his hands in his lap and sat silently for a moment, thinking about what he'd just said and how he'd sounded. "God, I guess I am. I don't think I realized how much I don't want to be back here. I'd better get hold of myself before tomorrow."

Phil leaned back. "Why is all this necessary? I mean, couldn't you make a perfunctory appearance, gallop around the country for a couple weeks with Elaine, then go back to Europe? What's the big deal? Surely they could make an excuse the public would buy."

"Not with the polls the way they are. When Billings called, he said that between APANS and the American Morality League they're really on the run this time."

"You mean that little twirp Dolan?"

"Yeah, Dolan was riding my father's ass about a lot of things, especially private schools in the South *and* the 'curious absence' of his only son."

"What the fuck is that supposed to mean?" Phil asked angrily. "Dolan probably wears black panties and a garter belt to bed when he fucks his old lady."

"I don't think he fucks his old lady. It's not nice," D.J. said. They both laughed.

"Is he really saying things like that? I mean directly to your father?" Phil asked, incredulous.

"Billings claims it's an issue. That huge fundamentalist faction is asking why I'm not on the scene. Besides that, Elaine and I have been married for so long and there's no bambino around."

"Yes, and those people are definitely pro–population explosion," Phil said, raising his eyebrows.

"So there you have it. Sonny has to come home and show his face with the little woman. I wouldn't be surprised if they put out a press release saying that Elaine was pregnant and then staged a miscarriage after the election."

Phil cleared the uneaten food from the table and came back with a huge bowl of chocolate mousse. "Here's the best part of the meal — dessert. It's the only reason I even bother to cook."

"Looks divine," D.J. said. "We've been talking about nothing but me so far. How have you been? How's everything between you and Jessica and how's CBS treating you?"

"Oh, God. Let's see, now. My life is so exciting, you have to promise not to get angina. I've been really good, actually. I joined a new gym, the one over on Sheridan Square. Naturally, I'm the only straight man in there and they all think I'm being a prima donna and a tease. I'll probably get raped before the summer is out."

"Well, you should have known better."

"It's the best gym in the city. It's the only one that has a full set of free weights in two-pound increments. Everyone else has nothing but machines. Besides, it's cheap and it's open Sunday. I think of myself as liberal and well integrated, so sooner or later I should be made to prove it. Why not in the shower? I just hope it's one of those big bruisers who's trying to overcompensate for having a tiny pecker."

"You're bad," D.J. laughed.

"So I'm fine physically. Mentally, too. Jessie and I have our ups and downs like everybody else, but generally we're okay. She can always make me laugh, no matter how mad I get at her."

"And work?" D.J. asked.

"Not bad," Phil answered. "Actually, they've been damned good. They've put me in the central newsroom and have me working for the nightly news now. It's a real opportunity. I figure all I need is one lucky break, one really good story, and they'll try me on assignment, maybe let me get in front of the camera once or twice on the locals. They do that, you know."

"Do what?" D.J. asked, not following what Phil was saying.

"Well, they'll put a guy in the newsroom, working on copy for the nightly news, and if he can come up with a story of his own that's good enough, they'll let him report it on tape for syndication to the local stations. That's why sometimes you'll see a news story on your local channel being reported by somebody you've never seen before. It's some guy like me in the newsroom who came up with a plum. It's kind of a bonus system, and it gives reporters incentive to hunt up good stories. So, while my job is really to put together stories for the anchors to choose from and for the wire, I have a chance to show what I can do on my own."

"What are you working on right now?" D.J. asked just as the telephone rang. Phil got up to answer it.

"They've got me on the convention," Phil said, talking as he crossed the room, "but I don't know yet if I'll be based in the studio or at the Garden. I'd love to be down there where the action is. Hello?" Phil said into the phone. "Sure, Terry, hold on. How are you? ... Good. It's nice to have you guys back. I hope I get to see you soon. Maybe you could come over for a drink or we could go out together some night ... Great, I'll call you in a couple days. Hang on, I'll get D.J."

Phil handed the receiver to D.J., who was already by the phone.

"Hello?"

"D.J., why didn't you call me?"

D.J. could tell that Terry had been smoking. "I did," he said, "but there was no answer. I tried before I came over here. Maybe you were in the shower."

"I didn't know you were having dinner with Phil."

"I hadn't planned on it. He called while I was taking a nap. I was going to try to reach you from here."

"I miss you," Terry said sadly.

"I miss you, too."

"Are we going to be able to be together tonight?" Terry asked.

"I don't see how, honey. They've got me on the seven-o'clock shuttle tomorrow morning."

"But Elaine isn't in town. You could leave from here. Or maybe I could come over to your place."

"We can't, Terry. We have to wait till I get back. I'm going to talk with Billings while I'm there. I'm going to tell him we absolutely have to be together more. Honest. I promise. I can't stand it any more than you can."

The line was silent.

"Terry?"

"What?"

"Please try to be patient. Trust me. It'll be all right. You'll see."

Silence again.

"I'll call you later," D.J. said.

But Terry had already hung up. D.J. called him when he got home, but there was no answer. He placed the last call at ten minutes to four in the morning and still there was no answer.

Washington, D.C.

A low-lying mist hovered gray and ethereal on the surface of the Potomac, slowly dissipating in the warmth of the morning sun. The arches of Memorial Bridge glowed a pinkish orange, and the trickle of automobiles crossing it from Virginia into the District of Columbia was slowing to make the turn near the Lincoln Memorial that would put them onto Constitution Avenue and take the sleepy drivers to their federal jobs. West Potomac Park was empty save for four figures jogging at a moderate pace along the northeast side near the Tidal Basin. Two Secret Service agents trotted about forty feet behind Elaine and Jessica.

Jessica had embarrassed one of them by offering to let him borrow a dance belt she had with her. "You don't want all that jostling to jeopardize the not-so-secret servicing you do on your own time, do you?" she teased, rubbing up against him and waving the black dance belt in his face. He turned crimson.

"I really think that blond one is cute," she said now to Elaine as they crossed the road and headed toward the polo field that borders Independence Avenue.

"Settle down," Elaine said. "He just might take you up on it."

"I wish!" Jessica laughed. "Hasn't one ever shown any interest in doing anything?"

"Of course not," Elaine said, feigning shock. "This is business for them; these guys are professionals."

"I'll bet that blond is professional," Jessica said.

"You don't even like blonds."

"I have never discriminated because of hair color. I'm an equal-opportunity lay."

"Not so loud, he'll hear you."

"Good," Jessica said, turning and jogging backwards so she could look at the blond agent. He smiled and she winked and turned back around.

"You're embarrassing me," Elaine chided.

"I think you're nuts not to take advantage of having a built-in 24-hour stud service. I mean, given The Arrangement," Jessica said, referring to Elaine's marriage. "After all, you can't be expected to dry up for four years, just because you've agreed to this insane virgin princess role."

"Jessica, don't start," Elaine warned in a friendly tone. "And, you know, you don't have to cheat on Phil every time opportunity presents itself."

"I don't consider fulfilling a bodily function cheating. After all, I'm only giving away a little bit of my body, not my heart."

Jessica had played devil's advocate with Elaine for as long as they had been friends and even more so since The Arrangement. In college Jessica nicknamed herself Sola and Elaine Luna, because Jessica's approach to life was rational, logical, pragmatic; Elaine, on the other hand, relied largely on intuition and feelings and was protective, even maternal toward her friends and toward D.J. in particular. Jessica saw Elaine's participation in The Arrangement as fulfilling the need to take care of someone. When the two of them discussed it, Elaine insisted that she did it out of deep friendship for D.J. and because he was in a tight spot with no way out. Elaine never complained about her situation, which irritated Jessica more than any other aspect of Elaine's attitude toward it.

They slowed to a walk on the other side of Seventeenth Street and cut across the grass toward Constitution Avenue and the White House beyond. Jessica took off one of the two sweatshirts she was wearing and tied it around her waist.

"You're going to catch a chill like that," Elaine warned.

"You don't actually think Phil doesn't chase skirts when I'm not around, do you?" Jessica asked, continuing her previous conversation, as she turned to see where the blond was. The two agents had also stopped running, and when she turned, the blond smiled and acknowledged her with a slight nod of his head. Jessica winked back.

"I certainly don't. Why would he?" Elaine answered, allowing herself to be drawn into this conversation, even though she knew Jessica would eventually turn it from Phil and herself to D.J. and Elaine.

"He's just dying to plunge me," Jessica said, untwisting a rubber band and letting her hair fall around her shoulders.

"What?" Elaine said, giving Jessica a quizzical look.

"That blond, I can hear him panting from here — and it's not because he's out of breath from running."

"Well, please try to control yourself for just a few more hours."

"I'll try, but I'm not promising anything," Jessica exclaimed. "I need fresh meat," she shouted, pounding her chest Tarzan-style.

"Jesus! What's gotten into you?" Elaine asked.

"Nothing yet, but I'm working on it," Jessica teased. "I can't help it, I'm horny. I have been since I woke up this morning."

They stepped onto the sidewalk near the black iron fence directly behind the White House South Lawn. Jessica walked over and leaned against the fence, looping her arms between the bars and gazing in. Elaine stood and leaned with her.

"Elaine?"

"Hmm?"

"We've been friends for a long, long time."

"Uh-huh."

"And I've just shared something really personal with you, because I trust you. I'd tell you anything, because even if I thought you wouldn't agree or even understand, I know you'd respect my right to have my feelings or ideas."

"Yeah."

"I've been your closest friend, your confidante in all of this with D.J. since the very beginning, and you know I love D.J. nearly as much as I love you. We've talked about The Arrangement and labored over it and dealt with all kinds of problems about it, from the decision to marry him to Terry's almost getting shot. But that was mostly in the beginning. It's been going on for four years, and here you are, faced with possibly another four years of it. I know I couldn't do it and I know why you did it in the beginning, but now, after so long with nothing really in it for you, at least nothing I can see, I have to ask you ... I mean maybe I should know, but I don't, so as your best friend and as someone who loves you and wants to understand this thing better — why? Why are you going to open yourself up to another four years of this charade? Please don't misunderstand. I'm not criticizing you or judging you. I just want to understand it better."

Neither of them had taken their eyes off the grand structure at the far end of the perfectly manicured lawn during Jessica's discourse. They continued to stare straight ahead now.

"I know you don't fully understand," Elaine said, softly. "I think maybe I've just begun this past year to understand it myself, and I guess I haven't discussed it with you because I don't know exactly what to say about it. Maybe there isn't anything to say about it. Your relationship with Phil is so different, and I'm not sure I understand that."

Elaine paused. Jessica waited.

"I don't know if you'll understand this, Jessie, but my love for D.J. is so strong and so deep, it transcends anything sexual."

Jessica was staring at her now, considering every word.

"I'd give up my life for him, Jessie. Without blinking an eye."

They stood for a few more moments without saying anything, then turned and walked slowly in silence, arm in arm, around to the side gate and into the executive mansion, where breakfast was waiting for them.

They had just been served when Claudia came into the room, carrying a clipboard, but looking radiant, as she always did. Even at seven a.m. she took the trouble to make certain her hair, her makeup, her clothing were all impeccable. The newspaper columnists generally agreed that not since Jacqueline Kennedy had a First Lady presented a more polished, more refined image for the women of America to emulate. She was also cast by the press as being a strict taskmaster and just as fastidious about the quality of her staff's work as she was about the clothes she wore. But no matter what was said about her by the media — and some had taken offense at her vitriolic replies to criticism of her husband and her condescending attitude toward the press in general — they all gave her high marks for being charming and gracious in public, even if some of them thought it calculating and contrived.

Claudia Wentworth Marshall was born the only child of a grocery store owner in California's Napa Valley. Her father was an alcoholic who left her and her mother when Claudia was in high school. A year later, her mother met Frank Wentworth, a physician who had stopped at the store to buy cigarettes. He was taken with the handsome woman immediately and returned every weekend for three months until she consented to marry him. The new family soon moved to San Francisco.

Frank Wentworth loved Claudia as much as he loved her mother, but he didn't believe in spoiling children, so, while he provided her with all that she needed, she very often did not get all that she wanted. Sometimes she would beg her mother to intercede on her behalf, but the 39-year-old woman, glad to be out of the valley and free from the heavy burden of the store, would do nothing to contradict her husband and risk her prized security.

As penurious as he was, Frank Wentworth was adamant about good education. He sent Claudia to Mills College in Oakland, then to the University of Southern California, where she majored in music. As a lark — and without her mother's knowledge — she applied for a secretarial job at the NBC studios, hoping to make some connections that might land her a singing job on television. A friend at the university had been hired by ABC as a singer in the chorus for a variety show and was making good money. Claudia hoped for the same.

She saw her break come after about five months on the job, when she was transferred from the main secretarial pool to the executive offices of *The Donald Marshall Hour*. Among the country's most popular singers, Donald Marshall had the top-rated musical program in television. His show had been on the air only a year and already he was tied in the ratings with *The Show of Shows* and *The Jackie Gleason Show*. His staff couldn't handle the mail and telephone calls, so off Claudia went to open letters, sign eight-by-ten glossies, and, one fateful day, when his private secretary was home with the flu, take dictation from Donald Marshall himself. It was love at first sight.

Within six months they were married, and Claudia gave up all thoughts of a career to take care of her husband, whose hit television program gave way within five years to the wave of rock and roll. Disappointed, but not bitter, Donald Marshall decided to pack up and leave Tinseltown. He took his wife and their only child, Donald, Jr., and went home to Arizona, where they retired to a family ranch north of Phoenix. Donald — a simple, self-made man — was content to work the ranch and dabble a little in local politics. But Claudia missed the bright lights and drama of Hollywood. Wanting to be a devoted wife, but also wanting more than a dusty ranch in what she — coming from the fertile Napa Valley — considered the middle of nowhere, a potentially liberating phenomenon became more and more apparent to Claudia as the next few years went by. Her husband, still popular with the established middle class, was responsible for the election of several political figures in the state, including two governors, a congressman, and a senator. It was at her insistence that he offered to vigorously campaign for the Democratic presidential candidate. And, while the man lost the general election, Donald Marshall once again became a household name, not for his ubiquitous presence on "golden oldie" radio stations, but for his ability to rally voters.

Claudia Marshall knew that her husband still had a lot of influential friends in the entertainment industry — and most of them shared his political point of view. Immediately after the unsuccessful election, which was lost to a more liberal opponent, Claudia arranged a private week-long retreat at their secluded ranch in Carefree, just north of Phoenix. She invited their good friend and neighbor Thaddeus Billings and a handful of the state's leading politicos, along with a couple of well-placed and well-heeled Hollywood producers. What was billed as a vacation from politics was later to be seen as the beginning of Donald Marshall's political rise, for it was at this weekend sojourn that Claudia, Billings, and the speaker of the Arizona assembly were able to convince Donald that he had the personal power and the political backing to become governor of Arizona.

The next three months were spent feeling out financial backers in the wealthy Scottsdale community. Money was also courted from certain Arizona farmers and friends back in Hollywood — friends who speculated that Donald Marshall's star just might rise to the White House. The handsome couple began making appearances all over Arizona speaking on behalf of neoconservative groups and railing against government intervention in the affairs of farmers and small businessmen. Strong stands were taken against abortion and for prayer in public schools, and a promise was made to crack down on welfare fraud. The sensitive and volatile issue of water was skillfully skirted so as to avoid alienating either powerful political allies in Arizona or rich financial backers in southern California. The candidate promised to appoint a governor's task force to propose a solution to the dispute over water rights from the Colorado River between Arizona and California.

The time was right, and fourteen months after announcing his candidacy, Donald Marshall became the first television personality ever to rise to the office of governor. His popularity lasted two full terms.

"Good morning, girls," Claudia said, seating herself at the head of the rosewood table and unfolding her napkin so the butler could serve her eggs Benedict. "I don't know where you two get the energy to climb out of bed so early and go jogging."

"I wish I had half your energy," Elaine said pleasantly and sincerely.

Claudia smiled appreciatively. "Well, Elaine," she said, watching as her coffee was carefully poured, "it's a completely different kind of energy."

"Yes, it is," Elaine agreed, adding, "what you do is much more draining than jogging, and you do it all day long."

"Not today," Claudia said, wagging her finger at Elaine. "Today we keep it to a minimum. After my morning appointments, the only major function on the schedule is the luncheon. By the way, Jessica, I've arranged for you to go with Miles Cameron, one of the White House press officers. I hope that's all right. That way the seating works out perfectly; there will be couples at every table. Miles is very attractive. I think you'll like him."

Claudia didn't know about Jessica and Phil living together. She wouldn't have approved, and the fewer things she had to disapprove of in D.J.'s environment, the better.

"That's fine," Jessica said. "I'm always glad to meet an attractive young man, especially one with such an impressive position. He's not blond by any chance?"

Elaine kicked her under the table.

"Blond? No, I don't think so. Does that matter?"

"Her horoscope said she was going to meet a blond today," Elaine said, giving Jessica a menacing look and another swift kick in the shin.

"Oh," Claudia said, laughing, "no, that won't be Miles, dear. Afraid you'll have to keep looking. There aren't a lot of blonds around here, come to think of it."

"Well, that ought to make it easier to narrow the field," Jessica said, just to antagonize Elaine.

Elaine changed the subject. "What time are we leaving for the center?"

"The luncheon is at one o'clock. The cars will leave from here at twelve-fifty, but Jessica and Miles will go on ahead. You should probably leave around twelve-fifteen, because I don't think they'll let you park in front. Miles will have to park in the garage. I'd better make sure he knows that," she said, making a note to herself on the clipboard. "Now, if I can free up the Vice President's limo, then you won't have to worry about any of that, but as of last night he was scheduled to use it all day.

"Then," she continued, "right after lunch we'll all gather on the terrace for photos. Then we'll return here, and you and D.J. will be driven to the airport. I know you have to be back in New York tomorrow."

There was no reason at all for them to be in New York on Sunday, but Elaine didn't press the point. She figured Claudia was anxious to have D.J. out of the way.

"So, you girls are free to do what you like this morning. They're having a wonderful sale at Garfinckle's if you want to do some shopping," Claudia offered enthusiastically.

"I think I'll just stick around and wait for D.J.," Elaine said. "I'm anxious to see him."

"I think I'll take the shopping spree," Jessica said. "My brothers' birthdays are next week and I haven't bought them anything."

"You have more than one brother with a birthday in the same week?" Claudia asked.

"Yes, I have twin brothers."

"How marvelous," Claudia said. "D.J. was supposed to be twins. Doctors then didn't know how to tell much, I'm afraid. I'll arrange to have a car for you. I'll have to see which driver is available." She made still another note on the clipboard.

"Oh, please don't bother. I can walk from here."

"Nonsense," Claudia said, obviously pleased to provide such luxury for her daughter-in-law's friend. "Why should you? This is the White House."

The First Lady excused herself, and the young women lingered to read the morning papers and have more coffee. In a few minutes, Claudia reappeared. She reminded Jessica of a ship's social director as she stepped just inside the doorway, clipboard in hand, and announced, "Gary James will meet you downstairs by the elevator at ten o'clock. He's the agent who'll be your driver. You'll recognize him from this morning. He said he went running with you girls." She started back out the door, then paused and poked her head back in. "Oh, yes, mind your horoscope, Jessica. My secretary told me he's a blond."

The elevator doors opened and D.J. stepped into the central hall of the family quarters. It had been redecorated since he was last there and now antiques littered the room. He had read about the redecoration project in the French press and of the criticism his mother had come under when she undertook the task, even though she had raised the two hundred thousand dollars it cost from private sources. D.J. could see that the money had been well spent.

He walked into the living room and recognized some of the furniture from their home in Carefree. This was obviously a concession to his father, since it was very casual- and comfortable-looking furniture. "Flop furniture" his father called it. Even so, the room was tasteful, and small details such as crystal vases and small lacquered boxes from Mexico were scattered here and there among the overstuffed chairs and sofas. The room was painted red, his mother's favorite color, and he couldn't help but wonder if it was the same red used in the VIP lounge at Kennedy Airport.

"Welcome home."

D.J. turned and saw Elaine standing in the doorway, looking sporty and fresh and very glad to see him. They hugged and kissed and sat together on a sofa exchanging stories and catching up on all that had happened in the previous year. They were genuinely happy to see each other, but there was a perceptible, if understandable, uneasiness. Their friendship had kept each of them going during several rough periods, and before the marriage, D.J. used to confide in Elaine whenever he had boyfriend problems. But when Terry entered the picture, he soon found that it was a much different matter, for while Elaine loved D.J., Terry became a threat to their intimacy together. She knew that D.J.'s love for this man was different and perhaps much stronger than his love for her. It was something she took a long time adjusting to, and she had preferred not to counsel D.J. on how to cope with the problems that arose between the two lovers. It was too painful for her, almost like counseling an adversary. D.J. picked up on it right away and stopped discussing Terry with her except when she brought him up. So it became Phil Kramer to whom D.J. turned when he absolutely had to talk to someone, and although not gay, Phil turned out to be a good friend to lean on.

"Have you seen your folks?" Elaine asked.

"No, I came straight up here. Thought I'd see you and get my bearings before I attempted that. Strangely enough, it's not something I'm dying to do," D.J. said.

"They're anxious to see you," she said, trying to make him more comfortable about it, but not exactly telling the truth as she perceived it.

"I'll bet they are," D.J. said sarcastically. "You look terrific, by the way. I should have told you that right away. Really great."

"Thanks. You're not looking bad yourself. France must have agreed with you. And how's Terry?" she asked, taking D.J. by surprise.

"Fine. He's fine. I had dinner with Phil last night. He told me Jessica came with you. Where is she?"

Elaine laughed and let him change subjects for a moment. "Oh, God. She's out of control today. We went running this morning and she kept putting the make on this blond pinscher who ran with us. She's so bad."

"Well, it's reassuring to know things haven't changed any in a year," D.J. said, laughing.

"Your mother offered her the limo to go shopping at Garfinckle's and guess who happened to be her driver? The blond. So she's off with him, probably in the trunk of the car somewhere. She's so funny."

"I'm glad somebody can relax around this place. What's the agenda for today, anyway?" he asked.

"There's a printed one around here somewhere. Your mother has it down to the minute. I hope the photographers have motor drives on their cameras, because they only have nine minutes for photos after lunch."

They both laughed and D.J. took her hand. "I'm glad to see you're handling all this nonsense so well. I was afraid it might have gotten to you by this time."

"Oh, no. They leave me pretty much alone. In New York I've gotten so used to the agent that I don't know he's around most of the time. Nobody's interested in me. Even the photographers have fallen off."

"I wouldn't count on that lasting with the primaries and the convention coming up.

"And with you home," she added, reaching for the newspaper on the coffee table. "Have you seen this?"

It was the photo Claudia had shown Billings the evening before.

"No," D.J. said, taking the paper and reading the short caption beneath the photo. "Donald Marshall, Jr., son of the President, returned home today from a year's sabbatical in France, where he studied acting at the Institute de Lyons. He will visit his parents in Washington tomorrow and then begin campaigning for his father's renomination."

D.J. looked up, confused. "'Campaigning'?"

"I don't know where they get that stuff. They just make it up in the newsroom. There's no plan for you to do any campaigning that I know of. In fact I only know about one dinner we have to go to and that's weeks from now," Elaine said.

"God, I hope you're right," D.J. sighed, putting the paper down and leaning back against the bright sofa cushions. "If there's one thing I don't want to do it's hit the campaign trail." He looked at Elaine earnestly, almost as though she were in charge of the campaign and could do something about it. "Really, Elaine, I don't want to do that. I won't do that."

Terry, she thought. "Don't worry about it yet, D.J." She patted his hand. "Like I said, I haven't heard a word about any plans, and those reporters make up things. They have to have three lines of type beneath the picture and so they say anything to fill it up. They're just guessing." She stood and walked to the window behind the sofa. "If it's Terry you're concerned about, I wouldn't be.

I'm sure you can see him often enough."

This was a test, D.J. thought. "Don't be silly. It's not that at all. I just don't feel like gallivanting around the country for two months. I want to stay in New York."

Elaine turned and knelt on the floor behind the sofa, resting her chin on her hands. "You're such a bad liar."

D.J. remembered the letter he had mailed to Terry that morning. Did he mean what he'd said or didn't he? Of course, but one had to keep peace in every quarter and Elaine was no one to alienate. She would be in a position to make his life miserable if she felt slighted or pushed aside, especially after he had been away for so long with Terry. "It's not that, Elaine. Of course, Terry's there, but—"

"I hope they don't put you at the podium anywhere and ask you to make speeches," she said, smiling. "People will see right through you." She stood up and came back around and sat next to him, taking his hand again. "D.J., I love you very much. I know you love Terry. I don't understand it, but I accept it and I respect your feelings. I don't want anything to happen to make you suffer or complicate your life any more than necessary. And most of all, I don't want anything to come between us."

"Elaine, I—" D.J. interrupted, but Elaine raised her hand and put a finger to his lips, stopping him.

"D.J., I've thought about this a lot while you've been away. What you and I have together is also very special. It isn't sexual, it isn't what you have with Terry, but in some ways it's more important. It has a value of its own. A friend, a true friend, who knows you, who taps deeply into you and everything you are, and loves you for what you are and in spite of what you are, is rare. It's hard to find and it's precious. You and I have that, D.J. We know each other so completely ... we have since the very first day we met. We clicked, and within weeks, maybe even days, it was as though we had known each other our whole lives. I know what you are and what you're not and I love you because of it all. I will always be there for you; I'll always protect you, always be the one person you know you can rely on. I think that's more important than a lover or a sexual partner, because very often a sexual partner doesn't or can't get deep into what you are. But a good friend can.

"Let's open this up again, like it was before Terry, when you used to come to me and say, 'Elaine, I saw Jesus last night, wait till I tell you what happened.' Remember those days? I do. We were so close. I miss that. Since you've been gone, I've had a lot of time to think. Terry is my competition, but not the way I once thought he was. Not for your love; only for your time and some of your attention.

"When you went away we were hardly speaking, and that was my fault. I had cut you off, made it impossible for you to talk to me about him. That meant you couldn't talk to me about an important part of yourself. I want to change that. I want us to be friends again — best friends. I love you, D.J., and I'm beginning to see just how much and in just what way."

D.J. put his arms around her and they sat locked together for several minutes before he spoke. "God, I feel so much better," he said, taking her by the shoulders and looking into her eyes. "You truly are the most extraordinary person I've ever known. How could I have lost sight of that? You are a 'great' person in the truest sense of the word. I love you, too, Elaine, and I'm so glad to be back here with you. I think I can face all this shit now."

"Of course you can. We can all face it together."

"But I worry about you," he said. "I feel so guilty about what you're doing with your life, the way you're literally giving up years of your life — maybe the best years — to do this for me. What about *you?* What about *your* needs?"

"Let me be the judge of what I need," she said, touching his face tenderly. "I'm still finding myself, D.J. I was pretty misdirected before I met you. Jessica and I used to be awfully wild, you know. It was meeting you that settled me down. Granted, at first it was because I thought you were the man for me. But even after you told me about yourself and the nature of our relationship changed, you had a calming effect on me. Then when this thing came up about getting married, it was perfect. Everyone thought I was nuts, but don't you see, it was just what I needed? It has forced me into a discipline that I was unable to impose on myself.

"Now I'm a successful professional woman who's good at what she does and I have good friends and I'm with someone I really love and respect. Don't forget, there are plenty of advantages to being, or having once been, the daughter-in-law of the president of the United States. I'm fine, D.J. I'm doing exactly what I want to do. I just don't want anything to jeopardize our friendship. Ever. I need you just as much as you need me. Maybe more."

D.J. kissed her on the lips. "Baby, if I were straight..."

"If you were straight, what?" she asked, daring him to finish the statement.

"If I were straight, you would be the only woman I would ever even think of."

Elaine looked around in all directions, as though they might be overheard, then leaned a little closer and whispered in her best Bette Davis voice, "But ya aren't, Blanche, but ya aren't."

The Kennedy Center luncheon went off without a hitch. D.J. and Elaine were the perfect lovebirds, holding hands the entire time and saying nothing, their faces locked in perpetual smiles as a result of a joint they'd shared with Jessica in the Queen's bedroom just before they left the White House.

D.J.'s reunion with his parents took place in the limousine. As they gathered beneath the east portico to get into the car, D.J. leaned over to Elaine and asked, "Which one is my mother?" For a moment Elaine thought she was going to have to go back inside to regain her composure. She kept the laughter down to several giggles, which clearly annoyed Claudia. The President just assumed she was giddy with joy at everyone being together again after so long.

After lunch they returned to the White House and went up to the family quarters. The visit was pleasant enough, and D.J.'s parents, especially his father, seemed genuinely happy to see him. His time abroad was discussed only in terms of the acting classes and some of the more popular places he'd seen in France. When, at one point, he began to describe a weekend trip "we" took to Chartres, the subject was abruptly changed and sympathetic glances cast toward Elaine. After forty-five minutes, Jessica entered and the party broke up with kisses and handshakes. Claudia and Jessica disappeared to round up the bags that had to be taken to the airport and the President excused himself to return to the Oval Office.

Billings rode with D.J. and Elaine to the airport in one car, and Jessica and the luggage rode behind in the Secret Service escort station wagon. Billings had a typed list of instructions and suggestions, which he began to go over as soon as they pulled onto Pennsylvania Avenue.

They would have the month of April free, but on May tenth there would be a dinner at the Waldorf Astoria given by the New York Bankers' Association; the following afternoon Elaine would visit a day care center in Harlem, and that evening they were to attend a special performance of a Broadway play sponsored by the Manhattan United Charities. The following day, Sunday, they would attend a picnic of the New York Jewish Guild in Central Park. There were to be no speeches and no statements, and a White House press aide would fly up to be with them in case they ran into any reporters they couldn't handle.

Other functions would be scheduled as appropriate and they would be briefed beforehand as to what the administration's positions were toward each event's sponsoring special-interest group. No statements were to be given to the media without the express approval of Billings or the White House Communications Office. Their schedule would be kept light, involving only secondary functions that required no speeches, statements, or press accessibility. Were there any questions?

D.J. looked at Elaine and squeezed her hand as he broached the dread subject with Billings, who sat facing them on a jump seat behind the driver. "We need to discuss Terry," he said, the words sticking in his throat a little. This was not the setting he had imagined the countless times he'd rehearsed what he was going to say to Thaddeus on the subject. He had thought they might be able to talk in more private surroundings, but he hadn't even seen Billings until they got into the car to drive to National Airport.

Billings eyed Elaine for her reaction. From the expressionless look in her eyes, he could tell she and D.J. were a united front. Very well, he decided, they would discuss Terry openly and frankly. "Terry will begin working with the New York Transit Authority starting next Monday. He will be part of a maintenance section that repairs buses. Nine to five-thirty, Monday through Friday, on call every other weekend. It pays twenty-one five per year, and there's potential for advancement if he's good at it."

This took both of them completely by surprise. They looked at each other, chastising themselves with their glances for not having guessed that Billings would have laid detailed plans regarding Terry. Elaine saw that D.J. needed time to regroup, so she occupied Billings momentarily while D.J. thought about how to steer the conversation to the heart of the matter.

"Have you discussed this with Terry? Perhaps he has other plans," she said.

"Terry had lunch this afternoon with his new boss. He has accepted the position and from what I can gather is looking forward to starting work on Monday," Billings said triumphantly. "He's going to be a very busy young man with his new responsibilities."

"Not too busy to spend some time with me, I trust," D.J. said, testing.

"Everyone's going to be busy from here on out, Donald, including you. There's not going to be much time for socializing."

Donald, eh? D.J. thought. So he wants to play tough. "I hardly call spending time with one's spouse 'socializing,' Thaddeus," D.J. replied tersely.

"You have only one spouse," Billings said sharply, growing irritated at having to have this discussion in front of Elaine. He had planned to take D.J. aside at the airport to discuss Terry and was angry that he had to talk about such an "indelicate" subject in front of a woman. "Until the campaign is over — and that includes the time from the convention to the general election — you will be quite married to Elaine. There's not going to be any funny business from here on, especially during the primaries. Your wife is your spouse, and the re-election committee will tolerate nothing else, either from you or from Terry."

"Look here, Thaddeus, if you think I'm going from now until November without seeing Terry, you're wrong. I'll go to my father if necessary."

Billings was growing red in the face. He hated having to struggle with a member of the family. Politicians and administration officials he could handle with ease; after all, he was the chief administrator and closest counsel to the top man, but he was only too aware of the President's deep concern and affection for D.J. and had for years avoided, at all costs, getting involved in any power struggle between the two of them, because in the end he knew that Donald Marshall's overriding priority was to protect his family. There could be no certainty that a confrontation among the President, Billings, and D.J. would result in Donald Marshall deciding in favor of his own political advantage. Billings considered it to be the President's one fatal area of vulnerability. When it came to family, Marshall acted out of instinct. His wife and son always came first.

"I'm speaking for your father," Billings said, treading out into deep water.

"That's funny," D.J. said sarcastically, "it sounds more like my mother."

It was all too clear to Billings that D.J. knew his parents well — much better than Billings would like. He retreated a little.

"This matter affects both your parents. It affects you and it affects the country, the entire world for that matter. It's not a game we're playing, and it's not our own personal interests that are the criteria for our decisions and our actions. There are larger concerns here, Donald, and it's time you and Terry realize that. It's time to start behaving like ... adults." He had almost said "men." That would definitely have proven catastrophic.

D.J. leaned closer to Thaddeus, resting his elbows on his knees and clasping his hands together. "Thaddeus," he said in what was almost a conciliatory manner. Billings took his cue and lowered his voice. "What is it, D.J.?"

"I am going to see Terry."

Billings looked to Elaine for help in reasoning with D.J. She sat stone-faced, obviously siding with her husband. Billings looked out the window and saw that they were leaving the George Washington Parkway and making their way into the airport proper. This was getting them no-where, and he didn't want to part with hostility between them. "All right," he said, "I'll see what I can do," implying that he would have to check with the President. "But wait until you hear from me and let's have a gentlemen's agree-ment. You will call me when you want to see him. At least allow me to do my job, to make certain that the conditions are right in order to protect your father."

"Agreed," D.J. said, "but I don't mean to be put off. I'm not talking about one visit every three weeks."

"Call me," Billings said as the car pulled up to the main entrance of the terminal. "That's all I ask."

The car door swung open and the three of them stepped out. D.J. walked to the escort car to get Jessica, as Secret Service agents formed a protective ring around the party, separating them from the quickly gathering crowd of trav-elers who were rushing to see who was in the limousine with the Secret Service escorts.

Billings stepped out, turned, and took Elaine's arm as she emerged from the car. He gripped her tightly, holding her in place, and she gave him a sharp look. "We're going to need you in this campaign, Elaine. In many ways. Reason with him."

"He's my husband, Mr. Billings," Elaine said, smiling. "It's my duty to honor and obey him. The First Lady taught me that."

New York City

The next few weeks grew increasingly difficult for D.J. as Terry fell deeper and deeper into depression over their forced separation. Terry was working at the job Billings had procured for him and seemed to be doing well so far as D.J. could tell. When they talked on the phone, Terry would not initiate discussion of anything except the two of them, but if D.J. could work the job into the conversation and pressed him long enough, Terry would eventually pick up on it and talk about it with considerable enthusiasm, telling D.J. of his accomplishments. He would speak of things he could fix that even some of the men who had been on the job for fifteen and twenty years couldn't.

While Terry's low spirits were a concern to D.J., ironically they were also a relief to him, because Terry's former pattern of behavior was not to get depressed, but to grow angry and rebellious. As discomforting as it was, D.J. would rather think of Terry home sulking than of him running the streets and increasing his use of alcohol and drugs, as he had done in the past. Perhaps the job really did help. But he knew it was no guarantee, and toward the beginning of May, Terry's phone calls started coming more and more frequently and more often than not in the early hours of the morning.

Elaine had been a great comfort through it. Their reunion had been the happiest part of his homecoming so far, and he felt closer to her now than ever before. They had even started sleeping together again from time to time — as friends. When the phone would ring at two or three a.m. and Terry would deliver his garbled lament and then hang up on D.J., Elaine would wait to hear the receiver being replaced on the hook and then come in and sit on D.J.'s bed and they would talk, or she would simply stroke his head and reassure him with the lies one always wants to hear in hopeless situations. Often she would end up climbing into bed next to him and they would fall back to sleep together.

The latest in the series of nightly calls was the most disturbing. D.J. was awakened by the phone a little after four a.m., but when he answered, there was only silence on the other end. He lay half-asleep with the receiver on the pillow next to his ear for a long time — so long that he thought perhaps Terry had already hung up. Finally the voice on the other end spoke: "Fuck all of you." Then there was the familiar click and eventually the loud dial tone in D.J.'s ear. So it has come to this, D.J. thought, trying to go back to sleep. Now I'm one of the enemy.

The following night, D.J. couldn't sleep at all. At two a.m. he got up and phoned Terry, but there was no answer. He tried again at two-thirty and once more at three-fifteen, but Terry wasn't home. At four he called for the last time. Nothing. D.J. went to the kitchen and made a pot of coffee, then sat on the sill and watched the dawn break over the Hudson. He couldn't go on like this. Something had to give, and with his father now losing ground in the public opinion polls over the APANS sale, it was going to be more difficult than ever to convince Billings that he and Terry needed more time together. They had seen each other only three times since their return.

The arrangement was that D.J. and Parker would meet Terry in front of New York University's Cardinal Newman Center across from Washington Square. The limousine would stop, Terry would climb in, and they would drive through Central Park or up the Henry Hudson Parkway, where they could talk and eventually make love in the slow-moving Cadillac. It was better than nothing, D.J. told himself, and tried to believe it. He would call Billings that afternoon to try to reason with him.

Arlington, Virginia

Billings and his dinner companions ordered dessert, brandy, and coffee. He had chosen Chez Andre in Arlington for their meeting because it was off the path beaten by most Washington officials and newspeople. They sat at a table in a far corner of the room. He had made polite conversation throughout the meal, hating to discuss business while trying to enjoy good food.

Steven Linwood, Washington lobbyist for Fairbanks Aircraft Corporation of Seattle, kept the conversation going, steering it away from APANS, until Billings decided to bring it up. Linwood was a handsome and athletic middle-aged blond with a Boston accent who went to work for

Fairbanks after serving as undersecretary of defense in the Reagan administration. His style was smooth as a titanium fuselage and just as unflappable.

Senator Owen Tugg of Washington sat with his back to the room, just in case someone from the Hill happened to be dining there. General Robert "Bombin' Bob" Gridding, chairman of the Joint Chiefs of Staff, wore civilian clothes, but his crew cut gave him away.

"Owen," Billings began after dessert had been served, "how do things look up on the Hill?"

"No way to paint things rosy, Thad," he answered. "It's not going to be an easy row to hoe. I'm getting nowhere with most of my distinguished colleagues. Even some party regulars are holding out."

"But for what?" Gridding said, jumping right in. "That's what I don't understand. Some of those boys own more stock in Fairbanks than I do."

"It's not money this time. You got to remember, this is an election year for most of them," Tugg said, raising his eyebrows and cocking his head.

"Bullshit!" Gridding said. "Cavoli would sell his wife if the price was right. Besides, he's not running for re-election. What the hell is his problem?"

"Well, Owen?" Linwood asked. "You know Sal better than any of us."

Tugg looked across the table at Billings and frowned. "He's waiting for Marshall," he said, as though Billings should have known the answer.

"Waiting for Marshall?" Billings asked.

"He's pissed," Tugg explained. "The President has called over a dozen senators in the past month. All the young bucks, the kids, as Sal puts it. He thinks he carries a lot of weight up there. He's never gotten over being beaten for minority whip. A call would go a long way. Even now."

Billings took a small pad from his jacket pocket and made a note in it.

"I'm worried," said Gridding, lighting a cigar. "It doesn't look good from where I sit." He blew a cloud of blue smoke across the table which Linwood immediately began to fan away. "Not one vote has changed in over two weeks and now I hear Packard and Stevenson are going to change their votes."

"You've been reading the newspapers again," Billings said and everyone but Gridding laughed.

"It's not a joke, Thad, and I don't see how you can take it so goddamn lightly. They might just be voting on your job."

"I'm not taking it lightly, first of all," Billings said good-naturedly. "I know probably better than anyone how crucial this vote is, but I also know we're going to win. The President is going to pull this one off and leave everyone with his jaw hanging."

"Has he got an ace up his sleeve we don't know about?" Tugg asked optimistically.

"Yes," Billings said, running a forefinger around the rim of his water glass, "but I can't go into detail about it. The element of surprise is essential."

"Can't you even give us a hint?" Gridding urged.

"Now, Bob," Linwood said, "if Thad says it's in the bag, that should be good enough for us. He hasn't been wrong yet."

"Well, I'm glad to see you're so sure," Gridding said, blowing more smoke in Linwood's face, causing him to close his eyes and fan the air once more. "From what I remember of the last look I had at Fairbanks's books, Steven, I'd say they're going to be voting on your job, too."

Linwood looked over at Billings, whose face was expressionless. "Oh, now, Bob, c'mon. Things aren't that bad," Linwood said, watching Billings for some sign of assurance that what he was saying was being confirmed by the President's chief of staff.

"Yeah, well, I'm thinking mighty seriously about selling my stock," Gridding said, leaning forward for emphasis.

Linwood's face registered uneasiness with that remark, but Billings took the men's attention away by announcing, "Maybe you'd like to sell it to me, since I'm looking to buy some."

All heads at the table turned in astonishment. "You're going to buy Fairbanks stock?" Tugg asked. "You're that sure of the vote?"

"I tell you guys, if you all pull your weight and do your part and stop acting like Henny Pennies, this thing will go exactly the way we want it. But what I'm seeing here, frankly, gives me some doubt about your loyalties."

They all began to talk at once, reassuring Billings that the White House could always depend upon each of them. Billings held up his hand for quiet. "Well, then, for Christ's sake, start talking positive. O ye of little faith! Your President has a plan and it will work, but you guys have got to fall in line behind him and give him your full and enthusiastic support."

He addressed each one in turn. "Owen, you can't go moaning and groaning through the halls of the Senate, wailing about how many senators aren't voting with the party. Start talking about how many *are* in favor of this bill. Emphasize the positive, make them think they're going to be left out in the cold if they don't support him. And let me assure you here and now, and you may quote me, they will indeed be left out in the cold — the November cold.

"Steve, you need to be sure you're in town more. I tried to get you all of last Thursday and Friday and you had flown back to Seattle. You can't lobby senators in Seattle. Now, the first thing you need to do is not only attend these various social functions that are going on around town, but throw a shindig yourself. And you'd better do it soon, because these guys are going to be hightailing it back to their districts as soon as they can for their summer recess. Most of them are commuting now, trying to save their asses in the primaries.

"Bob, you're complaining the loudest, and yet your department has probably caused the greatest setback. Who the hell sent that gofer up to the Hill to testify before the Senate committee? McCann had a field day with that little asshole. Why the hell you didn't go yourself we'll never know. If I had known you were sending someone else, I would have jumped on your ass so fast."

"It doesn't look good for me to—" Gridding began explaining.

"Jesus Christ, Bob. Nobody knows what kind of stock you have or how much. You're too goddamn paranoid. You don't send a lackey to testify before the Senate Foreign Relations Committee. They were so insulted, I'm surprised they even met with him. Now I'm telling you guys to dig in and get with it. The President is doing his part, but he can't do it alone. And to show you how sure I am — *if* you men pitch in — I'm offering to buy another five thousand shares of Fairbanks."

The group fell silent, the astonishment all over their faces, Linwood more shocked than any of them.

"That's right. By this time next year, Fairbanks will be filling so many APANS orders, they'll have to build another plant. But it can't happen without your help."

They all assured Billings they would start first thing in the morning to crank up their individual political machinery. They toasted the passage of the bill and then Tugg and Gridding said good night. Linwood stayed behind with Billings to pick up the tab. "Thank you," he said to the waiter as he took the receipt from his charge card. "Are you really going to purchase stock, or was that for their benefit?" he asked Billings.

"I'm prepared to buy the stock, but not in my name, of course," Billings said. "And naturally it depends on whether the price is right."

Linwood smiled. "The catch. I knew there was one waiting around the corner somewhere. I'll see what I can do. I have to go back to ... I mean I have to call Seattle tomorrow. By the way, do you have any news about the investigation that I might be able to pass on to the boss? He's pretty nervous. This thing has been dragging on for over a month now."

Fairbanks had supplied the major airlines with one hundred of its newest jumbo jets in the past two years, and within the previous four months, three of them had crashed because of what experts believed to be a poorly designed front landing gear. The remaining planes had been grounded for almost a month now while the FAA conducted an investigation into the matter.

"It won't be much longer. I should have a preliminary report on my desk by the end of the week. Have they made the replacements?" Billings asked, lowering his voice, as a couple was seated at a table next to them.

"Yes, that's been going on now since the first day of the grounding. The graveyard shifts have completed all but one or two, so far as I know. Of course, there's the one they've impounded. That will still show the first design."

"Well, if they did it right, and I'm not implying they didn't, no one will be able to tell."

"That's right, it wasn't the design, actually, it was the gearing material. That's been completely changed and wiped off the records. The three in question were flukes, so far as they know."

As they walked to the coat check room, Billings told him he would talk to him about the investigating committee's findings over the weekend. "At your cocktail party," Billings said, patting him on the back.

"My...? Oh, yes, the cocktail party I'm throwing next weekend, right." They laughed as they collected their briefcases.

"Well, well, well," a female voice said, slurring the words a little. Linwood blanched and Billings turned to find Bif Tucker's wife, Jenny, standing behind him. She was a thin, shapely blonde, noted around town for her acid tongue and her ample bust. She was wearing a dark green cocktail dress that clung tightly in all the right places.

"Good evening, Mrs. Tucker," Billings said.

"Jennifer," Linwood said, nodding in acknowledgment, and regaining some of his color.

"How nice to see you," Billings said. "What brings you all the way across the river? I thought this place was my little secret."

"Save it for your fans, Billings," Jenny said, not looking at him, but staring a hole through Linwood.

"Well," Linwood said, uneasily, "we're just leaving. Enjoy your meal." He nudged Billings toward the door, but as they began to move past her, Jenny reached out and grabbed Linwood by the sleeve of his jacket. "Hey, you," she said nastily. "Don't give me any shit."

Billings waited at the door while the two engaged in a short but heated argument. Finally, Linwood broke away and motioned for Billings to keep moving as he made his way toward the door of the restaurant. Jenny was now trying to prop herself up by leaning on a ficus tree. Once outside, Billings gave Linwood a look of great curiosity.

"If you must know," Linwood said, "we had a short thing last fall. I'm afraid it broke off rather unpleasantly and she takes every opportunity to embarrass me."

Billings said nothing.

"But I hear *you* have her in tow," Linwood said as they started for the parking lot.

"Me?" Billings said, thoroughly confused.

"I mean the collective 'you'; the royal 'you'; the White House."

"I don't follow you," Billings said.

"Oh, come on, Thad. Everyone in town knows she's sleeping with Cameron. I can't imagine I'm the only one who's figured out why. What I'd like to know is how Bif can be so ignorant of it. I guess it's like they say, the husband's always the last to know."

"Wait a minute," Billings said, stopping Linwood by grabbing at his arm. "You mean to tell me Miles Cameron is having an affair with Jennifer Tucker?"

"Oh, Jesus, Thad, you don't have to play dumb with me. I think it's great. What a way to get your info on his campaign, but how can you tell when she's telling the truth or when it's just the ramblings of an alcoholic? Oh, well, that's your problem. Good night," he said and turned and walked to his car.

The White House

Billings stood in the corner behind his desk staring at the large office he occupied as chief of staff. It was furnished with authentic antiques that had been found in one of the government warehouses shortly after the Marshall administration took office. In one of his last peacemaking gestures toward Claudia Marshall, Billings asked her shortly after Inauguration Day if she would decorate his office, since she had such an eye for color and had always done so well with the rooms she had undertaken in her homes. She protested at first, but was finally persuaded. In her penchant for warm colors, she had chosen oranges and browns. "It will help cut down the intimidation people will automatically feel when you call them in," she explained to Billings the day it was finished as she led him down the hall to see it for the first time. The walls were papered with a burnt orange linen and the carpeting was deep brown. The painting she chose for the only wall bearing artwork was a Remington that was mostly desert and blue sky with a lone horseman in the distance. The room didn't bother him, but he hated the painting. He thought it was depressing, especially for a working environment.

He stared at it now, wondering how he could have it removed without hurting Claudia's feelings and thereby bringing her vengeance down upon him. There was no way to have it removed or replaced without going through her secretary. His thoughts were interrupted by the buzzing of his intercom.

"Mr. Cameron is here," his assistant said.

"Yes, tell him to come in," Billings answered, sitting down in the high-backed leather chair. "Miles, come in and have a seat," Billings said, gesturing to the leather armchair on the other side of his large mahogany desk. "I won't keep you long, because I know how busy you are."

"That's quite all right," Cameron said, crossing his legs and positioning a yellow legal tablet on his thigh in order to take notes if it became necessary, as it usually did in meetings with the chief of staff.

Cameron was a slightly built, dark-haired fellow, thirty-four years old, a graduate of the University of California at Berkeley, and a former reporter for the *San Jose Mercury*. He met Bif Tucker through his older brother, who was Tucker's classmate at Stanford. The two men were teammates at the Olympics. When Tucker decided to run for the California Legislature, Miles and his older brother both went to work campaigning for him. At the time, Miles was just out of college and deeply interested in politics, but from the public relations angle. When Tucker won a second term, he asked Miles to come to Sacramento to work for him and Miles accepted, being genuinely devoted to Tucker's liberal politics and convinced that he was never going to get a chance at the *Mercury* to do more than chase fire engines and police ambulances.

In Sacramento, he quickly won the reputation of being an effective and articulate spokesperson for Tucker's office and the politics of the left. He moved smoothly and quietly around the state capital, winning allies and lining up votes on Tucker's bills. He was on everybody's party list, and when lobbyists came to Sacramento to solicit Tucker's endorsements, they knew to start by winning over Cameron. While other political aides who were successful at their jobs grabbed the spotlight and found themselves in the gossip columns of the *Sacramento Bee,* Cameron astutely avoided such publicity. His private life was his most valued possession, and he guarded it with the same vigilance with which he guarded that of his boss.

When Tucker married Jennifer White, daughter of a Marin County architect, the service was so small and simple that the press didn't even know about it until after it was over. He called them into the pressroom in Sacramento and announced it the Monday after the ceremony. It was this kind of protection and manipulation of the press that earned him their enmity. Having once been a newshound, Cameron knew exactly how to avoid them and even to throw them completely off the scent of their prey.

After his second term as a state senator, Tucker was appointed to serve out the term of a U.S. senator who was forced to resign because of ill health. His appointment was widely hailed by state politicos, and they all predicted an eventual run for the presidency. It came as a great shock to those who knew both Tucker and Cameron when Miles chose not to go to Washington with the new senator, but to take a position with a Los Angeles consulting firm.

Within the next two years, he underwent what observers called a remarkable metamorphosis. He divorced his wife almost immediately after moving to southern California, became a high-powered idea man within his firm, and, when Donald Marshall announced his presidential candidacy, was one of the first prominent businessmen in Los Angeles to offer his support. He joined the campaign, taking a leave of absence from his job, and worked closely with party headquarters in California. He soon became infamous for his ability to turn liberals into conservatives, or at least to garner their support for Marshall in the primary. Billings never trusted him, but finally conceded his value when the two most liberal precincts in the northern half of the state cast the majority of their primary votes for Marshall. Billings was outnumbered ten to one when he opposed bringing Cameron onto the White House staff in the Communications Office. He had no justification for not wanting to sign him up other than an instinctive distrust for the man. Billings lost.

Cameron came to Washington and was one of the most well-liked staff members at the White House. He continued to adroitly handle the press and was still as much of a phantom in his private life as always, but in Washington, where there are so many prominent people to gossip about, the newspaper columnists left him completely alone.

"As you know," Billings began, his hands folded on the highly waxed mahogany desk, "the First Lady is having a luncheon here on Thursday for the wives of the American Morality League. They will be naming her honorary chairperson of their annual fund-raising drive for retarded children."

"Yes," Cameron answered, his icy blue eyes fixed on Billings, waiting for the trap he always assumed was being laid for him by the President's right-hand man. "I approved the news release for it yesterday."

"Well, what you may not know is that while the women are having lunch, the President will be meeting with Horace Dolan in the Oval Office."

"No, I didn't know that," Cameron lied.

"Dolan is going to make some ... well, shall we call them 'requests' of the President, in exchange for his endorsement."

"That doesn't surprise me," Cameron said, smiling knowingly.

"We will consider some of those requests, and when the bartering has gone back and forth for a while, we will agree to one of them."

"And which one is that?" Miles asked.

"What I'm telling you here is confidential, Cameron. No one must know until after the meeting," Billings warned.

"I understand," Cameron assured him.

"We will agree to appoint his assistant to serve as undersecretary of education if we are re-elected."

The two men sat staring at each other, Billings trying to read Cameron's reaction, Cameron trying not to show any.

"Yes?" Miles said finally, inviting Billings to go on.

"Well, what do you think?" Billings asked.

Miles smiled and turned his legal tablet, pulling it closer. "Think about what?" he asked.

"About the appointment, of course."

"Mr. Billings," Miles said softly and without malice, "if you are asking me what I think about how best to announce such a thing after President Marshall is re-elected, I will have to give it some thought and get back to you. If you are asking me what I think about it as a political move, then you have my job here confused with someone else's. I'm part of the Communications Office; I have nothing to do with policy or campaign strategy. You make decisions; I only digest and disseminate them."

Billings leaned back in his chair, admiring the distance Cameron kept. He could have brought in anyone else from the White House staff and made the same disclosure and had instant advice on the political ramifications of such a move, but not with Miles Cameron. Not with foxy Miles Cameron. "What I meant was I want you to tell me how you would handle any leaks about it. Once we tell Dolan, you know it will leak. How do we face the press when they come back to us with questions about this?"

Cameron didn't miss a beat. "We tell them what we should tell them whenever they grab at rumors about future appointments. Future presidential appointments can only be made in the future, by future presidents. It would be a waste of time to comment on any crystal-balling that people might be inclined to engage in prior to the election in November. The President has urgent issues confronting him right now. Why and how would he take the time to consider future appointments of undersecretaries in a term of office he hasn't been elected to serve? Surely, there must be some important questions the press has to ask about things the President is dealing with currently."

Billings smiled in spite of his dislike for Cameron. The man was as wily as himself, and, while he didn't trust him and perhaps even feared him a little, he certainly had to admire him. He was not only good, he was quick on his feet. He only hoped he was in Marshall's camp, as everyone around the White House assured him.

"Very well," Billings said, "that will be our position. I'd appreciate it if you would give it more thought and try to anticipate what, if any, other complications might arise around this sensitive matter. As you know, we have to placate the moderates this time as well. They're not as pro-Marshall as they were four years ago."

"I understand," Cameron said. "Is that all?"

"Yes," Billings answered, rising to walk him to the door. "By the way," Billings injected, trying to sound as though it were an afterthought, "do you ever hear anything from your old boss?"

On the other side of the doorway, Cameron turned to face Billings. "Mr. Dannenbaum?" Miles asked, referring to the chief executive officer of his former consulting firm in Los Angeles and trying not to laugh at his own cleverness.

Billings gave him a quizzical look. "No, I mean Tucker. How's he doing these days? Thought maybe he'd try to woo you back into his camp. A presidential candidate could use a good pressman like you."

"I imagine you could tell me a great deal more about Tucker's campaign than I could tell you, Mr. Billings. After all, you and Mr. Stone receive all the information on the opposition around here."

Billings stared at him coldly. Was Cameron insulting him? "Funny," Billings replied, "I thought all the information came through your office."

Again, Cameron didn't pause, but shot right back at Billings, letting him know he wasn't playing with one of the junior varsity. "It does. After you give it to us, we tell the world what you want them to know."

There was a moment of silence in which Billings decided not to pursue this endless chain of double-talk, lest he be forced into a nasty confrontation. He laughed and held out his hand for Miles to shake, which he did firmly. "I see we have the right man in your job, Cameron. Carry on." With that, Billings turned and went back into his office, shutting the door behind him.

Miles Cameron proceeded down the hall to his office, where he too shut the door and pondered just why the chief of staff was calling in an assistant press secretary and telling him the most confidential of political campaign information. Just who did Billings expect him to tell? And how would Billings ever find out whether or not he passed the information along? He decided to cancel his plans for the evening and remain at home. It was just possible that Billings was having him watched.

New York City

Terry walked along the West Street waterfront near the abandoned warehouses, stopping once in a while to stare out across the Hudson. He had been walking aimlessly since he left the apartment of a man he had met the night before in Pete's, one of the seedier West Side bars. He had no recollection of anything that happened after they arrived at the man's Soho loft and began snorting large amounts of cocaine. When he met the man, he was already high on a double hit of sunshine acid he had taken before he left home in the early evening.

He didn't think he had slept, but he wasn't tired yet. He should call work and tell them he wouldn't be in, but there was no money in his pockets, only the keys to his apartment and half a quaalude. He entered one of the abandoned warehouses and walked toward the far end that opened onto the water. He was tense and depressed as he walked through the door at the far end and sat down on the concrete pier. He leaned back against the sheet metal wall, taking off his t-shirt and feeling the sun, warm on his chest. Suddenly he was back on the beach near Marseille where he and D.J. had spent a long weekend the previous summer.

He recalled the white sand, the sound of gulls crying above the blue water flecked with light, children playing in the foamy surf. He smiled to himself and reached his hand out to where, had he actually been in France, D.J. would be lying on the blanket beside him, but his palm came down on the cool, rough concrete. He withdrew it quickly without opening his eyes. A shadow blocked the sun above him, but he kept his eyes shut and waited for it to pass. In a few seconds, he felt the sun again, and then a tongue lightly licked his left nipple. He lay motionless as fingers worked open his buttoned fly. This was not why he had come here, but he was too weary to offer any resistance. When it was over, he drifted into sleep, the never-seen stranger having disappeared back into the dark, cool interior of the abandoned warehouse. He dreamed of the beach near Marseille, and in his dream, he was there with D.J. sleeping on the sand next to him. When he awoke, it was after five. He could go home, clean up, and be at the Ramrod before happy hour was over.

New York City

"What the hell is going on? Why can't I talk to my father?" D.J. shouted angrily into the phone at the nervous receptionist.

"Just a minute, Mr. Marshall," she said, "I'm connecting you now."

"Mr. Billings's office," the voice on the other end said.

"I don't want Mr. Billings, I want to talk to the President," D.J. demanded.

"Please hold for Mr. Billings," the voice said. There was some clicking, and the next voice D.J. heard was that of the White House chief of staff.

"Billings," Thaddeus said officiously into the receiver.

"Thaddeus, I want to talk to my father," D.J. said.

"D.J.," Billings said too warmly for it to be sincere, "how are things going in New York?"

"Thaddeus, why won't they connect me to my father's office?" D.J. asked, ignoring Billings's pleasantry.

"The President is in a very important meeting at the moment, D.J. Perhaps I can help you."

"This must be a real crisis; I've been trying to get through to him for two days now, and all I get is the runaround. What are you pulling?"

"Now, son, no one is pulling anything," Billings said as though he were speaking with one of his staff . "There have been a number of things that have demanded your father's attention here for the past twenty-four hours and he isn't taking calls from anyone. If you read the papers, you'd know your father is fighting an important battle on the Hill, and it's taking a lot out of him."

"Yeah, yeah, I know all about APANS. But since when can't he take five minutes to talk to his son?" D.J. asked, knowing full well that Billings had given instructions not to put D.J.'s calls through to the President, but to refer them to him.

"It's not that simple, I'm afraid. A five-minute interruption can break hours of concentration. It can completely ruin one's train of thought, especially when you're dealing with a matter this complex. Besides, we're keeping all lines open, so your father can have direct and immediate access to congressional offices, should there be any changes in votes on the Hill."

"Well, I'm sure it's important, but so is this. I have to see Terry. I don't know what's going on with him. I haven't been able to contact him for days now."

Billings was quiet for a moment. He had been so involved in the APANS fight on the Hill that he hadn't had time to keep very close tabs on Terry or D.J. If Terry hadn't been in touch with D.J., it could mean that he was slipping. He would have to do some intelligence gathering and get back to D.J.

"Look, I'll call you this evening with details of when you can see him," Billings promised.

"I'll be waiting," D.J. said and hung up in Billings's ear.

Thaddeus made a few phone calls and by the end of the day learned that Terry hadn't been to work for two days and no one knew where he was. He called Carl Stone and arranged to have Terry put under surveillance, but not through a federal agency. "Just have him watched, Carl. We need to know exactly what he's up to."

"Is he going to fuck us up?" Stone asked in his usual crude and abrupt manner.

"Not if we keep one step ahead of him. So long as I know where he is and what he's doing I can keep the lid on."

"That's what we thought last time," Stone said antagonistically, referring to Terry's dangerous behavior before being shipped abroad with D.J.

"Look, Carl, I don't need sermons, I need some cooperation. If you're too busy with the re-election committee, just say so, and I'll go elsewhere," Billings said sharply.

Stone chuckled, knowing Billings had nowhere else to turn for a clandestine operation like this. "I'll tail him for you. But this time, why don't you let me handle it? This sort of thing isn't up your alley."

"I'll let you know if I need any further assistance in the matter. For now, let's just roll on Snowman," Billings said curtly, referring to the code name they had given Terry after he was observed buying one ounce of cocaine a week the first time they had to watch him.

"You want the complete ski package?" Stone asked, meaning did Billings want him to tap the phone and provide photos.

Billings hated using coded language; it made him feel foolish. "Whatever appears appropriate. I'll leave that to you," Billings said.

"What's the scoop on Northwest?" Stone asked, referring to Billings's dinner with Linwood. "Is there going to be a signing?"

"I haven't heard yet. They'll get back to me in another week or so."

"Okay," Stone said, "I'll be in touch. I only need two days' notice for signatures."

Billings disliked discussing these things on the phone, but at times there was no choice. He wondered every time he hung up after talking to Stone if his own conversations were being recorded. It was a chance he had to take. Besides, the only person he could think of with the resources to do it was Stone, and he was on Billings's side. They were both working for one thing and one thing only — to preserve the presidency of Donald Marshall.

Thaddeus didn't care much for his brother-in-law, but he knew there was no member of Marshall's administration more loyal than Carl Stone, and certainly no one who could handle covert operations as deftly.

Carl had tried to go to college after high school, flunked out, and joined the army, where he became interested in intelligence work. He was good at it and rose through the ranks steadily, retiring after twenty years. After he was discharged from the army at age thirty-nine, he went to night school and earned a law degree, then went to work for a right-wing, archconservative group doing intelligence work and some legal consulting.

Some five years after Carl joined the group, the organization's president was arrested for lewd conduct in a public rest room in Mobile, Alabama, and hanged himself in the county jailhouse. Disillusioned and cynical, Carl quit his job and was soon grabbed up by Billings, who was looking for someone to gather information in Marshall's second campaign for governor. Carl met Billings's widowed sister-in-law, Rebecca, and they were married. She was forty-one at the time and had an only son by her previous marriage. The boy, Billy Dailey, a wild and rebellious young man, ran away from home shortly after his mother married Carl Stone. He went to Las Vegas and took a job in a hotel. After a fire broke out and four people died, Billy was charged with arson and eventually sent to the Nevada state prison.

Like Billings, Carl had little time for a family life and devoted all his energy to serving Donald Marshall, or at least serving Marshall's rise to power, and thereby his own.

New York City

D.J. lay motionless in the tub. When he had first gotten in, the water was so hot it turned his skin crimson, but he stayed there, telling himself the heat would burn out all the bile and venom he felt had built up in him over the last month. The perspiration ran freely down his face, and his hair lay limp on his head, several strands lying pasted to his forehead in banglike points almost to his eyebrows. Beads of moisture darted, quick as minnows, down the black tile walls around the tub, then stopped just as suddenly, as though trying not to be caught moving. The mirrored wall at the foot of the large tub was completely steamed over. Four large candles on the ridge of the tub provided light in the room.

D.J. suddenly felt a rush of cold air on his face and opened his eyes to find Parker standing in the doorway.

"You're really getting good at that, Parker," D.J. said, closing his eyes again and leaning his head back against the black porcelain.

"Good at what, sir?" Parker asked, adopting his subservient tone of voice, which could easily be taken as sarcasm.

"At sneaking up on me," D.J. said, sighing.

"Sorry, sir, didn't mean to startle you."

"Don't flatter yourself, Parker. You never startle anyone, except perhaps with your looks."

Parker paused to think that one over. He had been a member of his college varsity wrestling team and had participated in bodybuilding competitions before joining the service. He wasn't grotesquely developed, but he was phenomenally strong, and D.J. had no doubt that one smack of the back of Parker's hand would put any man out cold. It may have been one of the reasons D.J. enjoyed antagoniz-

ing him from time to time. He knew Parker wouldn't —
couldn't — hit him, but there was always that one-in-a-mil-
lion chance that he would forget himself, lose his perfectly
controlled emotions, and slap D.J.

"Do my looks bother you?" Parker finally said, deciding he'd play the little game with D.J.

"Bother me? How do you mean, Parker?" D.J. asked,
drowsily.

Parker took the liberty of sitting down on the closed
toilet near the foot of the tub and leaned forward, resting his
elbows on his knees. When he spoke this time, D.J. opened
his eyes, a bit startled at how close the voice was now.
Parker was wearing a white dress shirt with the sleeves
rolled up to the elbows; his striped tie was unfastened and
pulled ruggedly to one side. The top three buttons of his
shirt were open, revealing a blond, furry chest. For the first
time D.J. saw that Parker could be really attractive, even
sensual, and not just a brute force. His face was a Nordic,
chiseled face with a prominent, heroic jaw, high jutting
cheekbones, and deep-set blue eyes. Parker was smiling,
and D.J. saw him now as a handsome man that some woman might do very well to snag.

"I mean," Parker said, still playing the game, "are you
bothered by my looks?"

D.J. was enjoying this volley of *double entendre*. It had
been a long time since he had had the opportunity to spar
with someone, and Parker was always the perfect opponent, because he had to take extra pains to play carefully
with his boss. There was also the fact that so many levels of
meaning existed between the two of them. "Do I look
bothered?" D.J. quipped.

Parker leaned over the side of the tub and peered
through the water. "No, I guess not," he answered and
stood up, leaving D.J. wide-mouthed with surprise. It was
the first overtly sexual gesture Parker had ever made, even
if it was just a joke. "Oh," Parker said after opening the
door. "I almost forgot what I came in here for. Elaine will
be another hour at the hairdresser and Billings called." D.J.
turned and sat up in the tub at the mention of Billings's

name. "You can see Terry at ten Thursday night. He'll meet us at the usual place."

"Then he's talked to Terry?" D.J. asked.

"I don't know about that," Parker answered. "He didn't say, and of course ... well, it's not my place to ask questions like that."

"I just thought maybe he said something about having spoken to Terry." D.J. noticed Parker staring at his hands, which were gripping the side of the tub so tightly his knuckles were turning white. He released them and submerged them in the water. "Anything else I should know?" D.J. asked, his eyes open wide and sparkling in the candlelight. Sitting cross-legged now in the huge black tub, he looked like a child to Parker. All that was missing was a yellow toy duck or a sailboat. With the two of them like this, Parker standing, D.J. sitting in the water, Parker became acutely aware of his size in contrast to D.J. He could crush him if he wanted to. D.J. was completely vulnerable to him.

They stared at each other for a long, long time without speaking, just locked in each other's eyes, with nothing concrete in their minds, only the awareness of each other's size and physical proximity.

"What? I'm sorry, I was somewhere else," Parker confessed.

D.J. couldn't remember what he had asked. "Nothing, Parker."

Again, they stared at each other in the dim light.

"Well, then," Parker said slowly, realizing as he spoke that his mouth had become very dry, "I'll go."

"Okay," D.J. said.

Parker started to close the door, backing through it, his eyes still locked in D.J.'s gaze.

"Parker?" D.J. said just as the door was about to close. Parker opened the door and leaned into the room, his hand on the porcelain door handle, the white shirt pulling so tightly at his chest that his nipples were clearly outlined. "Yes, sir?"

"Thank you," D.J. said.

Parker smiled, and D.J. thought it was the first time he had ever seen the man smile at him. "My pleasure, sir."

As he said this, D.J. thought he noticed Parker's eyes shift downward toward the water again, but in the candle-light he couldn't be sure.

"And Parker," D.J. added.

"Yes, sir?"

"Stop calling me sir."

"Yes ... okay," he answered, flashing an even broader smile.

Parker closed the door and D.J. leaned back in the tub and let the water, which had turned lukewarm by now, cover his body again. Parker's changing, he thought. He's different somehow. I'm not sure exactly what it is, but he's ... nicer. He's become more human since we've returned. Maybe it's because he doesn't have the two of us playing tricks on him here; he doesn't have to have his guard up so much, doesn't have to be so defensive. But he's definitely different. I actually think I'm beginning to like him. And he could be a very useful resource if we became friends. Very useful indeed.

New York City

"What the hell is this? It looks like one of my brothers' cock rings with snot on it," Jessica said, taking a step back from the neon sculpture, more to get away it than to get a better look.

Jessica had invited Elaine to attend an opening in Soho at a gallery not far from hers where a mutual friend of theirs worked. Jessica was anxious to see it, because the gallery was new and her boss had heard it might give him some stiff competition. The friend had warned them that some of the pieces were "terribly *avant garde*" and that they should "be prepared to be shocked into a new sensibility." So far the two women had found the show to live up to the friend's warning in one way: they were shocked.

Elaine laughed and poked Jessica in the ribs. "Shh, someone will hear you."

"I hope the artist hears me. This thing is disgusting. What is that goop? I swear it's laminated snot. Touch it,

Elaine," Jessica teased, taking Elaine's hand and thrusting it toward the blue neon ring, which seemed to be covered with a thick, hardened mucuslike substance.

"Stop it," Elaine half shrieked, jerking her arm back and beginning to laugh uncontrollably. They had smoked a joint in the cab from midtown, and both were trying to control a laughing jag that had started when they were greeted at the door by a woman with a green flat-top hair-cut, who was wearing only a pair of stiletto heels and a Day-Glo g-string the same color as her hair.

"Touch it, go on, touch it, I want to see if it's sticky," Jessica said, still struggling with Elaine's arm.

"Straighten up, you two," a voice said from behind them. They turned abruptly to find one of Jessica's twin brothers looking scornfully at them.

"True, I should have known you'd be here," Jessica said. "What the hell is this thing supposed to be?"

"It's not *supposed* to be anything; it *is* a piece of neon sculpture," her brother replied, feigning indignation.

True Wood was twenty-four years old, five feet six inches tall, thin but well defined, and had hair so blond that in summer it turned white. His skin was a deep tan from the afternoons he was already spending on the docks at the end of Christopher Street. Both he and his brother Steffan worked as waiters in a Village restaurant.

"It looks like a vinyl sex aid to me," Jessica said.

"You're disgusting, Jessica. Please pretend you don't know me. Hello, Elaine, so nice to see you," True said, turning his back on his sister, who took the opportunity to pinch his ass hard as he took Elaine's hand and bowed slightly.

"Ouch!" True yelled, and the three of them began laughing so hard they had to leave the gallery. Outside, they leaned against the building and held their sides, the tears rolling down their cheeks. "You're such a genteel man," Jessica teased when she could finally talk.

"And you're such a piece of dog," he countered as the three of them began walking down West Broadway, Elaine's pinscher following a little farther back than usual.

"It really was awful," Elaine said, still wiping at her eyes. "There wasn't one piece that was interesting; it was all just disgusting. Even the colors were boring."

"If that's the most competition we have, my boss will make a fortune this year. I should get a bonus just for having attended the opening," Jessica said.

"Well, what shall we do now?" True asked. "How about a cocktail?"

"Ooo, that sounds deluxe," Elaine responded. "Let's go to Cafe Borggia, or better, let's go over to Pennyfeathers."

"I'd rather go to the Whitehorse," Jessica said. "We can drink like men there."

"Well, I'm buying and I say we're going to Tiffany's, because I'm looking for someone who's going to be leaving the gym at about five o'clock and I'm not taking any chances of missing him."

"God, True, you're such a sex machine," Jessica said.

"I hope this one doesn't keep hot pennies in the oven," Elaine teased as they all piled into a cab. The last time the three of them were together, True had told about going home with a man who got out of bed at one point, returned with a cookie sheet he had taken out of the oven, and proceeded to shower True with hot pennies. The image of True bouncing around on the bed trying to get away from the burning pennies still made Elaine laugh out loud whenever she thought of it.

At Tiffany's Elaine and True ordered coffee and croissants. Jessica drank a double Chivas on the rocks. True sat near the window watching the corner like a soldier on sentry duty.

"I thought you were seeing someone," Jessica said, poking True from across the table to get his attention.

"I am seeing someone," he answered.

"Oh," Jessica said with approbation. "This is just a friend you're looking for then."

"Give me a reprieve, will you, Mother Teresa? We have an open relationship."

"Does Kevin know that?" Jessica asked.

"Kevin is one of those people who thinks every romp in the hay is a rehearsal for a walk up the aisle," True said, pressing the side of his face to the window, trying to see farther up the street.

"Do you have a pencil, Jessica?" Elaine teased.

"That *was* a good one," Jessica chided.

"Well, it's true," he said, turning back to his companions. "He wants to get married, and I don't. I'm trying to train him. Sort of like you trained Phil," he said, smiling and blinking his long eyelashes several times.

"Don't get smart, buddy," Jessica said, making a fist and shaking it at him from across the table. "Phil and I have a good relationship. No demands and no complaints."

"Well, no demands anyway," Elaine joked.

"Shut up, best friend," Jessica said, waving her fist at Elaine. "This is a family feud."

"Yeah, if there's no complaints, how come I saw him spend thirty minutes in the shower at the gym on Monday? You cut him off or just getting too loose in your old age?"

"Faggots are so obnoxious," Jessica said to Elaine, stirring her Scotch with her little finger.

"Oh, I know what I wanted to ask you two," True said, animated now and friendly.

"He wants money, watch out," Jessica warned.

True ignored her. "We got our share confirmed yesterday. Do you guys want to come out to the island with us over Memorial Day? It'll be h-o-t out there. It'll be so much fun, come on, say you will. There's plenty of room and you could bring Phil and ... Oh, I guess D.J. couldn't come, could he? Maybe he could. Why not? Who's to know? Too bad he can't just travel around without those fucking pinschers. Nobody would recognize him most of the time."

"I'd love to True and I appreciate the invitation, but we're scheduled to attend something that day here in the city," Elaine said.

"Oh, fuck. Campaign shit?" True asked.

"Yes, some sort of luncheon and rally. A picnic, I think, in Central Park," Elaine explained.

"Oh, great, you can eat and get raped at the same time," Jessica said, breaking one of True's croissants and heaping butter on it.

"Well, what about you?" True said to his sister.

"Darling brother, just try to keep me away. I thought you'd never ask. Phil already told me you got the house. I find it very interesting that you told him before me."

"One very good, very big reason," True said, grinning. "I don't know why you won't share that man. Steffan and I could show him such a good time. I know he's got a good nine inches on him."

"Nine and three-eighths if you measure from the base," Jessica said, shoving the entire piece of croissant into her mouth and watching True's eyes bulge.

"Jesus! You are a sow. I bet you can't even take all of it. You're so selfish."

"Eat your heart out, honey," Jessica said, licking her fingers with a loud smack.

"Ohhh, ohhh, there he is. Let me out," True shouted and practically knocked Elaine on the floor as he bolted from the booth. "Bye, see you later. Thanks."

"Hey, you," Jessica shouted after him, but he was already through the door. "That little fartknocker didn't leave us any money, and he said it was going to be on him."

"That's all right, I've got money," Elaine said. "He's so funny; I love him. He's always chasing some man."

"Some hairy man. That's his only criterion. The guy has to be hairy. The more hair the better, unless it's on the top of his head. He loves a bald head and a hairy body. Blond, brunet, redhead ... it doesn't matter, just as long as he's hairy. He's so fixated," Jessica said.

"Isn't that funny how people focus on one trait like that? I guess for each of us there's some physical characteristic that turns us on."

"And Steffan is just the opposite. He only wants smooth bodies. What a pair," Jessica said, shaking her head and downing the last of her Scotch.

Just then True walked by the window with a tall, balding man in tow, whose forearms were covered with black silky hair. He had a tiny gold earring in his left ear, and as they passed, True winked at them through the window.

They paid the bill and walked out onto Hudson Street. The city was still hot, and the air was thick with exhaust fumes. At the newsstand near Christopher Street, Elaine bought a copy of *Vogue* and Jessica deliberated between orange and banana bubble gum. Neither of them noticed the two-column headline on the *New York Times:* PANEL FINDS NO FAULT WITH FAIRBANKS DESIGN.

The White House

The limousine carrying Billings back to the White House from Capitol Hill passed through the gate and curved up the drive, pulling around the news vans and stopping at the front entrance. Billings hurried inside, ducking the hordes of reporters he wouldn't be able to get away from if he entered through the west wing. He made his way straight to the Oval Office, where the President was waiting for him.

"Well?" Marshall asked before Billings even had time to set his things down.

"It doesn't look very good, Mr. President," Billings said somberly. "I calculate two votes swinging back to the other side, and there's a lot of rumbling among the undecideds. Baker of Wyoming wouldn't even see me."

The President leaned back in his chair and rolled a pencil back and forth between the index finger and thumb of his right hand as he thought. Billings sat silent, watching the President. Marshall picked up the phone and buzzed his secretary.

"Helen, get me Carl Stone on the line."

Billings suppressed a smile; he savored these moments when Marshall, who was usually easygoing, swung into cutthroat action. He would take a lot from people, but he would only be pushed so far and then he started applying screws that ended up making people wish they had listened the first time he spoke to them. The phone buzzed and his secretary announced that she was connecting him with Carl Stone.

"Carl?" the President said into the receiver as he drew dark circles on a page of the White House news summary sitting on the desk in front of him. Billings could see that the first page was a photocopy of the *New York Times* story on Fairbanks. "I want files on the nos and the undecideds. Projects, bills pending, block grants, patronage appointments, state function requests, and pledges for campaign appearances. I want them over here by seven this evening. And I want the files from Gasher on both Bakers, McCann, Tucker, Zimkowski, Stevenson, White, Packard..." He looked to Billings to supply more names.

"Jackson, Barnes, and Cavoli," Billings added.

"Jackson, Barnes, and Cavoli," the President repeated. "Hand delivered no later than seven, sooner if possible."

Stone repeated the names for Marshall and they hung up.

"Is there a double nine in the group?" the President asked, using campaign jargon, meaning was there a heavy domino, who, if he fell, would cause others to go down with him.

"Well, obviously, Tucker," Billings began.

"That's useless, don't you think? Even if he wanted to change his vote, he wouldn't align himself with our position before the heavy primaries, especially in the west."

"That's right, but I'm working on another angle in the meantime. I think if you could bring Zimkowski and Cavoli in, there'd be a good chance of roping Jackson and Hall and possibly even White. That could start the ball rolling. Especially since — and I hate to tell you this — Petri reversed his position today and is voting, as he put it, 'with Sal,' meaning Cavoli. They're both running in the primaries the day after Memorial Day, and it's close with them. It's a sixteen-man committee, and every damned one of them has aides out taking straw polls among the other senators. They don't want to recommend against the majority feelings. The mood up there this morning was that it's the Senate versus the White House on this one."

"We'll see about that," the President said. "I want you to call Hill at Interior and tell him not to move that offshore drilling permit off his desk until Cavoli comes around. And he's only to move it after he hears from me personally. That's an order only I can give him, understand?"

"Right," Billings said, making a note and beginning to feel the passion of hard-core campaigning stirring in him. They would grab every senator on the committee by his balls and drag each one across the line screaming if they had to, but they would never lose this fight.

"We are going to win this vote, Thad," the President said, looking deep into Billings's eyes with intense determination. "No matter what we have to do. Understand?"

"Yes, sir. And we will, I promise you."

The President took a deep breath. "What else do we have to address now? Let's get as much out of the way as possible before I start on this blitzkrieg through the Senate. At least let's get my desk clear so I can concentrate on these rascals with a clear mind."

"The rest of the campaign is going pretty much the way we called it. I think you're going to have to make one appearance in the Midwest."

"Before the committee vote?" Marshall asked, somewhat taken aback at Billings's suggestion. They had agreed several weeks before that he needed to be in the White House until this issue was resolved.

"Yes, I believe so, but it can be someplace safe like Cleveland or Columbus. Someplace where we know you'll get an enthusiastic reception. It will look good, make you appear strong and loved. We don't want to make the same mistake Carter made in '80. You need to get out among the people. If we do it right it'll be a great boost and probably raise your standing in the polls. Sooner or later, someone, most likely Tucker, is going to charge you with hiding in the White House."

"I suppose," Marshall said reluctantly. "But when?"

"I think you should do it this coming weekend, just before the committee vote. You have an invitation to speak at the Cleveland State commencement. We haven't given them a firm no yet, and they've been holding off asking someone else in the hope we would confirm. It's a plum."

"Very well, Cleveland it is. Get Thuronyi working on my speech."

"There's one other matter that we need to discuss," Billings said. "I hate to bring it up, but it's necessary."

"What is it?" Marshall said, virtually sure it had to do with D.J.

"It's about Terry," Billings said, mustering courage. Although it was D.J. who was pressuring him, Billings would never state it that way to the President. He always made Terry the villain. "He's getting a little out of control."

"What does that mean?" Marshall asked angrily.

"He hasn't been to work in three days, and he's harassing D.J. with phone calls at all hours of the morning. My sources tell me he's drinking heavily and is buying drugs again. This could get out of hand."

"Jesus Christ, they've only been back a few weeks — what kind of a weakling is he, anyway?" the President almost shouted, angry that he should have to deal with a matter so volatile and so out of control at a time when his position was being seriously challenged.

"I don't know, sir. All I know is what's being reported to me. I spoke with D.J. yesterday and he's very upset."

"Well, do something about it; that's what you're here for," Marshall said, moving some papers around on his desk, not wanting to go into the subject any further.

"But—" Billings began.

"Thaddeus," the President said, looking up, fire in his eyes, "I said do something about it. Anything. Just take care of it. I do not want to hear about it again. It's your problem from here on out. And you are not to discuss it with Claudia." There was a moment of silence as the two men stared at each other.

"Yes, sir," Billings said, almost weakly and with a little animosity that he should be saddled with this ugly task.

"Now I have work to do before those reports arrive from Stone."

Billings went back to his office and closed the door, slamming his papers down hard on the desk. As if I don't have enough to do, he thought. Now I have to control a queer drug addict two hundred miles away. Shit!

He called Carl Stone and told him he would now need daily reports on Terry's activity. He wanted every move monitored. "And keep him away from D.J. I don't care how you do it, but he is to be kept from approaching the President's son in public. I'll decide when they are to see each other. I want him watched closely, Carl. Very closely. I'm talking about a spy under every bed. And I want details. Call me tomorrow afternoon with a report on how you're doing it and what the hell he's up to."

New York City

The black limousine pulled around the corner at Mac-Dougal Street and stopped in front of the Newman Chapel. Terry stepped from the shadows of the entrance and got into the car, which immediately began making its way toward the Hudson Parkway.

The night was clear and the traffic moderate. D.J. and Terry held each other for a long time before either spoke.

"I've been so worried about you. What have you been doing? Where have you been? They told me you haven't been to work for three days. Were you sick?" D.J. asked, providing Terry with an answer.

"Yeah. I haven't been feeling too well," Terry said, thinking to himself that he wasn't really lying.

"I tried calling you," D.J. said.

"I haven't been answering the phone. I've been depressed, and I didn't want to worry you or get into a fight," Terry said.

"Well, when you don't answer the phone, I worry even more than if I know you're depressed. Promise me you'll answer the phone from now on."

"I promise," Terry said without conviction.

Had the light been better inside the car, D.J. would have seen how bloodshot Terry's eyes were, how drawn and pale he looked, how thin he had become. Terry hit the button that closed the solid divider separating them from the front seat, then began removing his clothes.

"Make love to me, D.J.," he said almost mournfully.

D.J. removed his clothes and made love to him, feeling how thin Terry had become as he ran his hands over Terry's body.

"I want you inside me," Terry whispered. "Please be inside me tonight."

They made love, Terry keeping his eyes closed the entire time. He was unable to reach orgasm. It was over in a matter of minutes and they dressed and sat in silence. Terry smoked a cigarette.

"What is it?" D.J. asked, taking Terry's hand. He was shocked by how bony it was. For a moment, he imagined he was holding the hand of a corpse.

Terry turned to him and D.J. could see in the moonlight how hollow his eyes were. "I don't know," Terry responded. "I guess I'm just no good without you. I'm having a hard time getting used to being back here. I hate being alone."

D.J. kissed him on the cheek. "I know. I'm sorry. I'm trying to do something about it. I'm trying my best."

Terry looked at him blankly and then back out the window. The moon made the river look fractured, a wide line of white brush strokes on a black canvas. It reminded Terry of a painting they had seen in a little gallery in France.

"Are you going to work tomorrow?" D.J. asked softly.

"What difference does it make?" Terry said and took a deep drag of his cigarette. It was almost like being in the car with a stranger.

"I think the job's good for you. It gives you something to do that you like and it helps take your mind off—"

"Off you?" Terry interrupted, turning to look at him momentarily, then returning his gaze toward the river.

"That's not what I meant," D.J. said, hurt.

"Sure, it is, D.J. I understand. You want me to be good and stay out of your hair. It's okay, I'm not going to cause you any trouble. No more fire escapes, I promise."

"Damn it, Terry, that's not what I meant. I'm just thinking of you. I don't like to see you depressed. You have to be patient," D.J. said, turning sideways on the seat, trying to get Terry to look at him.

"I am patient. I haven't called you lately, have I? I haven't disturbed you. I haven't made any scenes."

Terry was being too calm. D.J. took Terry's jacket from the floor and began rifling through the pockets until he found what he was looking for. "What's this?" he asked, holding up a white tablet. Terry took it impassively from him and held it up to the moonlight.

"Looks like a quaalude," he said, shoving it into his mouth. "Yep, it's a quaalude."

D.J. slapped him. Terry stared at him, D.J.'s action having said more about their situation than either of them could ever have articulated with words. "See?" he said. "No trouble from me."

"Stop it!" D.J. shouted. "Why are you doing this? Please stop. Please don't do any more drugs."

Terry continued to stare at him, his icy green eyes fixed, unblinking, on D.J. "You have dinner parties, close friends, and Elaine. I have drugs. It gets me through the day."

D.J. took Terry's hand in his, kissed it, and pressed it to his check. "You'll ruin everything we've worked so hard for if you keep this up. You'll ruin it all."

"Back off," Terry snarled, snapping his hand away.

D.J. was stunned. Terry never spoke to him like this.

"You really have a lot of nerve, sitting here telling me I'm going to fuck things up. Move in with me," Terry said.

"You know I can't do that," D.J. answered, hanging his head.

"See me at least every other day."

"I want to..."

"Go back to France with me."

"Terry, be reasonable."

"Let's move to California or New Mexico. Anywhere. We can run away and hide out. It would be months, maybe years before they caught up with us."

"Terry, what is all this? You know that's impossible..."

"Then back off."

The car came to a stop and they realized they were back in the city in front of the Newman Center. Terry opened the door.

"Terry, please...," D.J. pleaded, grabbing his arm. Several people out for an evening stroll in the Village were gawking now at the sight of the limousine.

"Call me when you need a blow job. You have my number," Terry yelled, stumbling out onto the sidewalk.

"Terry!" D.J. shouted, but he was already around the corner.

Parker jumped out and shut the back door, then rushed D.J. home. Inside the front door, Parker took D.J. by the shoulder. "You want to talk?" he asked.

D.J. looked at Parker for long time, trying to read what might be going on inside Parker, who was suddenly being so warm toward him.

"No thank you, Parker. I'll be all right. Really."

"You sure?"

"Yeah. But thanks, I appreciate it."

"All right," Parker said, turning toward the door. "I'm going to secure the outside. I'll see you in the morning."

"Parker?" D.J. said, grabbing him by the arm. The size of Parker's biceps sent a wave of emotion through D.J. It wasn't purely sensual, although he realized instantly that was part of it. Mostly it was a sense of security, a feeling that this muscle symbolized a kind of protection and reassurance that D.J. desperately needed to feel at the moment. He wanted to ask Parker to come in, to sit with him, even to sleep next to him and allow him simply to hold on to him through the night. Parker's blue eyes were sparkling in the lamplight. The scene was so romantic, so reminiscent of sweethearts saying good night after a date that it was all D.J. could do to keep himself from leaning forward and kissing him. "Good night, Parker. And ... thanks again."

"Good night, D.J.," Parker said and closed the door. D.J. watched through the curtains as Parker stood on the stoop for a long while. He wondered what he was thinking. And even more interesting, D.J. thought, would be to know what he was feeling.

Washington, D.C.

Miles Cameron waited for the cab to pull away from the front of the motel before he flicked the lamp on near the rumpled bed. He lit a cigarette and glanced at his naked torso in the long mirror above the dresser. He went to it, opened the top drawer, and removed a small tape recorder. He rewound it, hit the play button, and sat down next to it to listen to his recording of the evening's events. As he listened, he brought himself to a second climax. He pressed the stop button, leaned forward to the mirror, and kissed his smiling reflection.

The White House

Elaine and Jessica sat across the round table from each other listening to Mrs. Horace Dolan praise the work of the First Lady in aiding homeless children. Claudia sat at the head table next to the lectern, smiling broadly, and the contrast between the two women couldn't have been more startling. Mrs. Dolan wore a powder blue taffeta dress with a waist-length jacket. Pinned to the jacket was a corsage of gardenias so large it kept getting in her mouth and she had to continually bat it aside. The scent of the flowers filled the entire room and was making Jessica sick at her stomach.

The First Lady, on the other hand, wore a beige, tailored, linen suit with a strand of pearls over a white silk blouse. Her smile seemed permanently fixed to her face, and her eyes sparkled, as they always did. Jessica once asked Elaine if Claudia carried a small vial of tearing solution to give her eyes that special glint. The speech went on and on. This was Mrs. Dolan's first time in the White House, and she was going to make the most of it. Fran Altman, who was seated next to Elaine, played with her fork.

Meanwhile, in the Oval Office, the Reverend Dolan was giving a speech of quite a different nature. The president of the American Morality League sat uncomfortably in the stiffest chair in the room, which Billings had purposely placed in front of the President's desk and to which he had directed the corpulent minister when he entered. He shifted from one large buttock to the other now as he continued his rehearsed remarks to the President and chief of staff.

"The bottom line of all this," he said, rolling a fat cigar from one side of his mouth to the other and then removing it to flick the ashes into an onyx ashtray on the desk in front of him, "is that tens of thousands of good, Christian voters in the South are waiting to see exactly what stand you take on exempting those private schools from paying taxes. A lot of 'em have tried damned hard to meet the federal regulations on integration, but let's face it, they didn't organize those schools to educate coloreds. They did it to get away from 'em, to make sure that their kids got a decent education. They're all honest, God-fearing, tax-paying citizens who vote in the primaries and in the general election." The ashes from his cigar missed the ashtray and lay on the mahogany desktop. The President stared at them, imagining the look of horror and disgust that would be on Claudia's face if she were sitting there with them. He wondered if she would be able to control herself or whether she would jump up and brush the ashes into her hand.

"The President has sent a memo to the Departments of Justice and Education outlining proposed changes in those regulations," Billings said, "but you must remember, it isn't easy to change laws that are on the books and that have been in effect for many years. There are a great many people in this country who support those regulations, and a great many politicians in Congress who must vote as their constituents dictate."

"And there are a great many voters who feel just the opposite, Mr. Billings," Dolan said, leaning his rotund body in Thaddeus's direction. Thaddeus tried not to focus on the red stain on Dolan's tie. "They must also be heard and considered. They feel neglected, like they don't have a voice in Washington. That's exactly why they need some definite reassurance. Reassurance they can sink their teeth into, if you know what I mean."

"Such as?" the President asked.

"Such as a person in Washington to represent them, see to it their voice is heard," Dolan answered.

"That's what the Congress is for," the President said. "Those are their elected representatives here."

"If you'll pardon the expression, Mr. President, hogwash," Dolan said, his mouth still full of the fat cigar. "You and I both know that don't mean diddly-squat." Billings and the President exchanged a quick glance. "They need someone in the administration, someone who has access to you. Someone in the cabinet or close to a cabinet member."

"Are you suggesting, Mr. ... er, Reverend Dolan," Billings said, "that the President appoint one of your constituents to an administration post?"

"That would certainly be something they could sink their teeth into," Dolan said, smiling broadly, "now wouldn't it?"

"I really don't see how that's possible, Reverend Dolan," Marshall said, trying to control his temper at the man's audacity. Marshall saw him not only as an illiterate redneck, but even more repelling, he was slovenly and, worst of all, filled with hypocrisy. "I can hardly just pluck someone out of the crowd and make him part of this administration. That's not how the political process works."

"Isn't it?" Dolan asked rhetorically. "How'd Mr. Billings here get this job? Where'd you pluck him from? I don't remember voting for him."

"Mr. Dolan," the President said, purposely refusing to use his proper title, "in the course of obtaining political power, one relies on a great many resources and a great many people. When the time comes — if it ever comes — when the political reins are handed over to you, there are a great many, I repeat, a great many political debts to pay. Many more than can ever be properly or adequately paid, in fact. Those men and women who work hard to carry out the necessary tasks to obtain political office for their chosen candidate must, by honor and tradition, be compensated for their efforts. In the process of paying those political IOUs one takes a great deal of advice from those already in power. I don't just decide willy-nilly who I'm going to appoint to certain positions. They must be screened, they must pass certain tests, meet certain criteria, not all of which are designated by me. There are Senate confirmations, congressional approvals, committee recommendations..."

"Well, now, Mr. President," Dolan interrupted, "you just may have hit upon a couple of real important points. First of all, I happen to reach out every Saturday night to some one and a half million radio listeners in twelve states who hang on my every word. If you doubt that, just ask Senator Jenkins from Georgia. His opponent in the last election said some things about me that were not only untrue, they were downright nasty. That man lost his seat in the Senate, and before he went off half-cocked and said those things, he was way ahead in them professional polls.

"And secondly, I think you're real close to home when you mention women in your administration. Frankly, we don't think you got enough women working for you. And last of all, I don't think you'd find anybody more qualified to be secretary of education in your next administration than someone who has worked for more than twenty years with the school systems of North Carolina, especially when you consider that it was mostly all volunteer work."

Billings and Marshall looked at each other in total confusion.

"In fact, me and everybody I've talked to think it's about time you put someone in a cabinet post who is just a regular, ordinary person. Somebody who knows what it's like to be plain folk, instead of all these fancy lawyers and Ph.D.s. Me and most people I know think the best choice for a secretary of education next time would be someone like Georgina."

"Georgina?" Marshall asked, not having the faintest idea of whom he was speaking.

"Yessir. Nobody's got more feelings for education and little school kids than Georgina," Dolan said, raising his eyebrows and taking aim again at the ashtray. He missed.

"Who ... is ... Georgina?" Marshall asked, afraid he already knew the answer.

"Mrs. Dolan," Billings responded.

Marshall gripped the arms of his chair and gritted his teeth. "Out of the question, Dolan," he shot back.

The President's reaction and the look in his eyes were
not lost on the Southern preacher and he retreated immediately to a more acceptable position. "Of course, if that's not
possible, I suppose we could come up with somebody who
would be a suitable alternative. Somebody maybe like my
assistant, Lloyd Claggett. He's got a degree in business
administration from Ole Miss. I think either one would be
a real fine choice. Naturally, I think my wife would be a
smarter pick, but you boys know better about what'll get by
the Congress than I do. Speaking of family," he said, avoid-
ing the President's glare by holding up his wet cigar and
studying the long gray ash, "how's that boy of yours? The
play actor?"

"I really think it would be futile to try to nominate your
wife for such a position," Billings said quickly, before Marshall lost his temper completely and threw the man out. "I
don't see how we could possibly give a post like that to her
without being charged in the press with some sort of collu-
sion. Yes, I'm afraid that's out of the question. As for Mr.
Claggett, well, we'd have to look into his credentials and
see what post might be appropriate for him. After all, Reverend, it's rather difficult to promise a post to someone
when you haven't been elected to office yet."

"I guess what I'm saying is that if my flock thought that
by voting for you they would have a man in Washington
— or a woman — who would be able to get the ear of the
President on certain issues that they cared deeply about,
they'd be much more inclined to vote for you. I know I
would certainly be inclined to tell them to vote for you."

"I'll tell you what," Billings said, standing now to indi-
cate the meeting was over, "you let us think about this for a
few days, look into Mr. Claggett's background, and talk
with a few people. We'll get back to you with what we find
and perhaps we can discuss it further."

Dolan looked surprised, but not annoyed, that the little
conversation was coming to a rather abrupt halt. He didn't
recognize the look on Marshall's face as being one of contempt and near rage. "Sure, sure," he said, standing now
and crushing the cigar in the ashtray, hitting it for the first

time. "You boys think it over and get back to me. Plenty of time, plenty of time."

After they all shook hands, Billings showed him out, closed the door, and turned to Marshall. "Now, don't be too harsh. He's ignorant and contemptible, but he does reach out to a lot of people."

"Not for long," Marshall said, picking up the phone. "Helen, get me Jim Nickles immediately. Who the hell does he think he is?" Marshall said to Billings. "He's got to be the most arrogant, ignorant, slovenly pig I've ever encountered. I wouldn't give him a cabinet post if he came crawling on his hands and knees and convinced me he could finance my entire campaign."

"Mr. President," Billings said, trying to calm him down, "this will all look a little different tomorrow. Especially if we follow through with my suggestion of giving the man a powerless position. A million votes!"

"Not for two million votes," Marshall said, picking up the receiver in response to the phone's buzzing. "Jim? Donald Marshall ... Yes, yes, fine, thanks. Jim, I've got a real problem I think you can help me with. There's a radio station in North Carolina broadcasting with 50,000 watts. There have been a lot of complaints that transmission interferences are occurring all over the surrounding area. I think maybe they need to be cut back to about 10,000 watts for a while until we can fully investigate the situation and decide what should be done about it. Yes, it's station WDOL in Frankfort ... Uh-huh, that's right, but he's a God-fearing man of the people, Jim. I'm sure when he hears the common folk are complaining, he'll be more than happy to cooperate with you ... Oh, yes, one other thing. I think it will probably take until mid-November to resolve the issue. At least mid-November. See what you can do, will you? And report to me on your progress early next week, say, by Wednesday at the latest. Thanks, Jim. Sorry I had to bother you. Give my love to Christine and the kids." The President turned back to Billings. "Put Nickles and his wife on a list for the next state dinner and see that he gets his invitation early."

Thaddeus smiled, but it was a worried smile. "He still has the mails, you know."

It was the President's turn to smile. "Bulk rates change in June, Thad. That's been on the books for months. Some nonprofit permits are being revoked, especially religious-affiliated permits. Remember? Budget cuts."

Billings shook his head. "And you call me sharp. I'll bet you had this planned the whole time," Thaddeus said, feeding Marshall's ego in his own inimitable way.

The President smiled and rubbed his hands together. "Hey, Thad," he said, hardly able to contain his smugness.

"What?" Billings answered, seeing the Donald Marshall from the old days, before APANS.

"Fuck that son of a bitch. We'll win without him, and God will be on our side anyway."

"And so it is with great pride that I accept the honorary chairmanship of your worthy cause," Claudia said to enthusiastic applause, as the women rose to honor the First Lady. The applause grew louder, and heads began to turn toward the door. Elaine, who had been playing with the flower arrangement at her table, stood on tiptoe and saw the President being ushered into the room. As he passed them, he kissed Elaine on the cheek and greeted Fran Altman with a slight touch of the hand. He went to the head table and stood with his wife. When the applause died down, he tied the bow on his political package by assuring the women that his door was always open to them through his wife and that he was deeply interested in both their charitable cause and their political concerns. He then introduced his daughter-in-law, Mrs. Donald Marshall, Jr., "who came all the way from New York to join us this afternoon." Then the group retired, waiting for the Chief Executive and the First Lady to leave the room first. Elaine was immediately surrounded by women chattering and asking her for her autograph. She looked up just in time to see the door being held open for Jessica by the blond pinscher.

Great Falls, Virginia

Thad Billings and Carl Stone sat at table sixteen in Aluisi's restaurant in Great Falls Center. They had just finished one of the perfect Italian dinners the restaurant is famous for and were now sipping espresso with lemon. There were two items on Billings's agenda: Terry and Miles Cameron.

"The Snowman went to work today," Stone said, tearing open a packet of sugar and pouring it into his espresso.

"Excellent," Billings said, almost singing the word. "Do we have you to thank for that?"

"Not directly, but I'll gladly take the credit," he answered. "I think his new friend convinced him to go."

"New friend?" Billings asked.

"A spy in every bed, I believe is how we turned the phrase," Stone said.

"Isn't that a little risky?"

"Everything's a little risky, old buddy. Sitting here talking to each other is a little risky."

"But what's the purpose? Is this guy a dick or a social worker?" Billings asked wryly.

"Well," Stone answered, unable to hold back his smile, "I'm sure he wouldn't be where he is if he weren't a 'dick.'"

"Very funny, Carl," Billings said, unamused.

"You want the kid under control, don't you? Well, I'm giving him a good influence in his life and also getting the information you need."

Billings noted Stone's choice of the word "need," reminding him that he was in Stone's debt for this one.

"And who knows," Carl continued, "we may even get a nice drug bust out of this one if we can nab Terry's source. Two feathers in your cap if it works out right."

"Yeah, and a hot poker up my ass if it doesn't. I don't like it. It's too close," Billings complained.

"Look, you want me to pull him off?" Stone asked coolly.

"Not off, just back a little," Billings said. "I want the kid watched, not fucked."

"Nobody's complaining, but you. Not even the dick," Stone pointed out. "And if it helps the kid keep out of trouble, that is, out of the President's hair, what does it hurt?"

"What if Olivier gets wind of it?" Billings asked, using D.J.'s code name. "What if there's a row between him and the Snowman? I don't think either one of them is especially stable right now. Anything could set them off. If it ever got back to anyone that we had planted someone in the Snowman's bed, all our heads would roll. I think it's too risky, Carl. I want you to pull him back."

"All right," Stone conceded, "but I'll have to change operatives. We can't have a familiar face lurking in the shadows. You know, Thad, it's not easy to find the right man for this particular assignment. That isn't easy for most guys in this profession."

"I'm sure you'll be able to come up with someone," Billings said.

"I'll try, but it'll take me a while. I'll see what I can do. In the meantime, I'm getting great feedback. I can even tell you what he likes to do in bed."

"Spare me the details, Carl," Billings said, holding his hand up in a gesture that looked like a traffic cop stopping a would-be jaywalker. "What have you dug up on Cameron?" Billings asked, ignoring Stone's prurient interests.

"Nightcrawler," Stone said, supplying the newly acquired code name for Cameron and looking around for possible eavesdroppers.

"'Nightcrawler'?" Billings repeated, mocking this cloak-and-dagger business.

"Sure. He only operates at night," Stone explained in deadly earnest, either not catching or ignoring Billings's sarcasm. "This one is a little trickier. Very smooth operator. We haven't seen him anywhere near the house since that one time in March, but he was tailed to a motel in College Park. He stayed there until nearly three a.m. At around two-fifteen, Granola's wife emerged, got in a cab, and went home. He left about forty-five minutes later, and we followed him to his apartment. Interesting thing about this particular stakeout. He didn't go to the motel from the office, but wanted to look like he did."

"What do you mean?" Billings asked.

"He wore a suit and was carrying his briefcase."

"Maybe he went there straight from a meeting at some agency," Billings suggested.

"Nope. Left from home. Probably trying to cover up some lie he told her. At any rate, they are definitely seeing each other in an amorous setting. I doubt if they're planning Granola's campaign strategy," Stone joked.

"What about the husband ... Granola?" Billings asked, embarrassed by what he considered ridiculous names, but at the same time knowing full well that there was no place in Washington where a conversation like this could be held without the risk of someone overhearing. And you never knew who the someone might be working for.

"He's got a real classy woman he's seeing. Met up with her twice on the road. Once in New York and once in St. Paul. Same woman both times. No doubt."

"Any idea who she is?" Billings asked.

"We're checking. We're using out-of-town operatives in the cities where he's campaigning, and some of them are pretty parochial, but we got a telephoto of her and we'll run it down. Also, he's not that easy to tail closely, since he has his own agents assigned to him and they're constantly watching the crowd. I should know about the woman in a few days."

"What about the other side of the aisle?" Billings asked, meaning McCann.

"Forget Leprechaun. He's clean as a whistle. Never saw a guy so careful. We're still digging, but this guy's got his ass covered with lead. He even has one staffer whose job it is to check out every single contribution to his campaign that's over a hundred bucks. They track people down like they might be mass murderers."

"Well, anybody who tries that hard must have something in his background he's trying to hide," Billings griped.

"I don't think so, Thad. I think this one is really Mary Poppins in disguise."

"Okay," Billings said, handing the waiter his American Express card.

"How we doing on the little business deal out west?" Stone asked, leaning his chair back on two legs and picking his teeth with his fingernail.

"That's proceeding as planned. We should be able to have papers to sign by the end of the week. Can you arrange that?"

"Sure, no problem. All I have to do is tell Allen and he'll be at the prison within twenty-four hours. Make sure they get his name right this time, though. I don't want to go through what we went through with that last batch of stock. After all, the name isn't that hard to remember."

"I've already explained to Linwood what happened before. He forgot he was your stepson. He'll get it right," Billings assured him.

The waiter brought the charge slip for Thaddeus to sign, which he did after adding up the total. He tore off his own receipt and put it in his wallet. "That will make over 120,000 shares. And that's just our share, not including hers. Quite a tidy sum to be waiting for us when they release him. What are the doctors saying these days?"

Stone's tone of voice changed dramatically at the mention of his stepson. He was somber and a bit uneasy. "He's still having therapy twice a week. He's a lot better, but no one's making any forecasts as to when he'll be well enough to get out. And then, of course, he'll only be released into our custody. Rebecca's and mine."

"That's the idea, Carl," Billings said, patting him on the shoulder and smiling cunningly. "That's the whole idea."

New York City

Terry lit a candle on the nightstand, flicked out the lamp, and turned over on his back, propping the pillow up slightly under his head to better watch Rick undress near the closet. This new acquaintance was a friendly harbor in the storm of his life right now, someone who liked him and who was satisfied with little things, calm things, like cooking a pot of spaghetti and staying in all evening, or going to the Waverly for a double feature and then a short beer at Ty's and home again. The kind of thing Terry liked to do best, but could only do in the shelter and security of a relationship.

Terry knew little about Rick, but that didn't bother him and didn't seem important. Rick's personal life before coming to New York was never discussed. The closest they ever came to talking about it was one evening when Terry found a note on the dresser that said, "Call Jean."

"Who's Jean?" Terry asked as he emptied his pockets into a straw basket on the dresser.

"Jean?" Rick echoed in a puzzled tone.

"This note here. It says, 'Call Jean.'"

"Oh, Jean. That's a friend of mine in California ... She's collecting my mail for me. I have an unemployment check still due and she's going to forward it to me."

Terry had done practically no drugs since meeting Rick, except for pot, which they smoked regularly. Rick was new to New York and seemed rather untainted. He was quiet, observant, and made no demands. He spent his days looking for a job, while Terry worked at the bus maintenance yard. At five-thirty, when he got off work, Terry would meet him for a drink somewhere in the Village, and they would then spend the evening together. Rick asked few questions and seemed quite content just to hang around with him. They spent very little time in the bars, and never frequented the hard-core places. Terry was beginning to feel some tranquility about him for the first time since his return. He smiled as the lean, handsome young man crawled under the sheet. Terry snuggled close to him.

"You want to watch the news?" Rick asked.

"I don't care; it's up to you," Terry answered.

"Let's skip it. How about some music?"

"Good idea," Terry said, reaching over to the clock radio and flipping the switch.

"Come here," Rick said, pulling Terry over and positioning him so that he was straddling his chest. He ran his hands up over Terry's stomach and began to caress his chest. Terry threw his head back and drank in the sensation, feeling himself hardening in response to Rick's gentle touch. The hands moved around to the small of Terry's back and coaxed him forward until he felt himself entering Rick's mouth. He leaned forward, resting his hands on the wall above the bed. As he established a slow, sensuous rhythm of movement, he thought, There hasn't been anyone like this since D.J. He started to lose his excitement at the thought of his lover, but quickly dismissed the image of D.J. and concentrated fully on the moment. Within seconds, they reached their climaxes simultaneously, then collapsed together and slept intertwined.

Alexandria, Virginia

Thaddeus carried the three empty gin bottles from the bar in the den to the kitchen and placed them in the trash. They had each been full two days earlier, when he broke the seal on one to pour himself a drink after work. All that was left in the house was half a bottle of Drambuie. He poured some into a snifter and sat down at the kitchen table. The mail had been propped up between the salt and pepper shakers and he began to go through it. There were department store bills from Garfinckle's, Woodward and Lothrop, and Bloomingdale's; a monthly bill from Central Liquor for liquor he had delivered to his office, since it was against the law to bring it across state lines; and a letter from their daughter, Marjorie, in San Francisco.

She was working as a lawyer for the Department of Housing and Urban Development in Region IX headquarters and was dutiful about writing to her mother, who had found herself quite lost when Marjorie had left home six years before. That was when Rachael's drinking began to get heavy. The letter was chatty except for one reference to Richard, their son who had walked out of the house in Scottsdale one day seven years earlier and hadn't been heard from since. Marjorie said she thought she had seen him on the street, but she was on a bus, and by the time she got off at the next stop, the man had disappeared into the crowd on Market Street.

Thaddeus put the mail back where he found it and took a big gulp of his drink. He was sorry about Richard leaving home, but he didn't feel guilty. His son had just gone bad, the way some kids do, without any reason. Maybe it was genetic, maybe it was the crowd he was running with at college; but Thaddeus was certain it was nothing he or Rachael had done. They had provided him with the best of everything. Perhaps, Thaddeus told himself, they had made it too easy for him. Maybe they should have made him earn his way.

At any rate, his leaving was a surprise, and the break was clean and complete. Not a word in all those years, and if his friends had heard from him, they were keeping it a secret. Not even the police could come up with a clue. At first, Thaddeus was sad, then he grew angry, and finally he became resigned to it, but somewhere deep inside he knew there was a volatile bed of resentment toward Richard. It just wasn't a very kind thing to do to them, especially to his mother, with whom he had never had any disagreements.

Rachael knew that part of the reason was that Thaddeus was pushing him too hard to come into the automobile business with him. He would need Richard more and more as Marshall's career developed and demanded his attention, and he didn't like the idea of someone outside the family running things. But Richard wanted to go into forestry, and he and his father had many heated arguments over it. The environment was not one of Thaddeus's major concerns. When Richard was arrested for possession of marijuana, it was more than Thaddeus could take. The newspapers played it up and business fell off for a while. Donald and Claudia were sympathetic with him, but he knew that they couldn't weather that sort of thing politically again.

The night before he left home, Richard and Thaddeus had a heated argument. Thaddeus had stormed into Richard's room after learning he had failed one of his courses and found him smoking a joint. Rachael finally had to physically force Thaddeus out of their son's room, Thaddeus shouting that his son was a bum and an ingrate and warning that if he didn't change his major from forestry to

business administration and start accepting his family responsibilities, he wouldn't pay for Richard's tuition the next
semester. The feud over Richard's studies had been going
on for months, and the more they argued about it, the more
firmly entrenched they became in their respective positions.

The single clue Rachael had that Richard might be
leaving for good was one she realized only in retrospect:
when he left for class that morning, he kissed her good-bye
as usual, but instead of his regular "See you later," he had
taken her hand and said, "Bye, Mom. Be happy."

Thaddeus sighed, finished the Drambuie, and went upstairs. He undressed and put on his pajamas in the bathroom, then stood looking at himself in the mirror above the
sink. His face was beginning to show not only his age, but
the stress of his job. The lines around his eyes and mouth
were much deeper than they had been three years before,
when he and Rachael had first arrived in Washington. He
thought of all the before and after photos he had seen of
presidents. He remembered the frightening difference in
some of them, especially Lyndon Johnson. Marshall never
showed such signs of pressure. He looked just the same
today as he did the day he took the oath of office. But the
three years did not wear well on Billings.

What a failure I am, he thought, staring sadly at his
aging face. Never quite good enough, never the total success. Thaddeus's car dealerships were tremendously profitable, but much of it was achieved through kickbacks,
crooked deals, and the backing of some bad money in the
beginning. He married Rachael right after college, and they
had a good life up until the time he started working for
Marshall. He signed on with Marshall because the car business wasn't challenging him anymore and he assumed that
eventually Richard would take it over from him anyway.
But Richard turned out to be something other than what
Thaddeus had planned.

Even their daughter, Marjorie, driven by her father to
go through law school and make something of herself,
broke away. She had refused to marry a lawyer who was
very much in love with her and whom Thaddeus and

Rachael both thought would make a good husband. Marjorie, however, became caught up in her career and didn't want a marriage to interfere with it, especially since the man wanted to have a large family. He later became a noted criminal lawyer, which just made Thaddeus more disappointed that the marriage hadn't worked out. She went to work for HUD in San Francisco, and it was painfully clear now that Thaddeus and Rachael would never live to see any grandchildren.

Rachael had begun drinking heavily after Billings started spending his life with Marshall in his pursuit of the presidency. By the time they hit Washington, she was a certifiable alcoholic.

When this is over, Thaddeus whispered to his reflection in the bathroom mirror, we'll go back to Arizona and put our lives together again. Then he thought, This is the price one pays for power. I would do nothing different. Not one thing. I have done the best I could do at any given time. It's not easy.

He reached and flicked off the light, but remained motionless before the mirror. He wondered if his eyes would adjust to the dark and if he would be able to see himself in the mirror if he waited long enough. He stood there for nearly ten minutes, but all around him there was only a black void. He thought of Richard. He, too, was out there somewhere in the darkness, sleeping quietly, unaware that his father was standing in his pajamas, old and failed, somewhere in Virginia, thinking of him at that very moment.

New York City

"My tits are too small for that thing. It'll fall right off me," Jessica protested to Elaine, who was shoving her into a dressing room with a black bikini that had holes cut out of it in order to expose just a hint of flesh here and there.

"You can't go to Fire Island in that ratty old thing you wore last summer," Elaine said, closing the door and leaning against it so Jessica couldn't come out. "You're not getting out until you at least try it on. You'll be the hit of the island in it. Remember, you've got strong competition out there. You have to do something theatrical if you're going to get any attention."

"The only woman who would even be noticed on Fire Island on Memorial Day weekend is Bette Davis," Jessica said, struggling to pull off her blue jeans.

The small Bleecker Street shop was filling up with Villagers who were already shopping for the big weekend coming up at the end of the month. Since this store carried nothing but swimsuits and t-shirts, everyone began the search for swimwear there.

"Okay, it doesn't fit," Jessica said from inside the dressing room.

"Open this door immediately," Elaine demanded.

"I said it doesn't fit, I'm changing."

"You're not getting out, smart-ass, until you let me see," Elaine warned.

The door opened about an inch and then slammed shut. "I can't," Jessica pleaded.

Elaine grabbed the door and flung it open. Jessica immediately covered herself with her hands. "I look like Olive Oyl. This is ridiculous."

"Stop it, you fool, and move your hands, I want to see this for myself. I'll be the judge," Elaine said, stepping back for a full view.

Jessica lowered her hands to her sides and closed her eyes, mortified.

"Stand up straight," Elaine commanded. "I think it's sexy. You look perfectly wonderful. They'll go crazy over you. And what an interesting tan you'll get," Elaine added mischievously. "Phil will love it."

"Oh my God! It's Don Knotts in drag," a voice screeched from somewhere on the other side of the store. Jessica opened her eyes, screamed, and slammed the door shut, as Steffan and True came rushing toward the dressing room. "Call the paparazzi, a star is born. Open that door, you hussy!" True shouted, banging on the door. Steffan joined in, "You're under arrest in there, come out with your legs up."

"I hate you," Jessica shouted from inside the tiny room. "Get out of here. I'm not coming out until you two leave."

True winked at Elaine. "Oh, come on, Sis, we're just kidding. Let us see."

"Never!" Jessica shouted. "Get lost."

"Please, Jessie," Steffan begged. "We won't laugh. I think it's wonderful. Are you going to buy it?"

"Fuck off, twirp," Jessica said.

"I'm serious. I like it. You look great. Please let me see it. True's gone. It's just me and Elaine. Let us see, just once. Come on."

The three of them stood back and watched the dressing room door crack slightly. It opened slowly until Jessica saw True and slammed it closed again, but True grabbed it before she could get it latched and threw it open. There was a split second of silence, and then both twins became hysterical with laughter. Jessica slammed the door with such force that Elaine thought it would splinter.

"What's going on here?" the saleswoman asked, hearing the ruckus and watching True fall into a rack of designer beach pants.

"Get those fuckers out of here," Jessica screamed, "or I'll call the police."

The twins were helpless with laughter as the saleswoman led them toward the door by their arms. They were holding their sides and crying. Even the Secret Service agent was laughing. Jessica emerged, buttoning her jeans and hopping on one leg, while trying to get her foot into a sandal. "Where are those cocksuckers? I'll kill them. I'll kill them both. Where are they?"

"They're gone, settle down," Elaine said, trying to stifle her own laughter. "They were just having fun."

"Fun!? Is that what you call fun? I've never been so humiliated in my entire life. They're pigs, cretins, swine! Insensitive little bastards."

Jessica threw the bikini on the counter as she headed for the street, Elaine and the agent close behind.

Once outside, they caught up with the twins, who, still laughing, had gotten only a few doors down Bleecker.

"Hey, beefcakes," Jessica hollered from behind. The twins turned and upon seeing her became hysterical all over again, this time falling onto the hood of a car parked at the curb. "Hey, show us your meat. I hear you've got at least three inches," Jessica shouted, grabbing at True's Levi's. He was helpless with laughter, and before he could defend himself, she had succeeded in pulling his pants down. He wasn't wearing underwear, and to the delight of the assembling crowd, his genitals were on full display. True pulled frantically at his pants, but could not stop laughing, even in the midst of this crisis. Several men began applauding. Jessica gestured toward her brother and announced, "Ladies and gentlemen, Tiny Tim."

Steffan had crossed the street to escape her wrath, but he too was still convulsed.

"Come, Elaine," Jessica said, lifting her nose into the air and taking her friend's arm. "Let's go uptown. I'd rather deal with winos and bag ladies."

The White House

"It's coming on now," Billings said, hanging up the receiver on the President's desk. Carl Stone turned up the volume on the television set and stood back so the President, Secretary of State Gibbons, and Defense Secretary Smith, who were all seated on the sofa, could see the screen. Adam McCann emerged first from the Foreign Relations Committee hearing room and was rushed by reporters, making it nearly impossible for him to get to the microphones set up in the hallway.

"Senator," a reporter shouted, "what's the verdict?"

Always composed, McCann waited a moment so as not to appear as though he were answering a question, but making a statement to the press in general.

"Gentlemen, ladies, the Senate Foreign Relations Committee has just voted nine to six against the sale of APANS to the Sudan."

There was a flurry of activity and a bevy of questions shouted at him, which he proceeded to ignore.

"The committee," he continued, trying to overcome the noisy reporters, "the committee believes it would not be in the best interests of the United States, the Middle

East, or Israel to place such sophisticated military systems in the hands of a Mideast country in the fashion proposed by the President. Without a guarantee of some type of American control over the use of such military hardware, the committee feels there would be grave danger and unwarranted risk to peace and stability in the region, especially as it pertains to the state of Israel. We will, therefore, recommend to the Senate that the bill be voted down."

With that said, the senator made his way back to his office, fending off the reporters trailing him. The next picture on the television was Bif Tucker being interviewed outside his office.

"Senator Tucker," a woman reporter from one of the networks said, "what does this vote in the Senate Foreign Relations Committee mean to the presidential campaign?"

Tucker, looking impeccable in a gray three-piece suit and red club tie, spoke convincingly and with modesty, a campaign trait that made him popular not only with the electorate, but with the press as well. "It means at least two things, so far as I can tell at this point, Marilyn," he said, using the reporter's first name. "First, that the studied opinion of the members of the Senate committee — who have considered this issue long and hard — is that it is definitely not in the best interests of the United States government to put potentially dangerous military hardware into the hands of a third world power. Secondly, and perhaps most importantly, it means that the American people have been heard by their representatives in Washington. As you know, my position all along has been that this was a very risky proposition, and when the President's final proposal did not include any provisions for some kind of control over the use of these aircraft, it became obvious not only to me, but to all who had studied the matter thoroughly, that it was a risk we simply couldn't afford to take. If the White House had only pressed harder for some sort of safety mechanism in the package that would assure a responsible use of APANS, I think the outcome in the committee might have been quite different."

"Do you see this as being a boost to your seeking the Democratic nomination?"

"I don't think there's any doubt about the fact that the President is not as powerful with the Congress as he was three years ago. There has been a severe breach in communication between the White House and Capitol Hill."

"So you think this will hurt him, then?" the reporter pressed.

"Yes, I can't see how he can walk away from this vote without losing a great deal of the American public's confidence," Tucker said.

The reporter signed off and Stone turned off the set.

The President rolled up his shirtsleeves and went back to his desk. "All right," he said, "let's lay this out in detail."

The men gathered around the President's desk and began taking notes as he asked questions and gave instructions, laying out his strategy for them. The men present included not only Stone, Gibbons, and Smith, but Gasher from FBI, and White House Press Secretary Mark Baer.

"I want every program from every opposing senator's state where federal funds are involved scrutinized. Each cabinet member is to submit a one-page memo summarizing the totals of funds budgeted to the states for the coming fiscal year, breaking out what has been appropriated, what has been transferred already, and what is left to be paid. I want a report listing all block grants to every major city in every state, along with a call sheet for each mayor of those cities. And this time make sure that the family members' names are right. I don't want to ask the mayor of Los Angeles how his daughter is doing at UCLA and have him tell me he has no daughter by that name," Marshall said, looking directly at Baer, who had given him a call sheet once where all the names had been typed one line off and the President didn't realize it until he had made his third call, each time asking about the wife of the man he had telephoned just previously.

"I want this information by Friday, so you're going to have to work hard and fast and ask your staffs to put in plenty of overtime. This is critical, and we have to move now. Unless there are questions, that's all."

"Do you want to schedule another meeting of this group for later in the week?" Billings asked.

"No, but I want everyone to stand by," he said to the group. "No one is to leave town for any reason without checking with Billings first."

The men scurried off to their offices, Gasher and Stone remaining behind with Billings at the President's request. When the men were alone, the President spoke slowly, deliberately, and with grave concern evident both in his voice and on his face. "I'm not going to pretend to you three that we're not in trouble here. We are, and it's the most serious kind of trouble. I know it is widely known among top administration members that I am deeply worried about APANS. I haven't spoken with others about it, because I thought it senseless to alarm people until the committee voted, but now it's evident that the bill is headed for defeat. We cannot let that happen for many reasons.

"First, there is the obvious reason — defense. The Middle East is a hotbed of terrorism and anarchy right now, thanks to Libya. The Soviets are deeply infiltrating every country in the region. Intelligence sources tell us that if the Sudan doesn't get this hardware, they will turn to Russia. In fact, they have been negotiating simultaneously with the Soviets all along for their KMS System 3000. That means simply that they are in and we are out. Egypt won't have a chance; neither will the Emirates or Kuwait. It will only be a matter of time before the entire area is sealed off by the Russians, and all of Europe's oil, along with the Suez Canal, is totally under their control. I don't have to tell you that is an untenable position for us. It cannot and must not happen. Do you all understand that?"

The men nodded, each one beginning to feel the uncomfortable weight of his responsibilities heavy upon him. What they were being told, in effect, was that the military security of the United States was riding on this vote.

"Secondly," the President continued, "the effect this would have on our economy would be catastrophic. We could never recover from having this oil supply and the trade passage of the canal in the hands of the Russians. Nor could we long maintain any influence with European or Asian allies if we were to lose our military influence in the Middle East. Italy, for example, would have no alternative but to support every Mideast position in the United Nations. We would have no leverage in swaying the votes of critical issues in the General Assembly. Our allies are not going to vote with us and against the Arabs when the Arabs are controlling their factories and lighting their homes. Just as important, they are not going to be so easily maneuvered in trade agreements. International commerce would be in deep, deep trouble, and once we lose economic power with the Europeans, we will never regain it. We can take all our exported goods and mark them CARE packages.

"Finally — and this is only important so far as completing the economic and defense recovery program we've begun is concerned — we will surely go down to defeat in the election, if we even get beyond the primaries. That would mean a reversal of all our programs, whether the opposition party is elected to office or whether my good friend Mr. Tucker is elected. To put it closer to home, it means your jobs. So I expect a hundred and ten percent of your time and energy until we turn this thing around. Do whatever you have to do. Carl, rev up the party machinery in the states; double the airtime of those videos we're showing; get every available volunteer and party regular to man the phones. I want voters calling in their concern over APANS twenty-four hours a day, and I don't want them calling the White House. I want them calling the Hill.

"Glen, whatever you have in your files that will help me, get over here on the double. I don't care how secret, how dirty, or how seemingly trivial. I want every scrap of information you can put your hands on. That includes not only the no votes, but the undecideds, as well.

"Mark, crank up your staff for round-the-clock news briefings and releases. I want everything that goes to the media to relate in some way to APANS and how this country is teetering on the brink because the Congress is pussyfooting on this crucial military issue. The voters put us in office partly to beef up the military, so they'll be concerned about our defense going weak.

"Thad, I want every cabinet member who isn't involved in the ongoing operations of our effort here at the White House on the road. Personal appearances, speeches, testimonials, the works. I want full support on this, and I want it in the form of personal meetings. We are literally fighting for our lives here, and that's the message they are to carry to the people. Get some of them to high school and college commencement exercises. That impresses the voters. Starting tomorrow. Now, if you gentlemen will excuse me I've got some neck wringing to do. Just remember, failure is not acceptable this time. We must win this one ... at any cost."

The President stood and shook each man's hand as he left. There were no smiles on their faces. Billings and Stone stepped into Billings's office and closed the door. "Jesus," Carl said, flopping on the sofa under the painting Thaddeus hated, "he's really unnerved by this. I don't think I've ever seen him quite so panicky."

"He really believes what he said, Carl," Billings said, sitting in one of the chairs in front of his desk and putting his feet up on the one that faced it. "He believes the country is on the brink of disaster, both militarily and economically, if this APANS sale doesn't go through. And you know what?"

"What?" Carl asked.

"I agree with him. I think this one is purely unselfish. He's really not worried about losing the election that much. Sure, he wants to win. Who wouldn't? But that's not his primary motivation here. He really thinks the Middle East will fall to the Russians if we don't provide the Sudan with an adequate line of defense. We've done as much as we can for Egypt and they're holding their own, but not for long without being bolstered."

"Well, I'm not saying I disagree, Thad," Carl said, loosening his tie a little, "all I'm saying is I've never seen him so frantic. He was very lucid and articulate, even well organized in his planning, but there was a look in his eyes that I've never seen before. I guess it's like you say ... he really thinks the country is in danger."

"And he's at the helm. He certainly doesn't want to go down in history as the president who failed to protect his people from their number-one enemy. Just imagine the consequences of the Soviets controlling the Suez Canal, not to mention every drop of oil in the region. It's unfathomable. I only hope—"

Just then Thad's office door was flung open and Claudia appeared in the doorway in a fire engine red dress.

"Claudia!" Thaddeus exclaimed.

"May I come in?" the First Lady asked, closing the door behind her.

"Why, certainly," Billings said, jumping to his feet. Stone was already standing and straightening his tie. "Please sit down," Thad said, offering her one of the chairs near the desk, which she took.

"I was just leaving anyway," Stone said, moving toward the door.

"No, Carl, please," Claudia said, gesturing him to take his seat again. "I'm glad you're here. I want to talk with the both of you."

Carl cast an inquisitive glance to Billings and seated himself again on the sofa. Claudia smoothed her dress several times and straightened the belt at her waist. The men waited patiently. Finally, she clasped her hands together and rested them in her lap. "I'm worried," she said, looking at each man in turn.

"Worried?" Billings asked.

"About Donald. About the President."

"In what way, Claudia?" Billings said, adopting a personal, paternal attitude.

"It's this APANS bill. He's worried to death about it. He doesn't sleep, he's quiet and brooding, and when he does talk about it, it's in such negative terms. He thinks the Senate is jeopardizing the security of the country out of some sort of spite for him. He's taking it very personally, and it makes it that much more difficult for him to bargain with them. You know, to hold federal money out in front of them. He's afraid it's just making things worse, making them dig their heels in even harder. There must be something we can do to help him."

"I think he has things in much better control now," Billings said, trying to reassure her. "We just came from a meeting with him where he outlined a new strategy for lobbying the Senate on this issue. Everyone will be pitching in even harder now. I think we can do it."

"That's right," Stone agreed. "He's mobilized everyone now, the cabinet, the Communications Office, even state and local politicians. We're going to begin an all-out effort to get the voters to contact their senators and representatives. I think there's still a very good chance we can win."

"Do you really?" Claudia asked anxiously.

"Yes," Billings said, reaching for her hand. "It's going to be much better now. The President has the full support of everyone from cabinet officers to precinct captains. We'll pull it out, you'll see."

"Well, promise me if there's anything I can do, anything at all, you'll call on me. I don't know what it would be, but I'm willing to do whatever it takes to help in this. Promise me you'll keep me informed and let me know if I can be of assistance," she said, standing up now.

"I promise," Thad said, walking with her to the door.

"Thank you, thank you both. You're wonderful men, wonderful friends to Donald and me. We really are grateful for all you do. I hope you know that."

"We know," Carl said. "It's our honor to be of service to the both of you."

"Thank you," she said. "I'll wait to hear from you." She disappeared as quickly as she came, leaving the two men staring blankly at each other.

"Thaddeus," Stone said, thrusting his hands deep into his pockets and beginning now to pace back and forth in front of the sofa, "just how serious do you think this is? I mean, putting aside the President's feelings about the matter, what is really at stake here?"

Billings moved to the chair behind his desk. "I'm not sure I understand your question, Carl."

"What I'm saying is, naturally everyone is concerned about APANS — for a lot of reasons — and none of us want to lose the battle in the Senate. It would be a blow to the administration, to the party, to all of us personally. But what are the actual consequences to the country and to the world?" Carl stopped pacing and faced Billings straight on.

"I'm not sure I can think of it in those terms," Billings answered. "I don't mean to sound like I'm making a speech, but the good of the country and of the world, by extension, depends entirely on whether or not this president has any authority, any credibility, any power. This is a major issue. It has to do with his influence all over the globe, it has to do with his influence on the Hill and with his own people. It's clearly a test of all those things and, without a doubt, the most important test Marshall has ever faced. I think if we lose this one, it will very likely be the beginning of the end for this administration."

Stone sat in a chair in front of Billings's desk and leaned forward, resting his arms on the desk. Thaddeus recognized the look on Stone's face as being one of calculation, of which he was the master within the campaign hierarchy. He was taking Billings's answers to his questions and formulating a plan. Thaddeus could almost hear the mental wheels whirring.

"You and I know him better than anyone," Carl said, "with the exception of Claudia, of course. You've seen the psychological profile, you've worked with him from the very beginning. Claudia has never approached us before, not like this. She looked desperate. Is she trying to tell us something without betraying him?"

"Do you mean will he crack if he loses this one?" Billings asked bluntly.

"Well, that's putting it rather harshly, but ... yes. Will it undo his confidence in himself? Will he see it as betrayal and the end of his ability to move and persuade?"

"Well, he's not going to turn into another Nixon, if that's what you mean. He's not going to become paranoid and start cleaning house and fumbling the ball in public, but remember, he's never lost before. Not an election, not even a vote on the Hill. It's a remarkable record, and it's also a two-edged sword. The man is unfamiliar with defeat. I'm not sure how he'll react, but I do know he's committed to this. He's different from you and me, Carl. He deeply believes he's doing the right thing and that the people are behind him. He takes his office very seriously."

"And you? What do you believe?" Carl asked, a smug, thin smile etched on his face.

"I imagine I see it the same way you do," Billings said, staring intently at the heavy lead marks he was making now with a pencil on a yellow legal tablet — dark cyclonelike vortexes. "Whether APANS is right or wrong doesn't really matter. It's the Republicans against us and what they're trying to do is to make us look bad and get us out of the White House. I don't believe it makes a fucking bit of difference whether the Sudanese get the planes or not as far as peace in that part of the world is concerned. Just like Central America, the Middle East will always be in turmoil. When this crisis is over it'll just be something else, and whatever it is, our political opponents will jump on it and try to defeat us on that issue, too. It's politics, Carl, pure politics. And it's no different over there, just one crazy Arab versus another. They're all crazy for power. Look what they did to Arafat — drove him out, then murdered him. Look what they did to Sadat. They don't give a damn about their people. Give any one of them a chance and he'd invade every other country in the region. They're all little Hitlers. Our job has always been to keep the power balanced so that doesn't happen. Keep the Commies out and keep the power in any one man's hands limited."

"So it all equals out," Stone said, leaning back in his chair and sighing loudly. "Each crisis is meaningless, but each one is essential..."

"That's right. We have to win them all. This one is more important only because it's happening right before the primaries and our hides are at stake. Yes, we must win this one. When you're in the game to win, you've got to take every hand you play. If you don't play to win, you shouldn't be in the game. Let's face it, Carl, the men who occupy the White House are always politicians, not diplomats or statesmen or career foreign service professionals. We know politics, not foreign affairs. We all fly by the seat of our pants and hope to Christ that a war doesn't break out until we get out of here."

Stone sat quietly thinking, staring past Billings out the window.

"You have an idea, Carl?" Thaddeus asked.

"Operation Thunder," Stone said soberly, staring hard now at his brother-in-law.

"I've thought the same thing once or twice, but..."

"But what?" Stone said.

"Is there time? It would take weeks to put it into place again."

"It was never dismantled," Stone said, revealing a classified secret he had never intended to tell Billings.

"What?"

"We never wound it down completely. Things have been too hot over there to dismiss the idea completely. We could activate it and implement it within forty-eight hours if we had to."

"Are you sure?" Billings asked, both perturbed that he hadn't been informed and intrigued by the idea of using it now.

Operation Thunder had been a covert plan devised by the CIA under Stone's leadership to stage an attempted assassination of the Egyptian president in order to bolster support for the President's opposition to a Senate proposal to cut back arms sales to the Egyptians at a time when sympathy for the Israelis was running high in the United States. The administration had held that not giving arms to Egypt would make them vulnerable not only to the Israelis, who were better equipped, but to Arab countries in the Middle East who were becoming increasingly hostile to the Egyptian president for the westernization of his country. In the eleventh hour, Marshall convinced people that the Russians were ready to move in and overthrow the country and that they were the driving force behind the minor insurrections occurring throughout Egypt. The Congress approved

by a narrow margin the arms sale the President was propos-
ing; however, the discontent against the Egyptian leader
continued after the arms sale, so the same rhetorical tack
couldn't be taken with APANS.

"Every single man is ready to move on a few hours
notice. It would guarantee passage in the Senate. It'll scare
the shit out of 'em," Stone said a little too enthusiastically
for Billings's taste.

"He'll never approve it," Billings said.

"He doesn't have to," Stone answered fervently. "It's a
CIA operation and it's clean as a whistle. He'll never know.
No one will."

This was the side of Stone that Billings liked least. It was
also that facet of his personality which often frightened
Thad, but it was precisely what made him the perfect political strategist in an election campaign.

"They can all be trusted?"

"There are only two men who know every link in the
chain," Carl said. "They're career men, total indoctrina-
tion, machines of liberty."

Billings stood up now and walked to the window behind
his desk. He stood looking out for a moment to where the
azaleas were trying to blossom, then turned to face Carl.
"It's too risky.

"What isn't?" Stone countered.

"Maybe we won't need it," Billings offered, not too
convincingly.

"When you're in the game to win, you've got to take
every hand you play," Stone quoted.

Thaddeus turned back to the window. On the other side
of the glass, a cardinal sat staring at him from a slender
branch of a red maple. It cocked its head inquisitively from
one side to the other, as if trying to read Thaddeus's mind.
Billings waved his arm and the bird flew off. Birds looking
in windows had always been considered bad omens in his
house. A swallow had sat peering in the living room window the entire morning of the day his mother died. "Not
yet," he said, turning and sitting at his desk again. "Let's
not move on it just yet. Let's wait and see how things go in

the next few days, see if the President can change any votes."

"Well, I won't dismantle it yet, either," Stone said, discouraged. He stood to leave. "Unless you think we should," he added after a long pause. He waited for Billings's response.

"No. Don't dismantle it. It's good to have an alternative in place just in case, but I hope we won't have to go to such extremes."

"I'll call Bradley and tell him to give us a report on how fast the mission could be activated and completed — just in case," Carl said, still trying to monitor Billings, who was looking at him, but not concentrating on him.

"Yes, sure," Thaddeus said. "Do that much. See what's involved, but make sure it's airtight. We may need it, but let's hope not."

Carl moved to leave, but Billings stopped him just as he got to the door. "Carl!" he almost shouted.

Stone looked back to Thaddeus, who was now leaning halfway across his desk. "Yes, Thad?"

"You're sure this plan will work? It was scrutinized to the last detail?"

"Positive, Thad. It's absolutely foolproof. Think about it. Unless you're tired of Washington and want to go back to selling cars in Phoenix." He started to open the door, then closed it. "Oh, yeah, one more thing. You might want to think about that purchase we just made from Linwood. Without APANS, that's all worthless paper." Then he opened the door and was gone.

New York City

Terry took a deep breath and opened the stage door. The security guard recognized him from the day before and the day before that. Terry had been persistently trying to make contact with D.J., but he could only get through to Parker, so he had begun coming to the theater. He knew D.J. would be there already, because the curtain was at eight and D.J. had a little ritual of concentration and meditation that he went through before every show.

Before the guard could tell Terry that he had orders not to admit him, Parker appeared out of nowhere, as if he had been waiting for him. He took Terry by the arm and pulled him aside, out of earshot of the uniformed guard. Terry, who was a little incoherent from two 'ludes he had taken before he left work, lost his balance and fell against the water cooler, causing the water inside to gurgle and slosh around in its huge green bottle. He looked at Parker and smiled. "Hi, Parker. Long time no see. Miss me?"

"I thought I told you not to come here again," Parker snarled, clenching his hand tighter around Terry's arm.

"You did," Terry replied, looking around for D.J.

"Then what the fuck are you doing here? You're going to get all of us into one hell of a lot of trouble if you keep this up."

"I came to see you. Thought we might go for a cocktail. Hey, why don't we ask D.J. to join us? You'll have to ask him, though, 'cause I don't think I'd recognize him if I saw him."

"Look, wise guy, you two will see each other tomorrow night, like I told you on the phone yesterday. Now get out of here," Parker said, letting go of his arm and motioning toward the door.

"Oh, Parker, don't be so dull. You take your work too seriously. You're going to have a coronary one of these days. Then they'll have to replace you with someone nice," Terry said, smiling and looking past Parker for some sign of D.J.

"Come on," Parker ordered, leading him to the large metal door. Terry resigned himself to failure and fumbled with the door handle. Everything he did seemed to be in slow motion. Parker opened the door for him and Terry stepped outside into the alley, then turned and leaned against the wall, motioning for Parker to come closer so he could whisper something to him. Parker's face frowned in disgust, but he leaned closer. "What?" he asked.

Terry whispered in his ear, "Would you let me in if I gave you a blow job?"

"Get out of here, Terry. He'll see you tomorrow night," Parker said, closing the door.

Terry stood leaning against the wall for a while, trying to gather himself for the walk to the subway. All of a sudden, he was aware of a man standing next to him. He focused and saw the man was smiling at him.

"You look like you could use a cup of coffee," the man said.

"Coffee isn't going to help this. How about a drink?" Terry asked.

"Good idea," the man said. "I see you hanging out here a lot. You know someone in there?" he asked, motioning his head toward the stage door.

"Yeah, sort of, why?"

"Nothing in particular, just that I've seen you here a few times, so I figured you must know someone in the play. It's fun to know people in show business. Thought maybe you could get me a ticket for one of their shows."

"Ha!" Terry threw his head back and it struck the brick wall with considerable force. He didn't seem to notice. "They probably wouldn't even let me *buy* a ticket, let alone give me one," he said. "I'm a troublemaker."

"Oh, I get it, a star gazer, an autograph hound."

Terry laughed again. "Yeah, I'm trying to gaze at a star I been living with for over a year. How 'bout that drink?"

"Sure," the man said, as the two of them started down the alley. "Say, are you putting me on? Do you really live with someone in there?"

They walked down the alley and turned the corner without looking back. If they had, Terry would have seen Parker standing in the doorway, a brooding look on his face.

As soon as he learned that his drinking companion was a reporter, Terry excused himself and left the bar. The problem was that he couldn't remember how much he had told him up to that point. He knew he hadn't mentioned D.J. by name, only that he knew someone in the acting company and that it was someone he had been living with until they were recently forced to separate. Had he implied that it was a man? He couldn't remember. He did say his family had forced the separation because of his father's position. Shit! How could he have been so stupid? If only he hadn't been on 'ludes. It was Parker's fault. If Parker had let him stay at the theater or had let him in to talk with D.J., he never would have run into the guy or wanted to go cry on someone's shoulder. If anyone was to blame it was Parker.

Now he sat in the tub with a Kahlua and cream rereading Rick's note.

Dear Terry,
  Something urgent has come up and I have to go back to California. I tried calling you at work, but for some reason they were never able to put me through to your shop. I don't know if or when I'll be back. Thanks for everything.

Terry crumpled the paper into a ball and threw it into the open toilet. He relit the joint he had laid on the side of the tub and leaned back, inhaling deeply. The warm water swirled across his chest and sloshed the hairline at the back of his neck. He closed his eyes and thought of the beach near Marseille. Maybe he'll lose the election and we'll finally be able to live like normal people, he thought, toking the joint once more. How great that would be.

As the warm bathwater lapped at his chest and arms, he thought of the lover he had before D.J. and how he used to beat Terry. He remembered the day he threw all Terry's belongings out the living room window, including his stereo, and how humiliated he was, standing in the street below their apartment, his few things strewn all over the pavement.

A flood of memories came now. He remembered the time his father locked him out of the house one January night when he came home late from a date and how he had to sleep under the porch all night. He recalled the day his mother died, returning from the barn, where she had been gathering eggs in her apron for breakfast. He ran to help her, but it was too late, and after that the only image of her he could ever conjure was that of her lying in the yard, the seven brown eggs clutched unbroken in her apron. He remembered his Italian grandmother "deworming" him by bending him over the side of the tub and, with a rubber glove on her hand, shoving a Vaselined finger up his tiny butt. He imagined Rick packing his suitcase. He finished the joint and lay in the tub until the water turned cool.

Standing in front of the closet, he looked at each shirt individually, then at the entire wardrobe collectively. How can clothes look sad, he wondered and went to the narrow window that looked out between his brownstone and the one next door. It was overcast, and dusk was just beginning to settle on the city, casting an eerie blue light between the buildings, turning the bricks a strange purplish color. He leaned his bare shoulder against the window frame and pressed his forehead to the glass. How can bricks look sad, he mused, the finiteness of the world presenting itself to him in the cold, lifeless colors of the shirts, the dark bricks, the indifferent sky. He saw himself in all these things and, although he was unable to articulate it, identified with their ephemeral natures. He spoke aloud: "I don't want to be alone."

Terry then prayed for the first time in as long as he could remember, looking up toward the slit of darkening sky between the buildings, as though that might better ensure his prayer would be heard: *Make a miracle ... make him come home ... make us be together again. Please.*

New York City

D.J. sat in the window hugging his knees and looking out over the waterfront. A half-drunk glass of white wine sat on the ledge next to him. The moonlight danced on the choppy Hudson River. Elaine had gone to a reception following the play, but he had begged off, saying he was tired and would only be irritable and would inevitably end up making some rude comment to one of the patrons.

It had been only a few weeks, and already he was feeling trapped, manipulated, and completely impotent regarding his own life. How could he possibly see it all the way through to the general election? The past few nights he had lain awake until the early hours of the morning, aching for Terry's company. He longed for his companionship, for his special sense of humor, missed the way he wandered around the apartment always tidying things up, picking up socks and newspapers, carrying a cocktail with him wherever he went, keeping the music going on the stereo until D.J. would plead with him for some silence. "Silence hurts my ears," Terry would say, as he removed the record from the turntable, then went straight for the television set.

"I miss him so much," D.J. said aloud as he leaned against the window, touching one of the panes with his left index finger and watching the glass fog. He spoke to the lights twinkling along the river. "I miss you, Terry. I know you're out there somewhere, losing yourself in a mindless drug, and I know it's because we're not together. It's my fault, Terry. Don't ever blame yourself. I'm sorry, baby. I'll make it up to you. Hang on, Terry. Please ... hang on."

Cleveland, Ohio

Billings had just returned to his hotel room from the President's suite when a call came through from New York giving him the details of Terry's behavior and informing him that he was last seen in the company of a reporter from a smut tabloid. They were headed for some bar after he was turned away from the theater where he had tried to see D.J. before a performance. It appeared to the person on the other end of the line that things were clearly out of hand once again. Drugs, persistent attempts to talk with D.J. in public places, nightly visits to Village gay bars — the whole scenario was reminiscent of the trouble he had posed before the European exile.

It was more than Billings could cope with. The Cleveland trip was not going well for him. He had been able to protect the President from most of the demonstrations by rerouting the motorcade and bringing the presidential party into the hotel through a service entrance. Every reporter who got within earshot of Marshall was firing questions at him about the APANS sale and his dramatic slipping in the polls that worsened daily now. The President and McCann were even in every major poll, and one showed Tucker clearly ahead of the President for his own party's nomination by some six percentage points.

The president of Cleveland State, where Marshall was to give the commencement address, somehow had not been invited to meet the President at the airport and was miffed, according to a telephone call from his assistant; the flowers that were presented to the First Lady upon their arrival were red roses, which for some reason unknown to Thaddeus made her livid. When he asked an aide what was wrong, she said she didn't know for sure, but thought it might be because they clashed with the orange suit Claudia was wearing. At any rate, she refused to carry them, passing them to her secretary immediately after they were handed to her by the mayor. A member of the American Nazi party shouted over a hand-held speaker at the airport that the President was "handing the country over to kikes, niggers, and faggots," then proceeded to shout, "Where's your faggot son?" The Secret Service and several Cleveland police officers wrestled him to the ground, but his message was heard quite clearly by both the President and Claudia. Then, in the middle of the President's address, the chancellor's wife collapsed onstage right next to him, and his speech had to be interrupted while they carried her off to an ambulance.

Now, just when Billings thought he might be able to kick off his shoes and have a double Scotch, he was informed that Terry was again out of control in New York City.

"No," Thaddeus shouted into the phone so loudly that the Secret Service agent stationed outside his room came bursting through the door with his revolver drawn. "Don't do anything! I'll handle this myself. Just keep him away from Olivier!" He slammed the phone down, paying no attention to the agent, who was now retreating sheepishly back into the hall. Billings picked up the phone once more and in minutes was speaking with the governor of New York, whom he woke from a sound sleep.

"I want the entire company out of New York. I don't care where they go or how they get there, but have your brother get them the hell away from Manhattan for as long as possible," Billings ordered the governor, whose brother was the director of the Greenwich Performing Arts Center, where the acting company was based.

Billings seldom used his position to order such moves by state officials, but the governor was a senior party member, a one-time presidential nominee, and could be counted on for total support in a crisis. By seven-thirty the next morning, Thaddeus was informed that the New York Actors' Troupe would be leaving for a six-week repertory performance in Tucson.

Next, he called Carl Stone. "Now," Thaddeus said to Stone as he finished the last of the coffee which had been brought by room service, "I want Snowman out of the city, too. I don't care how or where, but I want him away from Manhattan for the summer and I don't want to hear that he's in Tucson."

Stone promised to take care of it and to get back to Billings with the details by the end of the week. Thaddeus picked up his briefcase and some loose papers, opened the door, and charged out into the hall past the agent. "Let's get the hell out of this fucking cow town," Thaddeus said to the pinscher, who was scurrying to keep up with him.

Air Force One, over Indiana

Claudia turned her face away from the window just long enough to see if anyone had noticed her brush the tear away. Her secretary was asleep in the seat beside her; the President was standing up in the aisle near the cockpit, talking animatedly with three staff members. She avoided the temptation to pull the white lace hankie out of her pink suit pocket — that would only call attention to herself. She wiped the tear on the seat cushion and returned her gaze to the world which stretched beneath her as far as she could see.

The Midwest divided itself into green and tan squares crisscrossed with blue and brown waterways and freckled with clumps of dark green trees. Here and there she could make out a farmhouse, a cluster of buildings, a village. Another tear coursed down her cheek. Why am I crying? she asked herself. What on earth is there that could possibly be upsetting me? Then, suddenly, as she spied a multicolored field, she remembered the roses and was forced to retrieve the hankie after all.

All her life she had fought her tendency to be superstitious, and, while she was able to keep it from people, it nevertheless remained a losing battle for her. Her best-kept secret, known only to her secretary, was her irrational fear of being presented a bouquet of roses before beginning a motorcade. For months after the Kennedy assassination, she dreamed of blood-covered roses falling into her lap and would wake from her sleep in a cold sweat. When the mayor thrust those flowers into her hands, she knew the trip was going to be a disaster, and, although no physical harm had come to anyone during their Cleveland visit, the entire visit was marred with unpleasantness and minor political disasters, from the Nazi harangue at the airport to the chancellor's wife fainting in the middle of Donald's speech. None of it came as a surprise to her in the wake of the incident with the roses. She was now terribly relieved that it was over and they were on their way back to Washington.

Distracted from her thoughts by Miles Cameron's raucous laughter, she could see that Donald was entertaining a group of aides with anecdotes, trying in his inimitable fashion to reassure them that he was not angry with anyone for the many *faux pas* he had endured in Ohio. It was so like him to weather difficulties in that way, regardless of whether they could have been avoided with more careful planning. It had always been his style to squeeze through a tight spot and later laugh it off and try to lift everyone's spirits so they would carry on with renewed commitment and not brood over what could no longer be corrected. "Scratch it," he would often say, "we'll do better next time." She loved him for that attitude and wished she could adopt it.

He had always been able to take the bumps much better than she. The more things went wrong, the angrier she became and the calmer he seemed to get. In the beginning, when he was just starting out in politics and she would go with him to make speeches and campaign for candidates, she wasn't able to control her anger at hecklers and urged him to retaliate when reporters would misquote him or refer to him as a has-been singer turned politician. She could endure the swipes the press took at her, such as taking her to task for keeping a .22 caliber pistol in her nightstand and carrying it with her wherever she went — even though she had a license to carry it — or their playing up her expensive wardrobe; but, when it came to the criticism of Donald, she struck out vehemently.

There were very few supporters when they started out. Virtually none in the press, only a handful in the entertainment business, and even many of their friends didn't offer their full support until after he had won the gubernatorial nomination. No one thought he could succeed at convincing people he was a serious candidate. When old friends and acquaintances in the recording industry would chide him or take a public stand against him, she never forgave them. Not so much because they were speaking out against the man she loved — although that was always part of it — but mostly because these were people who, in her estimation, never got involved, never became active in political issues until Donald, a hawkish conservative, gained political credibility, and their liberal interests became threatened.

It was her opinion that current entertainers should not mix in politics, and it was she who insisted that Donald never link himself with the entertainment industry once he chose to pursue a political career. She was a vigilant watchdog when it came to seeing that no movie stars or entertainers appeared on platforms with him, and it was with great reluctance that she agreed to a gala inaugural celebration that featured some of the biggest names in Hollywood. But as he pointed out to her after the election, "It's over now, honey. They can all come out of the closet and whoop it up for us. We won!"

Even though she acquiesced and in time let her old wounds heal, the scars never disappeared, and the friends who frequented the White House were not so much the entertainers they had once socialized with during Donald's television days as it was their business and political friends who had stuck it out with them and been supportive even in the toughest of times. Friends like Fran Altman. Claudia didn't see the two of them as having many enemies, but she once told Fran she believed she could list their real friends on the back of a small envelope.

"Maybe we would be better off if he lost," she heard herself whisper as she watched the Appalachians appear in the distance. "I miss the ranch. I miss our morning rides. I miss ... seeing D.J. more."

But she knew that was only a passing emotion, a feeling born of fatigue and weariness. The fighter instinct in her was too strong to give in. They would wage a hard campaign, and they would win. Their retirement could wait. The ranch would always be there, and after all, this was Donald's summit. He was the President, and he had a right to be the President for as long as he could manage to hold on to the job. And her responsibility as his wife was to see to it that he did.

The White House

Billings went over the list of items for Marshall, pausing after each report, waiting as the President either made a notation on his agenda or nodded for Thaddeus to continue. Most of it was routine information regarding staff operations, although some of it was related directly to the campaign. Except for APANS, which was still stalled and being badly battered about on the Hill, the news was not particularly disconcerting.

"The only caution signal we might want to pay attention to," Billings added as he concluded his report, "is some backlash from cutting the power on Dolan's radio station. He evidently has figured out it wasn't coincidental that he lost his wattage shortly after our little meeting. The lines have been humming for two days now with calls from his listeners, and the mail is starting to pile up in the mail room."

"How much?" Marshall asked, reaching for his coffee.

"A full bag this week, and it's still coming in."

"Wait and see, Thad."

"That's what I told them. There's some concern among the Secret Service, because a lot of crackpots have written in threatening you unless power is restored, but there's that sort of mail every day. I'm having them sort it by zip so we can try to get some idea of how far-reaching this is geographically and whether or not it's in vulnerable spots. We're strong in the South, especially in the Southeast, so it shouldn't affect the primaries. Claudia's scheduled to speak in Florida weekend after next at the opening of a new retirement center. That will offset some of the reaction, I hope."

"Just make sure before she leaves that we're not sending her into a combat zone," the President said, his voice marked with the troubled tone that was present whenever he talked about the First Lady going on the campaign trail. "I don't want her subjected to a lot of abusive reporters or angry demonstrators. If it looks like there will be any trouble, I want to pull her off of it. We'll send the Vice President's wife in her place."

Billings made a note of it. "Have you had time to look at the speech Thuronyi wrote for you for the Renfrow luncheon this afternoon?" Billings asked.

"No, I was going to do that in the car. I was even considering foregoing any formal speech at all. I've got to get back on the phone; I've only had a chance to go through about a third of the files Nickles sent over, and I'm not so sure any votes are going to change. I want to work on Cavoli this afternoon while I'm up there, but I haven't had a chance to look at his folder yet. Why? Do you have a problem with the speech?"

"No, not exactly," Billings replied. "There are a couple of comments in there that could be taken as partisan politicking and I think we should stay away from anything like that. We've put out a lot of advance publicity on your going up to the Hill for this, so there's going to be full media coverage and we should make sure it looks like you're going up there unarmed and friendly. You know — one of the good ole boys. It might be a lot better for you to use the jokes and ad-lib the comments."

"Good," Marshall said, "I'm more comfortable with that approach anyway."

Thaddeus left the President to review the Cavoli file and to go over the jokes that had been prepared for him. He gave the President's secretary strict orders not to disturb him for any reason; this get-together with both congressional bodies could have a decisive effect on his image in the polls as well as his PR with members of Congress itself and he wanted it to go as smoothly as possible. With that in mind, he had decided to wait until after the luncheon to bring up the matter of D.J. going to Tucson and Terry being whisked out of Manhattan. Actually, he wasn't convinced he needed to bring up the matter of Terry at all. Perhaps he would just let it ride until Marshall asked him about it.

The Capitol

The luncheon went far better than anyone had expected. Thaddeus was greatly relieved and felt somewhat better about the Cleveland fiasco, figuring this had a balancing effect. Marshall immediately began shaking hands and milling about from the moment he arrived at the Senate entrance to the Capitol. There was a party of senators and representatives at the door to greet him, and he spoke with each one in turn, asking about their families, the upcoming primaries of those who were about to run for their seats again, and special interests that each man had. He had never been in better form, remembering the names of wives and children and even recalling personal experiences he had shared with several of them at one time or another.

By the time the group had taken the elevator to the main floor and made their way to the rotunda, they were laughing and cavorting like schoolchildren. It seemed as though they had all just been waiting for the President to make this gesture. The men entered the noisy hall without formal announcement, but the gathered dignitaries sensed their presence, turned to face the President, and began applauding. Marshall waved, smiling broadly, and then held up the luncheon for thirty minutes by shaking hands and speaking with nearly half of the assembled crowd.

His remarks after lunch were witty and endearing, and there wasn't the slightest hint of partisan politics either in the remarks that any speaker made or in the ambience that pervaded the affair. He was applauded several times for his humor, and afterwards he carried out his plan of visiting several of the men in their private offices, an unprecedented act for a president. By the time he left the building, he had been assured of the votes of several uncommitted senators, and he had also convinced Cavoli and Baker to reconsider their positions. Cavoli even walked Marshall to the main entrance.

With things looking up as a result of the successful luncheon at the Capitol, Billings attacked the problem of Terry and D.J. with renewed confidence and with an innovative approach. He decided to break with his normal method of issuing directives and meet with the two of them personally. He arranged for Terry to be flown to Washington, where he was put up in the Georgetown home of one of the assistant directors of the CIA, where Billings would meet with them first thing in the morning. D.J. arrived a little after midnight at Andrews Air Force Base in Maryland and was driven in a military pool car without escort to Georgetown. He was shown to the upstairs bedroom by a CIA agent, seemingly the only person in the house; however, D.J. knew the gardens were filled with Secret Service.

He stepped inside the guest room and closed the door. A single votive candle burned on a stand beside the brass bed where Terry lay sleeping naked on top of the covers. A small radio was playing softly somewhere in the dark. The French doors to the terrace were open wide, and the sheer curtains that covered them blew gently in the warm breeze that carried with it the rich scent of honeysuckle, which grew on the side of the house.

D.J. undressed quietly and stood beside the bed looking down at his lover. He was still beautiful to D.J., even as thin as he was from the drugs he had been using heavily again. His ribs protruded so distinctly that each one could be counted, and his cheeks were sunken. But the chiseled features of the face and the solid structure of his jaw and nose remained classically elegant.

D.J. eased into bed next to him and gently laid his head on the pillow, facing Terry. As he let his body relax, sinking down into the mattress, Terry's eyes opened.

"I tried not to wake you," D.J. apologized.

"I wasn't asleep," Terry whispered. "I was waiting for you. Are you all right?"

"Yes, I'm fine, thanks."

They lay looking into each other's eyes for a long time. After several minutes of silence, Terry reached out and ran his fingers gently over D.J.'s face. "Be funny for me," he asked. "Make me laugh."

D.J. smiled. "I'm so glad to see you. I've missed you big."

"Remember the man who lived down the hall from us in France?" Terry asked. "The one who sweated so much."

D.J. laughed. "Yes, the one who used to stuff paper towels under his arms." They both laughed out loud now.

"You could see them sticking out of his shirtsleeves," Terry said. They laughed hard at the memory of the fat Frenchman, freed for a few moments from the shackles of their predicament. When they stopped laughing they kissed and lay in each other's arms.

"You know what my only problem is with all of this?" Terry asked softly, his head on D.J.'s shoulder.

"What is it?" D.J. asked, stroking Terry's hair.

"I like you best," Terry said. "I like you better than anyone I know, better than anyone I've ever known. That's why it's so hard for me to be away from you. I have more fun with you than with anyone else."

"I know," D.J. said, squeezing him gently. "I know."

"Do you want to fuck me?" Terry asked.

D.J. laughed and threw his head back on the pillow. "Jesus, you kill me."

"What's the matter?" Terry asked, propping himself up on one elbow.

"You say it like you were asking me if I want to borrow a pen or something."

"Well ... I was just being straight to the point. I thought you might want to." He laid his head back on D.J.'s shoulder.

"I've fucked you the last two times we've been together. You'd better watch out, you're going to make a top man out of me."

"It's okay," Terry said, squeezing D.J. around the waist, "I like you inside me." He planted a tender, sensuous kiss on D.J.'s left nipple. "I love you," he added.

"And I love you," D.J. said.

"Listen to what they're playing," Terry said softly, cocking an ear toward the radio. They lay quietly listening to the lyrics of the old song.

> *Dropping you this line to give you peace,*
> *And to set your weary mind at ease.*
> *I know that it's rough when you're so far away.*
> *Listen to the words I have to say...*
>
> *Our love will last forever.*

Terry kissed D.J. again. "Want to borrow my pen?"

Washington, D.C.

When the alarm went off, Terry was already sitting up in bed smoking. D.J. punched the clock radio with a vengeance, putting an end to the hard rock music that had rudely brought him out of sleep, then turned back toward Terry. "What are you doing up so early?" he asked, stretching.

"I woke up around five and couldn't go back to sleep," Terry answered. "Strange bed, I guess." He gave D.J. a forced smile and crushed out his cigarette. "They're already downstairs," he added.

"Who is?" D.J. asked.

"The pinschers. I heard the cars pull up about an hour ago. I'm surprised Parker's voice didn't wake you. He's been practically shouting all over the house, inconsiderate slob."

"You know, he's really not as bad as we've made him out to be. I've gotten to where I kind of like him," D.J. said.

Terry gave him a vacant, distant look that told D.J. he had said the wrong thing. He felt as though he had just pushed Terry away. There was a knock at the door and Parker stuck his head in. "Time to get up, you guys," he said, smiling. "Hi, Terry. How's it going?"

"Okay, Parker. Any coffee down there?" Terry asked.

"Sure. I'll bring you some," Parker replied and disappeared again.

"What's he being so friendly for?" Terry asked.

"He's been okay lately. Maybe he likes being back in the States. I don't know, but I'm not complaining. We'd better get dressed."

D.J. went into the bathroom and turned on the shower. After it warmed up, the two of them stepped in. For the next thirty minutes, they lost themselves in each other, lathering each other's body, caressing, playing, moving in slow motion through the steam. They made love to each other, taking turns, then embraced beneath the spray of water until they were both soapless.

"What's this?" D.J. asked, lifting the shiny metal washer that Terry had taken from their bed in Lyon and which now hung around his neck on a thin silver chain.

"Something I brought back with me from France. Kind of a souvenir," Terry answered, looking down at the circle of metal between D.J.'s fingers.

"But what is it?"

"It's a washer that was on our bed. I shined it up some and put it on this chain." Terry looked at him, slightly embarrassed. "I know it's stupid, but..."

D.J. took Terry's face in his hands and kissed him tenderly. "I love you more than anything in the world."

Terry lowered his eyes. "I love you, too. I just wish..."

"No," D.J. said, putting his fingers to Terry's lips. "Don't say any more. No more words. Leave it like this. Let us have the memory of this morning to take with us now. It's been so beautiful. Remembering this will keep us going until it can be beautiful again."

When they pulled back the shower curtain, two mugs of coffee sat steamless on the vanity. They looked at each other and both smiled. "Well, he hasn't changed in some ways," Terry said.

While they dressed, Parker came back upstairs and told them that Thaddeus would be waiting for them in the study. He wanted to speak with them before they left the house. This made Terry extremely uneasy, as he had never talked with Billings and only knew him through photos and stories in the newspapers and by the commands he issued from the White House, where for the past three years he had been running Terry's life, dictating Terry's every move. He didn't think he liked the idea of finally meeting Billings. Not because he was afraid of the man and his power, but because he was afraid of what he might say to Billings if he lost his temper. D.J. seemed to take Parker's message in stride, but grew silent after Parker retreated, which told Terry that he, too, had been put a little on edge by the imminent confrontation. When Terry had finished putting on his shoes, he stood and faced D.J. "Ready?" he asked, throwing his shoulders back like a recruit preparing for inspection.

"How come you're so brave?" D.J. asked, punching Terry in the stomach and forcing him to break his soldier-like stance.

"It's like finally getting to meet the Wizard," Terry joked. "Maybe he'll talk to us from behind a curtain. Better yet, maybe he'll send us back to Kansas."

For Terry, Kansas turned out to be Fire Island for the summer. And for D.J., it was Tucson with the acting troupe. Billings hadn't planned on sending Terry to the island, but D.J. convinced him that it was the perfect place; it was isolated, inhabited only by the kinds of people who couldn't care less about notoriety or publicity, since many of them were notorious public figures anyway and went there to escape. If Terry wanted to get drunk or do drugs, he would only look like everyone else around him. "And,"

D.J. added, "I would consider it a personal favor. I've never asked you for a personal favor through all of this, Thaddeus. I do understand your position and what we all have to do for my father, and I'm willing to cooperate. But Terry needs special handling if we're going to get through this unscathed. Regardless of how you feel about him or us together, try to understand one thing: I love him. Just as you love Rachael, I love Terry, and I want him protected."

Somehow this penetrated Billings. He thought of his wife's drinking problem, of how the press would run rampant with it and try to bring him down if they ever found out. He thought of how difficult it was for Rachael to live in Washington, where she had no close friends, and how lonely it was for her, seeing so little of her husband, of how she literally had nothing to do with her time and how at first she tried so hard to fit into the scheme of things. But Washington society was not very receptive to a plain-spoken woman from Yuma who didn't like politics to begin with and then found herself thrust into the middle of a presidential administration. Liquor was an easy tranquilizer and a common one for political wives. She was another casualty to power, but Billings reminded himself it was only for a while and recalled his promise to himself — when this was all over they would take a long trip and return to Scottsdale, where he would get treatment for her and put back together the life they had before they became bound to the political tail of Donald Marshall's cutaway.

"All right," Billings told D.J. and Terry as they sat facing him in the Georgetown study. "But I'm warning you," he exclaimed, pointing his finger at Terry, "any funny business and I'll lock you up in a cell until this is over. Understand?"

"Yes, sir," Terry answered. "No funny business."

"For now," Billings continued, "you'll go back to New York and stay put until I can find someone to stay with you for the summer. You can't be there totally alone, for your sake — as well as for mine," he said awkwardly, trying to add a touch of lightness to the conversation. It had never occurred to D.J. until now that Thaddeus might be a little anxious himself about this meeting. "As soon as I can get an agent assigned to protect you, then you'll hear from us."

"Is that really necessary?" D.J. asked.

"Someone has to watch him — for security reasons. I don't want anyone finding out who he is and then taking some potshot at him. The guy doesn't have to be tied to him, but there should be someone around. Don't worry, he won't cramp his style. Terry won't even know he's there. He'll never see him.

"Now then," Billings continued. "You will proceed immediately to Tucson from here and Elaine will join you in about a week. The publicity office needs her to help with final news releases about this six-week stint in Tucson. Besides, she says she wants to supervise the packing. Parker will go with you, and Rodney will come later with the car, which is going to have some modifications made to it. In the meantime, your transportation in Tucson will be provided by regional agents. You're going to be under heavy security out there, as will the rest of the family from now until the convention." He paused to give each of them a dour look. "I guess that's all," he said and stood up. Terry and D.J. stood too.

"I want to thank you, Thaddeus," D.J. said. "This means a lot to me ... to both of us."

There was a poignant silence as Thaddeus looked first at Terry, then back to D.J. "Regardless of how it may appear to you at times — to both of you — I do have some understanding of how difficult this is for you two. I know I'm an obstacle for you both, but I only do what I judge best for everyone. I need your help now and I promise that I'll do what I can to make it bearable for you, but it isn't going to be fun for a while. From now until the convention is over, we're going to be under a lot of pressure — all of us. You know, Rachael suffers through this much the same as Terry does. I know it's not easy, but sometimes there is simply no other way. All I ask is that you cooperate with me until we get through the convention. Then we'll see if we can't arrange something much more to your liking. I promise."

The three of them shook hands, and Billings left the two young men alone for a few moments before Terry was driven to the airport and D.J. was taken back to the White House.

"Be good for me," D.J. said, pulling Terry close to him.

"I'll miss you," Terry couldn't help but say, "but I'll be good. I promise. Do you think he really meant all that? I mean about maybe being able to arrange something for us after the convention?"

"He seemed sincere to me," D.J. said.

"I hope so," Terry said. "I really hope so. Call me from Tucson, will you?"

"Of course. As soon as I get there. I love you, Terry."

"I love you, too, baby," Terry said.

They stood holding each other until Parker tapped lightly on the door and announced that it was time to leave.

The White House

It was the end of the day, and Billings was tired. He had put off this meeting with Stone purposely, hoping Carl would be as tired as he and wouldn't feel like arguing. Thaddeus should have known better.

Carl came in, looked around his brother-in-law's office as though taking stock, then sat tentatively in one of the leather chairs.

"I want some new arrangements for Terry," Billings said. "I've spoken with him and D.J., and I think we've worked out an arrangement that's agreeable to all of us."

"You and D.J., eh?" Stone said sarcastically. "I didn't know we were negotiating."

"We're not negotiating, we're trying to be reasonable," Billings replied just as sarcastically.

"What's the deal?" Stone sat back in the chair and took his keys out of his pocket.

"As I told you when I called from Cleveland — I want him to spend the summer out of the way. Lost in a flock of birds of his own feather, as it were."

Stone began cleaning his fingernails with one of the keys. He waited for Billings to continue.

"I want to send him out to Fire Island for the summer."

"Fire Island!?" Stone exclaimed.

Billings turned now to face Carl and spoke with authority. "You and I should have learned one thing by now, if nothing else. He is nearly impossible to control. Neither you nor anyone you've assigned to him can keep him under wraps."

Carl bristled, but let Thaddeus go on.

"On the island, he may not stay off drugs and booze, but he won't be noticed. If you can get someone to stay with him and make sure he doesn't leave the island, everything should go smoothly from now until after the convention. It's only a little over a month. Surely you can manage that."

Stone kept his temper. He knew that Thaddeus had better access to Marshall and Claudia at the moment, and he didn't want the President to think he was either uncooperative or ineffective. "Do you have any suggestions as to how I should go about this?" Carl asked, trying not to sound antagonistic.

"As a matter of fact, I do. Whatever happened to that fellow you had living with him or seeing him?"

Stone smiled devilishly.

"Why can't you get him back to keep an eye on him? Terry trusted him, it seems. He'd be perfect for what we want. All he has to do is keep him company and keep him on the island."

"I thought you didn't like that idea. You told me to—"

"That was before. Things are different now. Can you get him back or not?"

"I suppose," Stone said, going back to his fingernails.

"Well, try. And make it fast, because D.J. is on his way to Arizona tomorrow and I don't want Terry alone any longer than necessary."

"Okay, I'll see what I can do," Stone said, putting his keys back in his pocket. "What about Operation Thunder? It's still ready to roll anytime we give the word. We ought to do it before the Texas and Ohio primaries."

"Scrap it," Billings said, reaching for his briefcase.

Stone had to stop himself from jumping to his feet. He gave Thaddeus an icy stare that froze Billings in his tracks. "Scrap it?" Stone asked, incredulous.

Billings's hand worked the handle of his briefcase nervously. "I don't see any point in it any longer," he said.

"For Christ's sake, Thad, we're behind in every poll being taken on APANS!"

Billings was flustered now and moved toward the door. "I don't want to discuss it now, Carl. There are too many things going on right now to be contemplating something like that. Just scrap it."

"We'll try," Carl said.

Billings reeled to face him "What do you mean you'll try? You'll do it, damn it, Carl. You'll see to it that nothing happens over there, do you hear me?"

Stone smiled thinly. "Sometimes movements like this aren't that easy to stop, Thad. Why do you think it's still in place? These political events just don't start and stop at will. There are entire religious sects involved, whole political movements. It's no different than Chile or Argentina or Vietnam or El Salvador."

"The discussion is over, Carl, and this issue is dead as far as I'm concerned. I don't want to hear about it again," Thaddeus said and left the room.

Stone banged his clenched fist down hard on the arm of the chair. "Fool!" he said aloud.

Silver Spring, Maryland

Jenny Tucker lay faceup on the motel bed, her hands manacled with handcuffs, her legs spread wide apart. Her breasts were bound tight in a black halter, and she wore a spiked dog collar around her neck. She raised her legs high into the air, and one of the black spike heels fell off her foot and landed on the floor.

"Fuck my pussy," she said lustily. "Fuck it deep."

Cameron knelt before her, working his cock with lubricant. "You can't get enough dick, can you, baby?" he said.

"Not enough of yours," she said.

"What about your husband? Doesn't he give you any of that big jock meat of his?"

"Who cares about it? I just want yours."

"Is his as big as mine?"

"It doesn't even come close."

Miles leaned forward and inserted the head of his penis into her. She moaned and gasped. "My God, you're big," she said.

"You want all of it?"

"Yes, yes."

"Ask me for it, then."

"Please give me all of it, please!"

"All of what?"

"Give me all of your big fat dick."

He rammed it deep into her, and she yelled loudly.

"Does Biffy Boy fuck you like this?" he teased.

"No, never like this. You're so big, so good. Oh, God. Oh, no!" she complained as he pulled quickly out of her. "What are you doing?"

"I've got something even bigger and better to put up there first," he said. "Just a minute." He disappeared into the bathroom.

She could see herself reflected in the mirror over the dresser and decided she was a pretty good-looking woman for forty-one. Bif would never play games with her, even when they were first married, but then he always had others to play games with.

"What are you doing in there?" she yelled.

"I'll be right out," he answered.

She strained to lean over the bed, looking for the lost shoe, when the door flew open and she was blinded by flashing lights, one right after another. She screamed and called for Miles. There were two men in the room, one causing the blinding flashes and another who leapt on top of her and was squeezing her breasts. She screamed as loudly as she could, but it seemed forever before Miles returned. Then there was scuffling and shouting and Miles fighting with one of the men. By the time her eyes could focus again, Miles was leaning against the door.

"My God, Miles, help me up. What's going on? What was that?" She was crying hysterically and straining at her handcuffs.

"Calm down, baby, calm down. It'll be all right," he said, unlocking the manacles and trying to hold her. She fought herself free and rushed to the window, pushing aside the gold-fringed drapes. Outside, there was no sign of the intruders. When she turned around, Miles was sitting on the edge of the bed, his head in his hands.

"Oh, my God, Miles. What are we going to do?"

Tucson, Arizona

Parker and D.J. left the jeep on the shoulder of the state highway and ran toward the sun. They kept up a steady but not exhaustive jog until they found a dirt road that seemed to wind endlessly into the desert. They ran in single file, once in a while passing each other to break the monotony, Parker preferring to be behind D.J. for security reasons, even though out here there was hardly cause for worry. D.J. preferred running behind Parker, as he was enjoying watching the agent's thick, sweaty body, which was clad only in frayed, blue cotton shorts. The letters "UT" were barely distinguishable on one leg.

Although it was evening, the sun was still intensely hot, and the sweat poured down Parker's back and stained the shorts dark blue around the waistband. There was also a dark blue impression which spread out from between his cheeks and worked its way halfway across each buttock. Twice, he had turned to check on D.J. and found him staring at his ass. The second time, D.J. just shrugged his shoulders and Parker laughed and shook his head.

They followed the road for about three miles, then D.J. took the lead again and turned off, heading down an arroyo and up again toward a small mesa. When they reached the top, D.J. stopped and surveyed what lay beyond: desert for as far as they could see. The sun was a burning sphere above the horizon, and the heat shimmered out of the earth toward the sky. They both stood with their hands on their hips, duly impressed by the vastness of the land before them.

"I had forgotten how beautiful this is," D.J. said, sitting down on a sprawling slab of rock that sloped out of the earth.

"Springtime is always the prettiest time of the year in the desert," Parker said, walking behind D.J. to the highest point of the rock, so he could have an even better view. "Did you see the Indian paintbrush and the bluebonnets while we were running?"

"No, where were they?"

"All along the way after we left the road. Sometimes you find whole fields of them."

"How do you know so much about the desert?" D.J. asked, lying back and feeling the last glow of warm sun on his chest and legs, even on his gluteals, where the sunlight was angling up his shorts.

"Went to school in Texas," Parker said, sitting down now just above D.J. and leaning back on his elbows.

"Where?"

"Austin."

"I didn't know that," D.J. said, realizing he had never thought to ask about Parker's background.

"Yep. Four years. I liked Austin a lot. It's not like most northerners think it is. It's all hills and lakes — really beautiful."

"Why'd you leave?"

"Job. I got a job in Washington."

"The Secret Service job?"

Parker half laughed, half grunted. "No. I had a job at the Veteran's Administration."

"The Veteran's Administration? Doing what?"

"I was a librarian."

"A librarian?!" D.J. exclaimed, twisting around to look up toward Parker, who was lying back on the rock now, his knees in the air, legs spread. D.J. could look right up his shorts and was surprised to see he wasn't wearing a jock.

"Yeah, a librarian."

"Gosh, I never thought of you as a librarian."

Parker raised himself up and shaded his eyes with his right hand so he could look at D.J. "Is there something wrong with being a librarian?"

"No, no," D.J. said apologetically, trying to keep his eyes off what he found to be Parker's most interesting physical attribute so far. "Nothing at all, I'm just a little surprised, that's all."

"Well, I wasn't a librarian for very long. I got riffed nine months after I started. After about six months of being unemployed, my roommate and I joined the Executive Protective Service."

"You went from being a librarian to working for EPS? What a switch."

"We were desperate. Jobs in Washington were really tight then. Reagan was in office, and he had not only put a freeze on jobs, but also ordered big cutbacks in non-essential positions. Librarians aren't considered very essential — until you need some information and you don't know where to find it. So Ben and I joined EPS. They were the only people in town hiring, and we both had college degrees, which put us way ahead of most of their applicants. So I went from guarding tomes of knowledge to guarding embassies."

"Who was Ben?" D.J. asked.

"My roommate then," Parker answered. "So that's how I got to this job."

"You quit them and went to work for Treasury?"

"It's all the same. EPS is part of the Secret Service. Boy, you sure don't know much about your own government," Parker said, only half teasing.

"I'm just an Arizona cowboy," D.J. teased.

Parker laughed and sat up again. "This really is an awesome country we live in. We're lucky. I can't imagine what it would be like to be born in one of the communist countries, where you can't do what you want, go where you want whenever you want to. It must be horrible."

D.J. sat up now, too. The sun was turning a dark orange as it approached the horizon. "I think about that, too. As much as I bellyache about the system, I wouldn't want to live anywhere else. I guess I'd even give my life for my country if it came to that." D.J. picked some small stones from near where he was sitting and began tossing them one at a time down the side of the hill. "What's it like to have to be ready to die for a stranger?"

Parker drew his feet up closer and hugged his knees, putting an end to D.J.'s voyeurism. "I don't think about it," Parker said, looking out over the desert. Somewhere in the distance, an animal was stirring up tiny clouds of dust. "I just know that if the moment comes, I'm trained to react, and that reaction could put a bullet in me. It doesn't mean it'll kill me. I tell myself it won't, anyway."

"But how could you, especially when you don't even know us — or like us, particularly?"

Parker looked at D.J. darkly. "That isn't true," he said, almost with vehemence.

"Well, I mean..."

"I do know you. How could I be around you twenty-four hours a day for practically three years and not know you?"

"But you probably don't like us. I mean we are a fucked-up bunch of people really. You didn't seem to like me and Terry much when you were first assigned to us. Tell the truth."

Parker looked away, setting his jaw and saying nothing. D.J. had seen that look before whenever he and Terry had been especially aggravating. He saw that look a lot in France.

"Tell the truth, Parker. I don't mind."

"It wasn't that I didn't like you."

"I know, you didn't relish the idea of having to lay your life on the line for a couple of faggots."

Parker's jaw jutted even more now as he clenched his teeth.

"I don't mind, Parker, honest. I can understand. I just don't see how a person could protect people he doesn't like or feel comfortable with."

"You guys didn't give me much of a chance, did you?" There was anger in Parker's voice. Aha, D.J. thought, now we're going to get at the resentment.

"What do you mean?" D.J. asked.

"You guys started in on me from day one. The first thing Terry said to me when we were introduced was 'If you don't like to watch men kiss, you'd better put in for a transfer.'"

"He had had a really bad experience with the pinscher before you. He assumed..."

"Well, he shouldn't have. All agents aren't alike." Parker was being firm, but not insolent, and D.J. could see that their behavior had actually hurt Parker's feelings.

"I guess we were pretty hard on you. I'm sorry, Parker," D.J. said, reaching up and putting his hand on Parker's knee. "I think most people think of pinschers as being bionic or having had all their feelings deprogrammed. You guys are so quiet and efficient that we just start looking on you as muscular shadows. I'm really sorry." D.J. took back his hand, afraid Parker might get the wrong idea. Or maybe it was the right idea. The more he got to know Parker, the more he liked him, and now he couldn't help but think that this was the kind of man he should have as a lover — someone with intelligence, sensitivity, good sense. Parker was a bold contrast to Terry, D.J. thought. But he loved Terry, for a lot of other qualities that Parker perhaps didn't have.

"It's okay now," Parker said. "I'm used to it."

"Terry's not so bad, you know. It's just that he hates being apart from me and he's not used to never having any privacy." D.J. laughed and tossed another rock down the hillside. "He used to think you watched us through the keyhole when we had sex."

Parker's face flushed noticeably, even in the glow of the setting sun. He lay back down on the rock and the two of them remained silent for a while. D.J. lay back, his arm brushing Parker's leg. He left it there, feeling the hairs of Parker's calf brushing his smooth skin. He liked the physical closeness now, after they had talked so personally.

"Ben wanted to be buried in the desert," Parker said. "Funny thing is he was raised in New Jersey. He'd only seen the desert once. On a trip we took back to Austin. I guess I'd like to be buried in the desert, too, except I don't know what difference it would make then. I wouldn't know where I was."

D.J. rolled over onto his stomach. "Can pinschers be married?" D.J. asked.

"Of course. A lot of us are. Funny thing, though, they like to hire men who are married, but once you're in, they prefer it if you're not. 'Cause of the travel and the danger factor."

"Were you married once?" D.J. asked uneasily.

Parker gave him a strange look.

"That ring," D.J. said, nodding toward Parker's left hand, which bore a simple gold band on the fourth finger. "I've always wondered what it was."

Parker looked at his hand and studied the ring for a second, then nudged D.J.'s shoulder with his foot. "Hey, that sun's almost gone. We'd better hightail it back to the jeep before we get stranded here. Desert's pretty spooky at night."

D.J. didn't press it. He didn't have a chance, since Parker was halfway down the rock and lighting out for the dirt road before he even finished his sentence.

McLean, Virginia

Carl Stone pulled into his driveway, cut the headlights, and let the car roll to a stop just in front of the garage door. He sat there for a few minutes with his eyes closed, letting his body relax and thinking of the black woman who had less than thirty minutes ago lain across the front seat, her mouth busy in his lap. The thought of it brought him to a state of arousal again, and he moved his hand between his legs, deliberating whether or not to masturbate. As he began to massage himself, the way she had begun massaging him after he slipped her two twenties and a ten, there was a tapping at the window on the other side of the car. He jumped and instinctively reached beneath the seat for his revolver, but before retrieving it, he recognized the face outside the car and, relieved, let the gun remain where it was. He reached over and flipped the lock, and the young man outside slipped quickly in and shut the door.

"That's a real good way to get shot around here, boy," he said.

The young man shrugged. "I thought you were falling asleep," he said. "Got a cigarette?"

"See if there are any in the glove compartment."

The young man opened the glove box and retrieved a pack of cigarettes. As he lit one, Carl could see his hand trembling. "Are you all right?" he asked, more out of curiosity as to what trouble the kid might be in than out of genuine concern.

"Yeah, I'm okay."

"But, of course, you're broke."

The young man looked at Carl with contempt, but said nothing.

"You strung out?" Carl asked.

"You know I'm not doing drugs," the boy said unconvincingly. There was silence. "Well, a little pot now and then, but that's all," he said, smiling weakly.

"If I could believe that, I might be able to help you."

His passenger turned and looked at him eagerly. "I swear it," he said. "I'm clean. Honest."

"I need you back on that kid in New York. Can you handle it?"

"I did it before, didn't I? I did just like you said. I didn't blow it."

"From what I heard, you were blowing it quite a bit," Carl said derisively.

"That's bullshit," the kid said, taking a deep drag on his cigarette. "How the hell was I supposed to get close to him without letting him get in my pants? Besides, if you close your eyes, a blow job is a blow job. You got your information, didn't you? That's all you care about."

"This time it may be a little trickier," Stone said. "We're putting him up on Fire Island, trying to keep him out of the way until after the convention. I need someone to stay with him twenty-four hours a day, and I mean twenty-four hours a day. He's not to leave the island under any circumstances. That would be your responsibility. You'd have to keep him there any way you could — even if it meant tying him up."

"Shit, that's no problem. If nothing else, I can keep him on downs the whole time. He liked me, anyway. He never got out of control once."

"Maybe it's you I'd have to worry about."

"Goddamn it, I came through before, and I'll do it again. Give me a chance. C'mon," the young man pleaded.

"There's no room for error in this one," Stone emphasized, sounding as grim and foreboding as possible. "Everything's riding on our keeping him under wraps — completely."

"No sweat. When do you want me up there?"

"As soon as possible."

"I'll need some money. Where will we stay?"

"That's all being taken care of. You'll have enough money to keep you, but it'll be delivered weekly. I don't want you spending it all the first day. Where are you staying now?"

The young man lit another cigarette, stalling for time.

"I see," Stone said. He reached into his wallet and handed the kid a wad of money. "Here, this'll get you to New York. Contact me in a couple days. Terry will have all the details about where you two will stay on the island. Just play along. Get on a Metroliner tomorrow and call me when you've made contact with him. I want to hear from you daily until you're out there, understand?"

"Sure," he said, stuffing the money into his jeans pocket. "Anything you say."

"And, Richard..."

"Yeah?"

"I mean it when I say I don't want him off the island. If you fuck this up, I'll be very angry. It would go very badly for everyone if this doesn't work ... even for your mother."

The young man paused, wanting to say something rude, but knew he didn't dare. Carl was not to be fooled with; besides, he needed the money desperately. "Don't worry, everything will be cool."

He opened the car door and disappeared as quickly as he came. Stone sighed, then smiled wryly. Fucking queers, he thought. They're everywhere.

Tucson, Arizona

D.J. slipped quietly from bed and went to the kitchen. In the Arizona heat, the terra-cotta tiles of the kitchen floor were warm beneath his feet even at two in the morning. He poured a glass of wine and walked to the living room window. The desert lay still and blue beneath the light of the full moon. He could see the truck with the pinschers in it parked at the end of the dirt road which ran from the highway to the white stucco house where he and Elaine would be living for the next six weeks.

Tucson was going to be a pleasant surprise for him. For the first time since he had been back in the States, he felt a sense of calm. Perhaps it was the desert, quiet and withholding, keeping its secret life to itself. Maybe it was the sky, immense and blue and dominated at all times by the raging sun or the icy moon. Or perhaps it was the little white hacienda with its red tile roof far on the outskirts of the city, removed from the constant traffic of society. Whatever the reason, he felt a sense of tranquility about him and thought that if he could somehow get in tune with his surroundings, he, too, might find some semblance of peace, if only for the short time he was to be here.

He turned to sit on the long white sofa which dominated the area in front of the large window and was startled to find Parker sprawled out on it in nothing but his white boxer shorts.

"Sorry," Parker said. "I was afraid I'd scare you if I said something. You looked pretty lost in thought."

"Well, you scared me anyway," D.J. said, plopping on the other end of the sofa and stretching his legs out next to Parker's. "Move over, you big lug."

Parker grunted and shifted, but their legs lay intertwined for lack of room.

"I take it you couldn't sleep either," D.J. concluded aloud.

Parker scooted up a little in a last effort to make more room for D.J., who buried his feet between the black cushions and Parker's ass. Parker let them remain there and didn't seem uncomfortable with the physical proximity.

"I don't know why I couldn't sleep. Maybe it's the heat, or maybe it's just being in a strange place," Parker said.

"I slept for about an hour, I guess, then woke up with a start and couldn't go back to sleep, so I'm giving in to the fruit of the grape. Why don't you get a glass?"

Parker held up a tall glass, which had been sitting on the floor next to him. "I'm way ahead of you, boss. This is my second one."

"Something bothering you?" D.J. asked, ignoring Parker's possible excuses for not being able to sleep.

"No, not really," Parker said, taking a swig of wine.

"Not really? Sounds evasive to me."

"It's nothing," he said unconvincingly.

"I love to hear about nothing. Why don't you tell me?"

"No, really, it's nothing. There's nothing wrong," Parker said.

"Well, there's something bothering me," D.J. offered.

"What's that?" Parker asked.

"I'm comfortable."

"What?"

"I'm comfortable here, and I'm not used to being comfortable. There's nothing wrong here, and it spooks me."

"Hey, enjoy it while it lasts. You deserve a break," Parker said, and nudged him with his foot for emphasis.

D.J. smiled. "There's something else, too," he said and took a drink from his glass, keeping Parker in suspense for a moment.

"What is it?" he asked, taking another drink, which D.J. took as a possible nervous gesture.

"You."

"Me?"

"Yeah, you."

"What about me?"

"I'm feeling really comfortable with you for the first time. It's almost like we're friends. That's new."

Parker got up and went into the kitchen for more wine. "Yeah, I kind of feel the same way. Does that bother you?" he asked from the kitchen.

"It doesn't bother me really, it's just different. I kind of like it, actually. Does it bother you?"

Parker returned and took up his former position. His shoulders took up nearly the entire width of the sofa. "It makes me curious and a little worried," Parker said.

"Worried?"

"Yeah, I'm not supposed to like you too much. Just be friendly with you. Friendly, but professional."

"Sounds like you're describing a hooker, not a pinscher."

Parker laughed. "Maybe there's not that much difference, actually. I'm selling my body."

"Well, with a body like yours, I hope you're getting paid plenty. People like me pay just to look at bodies like that."

"Are you trying to embarrass me?" Parker asked, almost coquettishly.

"No, I gave that up in France. You're too easy to embarrass. No challenge. So is that why you couldn't sleep?"

Parker squirmed a bit. "No, not really."

"I think I've heard this answer before. Want to try again?"

"First of all, I'm not supposed to talk to you about personal things, and secondly, I don't want you to think I'm coming on to you, like you and Terry are always saying about guys who are the least bit friendly to you."

"That's just wishful thinking on our part. Don't worry, I'm sure I couldn't get into your pants with a crowbar, although I'm just as sure you know after all this time that I'd like to. So now that we have that bullshit out of the way, why don't you loosen up and tell me what's bothering you? The hell with the rules. Let's break a few rules tonight."

Parker couldn't help but laugh, partly because of D.J.'s bluntness and partly because he was embarrassed by the flattery, which he greatly enjoyed.

"I'm not a rule breaker," he said. "If I was, I couldn't be a pinscher. It's not part of my profile."

"What is your profile, anyway? I've always been curious about it. What makes you tick, Parker?" D.J. said, poking him in the chest with his big toe. "Right there in your heart of hearts. What secrets lie hidden beneath that hairy pectoral?"

"We all have the same profile," Parker said. "Or at least we're supposed to. Young, strong, determined to succeed. Individualistic, but with a yearning to belong to a group. Heterosexual, but with strong ties to the tradition of male camaraderie. Low anxiety quotient, but afraid to go against the system. And above all, undying loyalty to any cause we subscribe to."

"God," D.J. exclaimed, "and all the time I thought you were human beings. I'm surrounded by bionic pinschers."

"You're practically right. So, you see, for me even to want to talk to you about anything personal is strictly against my psychological profile."

"And you want to talk to me? Or am I just flattering myself?"

"No, I do want to talk to you ... I guess. I mean, I've grown to like you. Like you said, I feel like we're almost friends."

"Is that so bad?"

"Of course!"

"You could get canned, right?"

"I suppose, but that's not it. What if my psychological profile is changing?"

"You mean what if you're becoming depinscherized?"

"Yeah, what if I'm losing whatever it is that makes me a good agent? How can I do my job?"

"Sounds like crap to me. You can't tell me that because you and I like each other you're not going to protect me as well. I think you'd protect me even better."

"Wrong."

"How so?"

"My job is to protect the country, not you personally. I always have to do what is best for the country, not what is best for you individually. If I ever had to choose between you and orders from my superiors, I'm supposed to choose my superiors, not you."

"That sounds like communism or something," D.J. remarked.

"Well, there has to be discipline. Without it everything would be chaos."

"I thought everything was chaos already," D.J. quipped, getting up and going to the kitchen for more wine. He brought the bottle with him when he returned. Parker was standing in front of the window looking out over the desert, his perfect body silhouetted against the eerie blue light outside. "So, if you could talk to me as a friend, what would you say that you're not supposed to say?" D.J. asked, curling up on the sofa again.

There was a long pause before Parker answered, and when he did, he spoke slowly. D.J. couldn't tell if it was because he was thinking as he spoke or if he was trying not to slur his words after three glasses of wine. "I'd want to be honest with you."

"Haven't you been?"

"I haven't been dishonest. I just haven't been as open with you as you've been with me."

"But in your position, you don't have to be. At least up to now, it hasn't been important. I guess what you're really facing is a decision about whether or not you want to alter our relationship slightly. I mean become friends, not just friendly."

"That's what bothers me," answered Parker. "I don't know why I feel like I want to."

"Maybe you just want to, regardless of whether you should or not."

"And that's the crux of it. It's the dilemma of what I want to do versus what I should do. You see, I want you to like me, and that is also not in the profile. Agents aren't supposed to care whether people like them or not."

"More bionic talk. You know, one way in which gay men have an easier life than straight men is the fact that they can openly express their feelings for other men. They can hug and kiss and show their affection for one another."

There was a silence of several minutes, and then Parker spoke, continuing to face the silent blue tableau of sand and mesquite, saguaro, and palo verde on the other side of the large window.

"I was in love once and I let it get away. Correction: I pushed it away, gave it up for security and for what I thought was right. I turned it away because I was afraid. Since then, I've seen a lot of couples, and you know what? You and Terry have the best relationship of all of them. You're the only gay couple I know, and my upbringing would have me believe that two men couldn't have any kind of meaningful or rewarding thing together, but that's not true. You guys have taught me that."

He took a drink from his glass just as a shooting star rocketed across the sky. "Now I want someone, too," he continued, "but I'm afraid it might be too late. Sometimes you don't get a second chance, especially in my line of work. Not many people will put up with it." He turned and came back to the sofa, stretching out again, his feet resting against D.J.'s side. "I'm just carping, feeling sorry for my-self. I don't have anyone to talk to. I hope you don't mind my bending your ear a little. I won't make a habit of it. It's probably just the wine."

"Is that where the ring came from?" D.J. asked.

Parker held up his hand, looking at the ring in the moonlight. He chuckled slightly. "No, that's another story entirely. Someone else I threw away. I don't know if I loved her or not."

"But you married her?"

"I married her. It was a mistake. My motives were all wrong."

"You must have cared for her — you still wear the ring."

"I wear the ring as a reminder."

"Of the mistake?"

"Of many things. Of the mistake, of having dishonor-able intentions, of being careless with other people's feel-ings. Mostly as a reminder that before I can be wedded to someone else, I have to be wedded to myself. If you don't love yourself, you can't love others, you can only be de-pendent on them. I won't make the mistake again."

"I wish we could make love," D.J. said softly, almost timidly, afraid he might be going too far out of bounds. The two of them had spent such a wonderful day together, being physically and emotionally close, sharing intimate thoughts and feelings. It seemed only natural that they should end it in an act of intimacy. There was a long silence.

"I don't know how, D.J.," Parker said, turning over onto his side toward the back of the sofa and hugging one of the cushions. "I'm afraid I wouldn't even know how."

D.J. lay looking at Parker's strong features and voluptuous muscles. He had crossed his right leg over D.J.'s body when he turned over. D.J. said, almost imperceptibly, "I could teach you." But Parker's breathing was already heavy as he sank deeper and deeper into sleep. Within a few minutes, D.J., too, was asleep, and he slept soundly until about three hours later, when he awoke slowly, sensing Parker's body next to him. The wine he had drunk made it difficult for him to gain full consciousness, so he wasn't sure if he was dreaming or not as he felt the huge arm wrapping around him, holding him close. D.J. squirmed back against Parker, nestling into his embrace, and the two men fell into a deep and tranquil sleep.

Chicago

Elaine spent the ninety-minute Chicago layover between New York and Tucson in O'Hare's VIP lounge drinking margaritas. She was using the drinks to calm down from the flight, which had been turbulent. Also, she had encountered an old college friend, who had been on the same plane traveling home to Chicago. They had sat together long enough to drink a glass of champagne and talk about old times.

The woman was married to a vice president of Sears, and they had been living in Chicago for almost seven years now. She wore simple but elegant and expensive clothes and talked at length about her husband and how little she saw him. She went on about how they had such a good time together, flying here and there to escape and be alone with each other. He was a thoughtful man, she said, attentive, considerate, affectionate, even as busy as he was. They enjoyed a good life together, and she had hobbies and interests to occupy her time apart from him. But she supposed Elaine had much the same kind of life, being the wife of the President's son. How exciting, how glamorous, just like in the movies. And then she was gone, back to her own first-class seat, and the pinscher was back in the seat next to Elaine.

The conversation had upset her, exactly why she didn't know at first. Now, at this little round table in the airport lounge, she contemplated it over her third margarita and came to the sad conclusion that it was because while the old college friend ostensibly had the same kind of marriage as she, the painful truth was that Elaine's husband could not give her the romantic interaction that completes a marriage. Toward the end of her cocktail, she went so far as to admit to herself that she wanted sex from time to time.

If only she could be as cavalier about sex as Jessica. She glanced over to the door, where one of the pinschers was not so subtly surveilling the comings and goings of the lounge patrons. She tried to imagine herself in bed with him, but it was no use. Perhaps before D.J. she could have, but now that she had been a wife for four years, she found it difficult to remember what she was like in her wilder days, when she and Jessica used to terrorize their favorite happy-hours bar after work. As she tried once more to picture herself and the agent standing naked in some hotel room, she saw a familiar face come through the door. It was Bif Tucker, and he was with a gorgeous blonde woman in a mink coat. They went to a table in a far corner of the bar, and he sat down while his companion found her way to the women's room. Elaine got up and went over in a genuinely friendly gesture, putting politics aside.

"Hello, Bif," she said, extending her hand.

He looked up at her and the color drained from his face, setting Elaine immediately on guard. She had hoped he wouldn't think she was going to put him on the spot. After all, she was only en route to Tucson; there was nothing remotely political in her motives.

"Oh, Elaine," he said, standing awkwardly and shaking hands. "How nice to see you. What are you doing in Chicago?" He was obviously speaking to her, but his eyes were riveted on the women's room door.

"I'm on my way to join D.J. in Arizona. The acting company is there for six weeks. I guess we're just two hapless travelers thrown together by the fate of our political connections."

He was staring at her blankly, and she realized he hadn't heard a word she had been saying. "Well, how are you?" she tried. "How are things going for you?"

"Fine, just fine."

There was a long, uncomfortable silence while Tucker looked first at her, then back toward the door.

"Well, I just thought I'd say hello. I have to run. I've a plane to catch. Nice bumping into you."

"Yes, yes. Same here. Give my best to your husband," he said, shaking her hand again.

Elaine headed for the women's room, feeling a little woozy from the margaritas and somewhat unnerved by the cold reception from Tucker. As she went through the door, the mink coat was coming out. Elaine stepped aside to let her pass, and for a moment, they looked directly into each other's eyes. The blonde was strikingly beautiful. She smiled as she passed by Elaine, and it wasn't until Elaine was finished in the bathroom and was checking her hair in the mirror that she realized what had struck her about the woman: she had one blue and one gray eye. Also, she was not Mrs. Tucker.

New York City

Terry opened his eyes, but they didn't focus, so he just closed them again and lay heavy and numb in the bed. He hovered between sleep and a drug hangover, trying to remember something, anything, from the night before. He recalled leaving the apartment and going to the Ramrod for a beer. He remembered the thick black hands that exchanged his money for three quaaludes, and he distinctly remembered walking into Pete's on Hudson Street and the bartender setting a beer on the bar before he even asked for it. For some reason, he also recalled picking up the beer and turning to face the crowded room, the faces and bodies spinning before him, as though he were a movie camera panning too fast. Everything else he could conjure up spun in the same fashion.

He saw a video game spinning and a Budweiser neon sign; bearded men in leather jackets, a man with feathers in his hair, and another with a shaved head and a long wire earring. There were sounds, too, loud music and the slap of hands on bare flesh; smoke and porcelain, blue tiles, the smell of urine and stale beer; he remembered the feel of stones and splinters, sawdust on his back, the sight of stern faces hovered over him, hands kneading his body, pulling at his shirt; he remembered a sense of smothering and being strangled, then air again, and large, calloused fingers forcing something into his mouth: pills. A deep voice saying, "Percodans, baby, they're good for you," then laughter and grunting; the rattle and reverberation of metal, like train wheels scraping and screeching on tracks, a hundred lights flashing in his face one after another, his body reeling and weaving, as he tried futilely to sit quietly somewhere, then arms under his shoulders and hands on his forehead; porcelain again and, yes, vomiting violently, then another bright light, and finally darkness.

He opened his eyes again, but it was no better than the first time. He mustered strength and moved his fingers to see if they worked, then his toes, his arms, legs, neck. He struggled to turn over, and as he did, he saw the blurred outline of a head and shoulders, a chest naked to the waist. He struggled to make his eyes work. At last he could make out another man lying next to him. Where was he?

"Welcome back to the land of the living." The voice was coming from the body lying next to him, which was slowly beginning to define itself more sharply. "I was beginning to worry. How you feeling?"

Terry grunted and rubbed his eyes, then looked again. The voice was familiar, and now the face was coming into focus. It was Rick, back just as quickly as he had disappeared.

"Where'd you come from?" Terry asked, his voice rasping.

"I got back last night. I finished up what I had to do in California and now I'm back. You're a hard man to locate on a Friday night."

"Yeah. Where did you find me?"

"You don't want to know, believe me."

"That embarrassing, huh?"

"Well, let's just say a good time was being had by all, except you."

"Now I really want to know. I'm sore as hell. Where was I?"

A gurgling sound came from the kitchen. "Coffee's done," Rick said. "How 'bout a cup?"

"Yeah, please," Terry grunted, struggling to sit up against the wall. While Rick was busy in the kitchen, Terry examined his body: a large scrape down the entire length of his back was smarting against the pillow. He found a small cut on his left hand and the beginnings of two bruises on his right thigh, and his ass felt like someone had beat him with a Ping-Pong paddle.

"Here you go, three sugars and cream, right?" Rick asked, handing Terry a large brown mug of steaming coffee. "You might want to soak in a tub for a while."

Terry sipped the hot coffee. "Seriously, where did you find me?"

"Well, when you weren't here, I left my bag in the hall and scoured the neighborhood bars, which took me almost two hours. I even went to Uncle Charlie's."

"You should have known I wouldn't be there."

"I thought maybe your tastes had changed since I left. When I couldn't find you by three o'clock, I figured I should give up until today, so I came back here, got my bag, and headed for St. Mark's.

"You met me on the way? Was I passed out in the gutter?"

"No, buddy. I found you at the St. Mark's baths, entertaining a host of eager soldiers, sailors, cowboys, and other assorted masqueraders."

"Jesus, the baths. I don't even remember."

"I figured I'd spend the night there. Cheap, you know? I couldn't get to sleep because there was all this slapping and grunting and groaning going on in the common room at the end of the hall, so I thought I might as well have some late-night or early-morning entertainment. I wandered down and there you were."

"How'd you get me out of there?"

"You'd have been real proud of me. I immediately realized I was outnumbered and that these guys weren't about to just let you go. They were having much too good a time. So I went back to my room, got dressed, then stormed in like some crazed uptown queen and threw a raging fit, pretending to be your lover. Those bruisers backed right off. I couldn't have cleared the room faster if I had yelled, 'Fire.' I found some clothes on the floor, which I assumed were yours, and dressed you as best I could, then hauled you back here. Thank God they were your clothes. It never occurred to me that they would be someone else's until we got here and I started looking for your keys. Luckily, they were in your vest pocket."

"I'm surprised the vest was still around."

"So was I, actually. By the way, if you decide to take that bath, you're going to have to clean up around the toilet. You decided to give up whatever it was you had eaten last night and some of it missed the bowl. I tried to direct your line of fire, but you were deadweight. Speaking of weight, you've gotten awfully thin in such a short time."

Terry said nothing. They sat drinking their coffee in silence, Terry's emotions scrambling inside him. This was the only person he had gotten close to since he and D.J. had returned, and he'd thought he wouldn't have to face him again — or his feelings for him. Now here he was sitting naked in bed with him once more, and D.J. was clear on the other side of the country. He decided instinctively that he wouldn't think about it. He'd just do what he felt like doing. After all, there was no telling when he would see D.J. again. It would be at least six weeks. He looked over at Rick, who was flashing the warm, affectionate smile Terry had missed so bitterly right after Rick had disappeared. "What are you doing in New York?" Terry asked.

"Just being with you for now. Isn't that enough?"

"How long are you here for?" Terry asked, trying not to sound hopeful or leading.

"Don't know. The summer at least. Guess that depends partly on you."

Terry smiled and sipped his coffee.

"First thing I'll have to do is look for a job. Can I stay with you for a while?"

"Sure. In fact if you play your cards right, you won't even have to look for a job."

"What do you mean?"

"How would you like to spend the summer on Fire Island?"

"Holy shit! Are you serious? How are we going to do that?"

"Just leave it to me and don't ask questions."

"Will I have to give up my body?"

Terry winked. "Maybe even your soul."

The White House

Thaddeus was just as glad to be working. Rachael had already started on her first Bloody Mary by the time he got down to a breakfast that consisted of juice and dry cereal, which he couldn't eat anyway, since the milk turned out to be sour.

Rachael sat across from him glaring and defiantly drinking her early-morning cocktail. "What if it was him? Just what if it was?"

"Don't start that again, Rachael."

"I wasn't even drinking, I tell you."

He gave her a look of disgust and headed for the back door, picking up his briefcase from the telephone stand near the coat rack.

"You son of a bitch," she screamed. "You don't even care about your own son. No wonder he left. Maybe I'll leave, too."

As he closed the door he heard the sound of crashing glass as the Bloody Mary hit the wall.

"Bloody Mary? Vodka and orange juice? Anything?" Marshall asked before sitting down at his desk in the Oval Office.

"No, thanks, I think I'll just stick with coffee," Thaddeus answered.

"So where the hell are we this week?" Marshall asked.

Billings shuffled some papers and began. "The best guess is that the APANS vote will come the second week in June, which is only three weeks away, so the campaigning has to crank up seriously for the primaries in Florida, Ohio, Pennsylvania, and Texas. Those fall one week after Memorial Day. Cameron is preparing a steady flow of news releases that will trickle out from now through Memorial Day, reporting on domestic achievements, the declining inflation rate..."

"Declining inflation rate?" Marshall challenged.

Thad sorted through the papers on his lap. "Monday's figures will show that for April the inflation rate after adjustment was 1.4 percent, the lowest in five and a half years."

"And unemployment?"

"Thirty thousand fewer applications last month than the previous month."

"Good, good. Can we keep that up until those primaries are over?"

"I think we can. We only have two more reporting periods until then. We won't release figures on Memorial Day, because it's a holiday."

"I'm not so sure those pollsters know what they're talking about. Did you see the morning paper? The most recent polls say I'm losing ground."

"Well, not exactly," Billings said, getting up to pour himself more coffee. "There's a lot of division about the administration's strength in the area of foreign policy. That should come as no surprise to us, given the heated debate going on in the press over the APANS sale. That's why the primaries in Ohio and Pennsylvania are so crucial. They fall just before the committee vote, and they'll be watching them closely. If they see you take those states, which are not as conservative as Texas and Florida, then they're going to jump on the bandwagon and vote for the bill."

"And the leadership issue? Gallup says I'm being perceived as a weak leader. How are we going to turn that one around?"

"First of all, the poll showed that there was only a 3 percent difference between those seeing you as weak and those seeing you as strong. Second, that's to be expected when we're having such a battle over a foreign policy issue like APANS. They go hand in hand. The bottom line revolves around those who would vote for you over the other candidates, and there's a clear 12 percent majority there. Tucker is the only one close, and he's too liberal to carry Texas or Florida. There's no challenge at all in those states. He's harping on one issue now, and that's APANS. He'll be blitzing Ohio and Pennsylvania on Memorial Day weekend and so will we. We've bought six hours of prime time on the networks for that weekend alone."

"Have you decided whether I should go to the ranch for the holiday or stay here?"

"You should stay here. We're flying D.J. and Elaine in. We don't want you flying off to Arizona, having a holiday, enabling Tucker to say you have time for vacations, but not for getting out to talk to the voters. In the meantime, you have to keep pounding away at the Senate. We need to call in as many IOUs as possible before the full Senate votes, and we have to get a majority of the committee vote, even if it's only a majority of one."

"Sounds like we're going to be busy for the next few weeks," Marshall said. "Tell me, Thad," he said, a kind of vacant look in his eyes, "do you think we're going to win this one?"

Billings knew he had no choice of answers. Besides, he didn't really know what he thought about their chances; he only knew that Marshall needed bolstering in times like these or he lost confidence. "We've never lost a big one yet and I have no intention of starting now."

The White House

Claudia woke gently, easing slowly out of sleep to the silence of the large room. She was wide awake now and disturbed by some unnameable uneasiness. Instinctively, she turned to touch Donald, but her hand came down only on disheveled bedclothes. She sat up and looked around. The room was dark except for the small night-light that glowed dimly in one far corner. Then she noticed a light coming from beneath the door of the little office off the bedroom. She assumed Donald was making his daily entry in his diary. She got up, slipped on her powder blue peignoir, and went slowly to the closed door. She pressed her ear firmly to it. He was on the phone. At first, she thought it must have been more APANS business and that he was probably pressuring some senator by phoning in the middle of the night, but then she heard him mention Elaine's name and something about the flight and the house and the weather in the desert. He was talking with D.J.

She returned to bed automatically, looking into the drawer of the nightstand to be sure her cold companion was there, and fell asleep before her husband came out of the study. She dreamed of riding her horse across the ranch, only in her dream the ranch bordered on the ocean. She was alone, riding toward two horsemen in the distance, who were poised on a cliff overlooking the sea. They wore western gear and large cowboy hats. When she neared them, the one closest turned and smiled. It was Donald. He had on brown chaps, a holster with a gleaming six-shooter, a red, white, and blue plaid shirt, and a white Stetson. He smiled broadly and touched the brim of his hat, then made a clicking sound, and his horse began to trot away.

The second horseman was turned looking in the opposite direction. She knew it was D.J. even though she couldn't see his face. She recognized his clothes as riding clothes she had bought for him on his sixteenth birthday, the year they had given him his own horse. She called to him, but he began galloping away from her toward the cliff. She called again and again, each time more frantically as he approached the rocky ledge, but he kept going until finally the horse tumbled over the side and went, with its rider, crashing to the rocks hundreds of feet below. She shrieked and sobbed as she scrambled down the craggy side of the cliff to where he and the horse lay in a heap of blood and rubble. Gulls were circling overhead, making a terrible ruckus. When she reached him, she turned him over on his back and held his broken body close to her, kissing his face over and over. She stroked his hair and rocked him, looking up to heaven and weeping for her lost son. She looked back at him through her tears, touching his face gently, then shrieked and dropped the limp body on the rocks as she recognized the face. It was not D.J. at all. It was Terry.

New York City

"Phil's really soiled about it," Jessica said into the phone, her mouth stuffed with Entenmann's cheese babka. She sipped coffee and hummed into the receiver, to maintain her territorial rights to the long-distance conversation, lest Elaine try to interject something before she was ready to end her tirade. "It's just not fair at all. He's worked so hard, and they had virtually promised him he'd be able to work at the Garden. And this assignment of all assignments — the ID book."

"What's the ID book?" Elaine managed to ask.

"It's some stupid fucking book that they have to have so the superstars like Jackson and Rather don't fuck up and say that's Senator What's-his-butt's wife, when it's really the wife of the Vice President. You know, it's like when D.J.'s father goes up to the Hill to address the Congress and they turn the camera on the audience during his speech and old Congressman Fartface is sleeping, so they flash his name on the screen beneath a shot of him keeling over into the secretary of the posterior, except they flash the wrong name and get sued for forty-four skyzillion dollars. It's a raw fucking deal. Poor pup."

"And there's no chance they'll change their minds?" Elaine asked.

"Evidently not. They say he's too inexperienced. What I really think is that they're jealous. That little Filipino they took away from NBC has been bitching about Phil's connections with the White House. She's saying he couldn't be unbiased if he had a story with any real meat on it. That cunt. I ran into her in the dressing room at Bonwit's last week..."

"What were you doing in Bonwit's? I thought you were so broke," Elaine teased.

"I was in there with Gloria, picking up something for her mother's birthday. Shut up and let me kvetch. Anyway, I should have stolen her clothes or set the little booth on fire."

"I'm really sorry," Elaine said. "I know how much Phil was looking forward to it. Isn't there anything he can do?"

"Well, now that you mention it, there probably is one thing that would get their attention, but I hate to ask. I've never asked anything like this of you before and—"

"Cut the prologue, what is it?"

"What about an interview with D.J.?"

"You've got to be kidding," Elaine said. "They won't even let him go shopping without a muzzle. They'd never let him give an interview."

"Why not? It could be real innocuous. You know, stuff like what brand of makeup do you wear and what's the hottest nightclub in Tucson? The kid needs a break bad and this is the best time. Maybe the only time. What if Marshall doesn't win?"

"Blasphemy! I guess I could ask, but don't get your hopes up."

"Well, then, what about you? Maybe he could interview you."

"That's more of a possibility. I'll check it out for you."

"I'll sing at your funeral."

"You'd better start rehearsing. If I know Billings, he'll kill me when I ask."

"You're such a kissy-face. I love you. How's everything going there? Are you surrounded by hunky pinschers?"

"No, actually it's been real quiet. D.J.'s driver is still in New York. He's a beefy, hairy blond. Keep an eye out for him. He has the car, so you could hump him in the backseat."

"Girl, how you talk! What's he doing here?"

"I don't know. Getting the car ready to ship or something. He's not coming till after Memorial Day."

"It wouldn't do me any good, I'm coming down with a cold or some dread virus."

"It's probably swine flu."

"I'm hanging up now. I've been insulted enough. Besides, I have to try to get Phil to plunge me before lunch. He's no good after he's eaten. Will you call me when you find out about the interview?"

"You'll be the first to know."

Washington, D.C.

Stone and Billings sat in the darkest corner of Harvey's on Nineteenth Street. Stone was on his second martini, Billings on his fourth Scotch. One of the behaviors Stone exhibited which told Thaddeus he was not a balanced man was his habit of never sticking to the same kind of liquor. When you were out with Carl, you could never order for him, because he switched drinks from bar to bar.

They had been discussing Rachael's drinking, which Stone's wife, Rebecca, was growing more and more concerned about. Billings was feeling remorseful and maudlin, and Carl took the opportunity to bring up Operation Thunder again, hoping to catch him at a weak moment.

"We have only two weeks left before the primaries, you know, and the polls are pretty discomforting. No APANS, no election. No election, no job for you and me, brother-in-law."

Thad was beginning to feel the effects of the alcohol, his words slightly running together as he spoke. "You're not bullying me into it, Carl. I told you, it's not necessary now."

Carl felt his temper rising. He knew his face was turning red as he clutched his cocktail glass tighter. "Don't be a fool, Thaddeus. You don't win a major piece of military hardware legislation with a smile. We're not even talking about the goddamned primaries. We're talking about the Senate."

"I'm talking about the primaries, not your childish espionage games with people skulking down alleys in the Casbah, sticking daggers into the backs of Moslems. Our problems are closer to home. It's a ridiculous plan, and that's why I didn't support it in the first place."

"If we don't win the Senate vote on this bill, you might as well stuff the primaries up your ass for all they'll be worth. Thaddeus, you can't have one without the other."

Billings stood up now to leave. "Carl, you're carrying this thing too far. I won't have another Watergate. You'd better back off. Frankly, I think you're losing your grip." With that parting comment, Billings walked away.

Stone sat smoldering. Thad was an amateur when it came to running a campaign, he thought. That's why Marshall had hired Stone in the first place: to collect information that Billings either didn't know how to get hold of or couldn't see the importance of. If I leave this in his hands, Carl thought, we'll lose both the Senate vote and the elections. He's a fool. He's way over his head with this job. He'll be the downfall of us all.

When he arrived home, Stone went into his study and picked up his private line, dialed the satellite communications number, and waited for the clearance. Then he dialed a series of nine digits and waited for an answer.

"Pilot central," the voice on the other end answered.

"This is weather forecast," Stone said. "Visibility report."

"Visibility clear for eighteen miles."

"Forecasting storm warning eight miles out, moving in at one mile per hour."

"Eight miles from ground zero. Check. Extended forecast?"

"Heavy thunder," Stone said.

"Heavy thunder," the voice repeated.

Fire Island

Terry stood on the concrete wall that kept the bay from washing into the patio and living room of the five-bedroom house next to the Belvedere Hotel in Cherry Grove. The diesel-driven ferries were busy bringing supplies to the island for the opening of the season. They labored through the choppy water between Sayville and the Pines, cutting across the bay in front of the house.

The house itself was unpretentious, a simple prefab structure that was about twenty-five feet from the plank walkway that wound all through the Grove and ended a hundred feet from the front door of the house, where it sloped down to the sandy earth at the edge of the Meat Rack, that mile-long thicket of laurel, oak, and strangling vine that separated the Grove from the Pines and served as nature's orgy room for the thousands of pumped-up male bodies that flocked to the island every summer to literally immerse themselves in male flesh. At any time of the day or night, the Meat Rack was filled with men performing every conceivable and inconceivable sexual acrobatic. It was a place of total abandon. One could walk from the Grove to the Pines and pass dozens of men in twos, threes, or larger sexual groupings, and they wouldn't so much as look up when people passed. Sex in the open was as commonplace as hailing a cab on Fifth Avenue.

The Belvedere was a huge structure that defied architectural definition. Surrounded by dense jungle, its blue-and-white towers rose out of the banyan trees and semitropical flowering vines, and could be seen from all over the island. Inside its long halls and circular staircases, a myriad of rooms and verandas were filled with cheap copies of Greek and Roman statues. Garish chandeliers hung everywhere, and paintings covered every wall.

The Belvedere was the phantasmagorical creation of the two men who owned almost half the property in the Grove, including the house next door where Terry and Rick were to spend the summer. The hotel loomed eerily over the roof, which was covered with skylights.

"This place is out of this world," Rick said, walking through the sliding glass door onto the patio.

Terry turned his attention away from the boats. "Yeah, it sure is. How do you like the gladiator?" he asked, referring to the eight-foot statue of a Roman gladiator that resided in one corner of the living room.

"It scared the shit out of me twice now," Rick said. "Every time I come out of the hallway, I think someone's standing there."

"Maybe we'll have to throw a sheet over him."

"Then I'll think it's a ghost. I'm going to have to remember him if I get up in the middle of the night, or you're liable to find me dead of a heart attack some morning."

"Well, I'm going to put on my swimsuit and head for the beach. You coming?" Terry asked.

"No, I think I'm going to lie out on the patio."

"Where's my shaving kit?" Terry asked, pulling off his shirt and throwing it on one of the chaise lounges.

"It's on the counter in the bathroom."

Terry retrieved a large pharmaceutical bottle from the leather kit and returned with a tumbler of orange juice and two quaaludes. He took one and handed the other to Rick.

"I think I'll pass," Rick said, staring uneasily at the thick white tab.

"C'mon, relax. There's plenty more where these came from, and I want to have a good time. Let's just mellow out. There's no one around, and there won't be for a couple days, so let's just turn to jelly and soak up this sun. Come on," he said, shoving the tablet at Rick.

"Why not?" Rick said, gulping it down.

New York City

Phil Kramer returned to his desk to find Gladys Nokatoma standing over it reading a telephone message slip.

"Can I help you find something, Glad-ass? Money? A hot tip? A rubber?"

"Oh, hi, Phil. I just took a message for you. Who do you know in Tucson?" she asked, holding on to the slip for an answer before she surrendered it.

"My grandfather is an Indian, darling, didn't I tell you? You're not the only minority here," he said, staring icily into her eyes as he inched so close their bodies were touching, her arm extended over her head, trying to keep the message out of reach.

"Is that why you're always so red-faced?"

He snatched the slip from her hand. "You didn't sit in my chair, did you?"

"No, why?"

"One can't be too careful these days about herpes."

"Very funny, Fill-up, I know damned well who that call is from. What are you up to?"

"Watch for it on the news, Mata Hari. Now, if you'll excuse me..." He pushed her aside and sat down.

"It won't do you any good," she said, walking away. "Not unless you're going to give the Republicans equal time."

Elaine answered on the second ring. "Phil? You're not going to believe this. In fact, I'm still in shock, myself. The White House said no regarding D.J., but okay to do me."

It was all Phil could do to keep from letting out a war whoop. "You're shitting me."

"That's not all," Elaine continued. "Hold on for this. Not only are they going to let you interview me, but they want you to do it at the convention right after the President's acceptance speech. Assuming there is one."

"My God! How the hell did you swing it?"

"Billings and the President are really pissed at the other networks for the way they've been hammering away at APANS. They said the only network giving them half-way objective coverage, or at least presenting their side of things, is yours."

"I can hardly believe it. I've got to get busy now. And they'll let me do it? They aren't insisting on Jackson or Rather?"

"They love the idea of you doing it, because that will make it so obvious that they're giving the interview away to be punitive. Don't take offense, but Billings loved the idea of — as he put it — 'the White House giving an interview to anyone other than the other two network anchor people.' So, unless something changes drastically, you're it."

"I'll never be able to repay you for this, Elaine."

"It's not necessary, Phil. You're a good reporter and a dear friend. I'm glad there's something we can do to repay you and Jessica for being so sweet to us."

"Now if someone from the network calls, it'll be confirmed? They're not going to say they don't know what we're talking about, are they?"

"No, no. You're to call Miles Cameron anytime, and he'll help make the arrangements. It's going to be chaotic there, as you well know, so you'd better get your plans firmed up right away."

"Don't worry, we'll be on the phone within the hour. Bless you, babe. You may have just made my career in a single interview."

"I hope so. Someone ought to get something out of all this."

"How're you and D.J. doing out there?"

"Great. It's so beautiful here. I could stay forever. D.J. loves it, too. I haven't seen him this calm or this happy in ... well, maybe ever. All he does is run in the desert. In fact, he and Parker have been out since before breakfast. He's running the poor pinscher ragged. They're running twice a day and sometimes even before bed. Give Jessie my love. We'll talk soon."

Phil straightened his tie, put on his jacket, and strode toward the elevator. Move over, Mata Hari.

McLean, Virginia

Carl Stone opened his front door to find a small man with disheveled hair, holding a notepad and pencil.

"Mr. Stone, if you could spare me just a few minutes, I'd like to ask you a couple questions," he said.

Stone started to close the door.

"It's about Terry Guidi," the man said a little too smugly.

Carl froze for just a second, opened the door, and stepped outside. He looked around and saw no sign of a camera anywhere. "Who are you and who do you work for?"

"I'm a freelance journalist and I'm just following up on a lead. I happened to meet Terry a few weeks ago and..."

"Look, bud," Stone said in his most menacing tone. "I don't know what you're talking about. And, furthermore, I don't like reporters coming to my home. I know you parasites have no scruples, so I'll tell you this just once: stay away from me."

"Just how close is Terry to the President's son, Mr. Stone? Are they just roommates? Rumor has it that the Committee to Re-elect the President has him on the payroll."

"I don't know where you guys get this garbage, but you're all wet. I don't know who or what you're talking about, and if you want some real good advice, you'll just forget it and get rid of the source who gave you this piece of trash. Otherwise, you might find yourself out of business."

"So you don't know this Terry Guidi? You never heard of him? You aren't aware that he was supposedly in France with D.J. Marshall and that they were living together while the President's son was studying in Europe?"

Carl grabbed the little guy by the lapels. "That's the kind of crap that gets people hurt in my business, pipsqueak. Who you working for, some smut paper or the Republicans?"

"Let go of me, Mr. Stone."

Carl let loose of his jacket and started back inside.

"Maybe you'd rather talk about your stepson? When is he likely to get paroled? Will he come home? Why don't you ever visit him? How will he support himself once he's out? Does he have a trust fund?"

Carl turned in the doorway, his eyes squinting, his face flushed. He pointed a finger at the reporter, who took one step backward. "Start working on your obituary, scum." And he closed the door behind him.

He went straight to his study, picked up his private line, and dialed a New York number.

"Hello?"

"Snowball is talking up a storm and I haven't heard word one from Caretaker. Call Sam and tell him to get on it. I want this stopped now before it goes any further, understand?"

"Yes, sir."

"And I mean stopped. I just had a little visit from a reporter. Do I make myself clear about the urgency of this matter?"

"Yes, sir. I'll call Sam right now."

"I'll assume everything is under control unless I hear back from you."

Stone's New York connection called every fifteen minutes until seven the next morning, but Sam never answered. There was, he concluded, no choice but to go himself, as risky as that might be. He went to the corner pharmacy, bought a bottle of Lady Clairol brown hair color, then went home and shaved his mustache. He packed a gym bag and called for train schedules to Sayville, but realized he couldn't go until Friday. There wouldn't be enough people on the island to provide adequate cover. He would have to wait until the weekend, when hordes of gay men left the city in droves for three days in Sodom. Very well, he would wait, and in the meantime he could continue to try to get hold of Sam. For the next two days, he stayed in his apartment and relentlessly called Sam's number. There was never an answer.

Fire Island

"I'm going to the store. Do you want anything?" Rick asked, pulling a pair of blue shorts on over his swimsuit.

"I don't think so. I'm going to take a nap," Terry answered.

He got a beer from the refrigerator, watched Rick walk down the plankway, then went to his room to roll a joint. The plastic bag of pot was on the nightstand, but there were no papers. He looked in the living room, then the kitchen, then went into Rick's room. There were none on the dresser, so he looked in Rick's pants pockets. He thought he found them, but it turned out to be a slip of paper with a phone number on one side and an address written on the other. The area code of the phone number was 703. Funny, he thought, Rick said he didn't know a single person on the East Coast. I wonder who it is?

Feeling mischievous and liking the idea of having something on Rick to tease him about at the appropriate time, he went to the phone and called the number. It rang several times, and just as he was about to hang up, someone picked up the phone.

"The Stone residence ... hello?"

"Uh, this is Rick."

"I'm sorry, this is the cleaning woman. Can I help you?"

"This is Rick."

"Mr. Stone is at his office, and Mrs. Stone is out. Would you like to call back?"

"Is there some way I can reach Mrs. Stone?"

"She's over at Mrs. Billings's. You could try there."

"Thanks."

"You want me to take a message?"

"No, no message. I'll call her there. That's Thaddeus Billings, isn't it?"

"Got me, honey, I just clean."

So that was how they're keeping tabs on me, he thought. Jesus Christ! Way back to when I first met Rick. But why Stone? It's Billings who runs the pinschers ... unless Stone and Billings are at it again and he's trying to pull something. He picked up the phone again to call D.J., but changed his mind immediately. D.J.'s line was always tapped. In fact, this line was probably tapped, too. He would have to call someone else, and he'd have to do it from the booth at the ferry slip. But whom could he call? And what would he say? Suddenly he felt very alone and very unsafe.

New York City

Phil and Jessica were in the shower when the phone rang.

"Who?" Phil said loudly, trying to jam part of the towel into his free ear to soak up the water. He changed ears. "Oh,

Terry? Where are you? We tried calling you last night. We wanted you to come for dinner."

"I'm on the island. Listen to me, I can't talk long. I'm scared."

"What's the matter?" Phil asked, listening closely now to see if he could detect any sign of drugs in Terry's voice. The voice was deliberate and strong, but the connection was bad.

"I'm here with this fellow I met. We came out early to avoid the crowds on Saturday. I just found out he's working for Carl Stone."

"What? You're not making sense. What are you talking about?"

"I met this guy about a month ago. I saw him a couple times, you know, just being friendly," Terry lied. "He showed up again a few days ago, and I invited him to stay with me at the house Billings got me on the island. This afternoon while I was looking for something in his room, I found a phone number and called it just to be funny. It was Carl Stone's home number. You know, the CIA guy who's running the campaign."

"Are you sure? There are a lot of Stones, you know."

"Not with sister-in-laws named Billings. I wanted to call D.J., but I know his phone is tapped. I don't know if this one out here is, but I suppose it is, so I'm calling from a pay phone. Will you tell D.J. for me? I need to talk to him, Phil. I'm spooked by this. They really had me fooled, and I don't know why they're doing it."

"Well, you know they want to keep an eye on you."

"Yeah, but why would he be reporting to Stone? Billings is in charge of all this. Even the pinschers report directly to him. Why Stone? That CIA crowd is nasty. I don't get it."

"All right, I'll get in touch with D.J. somehow and let him know. In the meantime, try to relax and enjoy yourself. It's probably nothing to worry about. You know how careful those guys are, especially when it comes to the re-election campaign. Guess what? They're going to let me interview Elaine at the convention."

"That's great. Good break for you, huh?"

"You said it."

"You'll call D.J. for me? And tell him to call me?"

"Sure."

"Tell him to be careful what he says. I'll probably have to go to a phone booth and call him back or something. He should call me from a phone booth, too."

"Okay, Terry. Take care."

Jessica was out of the shower by the time Phil returned to the bathroom. "Ahh, puppy toes, I was just getting going," Phil whined.

"We'll continue in the bedroom. I'm waterlogged. Who was that?" she asked, wrapping the bath towel around her.

"Terry. He's on the island already and says this guy he invited to spend some time out there with him is working for Carl Stone."

"What?"

"He found a telephone number in the guy's room and called it and says it was Carl Stone's home phone number."

"Did Stone answer?"

"I don't think so. That part was never clear. You know Terry: he was probably fucked up. There must be a million Stones in the world," Phil said, taking Jessica into his arms. "Let's play doctor."

"Why did he call here?" Jessica asked as Phil began nibbling at her left breast.

"He couldn't get hold of D.J. Wants us to deliver the message."

"What message?" she asked, barely audible now as the sensation of Phil's caresses swept her up.

"He wants him to call him. Oh, baby, the doctor is about to be in."

Sayville, New York

The lines for the ferries to Cherry Grove and the Pines were so long, they extended clear out to the dirt road by the parking lots and began intertwining. True, Steffan, and four of their friends, who also had shares in the house in the Pines, stood in line alongside the road, coughing and cursing the dust from the cars entering the unpaved lot to deposit weekend islanders and those going out to open their houses for the season.

"Oh, look," said Steffan, "there's Miss Stein."

Climbing out of a stretch limo near the ticket booth was fashion designer Maxwell Stein and three bodybuilders. They stood for a moment, adjusting to the bright sun and stretching after the long ride from Manhattan. Each was holding a champagne glass.

"The one with the 48-inch bust is the one in the new underwear ad," True offered to the group.

"I haven't seen that ad," said Dudley, one of the house-mates.

"It isn't out yet. Monique works for the agency that has their account. She was showing me proofs the other day. It's all done with airbrushes. He's really an Armour cheesedog."

"What?" Dudley asked.

Steffan interpreted. "No meat."

"Jesus Christ!" said True, who was standing with his back to the group, surveying the line of people queuing up for the ferry to the Grove. "Beefcake with hair."

Steffan turned to find the object of True's desire. It wasn't difficult. Standing in line about twenty feet away was a massively built man in a tank top. He was covered with hair.

"Honey, it's an illusion," Steffan commented. "Not a very well executed one at that."

"What are you talking about?" True said, unable to stop staring. "He's beautiful, sent from God just for me."

"Could be. That's Heavenly Ash he's wearing," Steffan wisecracked.

"What?" True snarled, annoyed that his twin was already bad-mouthing the scene.

"Clairol D-23, baby brother. It's the same color Marlene wears."

"Oh, it is not. You're always so critical, even when there's nothing to be critical about," True protested.

"Yeah?" Steffan retorted. "When's the last time you saw a brunet with blond body hair?"

"Oh, my God, you're right," True sighed. Then, "Who gives a fuck?"

"I'm sure you would," Steffan said, turning back to the group they were with as the line started to move toward the boat slip. Hundreds of people scuffled along in the dirt, carrying, dragging, and kicking their bags, boxes, and suitcases toward the turnstile.

"Now where the hell is he?" Steffan bitched, retrieving True's belongings, which had been abandoned several feet back and were being typically ignored by the passengers walking around and over his luggage. "There you are. I'm not playing bellhop for you, Miss Garbo, so stay in line. We're going to get on this one, I can tell by how fast we're moving."

As they got to the gate, True screamed. "Oh no, I forgot something. Here, Steffan, I'll catch up." True thrust his two bags at his brother.

"What the fuck are you doing now?" Steffan yelled, now on the other side of the turnstile. "Where are you going?!" he screeched.

"I'll catch the next ferry," True hollered back, walking away toward the road.

"Bitch!" Steffan muttered, kicking True's suitcases all the way to the dock.

True, meanwhile, sidled his way into line not far from the hunk of his desire, and when they boarded the ferry to Cherry Grove, he climbed over two rows of seats on the upper deck to sit next to him. The man paid no attention.

As the ferry slowly made its way out to the open bay, where it would pick up speed, the man took in the view along the banks, while True took in the view in the seat next to him. He was all muscle, but he was dressed wrong. He had on blue cotton and polyester gym shorts with white piping, way too baggy. Must be from out of town, True thought. And no tan at all. What self-respecting homosexual doesn't have a tan by Memorial Day? How can you go out on the beach without a tan? True lifted the bottom of his own shorts and checked his tan line. It was a little paler than he would have liked, but one afternoon in the sun would fix that. He looked up to find the man watching his self-inspection.

"Oh, hi. Mosquito bite."

The man smiled slightly, then turned away again. Hard to get, True thought. "My name's True," he offered.

The man turned to face him again. "Hi."

"What's your name?" True asked after a pause, sounding like he was talking to an infant and hoping he hadn't come off as too condescending with his attempt to let the guy know he should now enter into a conversation with him.

The man looked him up and down, then answered. "Frank."

"New in town, sailor?" True decided to try a lighter approach, since the guy seemed so uptight. It produced a faint smile.

"Yeah. Just in town for the weekend. Thought I'd see what the action is out here."

Hmm, that's direct enough, True thought. "There'll be plenty of it this weekend, but mostly it's over in the Pines. You have friends in Cherry Grove?"

Frank hesitated. "No, just a tourist. Guess I should have gotten on the other ferry."

"It's no problem, just a long walk. You can get there from the Grove, but you have to go through the Meat Rack."

Frank gave him a peculiar look, as though he didn't understand.

"The Meat Rack. You know, where everybody goes for bush sex." There was no visible response from Frank. "Or you can walk along the beach."

The ferry jolted forward, and in seconds, they were shooting across the water, the breeze blowing fiercely in their faces. It was noticeably cooler on the bay than it had been on the mainland.

"Some friends and I have a house in the Pines. Where are you staying?"

"Don't know yet. Someone said I should try the Belvedere."

"God, you'll never find a place this weekend if you don't already have a reservation. There'll be people camping in the dunes."

"Well, I may be one of them," Frank said, smiling again, this time more broadly and, True thought, more warmly.

"Well, if you need a place to stay..." True gave him the smile that always melted hairy hearts and let his thigh lean into Frank's. Frank jerked it away a little too fast. He tried to cover for it with an especially friendly tone in his voice and then letting his leg come to rest again against True's. "Thanks a lot, but I think I'll just wander around first and get my bearings. Besides, that wouldn't be fair to your friends."

"Oh, sure it would," True said, digging into his gym bag and pulling out a pen and a pad. "Here," he said, "this is the address. I don't know the phone number yet, but the house is easy enough to find. We even have a pool," he added as further enticement.

Frank took the address, glanced at it too briefly to read, then stuffed it in his bag. "Thanks, I appreciate it. Maybe I'll take you up on it." True wanted to believe him.

When they got off the ferry, True walked him to the Belvedere, since he was going to go through the Meat Rack to get to the Pines and it was on the way.

"This is a great place," True advised. "A little weirdly decorated, but a lot of fun. I spent my first summer here. Right up there in that room." True pointed to a corner room, which overlooked the island and the house next door. "The view's not as good as on the other side of the place ... unless you're a voyeur."

"Huh?" Frank grunted.

"You can see into practically all the skylights in that house," True explained, pointing to the green-and-white prefab practically hidden by the trees and brush. "Well, see you." He backed down the plankway toward the Meat Rack. "Remember, if you don't find a room..."

"Thanks," Frank called, waving as he went through the vine-covered gate that opened into the Belvedere's jungle.

True watched until he disappeared.

"Hey!" a voice shouted as True backed into the young man coming through the gate of the house with the sky-lights.

"Sorry," True apologized, looking over the dark-haired man in the blue Speedo swimsuit.

"That's okay," he said as he continued up the plankway toward the ferry slip, not looking back even once.

Jesus, True said to himself, I've only been here fifteen minutes and I've already struck out twice. I hope this isn't a preview of the weekend.

Fire Island

The Pines Pavilion had been so crowded all night that until four a.m. there had been a line to get in. The previous summer the entire island had been nearly deserted, but the discovery just before Thanksgiving of an immunizing vaccine against AIDS had changed all that. The disease that had threatened to decimate the gay population was now under control and the Memorial Day weekend on the island was the first fair-weather holiday since the vaccine had been introduced. Gay men were celebrating.

Nearly everyone in the Pavilion was on one drug or another, like Terry, who was tripping on a double hit of blotter acid; True, who was on the dance floor sweating out the Orange Sunshine and MDA; or Rick, who was standing outside on the second-floor balcony holding onto the rail and weaving precariously under a heavy dose of Percodans and quaaludes. Frank, who had come up to True earlier asking if he had any downs, may have been the only man in the building who had absolutely no drugs flowing through his veins. And he may have been the only one who needed them.

True watched now from the dance floor as Frank — his hairy body clad in only a pair of blue jeans and sneakers — made his way along the wall beneath the deejay booth toward the door. He stopped once, turned around quickly, then a few seconds later hurried past the bar and out into the morning.

"Hey! Where you going?" True's dance partner yelled. But True was already halfway across the dance floor headed for the door.

Terry walked along the beach toward Cherry Grove, the sky on the horizon shimmering a dark violet with the first glow of morning. The tide was coming in, and the waves broke off from the shore, then sent foamy hands rushing over the wet sand to grab at his bare feet. The double hit of acid was still working in him, and the dunes seemed to radiate a pink glow as if they were lighted from within. He heard crackling sounds coming from the woods on the other side of the dunes. He turned away from the beach toward the blue towers of the Belvedere, walking through the glowing dunes, which now seemed to undulate beneath his feet. He entered the Meat Rack. It was the shortest route to the house if he could remember which path to take.

He wandered for a long time, taking one path until it seemed to lead him back to where he had started, then branching off in an arbitrary direction when the path forked again. All along the way he could hear men off in the bushes, breathing heavily or groaning with pleasure or just moving through the brush. Every once in a while, he would pass someone walking in the opposite direction. Twice, he stopped to let people pass him from behind.

It was dark beneath the trees, as there was no moon, and he began to be frightened. He stopped and listened. There were no sounds at all, and that scared him much more than hearing men going at it somewhere in the distance. He hurried now, trying to suppress the effects of the drugs. Black vines clung at him as he rushed over the narrow, winding path. Leaves came out of nowhere to slap his face, and once, he stumbled over a log and fell, scraping his leg badly. He got up and ran, sometimes losing the path and hurling himself into the laurel bushes, which tore at his face with their sharp branches. He was sweating, and he could feel the trickle of blood on his cheek. He ran faster, and now there were sounds like voices all around him, as though others were running alongside, taunting him with words he couldn't make out. The trees were bending toward him, their branches grabbing at his body, and he could hear himself panting and whining like an animal. Suddenly something solid crashed against his shins, and he went down hard, falling forward, his face slamming against wood. He lay stunned for a moment, then slowly lifted his head. The plankway that led to Cherry Grove stretched before him. He had run smack into it.

Once in the house, he went around to all the windows and pulled the curtains, then turned on all the lights he could find switches for. The voices were gone, but now he was aware of sounds the house was making. The floor creaked under every footstep, and the roof made stretching sounds, as though someone were rolling something heavy from one end of the house to the other, pausing only at the skylights.

He went to the kitchen and drank a quart of milk to try easing the drugs, then went into the bathroom and took off his clothes. He stood in front of the full-length mirror, which was inside the shower, and examined his torn body. There were scratches and welts everywhere. Where the trees and bushes hadn't struck him, the mosquitoes had. He turned on the hot water and let it flow over him, standing directly beneath its spray. The room filled with steam, and his body began to relax, except for the occasional cold rushes that the acid sent shivering from the base of his spine up to the top of his skull. When the water began to turn lukewarm, he cut off the shower and threw back the shower curtain, crying out sharply and jumping back so hard that he struck his head on the mirrored wall.

"Hi, Terry," said the hairy man who called himself Frank.

"Jesus Christ!" Terry exclaimed. "How did you get in here? You scared the shit out of me, motherfucker."

"I thought you'd be glad to see a familiar face."

"What are you doing here, checking up?" Terry asked, trying to force himself into control over the drugs. He grabbed a towel from the rack alongside the shower and began to dry himself.

"Sort of. Got any downs?" Frank asked, helping himself to Terry's shaving kit.

"Get out of there," Terry shouted, stepping out of the shower and grabbing for the leather case. Frank snatched his arm and twisted it until Terry's eyes filled with tears.

"Get out of here," Terry ordered when his arm had been released.

"First, I want to know just who you've been talking to and what you've been saying. We've been getting some very disturbing reports about your mouth. And I don't mean what you've been filling it with."

Terry looked directly into the man's eyes, and the look frightened him. It was a look he had seen on the faces of strung-out friends, desperate for a fix. He looked wild and insane. Terry didn't care. He had his own drugs to worry about.

"Very funny," Terry said, wrapping the towel around him. "I haven't been talking to anyone. There's no one here to talk to, asshole, remember? That's the idea of being here."

"That's not what we hear. We hear you've been telling stories all around. And we don't like it. It could be dangerous. For you, as well as for us."

"I don't know what you're talking about. Now get out of here. I need some sleep." Terry moved toward the door, but Frank jumped up and blocked his way. "We're warning you. It could be very bad for your health if you keep it up."

"Does Billings know you're here? Or are you working for Stone, too?" Terry snarled. He could see by the wild, panicky look in the man's eyes that he had gone too far. "Look, I haven't been to anyone, honest. Why would I? It would only hurt me in the long run." Terry took a few steps backward as he watched the face flush. "What's the matter with you? You want a 'lude?"

The man took a step toward Terry.

"What have you heard? Tell me, and I'll tell you if it's anything I've said to anyone," Terry offered.

"You little cocksucker. How much do you know, anyway?" the man said, coming toward him.

"I don't know anything. What are you talking about? You'd better leave me alone. You could get into a lot of trouble, you know. I don't care who you're working for."

"You little asshole licker. What about Stone? Who's working for Stone? What did you mean?" He now had Terry pressed up against the wall next to the tub.

"Nothing, I didn't mean anything. I don't know——"

The huge hand came across his face with such force that it knocked him into the tub. Terry lay dazed for a moment, then tried to speak. "Please, honest, I don't want any trouble."

"You've been talking to reporters, cum-sucker. You're going to blow the lid off everything, aren't you? You're tired of being separated from your husband. You need more dick, and you're not getting it, 'cause you're such a little piece of shit. So you're thinking you'll just blow it all wide open and you'll be back with your he-man and get laid every time you want it."

Terry groaned as the room spun around now in slow motion. Whether it was the drugs or the result of the blow to his head on the porcelain tub he couldn't tell, but above him the skylight, the man's menacing face, and the light fixture chased one another in an endless circle. The man was still talking to him, but he couldn't make out what he was saying, only that the tone was jeering and hateful. He felt him strike several places on his body, but none of it was as painful as the reverberating throb in his skull.

He felt himself being lifted, shaken, and dropped back down into the cold tub. He heard the words "cocksucker ... motherfucker ... faggot," then he began to fall a long fall into increasing darkness. The light faded as it sped away from him, and his body was being washed with some warm liquid, then submerged into it. He was plummeting down into a dark, warm vortex, and suddenly far above him was another face. Was it Rick? Was it D.J.? It could be, but now it, too, was gone and there were loud noises and cursing again and someone else had been thrown into the vortex and was intertwined among his limbs. The light receded again, and then there was a shrill sound like the highest note on a violin. It increased until Terry thought it would burst his eardrums, then gradually faded away as the light, too, faded and vanished. Then there was nothing but darkness, yet he was conscious.

Far above him, the tiniest light appeared, and out of it came a woman. She came closer and closer, clutching something in her arms. It was wrapped in an apron. Her face was filled with light so bright he couldn't make out her features, but when she came close, she opened her apron and held something out to him. He looked into her hands and saw that she was holding a brown egg. He looked up into her face again and recognized his mother. She was smiling. She turned and walked toward the light, looking back in a beckoning way. Terry suddenly felt warm and comfortable, as though he had been wrapped in warm blankets. He moved behind his mother toward the light, she looking back after him every once in a while, the way a mother looks back after a small child on an outing to be sure she hasn't lost him. They moved into and through the blinding light. Terry sighed deeply, and then there was nothing.

The sun was completely up on the horizon now, its golden shafts of light fanning out over the island, warming the chilled wet bodies of the last of the dancers filing out of the Pavilion. Its beams fell romantically across the backs of one-night lovers struggling through the dunes toward their waiting beds; it pierced the trees of the Meat Rack and blinded men of leather releasing their semen into the mouths of revelers who weren't lucky enough to find love on the dance floor or at the bar. The sun, the golden, life-giving sun of morning, rose dispassionately on all the people of the island and all the island's houses, making the roofs steam ethereally.

True lay trembling against the green shingles of the house next to the Belvedere, the steam rising all around him like smoke from the floors of hell. Inside the house, Rick and Terry lay lifeless, their limbs intertwined on the blood-splattered, cold tile floor.

Cairo, Egypt

Hosni Khousoum waved and smiled warmly at the crowds of Egyptians that lined the route of his motorcade along Cairo's ancient streets. The sun beat down mercilessly on the open car, and Khousoum took off his hat to wipe the sweat from his head with a white handkerchief. The entourage stopped only once between the presidential palace and the military parade reviewing stand, so the Egyptian president could lay a wreath at the tomb of the unknown soldier. After a brief ceremony, the group climbed back into the black cars and sped to the parade site in a little, nondescript suburb of Cairo renamed Sadat after the former president, who had been assassinated there just a few years earlier.

Security was extremely tight, and even the presidential party had to undergo scanning with metal detectors as they entered the colorfully decorated reviewing stand. The orange, green, and white bunting hung limp in the stifling Egyptian heat.

While that security check was taking place for the VIPs, another security check was occurring at the entrance of the parade route. Lieutenant Abdul Hadaah was explaining to his commanding officer that his crew had all taken ill from something they had eaten the night before and he had had to recruit three new men from another unit. His superior officer listened intently and watched as Hadaah conducted a thorough and rather dramatic search of the replacement soldiers, then ordered them into the back of the military truck to wait their turn to fall in to the parade lineup.

Back on the massive concrete-and-brick reviewing stand, Khousoum, along with invited ambassadors, diplomats, and journalists, listened reverently as verses were read from the Koran. The religious ceremony completed, Khousoum, flanked by his vice president Abu Godzieba and his defense minister Fawzi Bouli, settled back to watch the hour-long military parade and air show.

The dignitaries chatted with one another, trying to ignore the heat. Several times, Khousoum stood and saluted as his soldiers marched by in perfect step, saluting their proud leader. The parade reverberated with fireworks, clicking heels, and the revving engines of heavy military armor. Mortars shot up little parachutes which gently floated back to earth carrying Egyptian flags and tiny portraits of Khousoum. Jet fighters shrieked by so close to the ground that many had to hold their ears. Khousoum laughed with pride, using his binoculars, a gift from an American general, to better see the acrobatic skydivers. He saluted the Camel Corps that patrolled the Egyptian frontiers in the more desolate regions.

A column of older military hardware, acquired from the Soviets during Mubarak's administration, rumbled by. The older equipment signaled that the military show was coming to an end.

In the third to last row of trucks and tanks, Lieutenant Hadaah sat calmly next to the driver of the truck that would pass closest to the presidential reviewing stand. As the truck drew parallel to the dignitaries, Hadaah ordered it to stop, but the driver, a young Egyptian from Alexandria, hesitated. Hadaah reached down and pulled on the hand brake, and the truck came to a jolting halt. In the stands, the dignitaries were looking toward the sky, where a formation of American F-14s were swooping low, trailing streams of red, blue, orange, and green smoke. As they passed, their engines made a sound like heavy thunder. The final trucks were now pulling around the stopped vehicle in front of the stand, assuming mechanical trouble, which was frequent in the Egyptian motor pool. Lieutenant Hadaah jumped from the truck and approached President Khousoum, who stood proudly to salute, assuming the young soldier was coming forward to pay his respects. Instead, once he was directly in front of his president, Hadaah pulled the pin from a hand grenade and tossed it into the stand. It exploded immediately, filling the president's face and upper body with shrapnel and felling several of those around him. Meanwhile, three gunmen leaped from the truck, ran forward, and sprayed bullets into the presidential party. A fourth gunman appeared at the side of the stand and began shooting people at random.

Godzieba tried to shield Khousoum with his own body, but it was too late; wounded in the chest, he also fell to the floor of the stand. No armed guards stood between Khousoum and the charging assassins; no sharpshooter fired from the upper levels of the reviewing stand. Several of the guards near the Egyptian president and many of the soldiers ran or ducked for cover. In seconds, it was over and the stand was washed red with blood, the moans and wails of wounded men and women filling the dry desert air.

Tucson

All day the yard had been noisy with the coming and going of vehicles filled with Secret Service, FBI agents, and local law enforcement officers. Along with Rodney's return with the limousine came a half dozen pinschers reassigned from Washington to Tucson. The President's chief of security had insisted that D.J. and Elaine cancel their planned visit to the White House for Memorial Day. Until they could gather all the facts surrounding the Khousoum assassination, every U.S. official was under added security. The first thing Rodney had done that afternoon after arriving with the refurbished car was to take D.J. out and show him the new bulletproofing and the blackened windows. He even operated the electric lead shields that sealed the windows two and a half seconds after the button on the dashboard was pushed.

All afternoon, the house had been surrounded with armed guards, and the road that wound past it was secured by guards who stopped motorists fifty yards away.

Elaine put the finishing touches on the potato salad while D.J. set the table. Parker and Rodney, whom Elaine insisted join them for their "indoor picnic," watched the evening news in the living room. The entire half hour was devoted to the assassination of the Egyptian president. D.J. put the last glass on the table and went in to stand behind the sofa where Parker was sitting. Barbara Jackson, CBS co-anchor for the evening news, was just coming back on the television screen following a live report from the network correspondent in Cairo.

"Vice President Godzieba's interim government moved quickly today to restore order in the stunned state of Egypt by imposing a one-year state of emergency. Already, he has begun ordering the arrest and interrogation of known leftists and radical religious fundamentalists throughout the country.

"Back in the United States, the assassination has further clouded debate in Congress over whether to sell sophisticated APANS military hardware to the Sudan. A Marshall administration spokesman contends that Khousoum's death means it is more important than ever to placate and bolster the Sudanese; opponents of the arms sale argue that the Egyptian tragedy is all the more reason to keep sensitive American military technology out of the region, since now there is blatant evidence of the Mideast's growing and deepseated instability.

"While Bif Tucker, President Marshall's leading opponent for the Democratic Party's nomination at next month's convention, could not be reached for comment, Senator Adam McCann, the leading Republican candidate and chairman of the powerful Senate Foreign Affairs Committee, was asking some tough questions today from his home in Montana."

McCann appeared on the television screen, standing on the front lawn of his home in Helena, dozens of microphones thrust in his face.

"There are some very disturbing questions this outrageous and tragic event raises that I think the President of the United States should be asking: How does a group of armed assassins get into a military parade of that sort, let alone manage to get into the truck closest to the reviewing stand? How is it that that particular truck happened to arrive in front of President Khousoum just at the moment when those jets were flying over distracting the spectators? And perhaps more importantly, do simple lieutenants really plan these kinds of things? I think not. I would hope an investigation of the most thorough and exhaustive kind will be immediately undertaken to find out who was really behind this heinous crime."

Jackson was now back on the screen. "A White House official who wished to remain unnamed told us today that the CIA is investigating unconfirmed reports that the assassination was backed by the Libyan government of Muammar Qaddafi and that there may be other assassination plots already under way around the world. Upon hearing of the assassination of President Khousoum, beefed-up security was ordered for all administration officials, leaders of the Senate and House of Representatives, and members of the Supreme Court."

"Okay," D.J. complained, "I've had enough already. Let's eat and try to have a good time this evening. Rodney, turn that thing off, will you?"

Rodney punched the television and the screen went blank, then he and Parker went to the table and sat down. D.J. was already seated. "Is there anything I can help you with?" D.J. shouted to Elaine in the kitchen.

"No thanks, I'll be right there," she said as the phone in the kitchen rang. "I'll get it," she shouted. After several minutes, she appeared in the doorway, her face white and drawn, tears in her eyes.

"What is it?" D.J. asked, fearing that something had happened to his father. He jumped to his feet. "Is it Dad? Is he...?"

Elaine shook her head. Rodney and Parker, seeing how upset she was, got up and retreated onto the porch. As the screen door closed behind them, Elaine spoke through her tears, her voice cracking as the words came out. "It's Terry, D.J. He's dead."

The White House

Billings had quite simply refused to talk with reporters. He was in his White House office when word came about Richard. Before he even started putting the pieces together, he called Rachael and told her to go to her sister's house. He sent a car for her, explaining that no matter how he felt and what he wanted to do, there was no way he could come home, with the turmoil that the Egyptian assassination had created at the White House. He would leave there as soon as he could and would pick her up at Rebecca's. In the meantime, their house would be searched and secured.

Thaddeus couldn't cry. He was too angry. Not only had his brother-in-law overridden his direct order to scrap Operation Thunder, thereby creating an international crisis and threat of war in the Middle East, but somehow he had also managed to involve Thaddeus's only son, whom he hadn't even heard from in five years, in the sordid political theatrics that Stone so perversely loved to engage in. It may be more than even I can tolerate, he thought, as he waited for Stone to enter his office.

Yet he knew there was no way he could extricate himself now without ruining both himself and the President. If he allowed the President to find out that the administration was in any way connected with Khousoum's death, Marshall would resign and the administration would topple. He couldn't even allow himself the luxury of mourning his son's death, because there was far too much to do now in the aftermath of the assassination. Could he possibly keep Richard's death from the President for even a short while? He would have to. How would he explain Richard's presence in the house with Terry? He couldn't even explain it to himself.

Stone entered the office and closed the door. Billings stood behind his desk, trembling with rage. He could barely speak. Stone, on the other hand, was cool and collected. He took a seat in one of the leather chairs and crossed his legs. He spoke first.

"I'm sorry about Richard, Thad."

Billings clenched his fists, and his eyes filled. He wanted nothing more than to kill this man. If he had had a gun in his hand, Carl Stone would be dead. He had never felt such raging hatred before. In this moment, he cared nothing at all for Donald Marshall or the administration or even the future of the American government. He wanted only revenge against this despicable, inhuman creature who had been the instrument of his son's death, a son whom he had hoped in time to be able to talk with and once more share his life with. A son he would now never see again.

"Richard came to me several weeks ago," Stone began. "He was desperate, he was broke, and he had nowhere to go. I tried to get him to come home, to talk with you and Rachael, but he refused. He said if I wouldn't help him, he would just keep moving on. I thought that maybe if I could keep him within reach, he might come around. I didn't want to put him on the dole, so I offered him work. I figured it was easy enough: all he had to do was spend the summer with Terry, keep him company on the island, and report to me once in a while. When he would report in, I would always talk about you and Rachael and how much you wanted to see him, how torn apart you were at his silence. I thought perhaps he would change his mind about not seeing you by the end of the summer. I—"

"Save it," Thaddeus snarled. "I don't want to hear any more of your lies. I have two things to tell you, and then I want you to leave. First, I intend to see that somehow, sometime, the world knows what you have done to Khousoum—"

"We had nothing to do with that, Thaddeus. That was completely out of our control—"

"I've already spoken with Bradley. I knew you couldn't do this without the cooperation of the man who's acting for you while you're heading the campaign, so I called him first thing. I also figured you couldn't tell him I knew nothing about it, since I'm running the show over here. I just called him and asked if things were secured as far as keeping the operatives in Egypt quiet. He assured me that they had already been taken care of. Murder seems to be the blue plate special this Memorial Day. So, like I said, save your filthy lies for someone who doesn't know you.

"Second, I want you to know that someday when you least expect it, in some way that you most dread, I will have my revenge. I don't know what it will be or how I will accomplish it, but before I die, I will see you suffer so greatly that you'll wish you had never met me. I'm looking forward to your and Bradley's report at the emergency cabinet meeting tomorrow. As chief of staff, I am very interested to know just how this 'tragedy' in Egypt occurred without our knowing about it. Now get out of my sight, Carl. The blood of my son is on your hands. I hope you enjoy the smell of it."

The White House

The President was the last to enter the cabinet meeting room. He seated himself at the table and opened the meeting by reading a telegram he had sent to acting president Abu Godzieba pledging the United States' support of his interim government and assuring him that American troops in the Middle East were being put on standby alert in case of any unexpected attack on Egypt by Libya or the Soviets.

Next, he instructed Secretary of State Gibbons to head the funeral delegation to Cairo. Secretary of Defense Smith was to work closely with the Joint Chiefs to see that there was an adequate troop deployment in the Mediterranean and to prepare the military to act instantly, should the need arise. Marshall would go on television in the evening to make a brief announcement regarding the actions the United States was taking and how his administration deplored this kind of violence and would not tolerate it.

He announced that the APANS sale must now go through at all costs, as the country's security depended upon it. "The Middle East is ripe for war, and the Soviets are obviously hard at work to stir up unrest there. State political leaders are to be given every resource available to convince the nation's voters of the need to push the APANS bill through Congress," he said. The cabinet members were all to hit the road to speak on its behalf. Naturally, it would be a major topic of his address on television.

"Now," Marshall said, sitting back in his mahogany-and-leather chair, "Will Mr. Stone and Mr. Bradley please report to this group just what took place in Egypt yesterday and, more important, how it took place and who was behind it?"

Stone whispered to Bradley, who was sitting next to him, then leaned forward and opened a folder that was sitting on the conference table in front of him.

"Mr. President, Mr. Vice President, members of the cabinet: The information we have been able to obtain from our sources and agents in Egypt and all over the Middle East leave us with a very disturbing conclusion. Not only was this assassination carried out at the instigation of a foreign government, but it is not the only subversive activity planned."

The group buzzed in reaction to this statement. Billings sat expressionless, waiting to hear the magnitude of the lie.

"Libyan forces supplied the assassins with their weapons — weapons naturally procured from the Soviets. This murder is the first of many that are planned. Even now, as I speak to you, we believe there is in existence a Libyan hit squad, a group of men trained to kill in cold blood and eager to lay down their lives for the cause of Muammar Qaddafi. They have been dispatched to the United States to carry out a plan to execute the President, the Vice President, every cabinet member, the members of the Supreme Court, the Joint Chiefs of Staff, and leading political leaders such as Adam McCann and the Speaker of the House."

Stone's voice was drowned out by the noise of the other men in the room talking in astonishment. Billings glared at Stone. He saw a thin smile cross Stone's lips and realized that Stone was Machiavellian not only in what he was doing here, but in his entire approach to life. If there was such a thing as evil, it was surely living within the soul of Carl Stone. He was perhaps, Billings thought, the only truly evil human being he had ever known.

"If you've been watching the news," Stone continued, "and you all should have been too busy for that today..." He looked to see if he had produced a chuckle among the group. He hadn't. "...then you've heard rumors of beefed-up security for members of the administration. Well, gentlemen, they're not rumors. Mr. Bradley, who, as you all know, is serving as acting head of the CIA during my temporary assignment with the Committee to Re-elect the President, has been working closely with Secretary of the Treasury Buchsbaum and Attorney General Haje to see to it that every person in this room, and all others who are crucial to the administration and the operation of the United States government in general, has been given personal security around the clock in the form of at least one Secret Service or Executive Protective Service agent. From the moment you leave this room you will be accompanied twenty-four hours a day by armed agents trained to protect you and lay down their lives to do so if it should come to that, God forbid."

Bombin' Bob Gridding turned to the President. "May I ask a question, sir?" The President nodded. "What specific information do you have concerning this hit squad? Do you know who they are or where they are?"

"Glen Gasher has the FBI staked out at every port of entry in the country. He has been working with the CIA to track down these armed assassins. So far, our intelligence sources have identified seven men: five Libyans, one Iranian, and one Cuban. We believe they are traveling separately under false names and identifications and are entering the United States from Canada and Mexico. Unfortunately, we have good reason to believe that they may already have entered the country. They probably did so prior to the Egyptian assassination, knowing that afterwards we would tighten our security. As we learn of their whereabouts, we will inform the President. It will be up to him to decide who, if anyone, should know their whereabouts. But, I assure you, we have taken every precaution to protect you and your families."

Stone sat back, closing the folder in front of him. He could feel Billings's icy stare, but did not acknowledge it. Bradley took over from there, explaining that the CIA had been watching covert operations in Egypt for a long time, but had no hard evidence that any attempt would be made on President Khousoum's life the day of the parade.

When he had finished speaking, the President wound up the meeting by urging them to get out and sell the American people on the need for APANS. "We must have this agreement for national security and for stability in the Middle East — at all costs."

Billings stood and left the room directly behind the President, Marshall's final words echoing in his ears. "At all costs." What price is there left for us to pay, he thought. And what price will we pay before it's over?

Tucson

D.J. rode with Elaine to the airport for her flight to New York and on the way home asked Rodney to drive him out to the desert. Parker rode in the front with Rodney; two other agents followed in a station wagon. They drove off the main highway and followed a dirt road to the base of a hill, which overlooked the city on one side and the vast desert on the other. D.J. got out and trudged slowly to the top of the hill. The Valium he had been taking since they received word of Terry's death made the climb seem more difficult than it normally would have. Parker leaned against the black limousine and watched his charge make an unsteady ascent. Rodney sat in the car and smoked.

On top of the hill, D.J. plopped down in the dirt and tried to weep, but couldn't. He hadn't been able to cry at all. He stared at the ground. It meant nothing to him. He looked out over the desert. The sky was azure behind him and orange in front of him as the sun eased itself down into the earth. These colors evoked no feelings in him, not even an aesthetic appreciation. He knew that partly it must be the drug, but mostly it was his sense of estrangement. He felt separate from anything living, anything of beauty or endurance. Halfway down the hill, a jackrabbit scurried from behind a cactus and scampered off in the distance. He felt no part of the planet beneath him, no kinship with a world he now felt himself trapped in.

He tried to find the rabbit in the distance, but couldn't. It's gone, he thought, out of my sight forever. Like Terry. The irrevocable finality of Terry's death now presented itself clearly to him, like the disappearance of that tiny rabbit — gone forever — and at last he wept, realizing as he sobbed there alone in the desert that he was also feeling a little guilty for his feelings toward Parker. But he couldn't deal with that now. He was rational enough to know that his feelings — for Parker or anyone or anything else — had nothing to do with Terry's death. But he was feeling just a little remorseful about allowing himself to want Parker. Later, he would realize that it was not only lust that drove him toward Parker, but a genuine attraction to his basic character.

When Parker came into the bedroom to say good night and see if there was anything he wanted before turning out the light, D.J. asked him to sit down on the bed. Parker eased himself down next to D.J.

"I'm sorry, D.J.," he said. "I wish there was something I could do, but there isn't."

"Yes, there is," D.J. said. "Help me find out the truth about what happened."

"The truth?" Parker said. "What do you mean?"

"I mean help me find out what really happened to Terry and Richard."

Parker scooted further onto the bed, making himself comfortable for a longer visit than he had anticipated. "You don't believe what they're saying?"

"Parker, I believe Terry was on drugs. I believe Richard was on drugs. But more than that I can't believe. I've been manipulated so much in the past few years — both Terry and I — that I never believe anything they tell me."

"But the Sayville police—"

"Fuck the Sayville police. And the state police. Ultimately they all bow down to Billings and the rest of them. Exactly what was Richard Billings doing on Fire Island? And why would anyone want to murder either one of them? There hasn't been a murder on Fire Island in fifty years. You go to the island to get away from this crazy society we live in, not to kill people. It just doesn't happen there. What would the motive have been? Terry didn't have anything anybody wanted, for Christ's sake."

"Drugs," Parker offered, repeating the official theory.

"Never in a million lifetimes. If there was one thing I would stake my life on it's that Terry didn't have more than a hundred dollars' worth of drugs in the house. It was a big thing with him. Too many of his friends in high school got busted for dealing drugs, and he would never stash them. Not even when he got a real bargain. He was absolutely firm about that rule. And he never talked about having drugs or did them in public where people could see he had on him. One of his friends on Long Island nearly died getting mugged for cocaine once after they had been handing it out at a party in the Hamptons. It just doesn't wash, Parker."

"Then why?" Parker asked.

"I just don't know ... unless someone wanted..."

"Unless what?"

"I don't know," D.J. said, turning over on his side away from the agent. Parker pulled him back to face him.

"Unless what, D.J.?" he persisted. D.J. looked at him vacantly.

"You don't trust me now, do you?" Parker asked, looking hurt.

"I don't know who to trust anymore. Let's just wait and see what happens," D.J. said. "Please turn out the light."

New York City

Rachael Billings had agreed to have her son Richard's funeral service on Long Island, where her brother and his family lived. Her aged mother lived there with them, and since the only other family she had was Rebecca, she saw no sense in having the service in Arizona, even though the family plot was there. After the funeral, she would accompany the body back to Phoenix for burial.

Elaine went to New York to be there the day of Terry's funeral, even though the White House wouldn't let her attend. She felt that someone should be there for D.J., since it was out of the question that he attend, and even though she couldn't go to the service itself, she might be able to sneak out to the cemetery on Long Island later and lay some flowers. She liked Terry, to the little extent she knew him, and always felt a kind of kinship of spirit with him, as they both had to give up D.J. to the other for long periods of time.

Rather than open up their apartment in the Village, she was staying with Phil and Jessica, who were going to attend the funeral. She lay now in bed running over the conversation the three of them had when she arrived a little after midnight. Phil told her about the phone call he had received from Terry and how terrible he felt that he hadn't taken him seriously. He had tried once to contact D.J. about it, but there was no answer at the house. Later, with the frenzy at work in preparation for the convention, he simply forgot. He admitted to Elaine that at the time he had thought Terry was probably on drugs or in one of his depressions over being away from D.J. Also, he thought that Terry had only assumed that the Stones he called were related to Billings. Now he was deeply disturbed about his cavalier attitude. Jessica confided to her that Phil had wept bitterly when they received word of the murder, that he was blaming himself for it and was virtually inconsolable.

There was more.

On Tuesday evening, they had a surprise visit from True, who was in a state of near hysteria, as only True could be when the world served up a heaping portion of reality. When they got him calmed down, he confessed what he dared not tell anyone else. Early Monday morning, as the Memorial Day tea dance at the Pavilion was winding down, he noticed that the man whom he had tried to put the make on coming over on the ferry was leaving the Pavilion alone. High on acid and unattached for the evening, he left the dance floor and followed him, thinking that maybe there was a chance they could get together. The man had approached him earlier that night asking for downs, so True assumed he was on some drug that had made him too high, which would make it all the easier for True to get him to acquiesce to a liaison, since both of them were apparently going home single.

True, being a summer regular on the island, had no trouble following the man without being detected, even on his drugs, which were by that time wearing off. The intricate pathways of the Meat Rack were as familiar to him after five summers on the island as his own neighborhood in Manhattan. He followed his prey to the Grove and saw him enter the house next to the Belvedere. He figured that the guy had not been able to get a room in the hotel after all, but had met someone who had agreed to put him up for the weekend. After all, with a body like his it wouldn't be difficult to find a weekend husband on Fire Island, even over Memorial Day weekend, when space was at a premium.

Seldom discouraged, True decided that if he wasn't going to get to dive into that sea of flesh himself, at least he could arrange for a show, so he went around the house to the wooden fence that separated it from the hotel and climbed up on the roof. He walked back and forth on the roof as quietly as he could until he found a skylight that afforded a view. It turned out to be the one in the bathroom, where someone was taking a shower. He had no sooner settled himself down on the green shingled roof, when Frank entered the bathroom and shut the door. At first, it was difficult to see anything, because the room was filled with steam, but eventually the shower was turned off and the steam cleared, rising mostly through the poorly insulated skylight.

The first thing he could make out clearly was Frank backing somebody up against the wall next to the shower. Then he hauled off and hit him in the face. True couldn't tell whether it was serious or if they were playing some kind of rough sex game. He saw the smaller fellow fall into the tub and then watched Frank pick him up and shake him and drop him back down, but he still couldn't tell if they were serious or not, because Frank then opened his pants and urinated on the guy in the tub.

Suddenly, Frank reeled around as someone else came into view. There was a struggle, and Frank had the new guy by the throat. True jumped back for a moment, trying to decide if there was any chance he could run for help, but realized that by the time he found someone coherent enough to be of real help it would be too late. He was also afraid that Frank might hear him and come after him, too. The next time True peered through the skylight, there were two people in the tub and Frank was rifling through a leather shaving kit. When he was finished in the bathroom, he ransacked the place as though he were looking for something. He went from room to room, tearing the place apart. True stayed put. He lay there until he heard the front door close and footsteps on the wooden walkway that led to the gate. He remained on the roof beneath the rising sun for over an hour, praying that Frank hadn't seen him and that when he finally climbed down, the massive beauty he had so feverishly sought all weekend wouldn't be waiting for him between the fence and the house.

True went immediately to the phone booth at the ferry slip and reported the incident to the police in Sayville, but when they asked who he was, he slammed the receiver down. It was a reaction he was later glad of, when he found out who was living in that house. He knew they would be hard pressed to find someone to pin it on fast, and he was, of course, the most likely suspect, even though he couldn't have possibly overpowered Richard and strangled him to death.

"I don't follow you," Elaine said, confused. "Why would they try to pin it on just anyone? Why wouldn't they look for the person who actually did it?"

"Because," Phil answered gravely, "it wasn't what they're saying. There couldn't have been enough drugs in that house for someone to murder two people for, and what drugs they had were left behind. Wouldn't it be much more likely for them to guess it was some sort of bizarre sex maniac? I mean with the urine they must have found on the bodies?"

Elaine grimaced at these sordid details. "Not with the house ransacked like that. He must have been looking for something."

"Yes, but not drugs," Phil said.

"What, then?"

"What if that person was looking for the only piece of evidence that would link him or someone he knew with the murder?" Phil asked.

"Like what?"

"Like that phone number Terry found. Carl Stone's phone number."

Elaine felt the color drain out of her face and fell back in her chair. "I can't believe that. They play rough sometimes, but not that rough. Not with Terry. There's no reason."

"Maybe they thought there was. Maybe they thought Terry was getting out of hand again, talking too much, or trying to leave the island. Maybe when he called Stone's house, they figured the jig was up and they had better send someone to find out what was going on up there," Phil posited.

"But they wouldn't have to kill him, for God's sake," Elaine protested.

"Maybe this bruiser didn't mean to kill him. True said he hit Terry hard across the face and Terry fell into the tub. Maybe he hit his head too hard. Maybe when the guy picked him up, he was trying to revive him. I don't know. All I know is that they sent someone to do something, and now Terry is dead and so is Richard Billings. I want to find out who it was, and who sent him," Phil said. From the way he said it, Elaine could tell that he felt it was a way of expiating himself for not getting Terry's message to D.J.

"But what makes you so sure someone sent him? How do you know?" Elaine asked.

Jessica answered. "There's something the police don't know or aren't telling. Perhaps True is the only one who does know. True and Steffan, that is. The first thing they noticed when they saw the guy on the ferry slip in Sayville was that his hair was dyed."

"His hair was dyed? Are they sure?" Elaine asked.

"They're sure," Jessica answered. "You can't fool a queen like Steffan when it comes to hair color. He spotted it right away."

"And that means one thing to me," Phil chimed in. "Whoever he was, he came disguised, and on Fire Island, that's the last thing anyone would have to worry about. There's only one reason for being on the island, and if someone sees you, it doesn't matter, because you'd both be there for the same reason. Unless one of you was there to commit a murder, or at least make trouble. It was murder all right, and I think when we find out who it was, that person will be very close to 1600 Pennsylvania Avenue."

It was after that that they laid the plan.

Elaine lay in bed now thinking of what she had to do that morning. She felt sick about it. Not so much that she had to attend a funeral, but that the funeral she had to attend wouldn't be Terry's. She got out of bed, still tired from the flight and from staying up half the night piecing this puzzle together. When she walked into the living room, Phil was on the floor with dozens of photos and clippings spread out all around him and Jessica was in the kitchen.

"How about some coffee?" Elaine called to Jessica.

"I was just bringing you some," Jessica said. She handed Elaine a bright blue mug and set another one down next to Phil. "Who's that?" Jessica asked, pointing to one of the photos from the *New York Times*.

"I wish I knew," Phil answered, sipping his coffee. "Is this sugar or artificial sweetener?" He looked up at Jessica and grimaced.

"We're out of sugar," she confessed.

"God! Put some honey in here, will you?"

Jessica disappeared into the kitchen again and returned a minute later. She stood over him now, watching him sort the photos. "Who's the blond?" she asked.

"I don't know that one either." He looked over at Elaine, who was on the sofa reading the morning paper. "Elaine, maybe you could help me with some of these?"

"What is it?" she asked, coming over and sitting down on the floor next to Phil, trying not to step on the photos around him.

"It's the ID file so far. I've got just about everyone identified, but there are a few mysteries left. I thought maybe you would recognize some of them. Everyone in that pile over there is still unidentified," he said, pointing to a small stack of photos and clippings by her foot.

"First one's easy," she said. "Marge Smith."

"The wife of the secretary of defense?" Phil asked.

"Right."

"I should have known that one. I'm slipping."

She went through the small stack and identified all but one person for him. "I think it's Justice Winthrop's son, but it's just a guess. I really don't know for sure."

"That's all right, you've been a terrific help. I'll find out. Thanks."

As Elaine got up to return to the sofa, something caught her eye. "Phil, who is that woman?"

"Which one?"

"This one," she said, picking up a copy of *Time* magazine and holding it so he could see the couple in the picture. "This blonde with Miles Cameron."

"Oh, that's an old one all right. It's from when he worked for Bif Tucker in Sacramento. You really don't know who that is?"

"No, I don't. Who is it?"

"It's his wife. Or, to be more accurate, his former wife. They were divorced right after he left Tucker and went back to Los Angeles. She's a real looker, all right. Bet you never saw a woman with one blue and one gray eye."

Syosset, Long Island

The service for Richard Billings was held in Syosset, at a small church on the bay. It was a simple funeral with a short eulogy and very little music. Afterwards, the mourners filed out and waited on the steps until the casket was brought out and placed in the hearse. Since the body was to be put on a plane for Arizona, there was no funeral procession from the church. The few people who had come to pay their respects — mostly Rachael's family — stood passively on the sidewalk and watched as the hearse drove away.

Elaine stood alone and waited for Rachael and Thaddeus to finish talking. It appeared as though they were arguing, although there was no shouting. Rachael kept looking away from her husband and he kept taking her by the arm, trying to get her to face him. Finally, he stalked off and got into a limousine, which then drove away, leaving her alone in the midday sun. None of the relatives approached her as she began to walk away from the church toward the bay. Elaine caught up with her and took her arm.

Rachael pulled her close and held tight as the two of them walked around the side of the church and across the lawn and stood looking out over Oyster Bay.

"D.J. and I want you to know how deeply sad we are, Mrs. Billings," Elaine said. Rachael wiped at her tears with one of her black gloves, tossed her head back, and breathed deeply. "D.J. asked me to tell you how much he wanted to be here, but the Secret Service wouldn't allow him to leave Tucson. I know how close he and Richard were when they were growing up in Arizona. He felt very bad when he heard the news."

"Thank you, dear, and thank D.J. for me, too," Rachael said, leading Elaine to a wrought-iron bench that looked out over the water. They sat down in the shade of a willow tree and Rachael took out a cigarette, offered one to Elaine, who declined, then lit it and inhaled deeply. "D.J. has his own mourning to do today, though," she said without looking at Elaine.

Elaine said nothing, noticing for the first time how striking this woman was and thinking what a beauty she must have been at one time, before the alcohol, before the loneliness. Rachael's naturally blonde hair was streaked with silver. She wore it pulled back from her face, a tortoiseshell comb holding it where it gathered behind her head. She had taken off the small black hat and veil she had worn inside the church, but she kept the sunglasses on. Her eyes roamed the water and the shore beyond as she spoke. The fragrance of lilacs was strong in the air.

"I was thinking of D.J. during the service. I felt sad for him. I thought, At least I am allowed to bury my loved one. He can't even have that simple solace." She turned now and looked at Elaine.

"You know about him and Terry, then?"

"Of course," Rachael said with a terse, sardonic chuckle. "These men who run and ruin our lives think they keep their secrets so well. They're fools. I look at them sometimes with their petty, egotistical little games and they remind me of children playing cops and robbers, so caught up in their own imaginings, their own desire to deceive and outwit one another. The only difference is that when they're called for supper, they don't come home. And when they shoot someone, the person really does lie down and die. Like my Richard."

Elaine squeezed her hand. "Did you know Richard was with Terry?"

"Yes. But Thaddeus didn't know I knew."

"He didn't?"

"He didn't know himself," Rachael said, stubbing out her half-smoked cigarette on the lawn.

"He didn't know? Then how did...?"

"Oh, my dear, we wives know so much more than they think we know. I spoke to Richard less than two weeks ago. He came to see me late one night, while Thad was at the office."

"He came to your home?"

"Yes, he was on his way here, to New York. He had a job to do for his uncle and—"

"For your brother here in Syosset?"

"No, no. For Carl."

"For Carl? I don't understand. How could he have a job to do for Carl without Thaddeus knowing?"

"Games, child, power games. Carl and Thaddeus have a long-standing rivalry. They really hate each other, always have. It's made it very difficult for Rebecca and me for many years. Anytime one of them has a chance to put something over on the other one or to make the other look bad, he jumps at it.

"Carl knew that Richard and Thaddeus hadn't spoken in years, so when Richard came to Carl down and out, he took the opportunity to rub it in Thad's face. Without him knowing it, of course. I'm sure he was just waiting for the right moment to tell Thad he had seen Richard and had helped him out of a jam. I tried to tell Thaddeus that Richard had been home, but he told me I was drunk. He was right. I was drunk when Richard came to see me, but nevertheless, he was there. I did talk with him."

"And he told you he was working for Carl?" Elaine asked.

"Yes, he was coming to New York to do a job for Carl. Of course, at the time, I had no idea it was to watch Terry."

"What makes you think he was watching him?"

"He told me later. He called me from the island a few days later when he knew Thaddeus would be at the office. He called me a couple of times, as a matter of fact. He was a sweet boy. He would have been closer with me if Thaddeus hadn't been there or hadn't been so stubborn. They just couldn't be around each other without having terrible fights."

"What did he say when he talked to you? Did he say anything that might have indicated there was trouble?"

"Not this kind of trouble, no. But I was worried about him. Richard was a very troubled young man and..." Rachael placed her hand on top of Elaine's to emphasize what she was going to say next. "You see, Richard wasn't gay. Don't misunderstand me, dear, I'm not being defensive. In fact, I probably would have preferred it. Wives of politicians secretly want their sons to be gay, I think, so they'll have a man around the house and get some of the attention they crave. But Richard wasn't gay, and that worried me, because Richard at one time had a drug problem and I knew that if he were spending the summer on Fire Island he was going to get bored and when Richard gets bored he turns — turned — to drugs."

"So you think the police were right, then? This was a drug-related crime?"

"No, this was no drug-related crime. Of that I'm quite sure," Rachael said emphatically.

"How do you know that?" Elaine asked, her curiosity growing along with her respect for this woman.

"Because Richard never lied to me. I asked him the second time he phoned how many drugs he was doing, and he said I shouldn't worry, that all they had was pot and quaaludes, and these were being sent to them to keep Terry placated and subdued. They were arriving through the mail in small quantities, so there was no way to overdose on anything and there was nothing hard enough to overdose on anyway. He even told me that Terry had a little LSD he was planning to take for Memorial Day, but that Richard wasn't taking it, because he couldn't handle it anymore, and besides, he had to keep an eye on Terry. So they weren't going around with large amounts of drugs for anyone to notice. No, it wasn't anything to do with drugs, Elaine," she said, looking far off across the water. A sailboat with a bright red, white, and blue sail leaned into the wind coming off the ocean.

"Then what was it?"

"I'm not sure, but I do know it had to do with Carl. Thad didn't know anything about Richard being with Terry, and he didn't know anything about Thunder, so I'm sure Thad wasn't involved. He's a stupid man, but he's not mean. He's just naive about some things."

"What's Thunder?" Elaine asked.

"It was some covert operation going on in the Mideast that Thad and Carl had argued about. All I know is that Thaddeus was opposed to it, whatever it was, and Carl was pushing for it. The only reason I know about it is because my sister and I — with nothing better to do — pieced together scraps of information we each had. These men, you see, never think twice about talking in front of their airheaded wives. What harm can a woman do? Honey, I could tell you things that would make your hair curl. Do you know who one of the major stockholders of Fairbanks Aviation is?"

Elaine shook her head, her eyes growing wider with the wealth of information this seemingly demure woman possessed.

"Hah!" Rachael threw her head back and laughed loudly. "Claudia Marshall. But it's not in her name. Look up the name of Billy Dailey in the stockholders billet. It's all in his name, but it's her money. Something called a revocable trust or an irrevocable trust. I don't know for sure. But it's her money all right. You see, she's still just a little girl who's afraid of being poor again. It's a farce," she said bitterly. "This whole government is a disgrace. No different from any other administration, but that doesn't make it any more palatable." She reached into her purse and pulled out a leather-covered flask. She offered it to Elaine, who shook her head politely. "By the time you're my age, you'll be carrying one of these," she said, taking a swig of the contents, "if you don't get out soon enough. I'm getting out, though. Starting today."

"What do you mean?" Elaine asked.

"I'm taking Richard back to Phoenix, and I'm staying there. I'm filing for a divorce. That's just between you and me, honey. At least for a week or so, till it hits the newspapers. I've had it, and I want out. I've lost my son, and my daughter's living in another world as far as I'm concerned, so I'm going to go have a good time with the few years I have left. The hell with all of them."

She took Elaine's hand and squeezed it tight. "I'm telling you all of this because it's not too late for you. You can still get out. I don't know exactly what your relationship is like with D.J., but you must love him a lot or you wouldn't put up with so much crap. Don't let it go on too long, Elaine. Get out while you still can. They'll devour you if you're not careful."

"Mrs. Billings...," Elaine began.

"Please, honey. Rachael, Rachael," she said, patting her hand affectionately.

"Rachael," Elaine said, flattered. "About the stock you mentioned. How do you know that for sure?"

Rachael sighed and played with her purse. "Several years ago, in a moment of rage and jealousy, Claudia Marshall did something quite irresponsible that put her in Carl Stone's clutches. Her best friend, Fran Altman, was in an embarrassing situation, one that eventually would have placed Claudia and Donald Marshall's futures in jeopardy. In order to avoid this, she—"

"Mrs. Billings?" It was a Secret Service agent. "We're running a bit late."

"Yes," Rachael said, "we're coming."

The two of them got up and finished their conversation as they walked back to where the limousines were waiting, one to take Elaine back into Manhattan and one to take

Rachael Billings to her new life. Elaine walked her to the car and the two of them embraced.

"Thank you for confiding in me," Elaine said. "I promise to be discreet, but I'm going to find out who killed them, Mrs. ... Rachael. I have friends who will help me, and I'm not going to rest until whoever did it is caught."

Rachael hugged her again. "Save *yourself*, child," Rachael whispered in her ear, then disappeared into the dark interior of the black car.

Elaine watched the limousine as it made its way down the little lane the church was situated on. Lilac bushes lined the way on both sides and their heavy, fragrant flowers bowed in the breeze the car made as it passed.

Suddenly, Elaine felt unsafe with her new knowledge. At that moment, as she watched the limousine carrying Rachael Billings turn onto the main road and pick up speed, she vowed that she could not allow herself to be left alone again. She must always have people around her. People she could trust. If only she knew which ones they were.

Somewhere over Arizona

"You simply have to rise up out of your own grief and attend to a higher need," Claudia said, concluding this part of her speech to D.J. and pausing for a few moments to sip her coffee and let what she had just said sink in.

They had been off the ground for less than forty minutes. D.J., under sedatives for several days now, tried to think about what his mother was saying. He had been roused from his sedated sleep a little before noon and told that he was to be ready to leave by one forty-five to meet Air Force One; he was being sent to California to help with the upcoming primaries. The latest polls showed Marshall losing ground to Tucker, and D.J. was told that his presence could help keep the President from losing California's sizeable delegate vote. The real reason, of course, was to get his mind off Terry.

"When Grandma Wentworth died just before the first campaign," Claudia continued, brushing some spilled sugar granules from her lap, "I thought I couldn't possibly be any use to your father. Our schedule was absolutely horrendous those first three months, but what I found out after I started traveling was that the campaign was a godsend. I had so much to do, so many people to meet with, so many appearances to make for your father's sake that soon I was carrying on a normal life again. If I hadn't had to do that, I probably would have sat around the ranch and moped and become terribly depressed. I may never have gotten out of it. It was the hectic bustle of the campaign that helped me get myself together. I'm sure it's the best thing for you. You'll see."

D.J. looked at her through a fog, as though some stranger had been sent to counsel him, to recruit him for this meaningless task. She was now giving him a smile, her eyebrows arched, her eyes waiting for an answer, as though he might say, "Gosh, Mom, you're probably right. Where do I start?"

"Who killed my lover?" he asked instead. Claudia flinched at the word.

"The police are doing everything they can, Donald." The use of his first name was supposed to warn him to change the tone of his remarks. "As soon as there's any kind of clue, you'll be the first to know. We're just as upset as you are about this. Your father—"

"My father can do one thing for me now. He can use his power to find the killer. That's all I'm interested in."

"And he will, darling. That's why he needs you now so very much. If he doesn't win re-election, he won't have the authority he needs to accomplish even that."

Parker approached and handed D.J. a manila folder. Inside were photos of several shabby-looking men and biographical data on them.

Claudia let D.J. leaf through them before she began. "Those men you're looking at have been sent to this country to assassinate your father and every other high-ranking government official in his administration. The CIA believes they are already in the country. Do you understand, D.J.? Someone is out there ready and trying to kill your father."

"The way someone killed Terry," he said tersely, closing the folder and setting it on the seat next to him.

"There's been enough killing," Claudia said, raising her voice just a little, distraught now at the thought of her husband being gunned down the way John Kennedy was gunned down and continued to be gunned down in her frequent dreams of that event. "And enough talk about killing. Please, Donald, if you love your father at all, help him now."

"Of course I love my father, but I don't want everyone to forget about what happened to Terry and Richard. There are two people dead, and I want to know why. I have to know why, and I'm going to find out, even if I have to do it alone."

Washington, D.C.

Bif Tucker took the envelope from the messenger, closed the front door, and made his way through the hallway, which was filled with campaign aides scurrying about. He stood in the living room, where three television sets had been installed several months before, before the very first primaries. He listened as the anchorman announced the latest tallies. There was a lot of shushing around the room as campaign supporters poised their pencils and clipboards.

"We now have a prediction for the state of Pennsylvania. With 63 percent of the precincts in, the votes line up this way: Tucker 1,633,121; Marshall 1,590,437. The winner in Pennsylvania when all the votes are counted will be Bif Tucker."

A loud whoop went up from the crowd. There was a lot of handshaking and congratulating. Ohio had already fallen into his column earlier in the evening. "Hey, Mr. President," someone shouted over the din.

"Not by a long shot," Bif shouted back, smiling in spite of himself. "We—"

"Shh, quiet! He's running down the other two now."

A young curly-haired woman turned up the volume of one set and turned down the other two. "In Texas, as predicted, the President is far out in the lead, with 1,876,900 votes against Tucker's 1,299,566. A clear victory for Marshall there. And in Florida, also as predicted, the President is carrying the state by a large margin. The count at this moment in Florida is 1,812,000 for the President and 1,000,390 for Governor Markham, running as a favorite-son candidate. Tucker is running third in Florida with 534,111 votes."

The crowd was quiet with this latest announcement and began milling about now, comparing notes and talking about which precincts in Pennsylvania were still out and if there was any chance of an upset there. Tucker patted his workers on the back and smiled as he made his way through the room and went into his study and closed the door.

He sat the large envelope on his desk and pulled up his chair. There was no return address, only a receipt taped to the front. It had a seven-digit number followed by two letters printed in red. Beneath that was printed "Central Delivery." The delivery boy hadn't been mysterious, but told him that he had no idea who sent it, that he was just paid to deliver, and that he hoped he won the nomination and could he have his autograph as well as his signature in the receipt book.

Tucker slit open the envelope and pulled out a half dozen eight-by-ten photographs and a ninety-minute cassette tape. He looked at the photos only fleetingly, then placed them back in the package along with the tape, and locked them in the top desk drawer. He took a deep breath and let it out slowly, then walked across the study to a cabinet that contained several bottles of liquor. He poured himself a straight whiskey, downed it, poured another, and began pacing the room.

He knew his sexual relationship with Jenny had left a lot to be desired over the past couple of years, but it had never occurred to him that she would sleep around, let alone get herself into a mess like this. More accurately, get him into a mess like this. Whoever it was would want money and a lot of it, and it wouldn't stop there. In a position of power such as Tucker held, there was always the possibility that these were foreign agents. How could she be so stupid?

The phone rang, but he let someone in the other room answer it. He would have to seek out someone he trusted to get the best legal and political advice. He checked the drawer again to make sure it was locked, then as he started for the door, someone knocked. It was one of his office staff, a young girl with red hair, who had dropped out of the University of Minnesota to work with his campaign.

"The phone is for you. He wouldn't say who it was, but said it was urgent."

"I'll take it in here," Bif said and closed the door.

"Hello."

"The tape is even better than the pictures, Senator," the voice said.

"How much do you want?" Tucker asked.

"Not a cent. You're going to need your money for your retirement."

"What is it you want from me? Who is this?" Tucker asked, his voice betraying him now as the gravity of the situation began settling in on him.

"An old friend, Bif. Tell you what. After you withdraw from the race, I'm going to let you finish out your term in the Senate. For old times' sake. As a sort of consolation prize."

"Cameron! Is that you? What the hell? Are you crazy? Is that you, Miles?"

"You have one week to drop out. One week exactly."

The White House

Gerald Baker, the senior senator from Ohio, led the group of six senators who emerged from the White House. He went straight to the crowd of reporters, the other men following and forming a semicircle around him. Senator Baker spoke.

"We have just come from a private meeting with the President on the very sensitive APANS issue that this country is facing. We asked for this meeting this morning in order to give the President a chance to share with us any information he might have that would affect the outcome of our votes next week on the bill before the Senate to sell this sensitive military hardware to the Sudan.

"I am pleased to tell you that the meeting was both cordial and profitable for both sides. As you know, the Senate has been extremely concerned about security in the Middle East since the tragic and barbarous murder of President Khousoum. President Marshall graciously agreed to share with us some of the classified intelligence he has been receiving about the situation in that part of the world.

"This is not a partisan issue. World peace can never become a political football. After meeting with President Marshall, Senators Wentworth, Jackson, Barnes, Cavoli, and I have decided to support the President and vote for the passage of the bill before the Senate committee. We will send the bill to the Senate floor tomorrow with full recommendation that it be passed unanimously as soon as possible.

"Speaking for myself, I can only say that I fear the country is on the brink of crisis due to the terrorist activities of the ruthless barbarians who are at the helm of the Libyan government. If we are to prevent armed conflict in the Middle East, and perhaps a nuclear war, we must move quickly to assist the smaller nations in that area of the world in protecting themselves from the threat of terrorism and communism.

"At this very moment, there are foreign agents somewhere in this country attempting to assassinate every influential leader of our government. The President assures us that everything possible is being done to track down these madmen and stop this evil plot. I myself intend to give President Marshall my full support in his efforts. This is no time for the leaders of our country to divide along party lines. I urge every American citizen to support the President in this cause."

New York City

"Are you drunk?" Elaine asked into the telephone.

"No, I told you, I've been drinking, but I'm not drunk. It was a fund-raising banquet at Moscone Center, and wine is all the pinschers will let me have at these things. Even then, they test every bottle. It's embarrassing." D.J. was slurring his words, and the cadence of his speech was uneven. He was indeed drunk, and Elaine knew it.

"I've been frantic. Why won't they let me call you? Why did they rush you out there before I got back to Tucson? And why are they making me stay here in New York?" she asked, knowing D.J. didn't have the answers, but finally venting the frustration of several days of unsuccessfully trying to get someone at the White House to take her calls.

"I don't know. They want me to help Dad out here. He's in trouble in the polls again, especially after Pennsylvania and Ohio. Are you okay?"

"Yes, I'm fine physically, but emotionally I'm a wreck. They've doubled my pinschers, and I can't go anywhere. I'm staying here at Jessica's now, because they won't let me go back to our apartment. Do they really think some Muslim is going to try to shoot me? Why would they care about me, for Christ's sake?"

"They're out to shoot anybody they can, I guess. Have you been out to Cold Spring Harbor?" he asked, meaning the cemetery where Terry was buried.

"No, I told you, they won't let me leave this place unless it's an absolute necessity. Jessica and True went out yesterday and laid some flowers for you. They said it's really a beautiful little place right on the water. Very picturesque and peaceful."

"Great," D.J. said sardonically. Elaine could hear him taking a drink of something. "I'm sure he'll be very happy there," he added.

"I sent you something his brother gave Phil at the funeral. It's a little metal thing he had on a chain around his neck. His brother said he thought you might want it."

"I got it today," D.J. said, fingering the polished washer as he spoke. "Thank you."

"D.J., what do you know about Rachael Billings?"

"She's Thaddeus's wife."

Elaine could see it was going to be fruitless talking to him in this condition. "I mean, what is she like? Can she be trusted? Does she tell the truth?"

"Sure, as far as I know. At least, when she's not drinking. She has a little drinking problem," he said, crunching an ice cube in Elaine's ear.

"Is Parker around?" Elaine asked, trying to hold her temper.

"Yeah, he's in the living room. Why?"

"Let me talk to him for a minute."

There was a loud thud as the receiver hit the floor. Elaine heard D.J. say, "Oops," as he started to walk away. In a couple of minutes, Parker came on the line.

"Parker, what the hell is going on there? How did he get so drunk?"

"I don't know, it just crept up on him from not eating."

"Well, for Christ's sake, make him eat something," she scolded.

"That's not as easy as it sounds," Parker said. "He's pretty depressed. We're doing the best we can."

"Well, then, you and Rodney force-feed him. He has to eat. When he doesn't eat, he just gets more depressed. Please."

"I'll try," he promised.

"How can I get in touch with you?" she asked.

"You can't. We have to call you, and it has to be cleared."

That told Elaine their conversation was being monitored. "Oh. Well, try to call a little more often, will you? It would be nice to talk with my husband more than once a week."

There was silence, then D.J. came back on. He was weepy. "Elaine, I miss him. I think I'm losing my—" The line went dead. Elaine tried to get the connection back. She even called back the hotel switchboard operator, but to no avail. She gave up and went out to the living room, where Phil and Jessica were curled up on the sofa.

"Well?" Jessica said.

"Did you learn anything?" Phil asked, setting a glass of wine down on the glass-topped coffee table in front of the sofa. Elaine sat up now, and Phil put his legs across her lap.

"He's drunker than a sailor, and we got cut off. They're tapping the calls," Elaine said with disgust. She poured herself some wine from the bottle on the table.

"Did you get to ask him anything at all?" Phil pressed.

"Not really. He said Rachael was okay when she wasn't drinking."

"She wasn't drinking at the funeral," Jessica observed.

"She had a flask," Elaine reminded them, "but she wasn't drunk. I'm worried. This is too out of control. I mean if they can't even keep D.J. from getting drunk, for Christ's sake. What good is he to them if he's going around to all these political shindigs half-corked? I don't like it. He's too depressed." Elaine ran her fingers absently through her hair, and her eyes filled with tears.

"Honey, things'll work out," Jessica said, trying to re-assure her. "At least he's safe with all those pinschers, and the convention is less than two weeks away. Soon, it'll all be over."

"But what about Terry and Richard?" Elaine protested, almost shouting, and causing both Phil and Jessica to start slightly. "Who the hell is going to do anything about that? Goddamn it, they can't get away with it. Someone has got to avenge them. It's not right, it's not right..." Elaine began to cry. "They're dead and nobody is doing anything about it," she said, weeping as she spoke.

Phil came over to her and put his arms around her. "We have to be patient, Elaine. Sooner or later, somebody will slip, and when he does, we'll move. We're learning more all the time. If we just stay low and keep our eyes and ears open, we'll be able to get them. But we have to be patient."

Elaine looked up at him through her tears. "If they don't get us first."

McLean, Virginia

Carl Stone was waiting at the door when the small mint green car pulled into the drive. The black lettering on the door read: "Government Interagency Motor Pool. Official Use Only." He took the package from the driver without saying a word, went inside, and watched through the window until the car disappeared back onto the street. Then he proceeded to his study, locked the door, and flipped on the desk lamp. He opened the large brown envelope and took out a smaller white envelope. He slit that open and pulled out a tiny scrap of paper. It had two items written on it in pencil, one on each side. The first was Stone's private telephone number. The second confirmed what he had suspected when he made the call to New York just two weeks ago. It was the address of the Nevada State Penitentiary. He felt justified now. There could be no doubt that Richard and Billy had been in contact. He lit a match and burned the scrap of paper in the large brass ashtray on his desk. Then he unlocked the top desk drawer, reached into the back, and withdrew a green address book. He turned to the M's and ran his finger down the second column on the page: Michaels, Donald. Warden, NSP, Jean, NV.

San Francisco, California

The limousine turned onto Powell Street and made its way through a flank of blinking red and blue lights, stopping directly in front of the St. Francis Hotel. One of the two newly assigned agents leaped from the front door of the car and began talking on his two-way radio; the other sat behind the wheel assessing the street for the quickest possible escape route should it be necessary. Rodney, who had been in the station wagon directly behind the car, now held open the door as D.J., with some difficulty, emerged. Strobe lights flashed and video floods blinded the large crowd of gawkers as he stood for a moment, whispered something into Rodney's ear, and then stared at him. Rodney's eyes squinted and darkened in response to the comment. D.J. laughed and headed for the hotel door. On the third step, he stumbled and went down on one knee. The crowd gasped and the strobes began flashing again, this time relentlessly, until Parker, now by his side, helped him up and rushed him into the lobby.

The elevator was waiting for them, but D.J. made a quick side step, and before anyone knew it, he was talking to one of the young bellhops, a dark-haired fellow with a mustache. Parker grabbed D.J.'s arm and pulled him away toward the elevator, leaving the bellboy wide-eyed and blushing. D.J. winked back at the young man as the elevator doors closed.

Once inside the suite, D.J. went into the bedroom and closed the door. Parker walked through the other three rooms, making his own search of the place even though he knew the two agents who had exited upon their arrival had gone over it thoroughly. He didn't like trusting his security to others the way others had to trust theirs to him. He stood in the middle of the living room loosening his tie when he noticed the bedroom door was closed. There was a split second of recognition before he bolted for the door. Inside, D.J. was lying on the bed, his shirt, shoes, and socks already off, the telephone receiver in his hand. Parker grabbed the phone away from him, jerked the cord out of the wall, and heaved it across the room in a fit of rage.

"What the hell is the matter with you — besides the fact that you're dead drunk again?" he asked D.J. through clenched teeth. D.J. rolled over on his stomach and buried his head in the pillows. "Leave me alone," he said, the words being lost in the pillows.

"I won't have a repeat of last night," Parker said. "Do you understand?"

"Go away," D.J. moaned.

"Come on, I'll help you get into bed," Parker said, lifting D.J. effortlessly and turning him over to unbuckle his belt. D.J. lay limp as Parker unzipped his trousers and pulled them off. The agent folded them, found a hanger in the closet, spied the suit jacket thrown on the floor in a corner, and hung that over the trousers. He hung the suit in the closet and set D.J.'s shoes outside the door in the hallway for polishing. When he came back into the bedroom, D.J. was still lying limp on the bed, his right arm twisted unnaturally beneath him. He looked like a corpse.

"Let's get under the covers," Parker said, tugging at the queen-sized down comforter that covered the bed. D.J. rolled over onto his stomach, and muffled words came out. Parker leaned over him, supporting himself with a hand on either side of his charge's naked body, and leaned down, his tie playing on D.J.'s back. "What?" he asked.

"Make love to me, Parker," he said, arching his back so that his butt pressed against Parker's precariously balanced torso.

"Come on," Parker said, lifting D.J. with one arm and pulling back the covers with his free hand, "let's get into bed."

"Only if you'll get in with me," D.J. answered, bending his legs and sliding them under the sheets. "Please? I'm lonely and you're the only..."

Parker was standing over him now, the temptation of it clearly visible on his face. Then, "You've got to pull yourself together, D.J. You've got to stop this awful behavior. You're getting completely unmanageable. No more drinking."

"No more drinking? That's all I have. I can't eat any food, because it might be poisoned. I can't go for a walk, because some crazed Libyan might be sitting in a tree in Union Square waiting to pump a bullet into my gut. I can't make any telephone calls because—"

"Because the calls you've been trying to make are not the kind of calls we want to read about in the newspapers." He pushed D.J. over and sat down on the bed. "Like the picture we're going to see on the front page tomorrow morning of you falling down the hotel steps."

"So what?" D.J. said petulantly and turned onto his side, placing his hand on Parker's leg. "Everyone stumbles once in a while."

"Not three times in three days. Not even Gerald Ford," Parker said and couldn't help smiling a little in spite of his anger about D.J.'s behavior, anger not only about the bad press and the possible repercussions it could have on Parker himself for not keeping D.J. in tow, but also because he was worried about what D.J. was going through psychologically. This depression had been unyielding since their arrival in California.

D.J. raised his arm, resting his elbow on Parker's thigh while his hand rubbed his chest, lingering as it passed over his left nipple. Parker made no move to stop him. "I feel so alone, Parker. It's bad enough to lose Terry," he said, choking a little as his eyes filled with tears, "but not to have anyone else to turn to afterward ... no family ... no close friends. You're my closest friend, I think." He chuckled. "Funny, when you think about it. About how Terry and I used to tease you so badly and how angry you used to get. I thought for sure you hated us and would ask for another assignment."

Parker smiled. He could feel himself hardening as D.J. continued to play with his chest. "I almost did."

"And now, you're the best friend I have. Besides Elaine, of course, who's a million miles away. Please sleep with me tonight, Parker. Just this once. Let me hold on to you. I promise I won't try to have sex. I'm too drunk anyway."

"You know that's not possible," Parker said, his voice cracking. He looked down and saw that his sexual arousal had produced a noticeable wet spot on his trousers. "I really have to go. I have reports to write." He patted D.J. on the cheek. "Sleep tight, soldier."

Parker turned out the light and went into the living room, closing the door quietly behind him. Rodney was standing in the middle of the room staring at Parker's crotch. Parker didn't have to look down to know what he was seeing, and he flushed with embarrassment as he moved quickly to the desk and sat down.

"How is our little problem?" Rodney asked, a nervous edge in his voice. He stood with one hand in his pocket, jingling a set of keys.

Parker pulled a sheath of papers from a briefcase on the desk and opened a folder that contained his daily log. "He's going to sleep."

"Are you sure? That's what we thought last night," Rodney said snidely, beginning to pace the length of the room, the keys jingling within his pocket.

"I'm sure. He'll be okay."

"Are you sure he doesn't have another room-service boy in there tonight? Did you look under the bed?"

"Lay off, Rod," Parker said. "Besides, we'll be out of here tomorrow night."

"You really like him, don't you? You two have a little thing going, don't you?" Rodney asked. Parker detected nothing menacing in Rodney's tone of voice. Rodney was clever enough to make this sound like it could be nothing more than teasing, but Parker knew him well enough to know he was agitated.

"What's the matter with you tonight? You've been jumpy all evening. Are you taking your pills?"

"What pills?" Rodney shouted.

"Whatever those damned pills are you're always popping. Maybe you need one ... or a drink. Jesus, I've never seen you so nervous." Parker began writing his report in longhand as he spoke, trying to sound removed from the conversation in the hope it would calm Rodney down.

"Those are just high-blood-pressure pills, I've told you, and...," Rodney began.

"Well, whatever they are, for Christ's sake, take one. You look like your blood pressure is through the roof."

"I just think he's acting like a fool. He's making our jobs twice as difficult as they have to be. He's being inconsiderate and careless, he's drinking too much and talking too much. He's making passes at the hotel staff..."

"What did he do to you this evening? Did he say something to you?" Parker asked, still writing.

"What difference does that make? He's always saying something to me. He hates me," Rodney said. He poured a glass of water from a pitcher on the bar and used it to swallow a pill, his back turned to Parker at the desk. Parker pretended not to notice.

"He doesn't hate you. He's been through a great deal, and he's having trouble handling it."

"He's a spoiled brat. He has everything a guy could want, and it's not enough," Rodney said, pacing again.

"The most important person in his life just died, for God's sake. He was murdered. Try to have a little compassion," Parker said, a little more emotional than he wanted to sound.

"You certainly seem to have a lot of compassion," Rodney answered, standing now with both hands in his pockets staring across the room at him. "How's that? Is there something you've been keeping from me, partner? Sweetie?"

Parker stopped writing and looked up at Rodney. His huge frame seemed almost to fill the room from where Parker sat. The buttons on his white dress shirt strained to keep the shirt fastened across his massive chest. Beneath the suit jacket, Parker knew that the white cotton fabric of the shirtsleeves were stretched just as tautly around his powerful arms. He didn't like to think about this man becoming violent. "Rodney, if you've grown dissatisfied with this assignment, you ought to ask for a replacement. You don't have to keep this detail if you're unhappy, you know."

"Are you going to suggest that to the boss? Are you getting ready to suggest I be replaced? Then the two of you could be alone. If I weren't around, you could be in there right now getting your rocks off." Rodney's eyes flared, and Parker could see that inside his trouser pockets his hands were forming into fists. Parker stood up to remind Rodney that he too was a powerful physical force to be reckoned with. Not as big as Rodney perhaps, but not small by any means.

"Rodney, I don't know what's eating at you tonight. I can only guess that at some point when I wasn't close by, the two of you had words. I know how antagonistic he can be when he's been drinking, but don't take it out on me. I'm doing the job I was assigned to do. It's not easy for me, either. Now, why don't you call it a night. You'll feel better in the morning, I'm sure."

"If he called you some of the things..." Rodney jumped as the telephone on the desk rang. He stared at it as though it were a bomb. "You'd better answer that," he said to Parker and took a couple steps backward.

Parker answered. The person on the other end of the line did all of the talking, and Parker sat back down and took notes. The call lasted about three minutes. Rodney poured himself a ginger ale and turned on the television, keeping the volume completely off. The eleven-o'clock news was just coming on, and the opening story was about the President's son being in town. The screen showed D.J. arriving at a dinner reception for him at the Mark Hopkins Hotel, then making a few remarks at the podium, then it cut to him pulling up to the hotel. The car door opened, and there he was getting out of the limo and pausing to whisper into Rodney's ear. The camera caught Rodney's glaring response as well as D.J.'s laughter, then it followed him up the steps and zoomed in when he fell. "The son of a bitch," Rodney muttered, then turned to Parker, who was hanging up the receiver.

Parker sat at the desk, staring blankly and not speaking. He looked ashen and confused. "What is it?" Rodney finally asked, coming toward the desk.

Parker looked up at him, then slouched back into the chair, and ran his hand through his hair. "I'm being ... reassigned," he said weakly.

"What?" Rodney said.

"They think the hit squad is in California, maybe right here in the city, and they're putting on three special agents. They're sending me to New York to replace somebody at the convention."

"Lucky you," Rodney said. "I wish they'd recall me."

"But they've already added two new guys out here. I thought *they* were supposed to be the experts. Why would they pull me off now? It doesn't make sense. There's no time to orient anyone to D.J. It's just crazy." Parker was staring blankly at the desk.

"They pull stuff like this all the time," Rodney offered disinterestedly. "That's why they drill all that stuff into you at the academy about never questioning your superiors. Security men are just well-trained dogs. When they say move, people are supposed to move. In a week, you'll be glad. This assignment is a bitch, anyway. It'll be easier at the convention. It's a piece of cake. You'll have the whole New York Police Department to back you up."

"I just don't get it," Parker said.

Rodney downed the last of his ginger ale and filled his mouth with an ice cube. "When do they want you back there?" he asked, trying to talk through the ice.

"Tomorrow," Parker said blankly. "Tomorrow evening."

Washington, D.C.

The old Senate Caucus Room was filled with reporters from every segment of the media. The back of the room was lined with television cameras, and technicians were making last-minute adjustments to the lights when Bif Tucker, his wife Jenny on his arm, strode into the room followed by a cortege of campaign advisors and Secret Service agents.

Bif went straight to the podium in front of the room. Jenny started to take a seat behind him, but he took hold of her arm and pulled her next to him. The grip on her belied the forced smile on both their faces, but no one other than the two of them and a single viewer watching this press conference on a television in a small office at the White House was aware of it.

"I have a brief statement," Tucker said. "There will be no questions afterward."

The crowd of reporters buzzed as they wrote. The lights from the back of the room blinded Jenny, and she rubbed her eyes, causing her mascara to smudge. She looked like she had been in a fight and lost. One of her false eyelashes dangled precariously from her lid. She yanked it off and held it in her right hand.

"I am announcing today that I am no longer a candidate for president of the United States," Tucker began. In spite of themselves, the reporters gasped.

"While we did enjoy significant victories in Pennsylvania and Ohio just one week ago, the losses we took in the South, coupled with our prognosis of the political climate in those states where we have yet to face our opponents in primaries, particularly in New York, lead me to only one conclusion: to continue to seek the nomination would be irresponsible. In the best interests of my party and the country, I am releasing my delegates to vote their consciences.

"I want to deeply thank the thousands of people who have worked so hard for me throughout the past twelve months and I want to thank the millions of people who voted for me in the primaries. But my duty now, as it always has been, is to my country and to the Democratic Party. To continue to seek my party's nomination would just further divide the party, and it is my conclusion that the outcome would not justify that divisiveness.

"I would like also to take this opportunity to thank the press for what I consider to be fair and objective coverage of my campaign. We have had our differences at times, but on the whole, I have no complaints. I think you did an excellent job. I will continue to serve out my term as senator from California and then we'll see how things look at that time. Thank you, ladies and gentlemen."

Dozens of reporters began shouting questions as Tucker led Jenny out of the room. His press secretary was at the microphone repeating over and over, "No questions, folks, the senator said no questions."

Jean, Nevada

The corpulent man in the light blue suit sat in the antiseptically clean room mopping his brow. There were no windows, and the air-conditioning vent in the wall near the ceiling gave no indication that anything was moving through it at all. The room was pale green, almost white, with a highly polished mahogany table in the exact center of the floor. On either side were two green plastic chairs, the kind that are usually found in high school cafeterias. There were two doors with wired glass windows that faced each other from opposite walls. One led to a long corridor off the visitors' entrance. The other led to another corridor, which in turn led to a series of locked antechambers and finally to a block of cells that were more like hotel rooms than prison cells. These rooms housed minimum-security prisoners and were isolated from the rest of the complex.

After the man had been in the room for ten minutes and had sweated through his suit, which was now dark blue under the arms and along the spine of the jacket, the door facing him opened and the prisoner was led in. The guard closed the door and stood on the other side watching the exchange through the window. Both the corpulent man and the prisoner assumed they were being overheard.

"What is it this time?" Billy Dailey asked.

"Just a few signatures," the man said, opening a briefcase. "Three signatures and then you can go."

Billy watched as the man spread out the thick documents and certificates on the table. His eyelids were heavy, and the man noticed he could hardly keep them open at times.

"They moved me, you know," Billy said, his words spaced far apart, as though he had to think of each one before saying it. "Why'd they do that?"

"We thought it would be more comfortable for you. Give you some privacy, get you away from the less savory characters in here."

"I didn't ask to be moved," he said. There was no emotion at all in his voice. "Why'd they do it?"

"I told you," the man said flatly, "so you'd be more comfortable. Here you go, son. Just sign on the lines marked with an 'X.'" The man handed Billy a pen, which the young man took and held with some uncertainty.

"What if I don't sign?" he asked, trying to focus on the man's face, which was dripping with perspiration. "What if I don't want to sign any more papers?"

"It's for your own good, Billy. It's your insurance, so to speak. I've explained this to you before. This is your family's way of making sure you're taken care of when you get out of here." He took a handkerchief from his hip pocket and mopped his forehead.

"They're giving me some different kind of medication. I want you to find out what it is and make them stop it. The other stuff was bad enough, but when they moved me, they started this new stuff. It makes me sleep all the time, and I can't remember things."

"Okay. I'll find out about it. Here, son, sign this one first."

Billy signed the paper laboriously, then shoved it toward the man. "Oh, wait," he said, grabbing the paper back. He went over the last two letters of his name again as the perspiring fat man arched his eyebrows and rolled his eyes in exasperation. "Okay," Billy said, sliding the paper toward the fat fingers waiting impatiently on the other side of the glistening tabletop.

"Now these," the man said, holding the certificates for him while he scrawled out his name.

"Atta boy," he said, gathering up the papers and putting them in his briefcase. He rose and held out his hand toward Billy, who simply raised his head and blinked at him.

"Please get them to stop this drug, okay? I don't like it. I haven't done anything to them. I don't give them any trouble. Will you ask them?"

"I'll do what I can, Billy. Good luck, son." And with that the man left.

The White House

Billings walked into the White House approximately forty-five minutes after receiving the call saying that the President wanted to see him on a matter of utmost urgency and, even though it was Sunday, could he come immediately and meet with him in the family quarters.

He racked his brain during the ride into the city. What could be so urgent that he would call him in on a Sunday? It didn't sound like anything to do with business, since they were meeting in the family quarters. Perhaps something had been discovered about the murders. Perhaps somehow Carl had slipped up and the crime had been traced to him. That would be fine with Thaddeus, except, of course, if Carl were backed into a corner, there was no telling what he might say. He might even spill the beans about the stocks he and Thaddeus had been purchasing for Claudia.

No, if anything had been uncovered about the murders, he would have been informed first. The authorities wouldn't go directly to the President with it, especially since they could only get to him through his chief of staff.

Maybe it was the stocks. Marshall might have found out about that. But how? He never bothered himself with financial matters. He didn't have the time, and since taking office, he really didn't have the interest. The last thing on earth he was concerned about was his finances — unlike his rags-to-riches wife, Thaddeus mused. He resolved to keep cool and play this scene by ear. He would just have to wait and not try to guess what was about to be sprung on him.

When he reached the elevator that led up to the second-floor living quarters, Carl Stone was waiting there. "Carl," Thaddeus said, nodding in greeting without emotion, lest the Secret Service agent standing by the elevator detect some unpleasantness between them.

"Thaddeus," Carl acknowledged. "I should have guessed you were behind this little meeting."

The agent opened the elevator doors and the two men stepped in. When the door closed and the elevator began to move slowly upward, Carl spoke again. "You want to give me a little hint as to what this is about? Have you broken down completely and confessed all to Daddy?"

Thaddeus controlled himself, but as he responded to Carl, his mind was filled with the image of emptying a revolver into Stone's midsection. "I assure you, I'm just as much in the dark as you are."

"I hope so, because everything that has gone on around here has been with your full awareness," Carl said in warning.

Billings had a sinking feeling in his stomach. He knew that Carl would stop at nothing now to save himself, even if it meant incriminating Thaddeus in Operation Thunder and the fiasco on Fire Island and God knew what else. For the very first time, Thaddeus wished he had never met Donald Marshall.

"Old buddy, old partner, old ... brother-in-law," Carl said, slapping Thaddeus on the back as the elevator door opened, revealing the bright red hallway of the President's residence. Thaddeus jerked away from Carl's hand as the two of them stepped out and were led by a butler into the living room, where the President and Claudia were waiting.

The President stood near a window. Claudia sat on the sofa, nervously wringing her hands. Marshall motioned them to sit down without speaking, then stood silently for a moment, observing them and trying to detect how nervous each man was. Billings thought it a serious mistake to hold this meeting in the family apartment. Once again, Marshall was acting on his own instincts, without Thad's advice, and his instincts once again were wrong. If he wanted to intimidate the two of them, he should have held this little soiree in the Oval Office, where his power was evident at every turn. Carl lit a cigarette without asking. He got up and took a crystal ashtray from the coffee table in front of Claudia, then sat back down and balanced it on the arm of the chair. Too much bravado, Thaddeus thought, even for Carl. He's bluffing about how calm he is.

Nothing was further from the truth. Carl was completely tranquil, even hoping for a confrontation. He had put up with these incompetents long enough and had gone unappreciated the entire time. Who did these worms think they were, anyway? If it hadn't been for his covert intelligence gathering and strong-handed tactics, Donald Marshall would be nothing more than a former Arizona governor and has-been, second-rate crooner, Claudia Marshall would be in a mental institution from worrying about being indigent in her old age, and Thaddeus Billings would be selling used cars in Prescott. Fuck all of them!

"I received a very disturbing telephone call this evening," Marshall began. He was wearing baggy pleated trousers and a white oxford-cloth shirt open at the neck. His hands were thrust deep in his pockets, and he shared his cold glare with both men equally. He ignored Claudia, who sat where he couldn't see her face. She was looking pleadingly at Carl, as if she knew he was recklessly lacking any anxiety over this encounter. Every now and then, she would look down at her lap or glance at Thaddeus and give him the thinnest smile.

"From whom?" Carl asked brusquely, flipping an ash into the ashtray. Thaddeus winced at his tone of voice. This was not going to go well no matter what it was about.

"From my son!" the President said dramatically.

Claudia and Thaddeus both closed their eyes momentarily at Marshall's booming voice. Although his immediate reaction was to seek out and punish the agent who let D.J. get to a phone, Stone didn't miss a beat. "What'd he have to say?" he asked cockily.

"A lot," Marshall answered, considering the empty chair he was standing next to, but deciding he had an advantage by standing.

"Well, let's hear it," Stone said. "Obviously it's earth-shattering, or we wouldn't all be sitting here without a drink."

"That does sound like a good idea," Claudia said, rising. "Would anyone else care for one?"

"Sit down, Claudia," Marshall said. She sat back down on the sofa and played with her skirt.

"For one thing, he tells me he doesn't think that Richard's being on Fire Island was coincidental. He thinks he was sent there by someone to watch Terry. He says I should ask the two of you."

"Well, isn't he a little talent?" Carl chided. "Maybe we ought to change his code name to Sherlock."

"I knew nothing about it," Billings said, almost shouting.

The President looked at him, trying to read his face for honesty.

"Shut up, Thaddeus," Carl snapped. "Of course Richard was sent there to watch Terry. On your instructions, Mr. President."

"On my instructions?!"

"That's right..."

"I don't understand your attitude, Carl. I'm not sure you're taking this very seriously," Marshall said, attempting without success to gain control of the exchange. It was clear to everyone present that Carl was on the upswing and was going to get nasty.

"Carl, Donald just meant—" Claudia interjected.

"Claudia, I suggest you keep completely out of this," Stone said fiercely. Claudia read between the lines and shut up.

"You told both Thaddeus and me that Terry was to be kept under wraps and out of trouble. You told each of us on separate occasions — and I quote — 'Do whatever you have to do,' and that's just what I did. Richard Billings was the perfect watchdog. He was harmless, he was reliable — when he wasn't on drugs — and he didn't mind buggering the kid once in a while either."

At this last remark, Claudia gasped. Thaddeus was still smarting from the comment about Richard and drugs. "Carl!" Marshall shouted and took a step forward.

"Save it for your fans, Mr. President. Let's call a spade a spade. Everyone here knows both your son and Terry were queer for each other, and it just so happens that Richard swung both ways. Why the big act pretending it's not so? Let's at least be frank with each other."

"I won't listen to talk like that in my own house," Marshall said.

"I pay for this house too, Mr. President. If you don't want to listen, that's your business, but I'm going to have my say. You wanted the kid muzzled and kept muzzled till after the convention. Well, there was only one way to keep that guy quiet and that's drugs and sex, so that's what we gave him and plenty of it. If he went around flashing his drug stash, that's his problem. Somebody saw it and wanted it and he didn't want to give it up and so the guy took it and bashed his skull in, to boot. That's not my fault. I'm just sorry that Richard had to walk in on them and become a victim of your 'son-in-law's' drug habits. That's something no one could have foreseen, but as we all know here at the top, you take a lot of risks getting here and even more staying here. We all pay a price — some more than others."

Carl got up and went to the bar and poured himself a straight bourbon, while the others recovered from his speech.

"That price is too high for anyone to pay," Marshall said, deciding to retreat to the chair after all. "I don't want anyone else to pay for my presidency with his life. Nothing is worth that."

"Save that for the voters," Carl said callously. Now he was the one standing. "You've clawed your way to the top over a lot more than two corpses."

The three listeners raised their eyes now in astonishment. Was this man unbalanced? Was this the man who was running the re-election campaign? This man headed the CIA for three years?

"The irony is that you've made a good president — and you're going to go on making a good president for another four years if you let me handle it. No one else will have to get hurt. I've got every base covered."

"Then why have you pulled my son's primary agent back to New York?" Marshall spoke with renewed vigor.

"What?" Thaddeus asked, incredulous. "You did what?"

Carl looked a little nervous for the first time since the conversation started.

"That's not your responsibility. His security is directly under my jurisdiction," Thaddeus said, indignant. "Why didn't I know about this?"

"You see?" Carl said, recovering. "You're so busy trying to keep things together here, you didn't even know he had been reassigned. That just proves my point: I need to handle things if they're going to go smoothly."

"I wouldn't call murder exactly smooth," Marshall said quietly.

"What's the meaning of this?" Thaddeus asked. "How dare you do such a thing. Parker is..."

"Parker is getting — how shall I put this delicately this time? — a little too friendly with D.J. It's becoming a security risk. He had to be removed."

"Carl," Claudia said, pleading with her eyes again, "is D.J. in any kind of danger?"

"No, but the campaign is. Thad thought — we all thought — it would be a good idea for D.J. to get out and hit the trail. Thought it would get his mind off Terry. Well, that backfired. He's been depressed and drunk for the entire trip. For three nights running, he has caused scenes in the hotel lobby, and two nights ago, he was found in his room with one of the boys from room service. I don't need to tell you we can't have that."

"Still, you should have told me," Thaddeus countered. "I would have handled it."

"I didn't think you should be bothered," Carl said between sips of his drink. "You have enough on your mind with APANS. This is campaign stuff. It's my territory. But you don't have to worry, it's being taken care of now."

"How is it being taken care of?" the President asked.

Thaddeus shook his head at Carl, hoping he would get the message and not go into Operation Thunder. That would be certain death with Marshall. He would simply resign as president.

"I've decided," Carl began slowly, "that in order to cinch up the last round of primaries, which includes both California and New York, we're going to go after the sympathy vote. You're neck and neck with Tucker in both states, and from all indications, he's picked up even more support since he's withdrawn. He can't get his name off the ballot now. It's too late, and all the polls predict that he's going to walk away with California and possibly even New York. We can't have that. The *New York Times* this morning talked about a 'draft Tucker' movement at the convention in spite of his dropping out. Between now and the general election, the Republicans will gin up the most godawful rumors. They'll probably have people believing you blackmailed Tucker into pulling out."

"And what is this master plan of yours?" Thaddeus asked, wishing now that he, too, had a drink.

"D.J. is about to disappear," Carl said triumphantly, as though he expected their reaction to be a round of applause. Instead, he got incredulous stares and gaping jaws.

"What!!?" Thaddeus cried. "I hope to Christ you're not planning what I think you're planning."

"I'm not planning anything at all," Carl said, refilling his glass at the bar. "The plan is being carried out even as we sit here having this friendly conversation, this little gathering of old friends in the living room."

"This is too much!" Billings said, leaping to his feet.

"No, Thad," Carl countered, shouting now, his face red with rage as he stepped over to him and shouted him back down into his chair. "It's just right, and you're never enough! You're a wimp and a coward. You've never been daring enough to take the chances that were necessary to push things over the top, to make plans actually work. You're an idea man, but you don't know how to make things happen. You're ineffectual, Thaddeus. Face it. You know how to call the plays, but you can't carry the ball."

"All right, Carl, settle down," Marshall said, getting to his feet. "I think you're overstating things here. Thaddeus has been the real brains behind my career for over ten years. If it weren't for him, APANS would—"

Thaddeus leaned forward and buried his face in his hands. He couldn't watch the President's face while he heard what he knew was coming.

"Ha! APANS! APANS?" Carl shouted at Marshall, almost hysterical. "Would you like to know about your precious APANS? Well, I'll tell you."

"Carl, no, please," Thaddeus begged, not looking up.

"After your embarrassing procrastination in moving people to lobby for it, Mr. President, it was more than evident that APANS was going down the toilet fast. So Mr. Billings and I—"

"I had nothing to do with it!" Thaddeus shouted, looking up now, his face flushed, his eyes red.

"Don't be too modest, now, brother-in-law, I'm going to give you some of the credit. Granted, it was only at my insistence that he went along with it, but nevertheless, he finally did agree—"

"He's lying!" Billings shouted, then repeated it over and over until he was no longer audible. Meanwhile, Carl went on.

"—he finally did agree to Operation Thunder."

"Operation Thunder?" Marshall repeated.

"Yes, Operation Thunder, an old CIA plan that was started up a couple years ago, but was never carried out. Yet it was never totally abandoned. It was back during one of your even weaker periods. You were about to lose your first battle over the defense budget and I, your faithful and humble servant, together with some colleagues at the CIA, put together this little plan. It was to be an attempted assassination — attempted, mind you — of the Egyptian president. Just a little scare to wake up the Congress and the American people as to how tenuous, at best, peace can be in that part of the world.

"Well, as you sometimes do, you pulled out of the nosedive. You gave a stirring State of the Union speech and Congress rallied behind you, so we put Operation Thunder on hold. Luckily for you, we didn't dismantle it altogether, because your handling of APANS was a disaster. When it became apparent to us that APANS was lost and that the communists would take over in the Middle East within months after the bill's defeat, we rekindled Operation Thunder. Unfortunately for Khousoum, he had more enemies than anyone knew, and they got to him. However, luckily for us, it turned the tide of popular opinion and brought the majority of the Senate and the House around to our side — that is, your side. APANS will pass the Senate vote next week, and the world will sleep easier."

Carl stopped talking and smiled as his audience digested the incredible tale. Claudia stared blankly at him, as though he had just removed a mask, revealing another face entirely, one she had never dreamed existed.

The President sat dumbfounded, trying to decide if this were some sort of bad joke or wild delusion. Thaddeus leaned back in his chair and sighed deeply.

"Is this true?" Marshall finally asked Billings.

"Yes," Thaddeus whispered, unable to summon his full voice. "Yes, it's true."

Marshall rose and went to the window. The Washington Monument blazed against the dark sky, like a giant white sword sticking out of the earth. Carl returned to the bar for still another whiskey.

"You realize this means I will not be able to seek re-election," Marshall said. Claudia put her hand to her forehead.

"Of course you'll seek re-election," Carl said, pouring another drink and plopping fresh ice into the glass. "You've already won re-election. No one can stop you now. You have no competition. It's yours for the taking."

"I couldn't possibly hold this office knowing what I know now. The very thought of—"

"Don't be dramatic," Carl said, raising his glass in a toast. "That's bullshit, and you know it."

"Carl! You goddamned son of a bitch. Do you realize what you've done? You have assassinated the president of one of our allies. You have stained the presidency forever," Marshall raged.

"I have prevented World War III," Carl said calmly. "I have also assured your re-election, which is for the good not only of the American people, but of the world as well, and..." He looked at Claudia. She grimaced and closed her eyes.

"...well, let's leave it at that. Tomorrow, D.J.'s light plane will be reported missing..."

Claudia's eyes popped open and her hand went to her mouth.

"Don't worry, he's safe. He's out of harm's way and someplace where he won't embarrass us before the nomination. Tuesday, you will win the primaries in California, New York, and Washington State, thus being assured of the nomination, and the following week, you will be renominated as the party's presidential candidate. You will have survived a fierce battle on Capitol Hill, and the trauma of having your son missing and feared dead, yet still you carried on business as usual, proving without a doubt to the American people and the world at large that you are one of the greatest presidents this country has ever had."

Carl downed the rest of his drink and set the glass on the bar. "Now, if you'll excuse me, I haven't had my dinner yet."

As Stone headed for the hall, the President spoke, softly, but firmly. "I want your resignation on my desk by tomorrow afternoon, and I want D.J. returned to this house by tomorrow evening."

Stone whipped around, his eyes wild, his face contorted with rage and enmity. He walked slowly toward the President, pointing at him as he spoke. "No! Now you listen to me. I made you what you are. I put you here with my dirty deals and my nasty little covert operations. I've covered your bunglings, I've done my job and Thaddeus's, too, for the past four years, and I'm not going anywhere. Neither are you. You're going to go through with this, and you're going to win. You are the President and you will be the President for another term. Your son will be missing for two weeks, and when he's found, you'll be a demigod, and three months after that, you'll be re-elected. Billings will be chief of staff, and I will return to the CIA, and everything will go back to normal. And if you think I'm kidding, then you just think again.

"No one in this country, least of all the media, is going to believe you didn't mastermind this whole chain of events. You're the President, you're the boss. The buck stops on your desk. Not only would you be disgraced, you'd probably go to prison, and more important, it would ruin this country. We could never survive an international scandal of that proportion.

"And if that isn't enough, because I know that sometimes your sense of duty to your family outweighs your common sense, think about this: your wife happens to be a major stockholder in Fairbanks Aviation, the manufacturer of APANS. The stock was purchased just before the Senate vote. So if you're ready to send yourself, your staff, and this country down the rat hole, you'd also better be ready to send your wife to prison, too. Now I suggest you all get a good night's rest and get a grip on yourselves. Somebody has to run this country while I'm out running the campaign."

Carl turned and walked out of the room, closing the door behind him, leaving the three of them alone with one another in the dreadful silence.

San Francisco

Parker called the desk and asked for his luggage to be taken to the lobby. He checked once more to make sure he hadn't forgotten anything, going back into the bathroom twice. Then he went next door to D.J.'s suite. Rodney was flopped on the sofa reading the current issue of *Self-Defense* magazine. He motioned toward the bedroom when Parker asked where D.J. was.

D.J. was just getting out of the shower. He walked out of the bathroom and found Parker standing by the door waiting to say good-bye. He wrapped his towel around himself and sat on the foot of the bed. "Is it time already?" he asked, combing his hair with his fingers.

"My plane is at 8:15."

"Who's taking you to the airport?"

"I'm taking a cab."

"That's not necessary," D.J. said. "Surely—"

"I want to," Parker interrupted, moving to a silk-covered chair near the bed and sitting down. "I prefer a clean break."

D.J. laughed and threw himself back on the bed.

"Is that so funny to you?" Parker asked, sounding confused or possibly even hurt.

"No, that's not funny. It's ironic. I had this strange long dream last night that it reminds me of. I've been debating whether or not to tell you about it." He leaned up on his elbows and looked at Parker. "Do you want to hear it?"

"Sure."

"It involves you," D.J. warned.

"Tell me."

"Somehow you and I managed to escape all this. It was as though everyone in our lives who complicates things disappeared, and you and I were asked to do nothing more than raise birds."

Parker smiled and settled back into the chair.

"We were asked to re-establish the rare and beautiful Quetzal bird of South America, which is on the verge of becoming extinct. Are you familiar with it?" D.J. asked.

Parker shook his head.

"Well, the important thing about it is its colors. It has a comb like a cockatoo and a long tail. Its feathers are brilliantly colored: iridescent blues, deep purples and scarlets, vivid yellows. At first, we were frightened, because it meant such drastic changes, living in the jungle and all, but we agreed to do it.

"We were given two mated pairs and went off to live in our thatch hut. It was very real. There were even those details that are impossible to explain, things like learning how to do things I don't really know how to do. We learned to repair the thatched roof and to fix the jeep; we pumped water from a well we had dug and found natural ways to repel insects and bugs in our garden. Mostly, though, we were happy. And I guess we ... we were in love."

Parker smiled, and there was the slightest hint of a blush on his face.

"We walked hand in hand a lot and wore little or no clothing most of the time. We worked hard and lived on fresh fruit and vegetables. I remember there was no electricity, but we didn't seem to mind.

"The birds thrived, and after a while, we had a large brood. They were very tame, but we had to keep them caged so nothing happened to them before the project was over. Finally, the experiment came to an end and it was declared a huge success. We had photographed them during the whole time we were there, and they were tremendous photos that were published everywhere. All the magazines published them, and the bird became an international symbol of hope.

"After we filed our last report and the hoopla had died down, there was nothing left but the final act we had always known we would have to perform. We woke early one morning, and you got up and performed some ritual while I watched from the bed, half-asleep. It was lovely to watch you. You were very tan and your hair had gotten long and your body was even more beautiful than it is now from all the hard work we had to do to stay alive in the jungle. I knew as I watched you that morning in the early light, moving about in and out of the shadows, that I would love you forever.

"We ate nothing and were very quiet. The air was cool and still, and as we left the hut, the birds in the trees stirred. We walked to the huge makeshift cage we had built, which encompassed nearly an entire acre, and as we approached, I saw that you had gotten up during the night while I slept and had decorated the cage with boughs and flowers and had rigged up a pulley to lift open the top. Most of the birds, who were still roosting from the night, awoke and watched as we neared them. We stood there quietly, holding hands, not sad, but moved to tears by what we had to do.

"Slowly, but unceremoniously, you hoisted the top of the cage. At first, there was no movement. You looked at me for some sign, then continued watching. Nothing happened. Then suddenly one of the wild birds on the other side of the compound broke the silence with a morning call. We were both startled and turned to look. All at once, there was the roar of wind and thousands of birds inside the cage took to the air at once. They rose like a funnel of color out of the opening and filled the sky in every direction. It was over. I turned to look at you, and you were gone, too, and it was no longer dawn but dusk, and all over the compound and on the edge of it in the trees were hundreds of thousands of fireflies twinkling. I have never seen anything so beautiful as those tiny, mysterious natural lights blinking among the trees.

"I began walking slowly back to the hut, when I noticed on the ground a single firefly lying in the dirt. He wasn't flashing on and off, but just lying there, his light fading slowly, pulsing faintly. I leaned down and gently placed him in the palm of my hand, watching the tiny golden light pulse more and more faintly until finally it stopped glowing completely. And then I wasn't there any longer either. The dream went on, but I was no longer in it. It went on for a long time, but it was just the compound: the hut with its thatched roof, the empty cage, its giant makeshift roof askew, a bucket tipped carelessly on its side near the well. There were no birds, no animals, not even any of the insects that had bitten us so incessantly. Nothing living remained in the compound. Everything had fled. And then I woke up."

When he finished, D.J. sat upright and folded his hands between his legs; the towel, having unwrapped itself, now covered barely half of one thigh. He seemed unaware of his nakedness. "That's quite a dream," Parker said.

"Do you believe in dreams?" D.J. asked.

"Believe they mean something or believe they come true?"

"Both."

"I believe they tell us something about what's going on inside us, but I don't know about dreams coming true. Dreams are just dreams," he said. The room was dark, except for the slices of pink light that cut through the partially opened copper-colored miniblinds and fell across the bed and D.J.'s naked body, painting him in horizontal stripes.

"Not in our family," D.J. said. "Dreams are serious business for Marshalls. My mother's dreams come true." He rose from the bed and walked to the window, peering out at the skyline and the choppy bay beyond the Embarcadero. The towers of the Golden Gate poked through the top of the fog bank that was rolling into the harbor. His silhouette was all Parker could see against the light coming through the blinds. His buttocks, whiter than the rest of his body, reminded Parker of their night together on the sofa in Tucson.

"My mother had a premonition about the Khousoum assassination before it occurred. Did you know that?" he asked without turning from the window.

"No, I didn't," Parker answered. "I've heard of things like that, I mean people who have that kind of power or gift."

"In many ways she's a very odd woman. She's had dreams come true before. They always have to do with some impending disaster. She dreamed her stepfather died the night before he had a massive coronary. She dreamed my father was seeing another woman once, not long after he began his second term as governor. She confronted him with it," D.J. said, turning to face Parker now and running one finger along the edge of the lamp shade on the table between him and Parker, whose eyes followed D.J.'s finger back and forth on the pleated silk shade as he spoke. "She had no evidence, no hard proof. She just went into his office, shut the door, and asked him. He was so taken aback, he admitted it."

"I had no idea," Parker said.

"Very few people know about it. I found out only long after it happened."

"I can't imagine it. They're so devoted to each other," Parker said. The lamp shade hid most of D.J. from Parker's view. He could see only his eyes over the top of the shade and his midsection and thighs below. D.J.'s genitals dangled at Parker's eye level less than a foot away. They were almost iridescent in contrast to the dark tan of his legs.

"She took it very hard. I guess it was the only time she ever acted out of character; she had an affair of her own, a brief one, but it still haunts her. I think that's why she's so totally devoted to him now, as sort of a way of expiating an infidelity she can never quite forgive herself."

"What was your father's reaction?"

"I'm not sure he ever found out. If he did know about it, I don't think he knew who it was, because the man still works for him, and I don't think he would allow that. He's too proud."

"The guy works for your father?" Parker asked. "Now?"

D.J.'s eyes peered down from over the top of the shade as he spoke the man's name. "Carl Stone. You see," D.J. continued, walking over and lying across the bed, faceup, talking now to the ceiling, "my father is really a decent man. Terry never could understand that. He only saw or felt the political side of him. My father is dedicated to old-fashioned principles. Oh, he slips up, like having that affair — he's only human — but he values loyalty and hard work and commitment and dedication more than anything. He's pretty honest, too — for a politician. But he has this really fatal flaw: he's a poor judge of character. He surrounds himself with men who will serve him blindly, or seem to, and he thinks they're his friends. Once you have my father's friendship, you have it for life. He'll stick by you no matter what, unless you really do him wrong. It's impossible for him to imagine someone betraying him. It's a huge contradiction for a politician, but I guess he's not the first. I can think of a lot of presidents who surrounded themselves with crooks and wouldn't believe it when they were exposed."

D.J. rolled over on his stomach and twisted his body a little so he could see Parker. "Make love to me, Parker."

Parker went over and sat on the bed and placed his hand on the small of D.J.'s back, rubbing him gently. "I can't.

For a lot of reasons. Mostly, because I have to leave. I'm going to miss my flight."

"Miss it, then. I want you. I don't want you to leave," D.J. confessed.

"I have no choice. There's nothing we can do about it." His dark hand came to rest on D.J.'s white butt.

"I tried to keep you here," D.J. said, turning and reaching inside Parker's jacket, where he slipped two fingers through the opening of his shirt. The feel of Parker's firm chest sent a flood of desire through D.J.'s body, and he wriggled his ass beneath Parker's hand. Parker's fingers rested against D.J.'s opening, and he wanted desperately to take him right then. He wanted to make love to him for a long time, holding back his orgasm until he could no longer stand it and then exploding inside him. He admitted in this moment what he had not allowed himself to admit for weeks. He had fallen in love with D.J. Perhaps he had been in love with him from the beginning. Maybe that's why he had felt a hostility toward Terry.

"I called my father last night," D.J. said, "and I got through. He didn't know you had been reassigned. He was concerned about me. I could hear it in his voice. He really does love me, you know. He's a good man, Parker. Like you."

D.J. reached up and pulled Parker to him and kissed him long and tenderly. Parker squeezed D.J.'s ass, then pulled D.J.'s body tightly against his own.

"Parker, I think I'm falling in love with you. Please don't leave me. I'm afraid. Please..."

"Shh," Parker said, putting his fingers to D.J.'s lips. "This is only going to make it more difficult. I have to go. But I promise I'll be back. Somehow, I'll be back. Maybe you can fix it with your father. I don't want to go, but I have to."

D.J. put his hand on Parker's cheek. "Parker, do you ... feel anything for me? Am I..."

"I think I love you, D.J.," he said, and they kissed one last time.

South San Francisco

The white laundry truck pulled off Route 101 and headed down Bayshore Boulevard just above Candlestick Park.
At Tunnel Road, it made a left and followed the dimly lit
street into the warehouse district. At Scavenger Road, a
dead-end alley leading to a row of furniture warehouses, it
turned left again and stopped at the second loading dock.
Two men in white uniforms got out and opened the back of
the truck. They brought out D.J., still unconscious from
the powerful tranquilizer Rodney had slipped into his
drink, and quickly placed him in the back of the brown Jeep
Wagoneer that sat in the dark, its quiet engine idling
smoothly. As soon as the door clicked shut, Rodney pulled
out and took Beatty Avenue back onto the freeway.

All night the vehicle moved east toward the Sierra Nevada. D.J. slept deeply, not even shifting positions. He
dreamed, but would not remember the dream when he
woke. In the dream, Parker was suspended naked above
him, held as if by invisible wires. He was shouting at D.J.,
but no sound came from his throat. His face was contorted
in frustration and fear as the wires lifted him up, away from
D.J. into a black void, his arms futilely flailing the air, his
blond hair flying as he twisted and shook his head. Then the
blackness opened, and with a deafening final scream that
caused D.J. to shake uncontrollably, he disappeared into a
blinding light that D.J. could not bear looking into.

New York City

Jessica stood in her bra and panties in front of the open
window, drinking iced coffee. Elaine, in a pair of D.J.'s
running shorts and a t-shirt of Jessica's that read, "Substan-
tial Penalty for Early Withdrawal," sat on the sofa talking
on the telephone. Someone on the street three stories below
shouted something at Jessica. She hollered back at him,
"Not even with somebody else's mouth," and looked away.

The city was unusually hot for June, and the stoops and
sidewalks all up and down the street were filled with children and their mothers, mostly Italians speaking in their
native tongue, scolding, cajoling, laughing, shaking their

heads at the latest gossip. The tree in the lot across the street seemed especially green. Jessica marveled at how it could even be alive in the humid, polluted air of Manhattan. Down at the corner, where Downing intersected Greenwich, several cars honked impatiently and someone was cursing. She looked at the pinschers' cars pulled up on the sidewalk in front of the vacant lot where the tree stood. Extra agents had arrived even before the three of them had been awakened by the call from the White House at 7:15 that morning. Two of the pinschers sat inside one of the station wagons with the air-conditioning running. The car idled noiselessly, contributing to the air it made Jessica nervous to breathe. She heard the click of the receiver and turned to Elaine. "What's the latest?"

Elaine collapsed backward against the sofa and sighed deeply. "Claudia says they're getting all their information from the press. The first reports were wrong, though. The plane didn't go down in the Sierras. They think it went down in the Coastal Range."

"Who was flying, Wrong Way Corrigan?" Jessica asked sourly. Elaine looked at her blankly. "I'm sorry, I'm not making fun, I'm just suspicious. I can't help it. I think Phil was right this morning. It's just too convenient. First Terry, then D.J., just when he was getting a little unwieldy."

Elaine sipped her cold coffee and made a face. "Here," Jessica said, taking the mug from her and going into the kitchen, "I'll give you a warmer-upper."

"I can't allow myself to believe that, Jessie. I just can't accept that anyone in his right mind would try to do something to D.J. How could they think they'd possibly get away with it? They're fighting the state police, the FBI, the Secret Service, and probably the CIA by now."

Jessica returned and handed the mug to Elaine, turning the handle toward her. "Unless," she said, raising her eyebrows for emphasis, "it was one of *them* who did it."

"Now I think we're getting a little too paranoid," Elaine protested. "How could they pull something like that without the President knowing? And why would they? No, it doesn't make sense. Claudia says they're looking into the possibility of the Libyan thing. The FBI thinks maybe that hit squad had something to do with it. They were reported to be in California, which is why they beefed up D.J.'s security. God, I hope they're wrong."

"A lot of good it did to beef up the security. They were better off when it was minimal," Jessica said, sitting on the other end of the sofa and crossing her legs lotus-style.

As they were sitting there silently, trying not to be so glum, the door opened and Phil came in carrying a large brown bag and looking excited.

"What are you doing home in the middle of the day?" Jessica asked. "I thought you were up to your ass in convention stuff."

Phil opened the bag and pulled out a Federal Express envelope. "This arrived about an hour ago at the office. It's for Elaine." He handed it to her. "It's from Rachael Billings," he said. "I opened it before I realized it was for you. I think it's really a hot item."

Elaine reached into the envelope and retrieved a small leather-bound book and a letter from Rachael. She read it aloud.

"Elaine, this was a journal that Richard was keeping when he was murdered. I won't go into how I came by it, but I think it will interest you, especially the entry on the page with the paper clip. I thought you should have it right away. The only way I knew how to get it to you was through Phil Kramer. Maybe it will help. Love and good luck, Rachael Billings."

Elaine turned to the clipped page and read the entry silently, then looked up at Jessica, who was saucer-eyed. "Jesus!" Elaine exclaimed.

"What? What is it?" Jessica asked, sitting straight up. "What does it say?"

"Richard and Billy—"

"Billy who?" Jessica interrupted.

"Billy Dailey, Rebecca's son by her first marriage, the one who's in prison. Richard and Billy were pulling a scam on Carl Stone and Thaddeus."

"What kind of scam? What are you talking about?" Jessica asked, bouncing up and down where she sat.

"About the stock," Elaine said.

"Wait a minute, Elaine," Phil said. "Start from the beginning. What stock?"

"Well, there are some things I haven't told you. They're kind of confidences. I mean, I didn't know if I should say anything yet. Rachael told me a couple things after the funeral that I've been trying to piece together, trying to figure out if they might have anything to do with what's been going on. I guess I should tell you now. Maybe together, the three of us can make some kind of sense out of it."

"What?" both Jessica and Phil said at the same time. Phil sat down on the floor next to the sofa, leaning forward in rapt attention.

"Well, Rachael told me that Claudia is a major stockholder in Fairbanks Aviation, owning stock bought through Billy Dailey."

"Jesus Christ!" Phil exclaimed. "That's a conflict of interest. At least, if she bought the stock after entering the White House and before the APANS bill."

"Well, that's the part I wasn't sure about. I don't think Rachael was quite sure either, but this makes it definite," Elaine said, holding up the diary. "According to this, Billy signed two stock purchases within the past four months, the most recent one being about a month ago. Also, according to this, there was to be one more, bigger than the other two combined, sometime last week, just before the Senate vote."

"But," Phil said, playing sleuth, "how could they prove it was signed then? Surely they would have backdated the certificates."

"That was the scam," Elaine said, holding the book up once more and gesticulating with it to make her point. "Billy signed each one with a code. Instead of making a 'y' at the end of his last name, he wrote it to look like a 'j' and dotted it, to prove it was done after he was in prison. Those three signatures are different than he has ever signed his name before."

"I'm not sure that would mean much, though," Phil mused. "They could say he was just on drugs or something when he did it and it came out sloppy."

"But," Elaine continued, "the 'j' doesn't mean he was sloppy about his name. It stands for something."

"Stands for something? What does it stand for?" Jessica asked, cocking her head like a spaniel.

"It stands for Jean," Elaine said, smiling.

"'Jean'?" Phil repeated.

"Jean," Elaine said again. "Jean, Nevada. That's where the prison is."

"Hmm," Phil reflected, "that might just work. And you say Stone and Billings were in on this stock business?"

"According to this diary," Elaine said. "Rachael didn't tell me that part. She just told me to look up Fairbanks's records and see who the major stockholders were. She said one would be Billy Dailey. I figured then that Thaddeus had something to do with it, because she was really down on him at the time she told me." Elaine almost mentioned Rachael's plans to divorce Thaddeus, but remembered that Rachael had asked her to keep it confidential, especially from the press, until she had time to file the papers.

"Well, how would this fit in with the murder or D.J.'s disappearance?" Jessica asked. "I don't see the connection."

"I'm not sure there is one," Elaine said, "but it certainly does prove that those two are capable of anything. Can you imagine being involved in a scheme like that right under the President's nose? Maybe they found out and sent someone to kill Richard and he ended up killing both of them. But that sounds too excessive. Thaddeus wouldn't kill his own son."

"Do you think Marshall is in on it?" Phil asked, ready to lay blame at the top and thinking of the scandal he might be on the verge of uncovering.

"No, I'm sure he isn't," Elaine said. "First of all, you don't know him like I do. He's really a very moral man in his own way. He might twist arms and hold things over people's heads to get them to vote his way on a bill or support his programs, but he'd never use the office for personal gain. It's a peculiar kind of ethic, but there is some sense to it. It has nothing to do with his concept of the public trust and all that crap. No, he's no Nixon, I'm sure of that."

Phil got up and fetched himself a cup of coffee from the kitchen, complaining about there still being no sugar in the apartment. "The part that doesn't make sense to me," he said, returning to the living room, "is why Claudia would do it in the first place, and second, why she would conspire with someone right there in the White House. Surely someone would get wind of it and tell Marshall."

"Claudia is deathly afraid of being poor," Elaine explained and waited to see if Phil would buy it.

"That's not reason enough to pull a deal like this on her husband and jeopardize the presidency. She has too much to lose. Why would she think she's not going to be taken care of for the rest of her life? They're a regular Ozzie and Harriet, those two." Phil returned to his spot on the floor in front of the sofa.

"Well, she did grow up in pretty rough circumstances," Jessica posited.

They both looked at Elaine, waiting for further explanation.

"All right, all right, but you have to swear yourselves to secrecy on this. If it ever got out we'd all be murdered in our sleep." She got up and went to the front door, opened it, and looked to see where the pinscher was. He was sitting in a folding chair right outside the door. He jumped up when she stuck her head out. "Everything all right?" he asked.

"Fine, fine. I thought I heard voices out here, that's all. I guess I'm just a little jumpy." She closed the door and herded her two friends into the bedroom and closed the door. The three of them sat cross-legged on the bed while Elaine revealed the terrible secret that D.J. had shared with her long before.

"Claudia Marshall and Carl Stone?" Jessica gasped. "How soiling. Do you think Marshall ever knew?"

"D.J. and I doubt it. Why would he keep Stone around if he knew?"

"Yeah," Phil agreed. "No man would be cuckolded and then keep the cuckolder on the payroll. He doesn't know."

"There's more," Elaine said nervously.

"More?" Phil exclaimed.

"The President is having an affair with Billings!" Jessica shouted.

"Shh!" Elaine warned, looking toward the closed door. "For God's sake, if you're not going to be serious..."

"I'm sorry. Go on," Jessica apologized.

"Even D.J. doesn't know about this one. Rachael told me about it at the funeral. She told me I had to know this so I could protect myself if it ever came to that. I don't know if you'll remember this or not. I was really too young to have paid much attention at the time it happened. When Marshall was governor, Claudia only had one really close friend, Fran Altman."

"She's still her only friend, isn't she?" Jessica asked. "Remember her at the inauguration? What a gauche woman. She wore a neon blue dress and was literally dripping with diamonds."

"They're best friends. They went to school together and have been like sisters ever since," Elaine continued. "Her husband, Todd—"

"The southern California land baron," Phil annotated.

"Right," Elaine said. "Not long after Marshall was elected governor for a second term, Altman was hit with a palimony suit by this blonde tart from Hollywood. It was a huge scandal. She had been carrying on with him for something like ten years, and when he tried to dump her, she took him to court. It was really nasty. She sued him for ten million dollars and brought out pictures of him in the nude and wearing all these ridiculous costumes. His wife was mortified. Well, just before the trial, old Altman up and died, leaving a bereaved widow and this screaming trollop suing his estate trying to get her hands on the money. Claudia was devastated."

"Why Claudia?" Jessica asked, sipping her coffee and finding it had gone cold again. She put the mug on the nightstand.

"Because now she didn't have anyone to play governor's wife with. Also there were a lot of shady deals that Altman had pulled off that Marshall supposedly had profited from in exchange for political favors. Marshall and his press people wouldn't allow Fran to be seen in the company of the governor's wife. They were even forbidden to talk on the telephone, in case someone was tapping the lines. His political advisors were trying to work out a strategy for getting him off the hook if things got really hot, and they wanted to keep his association with Fran at a minimum. So Claudia, unbeknownst to anyone, comes up with a brilliant idea, which she proceeds to carry out on her own."

"Brilliant and devious, I'm sure," Phil said.

"The plan was this. God," Elaine said, "I hope I'm doing the right thing. D.J. can never know this. No one can."

"Go on," Jessica urged.

"Remember," Phil added, "D.J.'s life may depend on this."

"A plan was laid to get rid of the blonde."

"You mean..." Jessica gasped.

"Will you shut up and let her finish ... darling," Phil said, glaring at Jessica.

"Claudia arranged — tenth-hand, I'm sure — for this old boyfriend of the blonde's — some wacko she had been hooked up with at one time in some sort of religious cult — to move back in with her, and a deal was struck. He was to shut her up any way he could. If it got violent, he was to turn himself in to the L.A. police. In return, he would be provided with the best lawyers money could buy. If he went to jail for any crime he might be convicted of, he would be paid one million dollars for every year he spent in prison. In California, you're eligible for parole in seven years on a murder charge. The minimum they would pay him, regardless, was five hundred thousand dollars."

Her two listeners were speechless.

"I know it's incredible, but it's true. You can look it up in the newspapers. The guy was tried and acquitted for her murder. By the time they were finished with the trial, Blondie was shown to have slept with every major politician in the western half of the country, along with several movie stars and a few foreign diplomats. She was also shown to be more than slightly kinky, and it was proven that she had tried to blackmail a couple of her johns. The boyfriend went off to the funny farm for about two years and was then released, and Mrs. Altman, in just a few short months, having been vindicated, was hooked to the arm of Claudia Marshall in almost every photograph that's been taken of her since. There was a lot of sympathy for her and a lot of plaudits for Claudia's magnanimous attitude in choosing to remain close friends with her much maligned bosom buddy."

"But wait a minute," Phil said, playing devil's advocate. "Who could Claudia possibly trust to pull this off without blackmailing her in the end?"

Elaine gave a thin smile and said, "Who do you think? Who is even more devious than she is and who was she close to at the time who might have those kind of connections?"

Phil and Jessica looked at each other and came to the same conclusion at the same moment. They said the name together: "Carl Stone." They looked back at Elaine for confirmation.

Elaine stood up, took a few steps, and turned back to face them. She spoke slowly, as she came to a conclusion of her own. "And who says he didn't decide to blackmail her after all?"

McLean, Virginia

Carl Stone went into his private study at the prearranged time and waited by the telephone. He had barely sat down when the phone rang.

"Yes?" he said into the receiver.

"Camper here," Rodney said.

"Go ahead."

"Everything went like clockwork. The kid is sleeping like a baby."

"Good," Stone said, the relief in his voice evident even to Rodney. "Let's keep this smooth. I'm still trying to believe how badly Sam bungled the island job. We're still looking for him. It looks like he may have left the country."

"Figures," Rodney said flatly. "When do you want to hear from me again?"

"Not until after the convention. Unless something unexpected happens, of course. But you're too professional for that. I should have sent you on the island errand. What a fiasco."

"I'm at a phone booth," Rodney said. "I'd better get back to the cabin before he wakes up."

"Call me on the twenty-fifth. Same time," Stone said. "And be careful."

"Roger," Rodney said, and hung up.

The White House

"You're too upset to discuss this now, Donald," Claudia said, pulling the covers up and tucking them around her waist. She was leaning against the headboard of the bed, the book she had been reading lying facedown in her lap.

"This is as calm as I've been about it in twenty-four hours," he said, pacing at the foot of the bed, his hands stuffed into the pockets of his blue silk robe, "which is why I brought it up. We have to discuss it. I want some answers, Claudia. I've gone over and over it, and I can't imagine why you did such a thing without consulting me. And keeping it a secret! It's beyond my comprehension. Putting aside the compromising position it puts me in as President, I'm more concerned about what it says about our marriage. Where is the trust? The honesty? Why, Claudia, why?"

"Donald," she began, clutching the book to her breast now as though it might shield her from his anger, "it was like an insurance policy, in case anything would ever happen."

"What could happen? We're exceptionally well off. We have the ranch, we have stocks in the blind trust, we have my pension from the presidency. It makes no sense at all. Insurance against what?"

She clutched the book tighter. "I love you, Donald. I'm sorry about it. Can't we just forget it?"

"No, damn it, we can't just forget it! Do you have any idea what will happen if the press should find out about this? I would have to resign. I should probably resign anyway. I'm the President of the United States, Claudia. I have a public trust, a public responsibility. I'm supposed to be exemplary, above reproach, for God's sake." He was gesticulating wildly now, standing at the foot of the bed and facing her.

"It's different for a man, Donald!" she shouted, startling herself a little at the sound of her voice. She continued in a more modulated tone. "A man can do what he wants, but a woman is left to her own defenses."

"What the hell are you talking about?"

"I'm talking about if something should happen," she said.

"I've got more life insurance than any reasonable man needs. If something should happen to me—"

"That's not what I mean."

He stared at her blankly for a moment and then there appeared a look of recognition, followed by exasperation. "Jesus Christ, you're not going to bring that up again. That's ancient history. One small indiscretion ten years ago, for God's sake. Can't you let it alone?"

"It wasn't ten years ago, and, no, I can't let it alone. I worry about it. I dream about it. There's no guarantee that it won't happen again. My father—"

"Your father and I are not the same man. I am not going to leave you, Claudia. I love you. I could never love another woman. My God, we've been married for thirty-four years. Be reasonable." He collapsed into an overstuffed chair near the nightstand.

"That sort of thing has nothing to do with reason. It's completely a result of biological urges. One can't always control them. Men do foolish things," she argued in defense of her fears.

"Not half as foolish as what you've done."

"I didn't know he was going to put that money into Fairbanks. I just asked him to invest it for me. It was money we could always use. It would be there for us if we ever needed it. It was a long time ago. I thought he just bought some ordinary old stock and then I forgot about it." She looked at him to see if he believed her. His eyes were closed, his head tilted back against the back of the chair. "I'm sorry, Donald. I love you more than anything. I never meant to do anything that would hurt you. You're my whole life. I live for you. Tell me what to do and I'll do it. Anything, just name it."

"I don't know," he sighed. "I'll have to think about it. I don't even know whom to ask for advice. I can't take the chance of anyone else knowing. I guess I'll have to talk to Carl. Maybe he can dispose of the stock in some way that will look like it was never yours to begin with."

"Donald, no," she blurted out. He gave her a look of scorn and incredulity. "I mean ... it's so much money, darling."

"You'll do what I say, Claudia," he said threateningly. "From now on, you're going to do exactly as I say. And there's another thing you may as well know right now." He rose and walked to her dressing table and stood silently for a moment, lightly touching the tops of several bottles and jars that stood crowded in front of the oval mirror. He turned, dug his hands deep into the pockets of his robe again, and drew himself up with a deep breath. "I'm going to refuse the nomination. The men I've chosen to help me run the country have betrayed me. They've made a mockery and a disgrace of the trust this office holds. I'm ashamed of what has happened under my leadership, and I can't allow it to continue. I cannot run again."

"Donald, you're not serious!" she exclaimed.

"I am most serious. What's more, after I'm out of office, I intend to set it all down on paper, every sordid detail, and make it public, so that the American people will know how power corrupts and how even when a man thinks he is doing the right and good thing, he is fallible and can actually lead the country to ruin."

"Donald, you can't do that," Claudia said, barely able to speak. "You simply can't."

"We'll see about that, Claudia," he said. "No man is above the law. No man is above reproach. These men can't be allowed to get away with what they have done. I will just have to bear the consequences. Next week, when they complete the first ballot I'm going to announce that I am not a candidate. That way, they will be free to choose someone else before the convention is over. To do it sooner would throw the party into complete chaos, and every viper who has any political hold over delegates would throw his hat into the ring. It would divide the party too badly. First, they must vote, and if they nominate me, I will decline and the delegates will have fulfilled their responsibilities according to the law. They will then be free to vote their consciences. It's the only way. I have no other choice."

The Sierra Nevada

D.J. sat on the porch of the cabin and watched the trees disappearing into the blackest dark of night, night as it exists only in the forest. Soon, he literally would not be able to see his hand before his face. From where he sat on the wooden steps, he could hear Rodney clinking and sloshing the dinner dishes in the sink. At first, he had believed the story Rodney told him about the Libyans being in San Francisco and how in order to protect D.J. it had been decided he should be hidden. But the more he thought about it, about the fact that only Rodney and no other agents were with him and how they didn't even have a radio in the cabin, he concluded something very clandestine was going on. He thought perhaps his father didn't even know what was happening. He fingered the washer that hung around his neck now the way it had once hung around Terry's, and renewed his determination to convince Rodney he didn't for a minute doubt his story. He had been completely cooperative since waking up less than twenty-four hours ago. Rodney, who was right now watching him from the kitchen window, hadn't let him out of his sight for an instant.

Somewhere above him, an owl hooted, and off to the side of the cabin, something stirred on the pine needle floor of the forest. He had no idea where he was or even where the nearest highway might be, but he knew that before long, he would lay a plan to escape and take his chances getting out of there. In the meantime, he would have to ingratiate himself with Rodney. Any way he could.

New York City

"I can't believe that every fucking channel is carrying nothing but these goddamned election returns," True bitched, flipping the channel selector on the television wildly.

"And, naturally, the cable would be out tonight," Jessica commented, shaking a bottle of nail polish. She was sitting in her lotus position at one end of the sofa. Phil leaned against the other end, going over files from the office.

"Are you sure you paid the cable bill?" she taunted him. "This has been going on for two days now." He ignored her.

"And so with his victories in New York and California tonight," the news commentator said as the tallies for Marshall being flashed on the screen kept increasing even as he spoke, "President Marshall will go to the New York convention with enough delegates to sew up the nomination on the first ballot."

True turned the volume off. "Well, does anyone want to play gin?" he asked the group.

"I'll play," Elaine said, closing her *Harper's Bazaar* and sitting up on the floor. They sat facing each other, playing cards and watching the silent television screen. Jessica worked on her nails while Phil read and made notes.

"Yoko Ono was right," True said, discarding the jack of diamonds, which Elaine picked up, "the television is the twentieth-century fireplace. It's much more amusing without sound. Jesus, now they're going to show clips of the President again. Between the primaries and this missing airplane business, I'm going to go nuts."

Elaine and Jessica turned their attention to the screen. Phil kept working. First, they showed the President making a statement with the First Lady weeping at his side. Then they showed some photos of D.J. and Elaine at their wedding. There was a series of still photos, then a reporter came on, then they cut to a videotape.

"I haven't seen this clip before," Jessica said.

Phil looked up. "Yeah, I saw this earlier. It's from KPIX, our affiliate in San Francisco. It's local coverage of that shindig he went to last Saturday."

"Turn it up, please, True," Elaine asked softly.

"...last photos taken of the President's son on Saturday after a reception and fund-raiser he attended at the Mark Hopkins Hotel."

The tape showed the limousine pulling up to the front of the St. Francis and Rodney, his back to the camera, opening the door. Then there was a shot of D.J. whispering in his ear and Rodney turning to look at him. The camera zoomed in to catch the looks on both faces. True cried out, "Wait a minute!" and began crawling closer to the television screen. "That's him. That's him!"

The three of them looked at True as though he had lost his mind and waited for an explanation. True leaned back on his haunches, pointing at the television screen. "That's the man from the island. That's Frank with blond hair." His voice was a monotone now as he announced his terrible news. "That's the man who killed Terry."

The White House

Marshall, Stone, Billings, and six members of the cabinet sat in the Oval Office watching Miles Cameron, who was on the telephone. He was waiting for the voice on the other end to relay information, which he in turn called out to the men in the room. Billings and one of his staff were making hash marks on clipboards as Cameron called the votes.

"Targowski, aye. Treadwell, aye. Truesdale, nay."

"Cocksucker," one of the men said. The President stared straight ahead at Cameron.

"Valencia, aye..."

"One more," Gibbons muttered, "just one more."

"White, nay. Wilson, aye...," Cameron shouted. The room broke into applause and shouts of victory. Marshall smiled and accepted congratulations, while Billings and his aide moved closer to the phone to get the few remaining votes Cameron was still calling out. When he was finished, Miles quieted the group. "Mr. President, I am happy to officially report to you that the United States Senate has just passed Senate Bill S. 1386, the proposal to sell Airborne Protection and Neutralization Systems to the Sudan." There was more applause and cheering.

Marshall thanked everyone for his help and support in the long, hard battle to make the Middle East safe from the threat of Communism, then he excused himself and went upstairs, leaving the group elated at the victory, but uneasy at the behavior he was exhibiting for the third consecutive day. No one was more uneasy about it than Carl Stone.

The White House

Claudia opened the long top desk drawer in Marshall's little study off their bedroom and slipped out the large leather-covered diary. She opened it and found the page printed "Sunday, June 12."

She smiled affectionately at the sight of his fastidious script, but her smile soon faded.

My entire presidency has been jeopardized by the men around me. I have learned this evening some startling and disappointing facts. The bottom line of it all is that I am responsible for the death of a foreign head of government and possibly the deaths of two young men, both innocent victims of an egregious and dishonorable power struggle within my own administration. It is no longer possible for me to consider accepting the nomination of my party for a second term. I will, however, have to allow the convention to convene and go to the floor with the first ballot, lest the party be completely torn asunder with the news at this late date that I will not run. That would only jeopardize the unity we have worked so very hard to build over the past five or six years and hand the

Republicans a distinct advantage in the general election.

The most disturbing news, however, is that Claudia has somehow been involved in financial dealings without my knowledge. It is ruinous enough that it violates the trust that has been placed in my hands; it is almost heart-breaking to think she would engage in something like this without my knowledge. I thought that of all the people in my life — past and present — she was the single one I could trust implicitly and unquestionably. It turns out I was wrong.

Yet I cannot be too harsh with her, and I cannot bring myself to judge her. Her lot is a difficult one, being in the spotlight as she is, having to be on camera, as it were, and never make an error. She works hard, and our lives have been completely disrupted by this office. I love her more than I have ever loved anyone and I know she would never deliberately do anything to hurt or con-tradict me. Once again, it appears as though she has been misled by one of the very men I chose to advise us. So even this, it turns out, is my fault.

I could never stop loving her. I could forgive her any-thing with the single exception of infidelity. Even though I have been unfaithful to her — only once in my life, thank God — I could never live with her infidelity to me. I know it is a double standard, and I guess it is just another piece of evidence proving that I am indeed "old-fashioned." What's good for the goose is not good for the gander in this regard.

So I must close this chapter of my life, take my lov-ing wife back to the ranch, and begin the traumatic and heartrending task of setting down for historians what shameful wrongs were perpetrated during the Marshall administration in the White House. I hope the American people and the people of the world will judge me kindly. I hope my son will forgive me for ruining his life. I will not blame any of them if they do not.

The irony is that it will probably be good for Claudia and I to go back to Arizona. I miss our life there, away from the world, alone in the desert. We will grow old together — I should say older — and spend lovely days in each other's company, simply caring for each other and living a peaceful existence. We will have no grand-children, I suppose, but we will have D.J., and, if God is kind, D.J. will want to be near us. We will be a family again. We will have peace and tranquility and love. I could do much worse than that. So long as I have Claudia I know I am taken care of. I have done my best and I have failed. I will take my leave and go live out my days among the saguaros.

She wiped a tear from where it had fallen on the page, closed the book, and replaced it in the desk. She was in bed reading by the time the President came upstairs. He un-dressed silently and got in bed, pressing close to her and wrapping his arms around her waist. "Hold on to me, mama," he said. She put her arms around him and stroked his hair. They both cried noiselessly and fell asleep in each other's arms for the first time in over two years. Claudia fell asleep vowing to herself that her husband would never find out about her "infidelity," as he put it in his diary. She could never live without him.

For the first time since living in the White House, Clau-dia went to sleep without checking the nightstand drawer.

New York City

The entire eighth floor of the Pierre Hotel was sealed off. One elevator, normally used only for service to the upper floors, was secured for use by the First Family and Secret Service agents. Entry to the elevator could be gained only by going through a ground-floor corridor and past four security checks. People were then taken to the eighth floor by an agent operating the elevator. Emergency mea-sures called for access to the elevator from the mezzanine level, where two additional agents and New York City police had secured one of the main ballroom's anterooms, should the need arise to enter or exit on that level.

Elaine had been picked up at Jessica's and driven to the hotel prior to the opening of the convention at Madison

Square Garden. She was to occupy a suite of rooms at the opposite end of the floor from the President's suite. She had just been briefed on the security procedures and was inspecting the rooms when she heard a familiar voice and turned to see Parker standing at the door to the sitting room talking to another agent. He looked at her and smiled, but kept talking. When he was finished, he walked to the bedroom door and greeted her warmly. Elaine looked like she had seen a ghost.

"Are you all right?" he asked.

"But ... I thought..." She moved to the bed and sat down.

He walked over to her. "Is something the matter?" he asked, fearing that she was ill.

"Parker, what are you doing here? I thought you were with D.J. I thought you were lost," she managed to say, feeling light-headed with confusion.

Parker stood upright, looking somewhat ashamed and feeling guilty. "No, they reassigned me the day before the accident," he said in a low voice. "I thought you knew about it."

"I had no idea. They said three men were with him in the plane and they didn't give any names for security reasons, but I assumed you and Rodney..."

"Rodney, yes. Rodney went down with him, along with two other agents they had assigned to him after they heard the Libyans might be in San Francisco, but I had received orders the night before to return to Washington the following day for reassignment."

"But why? Why after all this time would they reassign you?" she asked, dumbfounded.

"I don't question my superiors. I just carry out my orders as they're given to me."

"Parker, close the door, will you?" she asked.

He closed the door and returned to where she was sitting.

"Sit down," she said, patting the bed next to her. He looked at her anxiously. "Just sit down, will you, please?"

He sat.

"Can we talk here without being overheard?" she whispered.

Parker hesitated for a moment and Elaine rolled her eyes in exasperation. "For Christ's sake, Parker, are we bugged or not?" She was growing impatient.

He shook his head. "It's okay," he said.

"Parker, something very weird is going on," she said.

"What do you mean?" he asked.

"I mean things aren't on the up and up with all this."

"I don't understand," he said, genuinely perplexed.

Elaine studied his face trying to detect whether he might be part of the plot. He was too sincere in his confusion, she decided. Besides, she knew that D.J. had grown to trust him and that a strong bond had formed between the two of them. She also knew that D.J. was just as unerring in his judgment of people as his father was foolish.

"I have reason to believe that D.J. is being held against his will. I don't think his plane is missing at all."

Parker's face reflected his incredulity. "Elaine," he said, "I know this has been a terrible strain on you, but..."

"Parker, we've all been duped and I have strong reason to believe someone in the White House is behind it. I've come by some information that is very incriminating for certain people close to the President."

"I really don't understand what you're talking about. What do you mean, 'duped'? Incriminating for whom?"

"Parker, why weren't you on that plane with D.J.?" she asked pointedly.

"I told you, I was reassigned," he said, feeling as though he were being accused of disloyalty.

"You were reassigned after almost three years with D.J. and told to pack up and leave within twenty-four hours?"

"That's right," he said defensively.

"Doesn't that strike you as being just the least bit unusual?"

"Well, I don't understand it, but..."

"Neither do I ... unless..."

"Unless what?" he asked, trying to follow her line of thinking.

"Unless someone was planning something and wanted you out of the way."

"Why would anyone want me out of the way and what would they be planning?"

"You are the only pinscher not on a rotational duty with D.J., right?"

"That's right," he said. "I'm the 'k' agent."

"The 'k' agent?"

"The constant," he clarified. "Each First Family member has one constant, one regular agent that doesn't rotate. It's a security measure, so that at least one agent knows the nuances of the person's behavior."

"Isn't it unusual for a 'k' agent to be reassigned?" she pressed.

"Well, it's done from time to time," he said, thinking back in an unsuccessful attempt to recall other cases.

"Within twenty-four hours?" she continued.

"Well, no, that part wasn't standard procedure, but then, with the hit squad report, it may have been necessary."

"Who replaced you?" she asked.

"I ... I don't know," he confessed.

"Is that standard procedure?"

"Well, no. Usually the 'k' agent would have to orient the replacement, tell him what to watch for, give him some clues as to what to expect, what the person's habits were, that sort of thing. Otherwise, it's hard to tell when the person is acting peculiar or ... well, you get the idea."

"Yes, and you weren't asked to orient anyone. What was so urgent about you getting back to Washington?"

"I don't know. They reassigned me to the convention. In fact, now they've reassigned me to you, starting tomorrow night."

"Parker, I have proof that someone very close to the President was responsible for Terry's death," she said, exaggerating a little in hope of gaining his allegiance.

"That's preposterous," he said. Elaine sensed it was his training speaking and that the remark did not come from his heart.

"Parker, how did you find out you were being reassigned?" she asked.

"I got a phone call on Saturday evening," he said. She could see that he was beginning to waver. He was starting to consider that she might really know what she was talking about.

"Who called you?"

He paused. "I don't think I should..."

"Who was it, Parker?" she asked firmly. He just stared at her, turning things over in his mind.

"All right, let me ask you this," she continued. "Who do you take your orders from?"

"Mr. Billings. All of D.J.'s agents are responsible to him. We have been from the start."

"So it was Billings who called you?"

"No, it wasn't."

"Then it was one of Billings's staff members?"

"No..."

"Who was it, Parker? Who pulled you away from D.J. so that he could be gotten out of the way? Who was it who knew that you were too close to the President's son to allow anything potentially harmful to happen to him?" She was trying to keep her voice down, but she was extremely agitated now. Parker was wrenching inside. He didn't know if he would be violating security by telling her. He didn't know what she was up to or if she could be trusted. His impulse was to get up and leave the room, but his allegiance and now even his affection for D.J. wouldn't allow that. He looked to Elaine for sympathy, as if to say, Please stop this.

"Never mind, Parker, I'll tell you who it was. It was Carl Stone, wasn't it?"

He nodded his head. "Yes...," he said, reeling now with the possibility that his leaving may have resulted in some harm coming to D.J. "Yes, it was."

"Then I'm right. Because Carl Stone is the man who sent someone to Fire Island to muzzle Terry. Only the strongman he sent didn't do a very neat job. He muzzled him all right, by killing him. And then he had to kill an eyewitness as well."

Parker put his hands on the mattress as though to steady himself.

"Do you know who Stone sent to the island, Parker?" Elaine asked, pushing him to the limit.

"No, I don't. I don't know that he sent anybody," he said, trying to get his bearings, feeling betrayed.

"It was your partner, Parker. It was Rodney who killed Terry and Richard," she said bitterly.

"No, that's not possible. It couldn't have been Rodney. We were in Tucson when Terry was murdered."

"No, Parker," she said. "*You* were in Tucson when Terry was killed. Rodney hadn't joined us yet. Rodney arrived the day after."

"That's right," Parker said thoughtfully. "He was bringing the car. He had to wait with the car while they made the changes." Parker was staring blankly at the floor. "There must be some other explanation." He turned and looked at Elaine. "What makes you think it was Rodney? Why do you suppose it was him?"

"I don't suppose, Parker. I know."

"How? How can you possibly know?" His voice was filled with desperation. He wanted her to be wrong. If she wasn't, it meant he had been deceived and used by those he had put his faith in.

"Because there's an eyewitness. Someone saw him do it."

"Are you sure? Are you positive? This person could have made a mistake."

"No, Parker, there's no mistake. And now Rodney is someplace with D.J., and that means D.J.'s life is in danger, too."

"My God," Parker exclaimed.

Elaine put her hand on Parker's shoulder. "I'm going to need your help, Parker, and your protection. You're the only one I can trust."

"Have you told the President?" he asked.

"I can't get to him. I've tried to get through, but they won't let me talk to him. Besides, I'm not sure he'd believe me."

"What about Mrs. Marshall? Have you tried to talk with her?"

"That's not possible," Elaine said.

"Sure, it is. They'll let you talk to her. She'll be here tomorrow," he offered.

"I can't tell her," Elaine said. "I think she's being black-mailed by Stone."

"What?" This was almost more than Parker could comprehend.

"It's very complicated, but it wouldn't be wise to try to talk to her about this. That's why I'm going to need your help. You are the only person I can trust. I can trust you, can't I?"

"Of course. You know you can, but what can I do?"

"You can do two things. First, you can keep your eyes and ears open. Second, you can stick to me like glue. If Stone gets wind of my knowing anything, I'm in big trouble."

"What are you going to do?" he asked.

"I don't know yet. But if D.J. isn't found by Tuesday, the day I'm supposed to be interviewed by CBS, then I'm going to tell everything I know and let somebody else take it from there."

"I'll do anything I can, Elaine," he said, still trying to digest and believe her incredible revelations. "At any rate, I promise no harm will come to you. I'm your new 'k' agent starting tomorrow, so I'm with you round the clock."

Elaine took his hand. "I'm scared, Parker, but I've got to go through with this. I'd never forgive myself if some-thing happened to D.J. and I thought it was because I hadn't spoken up. But I have to do it at the right time and to the right people. The only way is to blow the thing wide open so they can't try to shut me up, too."

They walked to the door, Parker looking and feeling somewhat dazed. He started to open it, but Elaine put her hand on his and stopped him. "I know that this must be very difficult for you to believe," she said, looking at him with compassion. "I know how dedicated you are to your job, and learning that one of your fellow agents — someone you went through the academy with and all — might be a murderer must dash a lot of your beliefs about the service."

"Elaine," Parker said, his voice etched with surprise that she didn't already know what he was about to tell her, "Rodney isn't an agent."

"What?" she said, not comprehending.

"Rodney is CIA, not Secret Service. He came on board with Carl Stone."

New York City

The lobby of the Pierre was jammed with New York police officers, White House staff members checking into the hotel, and reporters from all over the country jockeying for position to catch the political figures who would be coming and going, making deals with White House staff, bargaining for delegate votes, and making promises they hoped they would be able to deliver on when the time came.

Bif Tucker and Jenny had just come down from the fifth floor, where Bif had been striking a bargain with two members of the Committee to Re-elect the President. He was billing himself as the great party healer, hoping, since no one knew why he had withdrawn, that he might be able to walk away with the pledge of a cabinet position in return for urging his delegates to cast their votes with Marshall on the first ballot. He was counting on Miles Cameron to cool off between now and then, and even if he didn't, Bif had no plans for Jenny to be around much longer. Her marriage to him had turned into a political liability he couldn't afford. He figured he was better off dealing with the stigma of divorce than with photos of her in the buff on the front page of some tabloid.

As the two of them made their way through the lobby, Miles Cameron emerged from the Oak Room cocktail lounge and nearly collided with them. There was a tense moment as he and Jenny did a little two-step one way and then the other, trying to get around each other. Finally, he stood aside, smiled at the two of them, and tried to make a little joke. "We really shouldn't dance in the lobby," he said.

Jenny Tucker took one step toward the door, turned on her heel, and spit in his face. The photographers' flashes went off like a Fourth of July pyrotechnical display as the couple rushed from the hotel, leaving Cameron wiping his face with a handkerchief. "I guess she had started picking out furniture already," he said to one of the reporters.

New York City

"I wish you didn't have to go in today," Jessica said, snuggling closer to Phil, her face pressed tightly against his chest.

"Mmm, me too," he said, nudging her belly with his still-erect cock.

"Has that thing grown since last week?" she teased.

"Nope. It's still nine and three-eighths delicious, tensile inches."

"Mmm, a perfect fit," she said, wriggling against it.

"Would you like to try it on one more time before I leave?" he asked, rolling over on top of her and brushing her hair aside.

She looked up into his sparkling brown eyes. "I love you very much," she said, wrapping her arms tightly around his back. He slipped inside her again and lay motionless, already on the verge of orgasm.

"I hope everything is going to be all right," she said.

"Everything will be all right, just as soon as Elaine can tell somebody what she knows. The interview is the perfect place to do it. No one will dare harm her after that, but we've got to get some hard evidence between now and Tuesday. Something we can take into court."

Jessica squirmed against Phil's groin. "Watch out," he said. "I'm close."

"Already? God, you're easy."

"It's just because you're such a voluptuous woman," he said.

"Right. The most voluptuous skin and bones in Manhattan," she said. "What if we don't get anything concrete? What if we can't prove that Stone had something to do with the missing plane?" she asked, her voice filled with worry.

"Then we have to go with True's story and with the diary. It's not much in relation to D.J.'s situation, but it may be enough to squeeze a confession out of Stone."

"Stone will never break, you know that. Elaine says he's the toughest cookie in the batch ... Ohhh...," Jessica moaned as Phil pressed deeper into her.

"Well, maybe it's grown a little," he joked, giving a quick thrust. Jessica moaned again and threw her arms back above her head. He let up, his body resting heavily on top of hers.

"But Billings might crack," he said, panting slightly. "He's under a lot of pressure now with his wife suing him for divorce and his only son a victim of all this shit. I'd lay my money on his coming clean once all the dirt is out."

"I just don't want anything to happen to Elaine ... or you or True because of all this," she said, grabbing onto the brass poles in the headboard. "God, I wish you didn't have to go to work."

"Convention time, honey. We all work round the clock for this one."

"Are you going to come in me again?" she asked, putting on her sexiest, most throaty voice and licking her lips in mock sensuality.

"I just did, kitten breath."

"You cow," she bellowed.

"You vixen," he retorted. "Let's take a shower. I think I have one load left and I promise to wait until you come first."

Alexandria, Virginia

Thaddeus sat in a plastic lawn chair on the patio, drinking a cold bottle of Stroh's. On the white metal table next to him was the Sunday *Washington Post*. The front page of the Style section carried a clip in the "Personalities" column about Rachael's filing for divorce. Next to the paper was a photo album filled with family pictures from the early years of their marriage. There were photographs of him and Rachael and Richard and their daughter, Marjorie. Some had been taken when each of the children was born. There were others of all of them on vacation, of the kids' high school graduations, of parties in the backyard of their Scottsdale home, and even one of Thaddeus standing in front of his first automobile showroom in Mesa. The last photo in the album was of Richard standing on a huge rock in Yosemite. He was holding a beer in one hand and waving with the other. Thaddeus had never seen it before. Richard must have sent it to Rachael and she inserted it without showing it to him. He probably wouldn't have had time to look at it anyway, he thought. He would have been too wrapped up in some political crisis. He got another Stroh's from the refrigerator and stood in the kitchen doorway, looking out at the garden, which was starting to look shabby with weeds. Rachael had always tended the garden, never allowing the boy who mowed the lawn and trimmed the shrubs to work in it. She considered that to be her territory, and no matter how heavily she had been drinking, she always tended her flowers fastidiously and with great affection.

Well, he thought, his lips curling in a sardonic half-smile, now your total life is a failure. First Richard, then Marjorie, then Rachael, and now the President. What a waste. He sighed and sucked on the beer, noticing that in one part of the garden the weeds were as high as the columbine. I'm tired, he thought, thinking of the gas stove in the kitchen. He couldn't do that. At least not yet. He had to see Marshall through this crisis. He may be responsible for the administration's fall, but he would stick it out to the very end and take what was coming to him. Also, he would try to protect the President from as much slander as possible, taking full responsibility for what had happened and trying to see that Carl was held accountable for Operation Thunder. Poor Marshall, he thought. He really doesn't deserve all this. Poor Richard, poor Rachael, poor everyone. What a pitiful bunch we are.

McLean, Virginia

Carl Stone made the last entry in the computer file, pressed "Enter," waited for the signal that the data had been stored and password-protected, then flicked off the terminal at his desk. He locked the top drawer, checked each of the side drawers to make certain the latch had been tripped to secure the entire desk, then made his way to the elevator that would take him down to the garage.

As he descended into the bowels of the CIA complex, he smiled with pleasure at his new strategy. Bradley would make an excellent CIA director. After all, he was Stone's protégé. He should have no trouble now convincing Marshall that Billings was not the person who should be at the helm of the White House staff. Yes, he himself was the only one left in the administration who could handle the job of White House chief of staff in the new Marshall administration. The very idea that Billings should continue in that position now was ludicrous. The man couldn't even control his own wife; how could he be expected to manage the affairs of the White House?

Imagine, he thought, allowing his wife to divorce him at a time like this. What a pathetic fool he is. Someday, when this is all over and the smoke has cleared, Marshall will thank me for what I've done.

He could see his picture on the cover of *Time* magazine. Carl Stone: the real power behind the presidency.

Jean, Nevada

Rachael Billings and Rebecca Stone stood in the stark hallway before the door to Billy's cell, listening to Donald Michaels, warden of the Nevada State Correctional Facility, explain for the fourth time that Billy wasn't feeling well and had been on some pretty strong medication. "It's nothing really serious, mind you," he said nervously to the two women, directing his comments mostly to Rachael, since Billy's mother seemed much too agitated to hear what he was saying. "It's just an infection of some sort, but the doctor didn't want to take any chances of it not clearing up completely, so he's prescribed a rather strong antibiotic and the side effects..."

"Just open the door, Warden," Rebecca said, staring at the knob where his hand lingered. "I want to see my son."

Reluctantly, Michaels opened the door, and the three of them stepped inside the small, pale green room. It was furnished with only a dresser, a chair, a toilet in the corner, and an uncomfortable-looking metal bed just large enough to accommodate one person. Billy lay on the bed in a pair of gray boxer shorts. He seemed to be unconscious, but when Rebecca pulled up the chair and sat next to him, speaking his name softly, tears running freely down her face, her son turned and opened his eyes. He tried to focus on her, but it was apparent he couldn't tell who it was. His pupils were dilated, his face ashen. He was twenty pounds thinner than the last time his mother had seen him. He gave up the futile attempt of trying to see who had sat down next to him and closed his eyes again.

"Billy, it's Mother, baby. It's Momma. Are you okay?"

He opened his eyes again, and his words came slow and garbled, but she could make them out. "Mom, is that you? Is my mother here?"

The warden was sweating profusely, his shirt beginning to darken as the perspiration soaked through. He tugged at the necktie, which now seemed to be choking him. "If you had given us some advance notice, Mrs. Stone, we could possibly have reduced the dosage a little and..."

Rebecca, now in full control of herself, her maternal instincts rising to the rescue of her only son, whipped around and stood up. With her face just inches from Michaels's, she spit the words at him: "I don't know what you're doing here, Warden, but it's obvious my son is not being cared for properly. I think it's just as obvious to anyone who knows him that my husband has had a hand in this. I don't know what the two of you are trying to pull, or why you don't want me to talk with my son, but I assure you he will be out of here within twenty-four hours. I'm not without my own resources, you know."

"Mrs. Stone, I—"

"Momma," Billy cried out, searching the room vainly to find where the voices were coming from. The three people next to the bed formed one large blur in his vision. "Please get me out of here. Please help me. Don't leave me here."

Just then an orderly dressed in white smock and trousers appeared at the door with a syringe. The warden's face contorted with rage. "That won't be necessary, Trevitt," he said through clenched teeth, furious that the order he had given upon the women's arrival had not reached this man.

"Keep away from my son, young man, or you could find yourself in this place for a long, long time, and not as an employee." It was now clear to Michaels that this woman was not going to be railroaded or dismissed. "I will use your telephone now, Warden," Rebecca announced.

The White House

Claudia looked up over the raised lid of the suitcase as the President entered their bedroom. "I've packed everything but the clothes you'll wear tomorrow. Do you want that red silk tie to go with the navy suit you're going to wear Tuesday night, or do you prefer the blue-and-silver stripe?"

"Either one will be fine. What do you think?" Marshall asked, setting a cordovan leather shaving kit down on the bed beside the suitcase.

"I think the stripe is more formal, Donald," she offered, "especially considering..." She looked up at him, a sad smile on her face.

"I appreciate your understanding, Claudia," he said, taking her into his arms.

"I'm the one who's grateful," she said, hugging him.

"You realize, don't you, that I have to do this?" he asked, holding her back almost at arm's length and looking into her eyes.

"Yes, Donald, I only wish I weren't the reason for it. That breaks my heart so. I've only wanted to be strong for you, to be an asset, an ally..." She began to cry, and he held her close again.

"Hush. You aren't at all the reason. If the stock were all I had to worry about, I'd brush it off in a second. I'm sorry I was so cross with you. I do understand why you did it. No, it's not the stock at all, it's all the other shameful acts those two have been perpetrating." He walked around her and sat on the edge of the bed, running his hand through his hair, which had grown noticeably more gray in the past few months.

"The assassination is unforgivable," he said sadly. "And if Carl is responsible for the deaths of those two young men, well..."

She sat next to him and took his hand. "I understand, dear, but please don't torture yourself anymore. None of it was your fault, and you're doing the most honorable thing you can do to compensate."

"I just can't believe this is really happening," he said, looking up as though some divine aid might be found flooding through the ceiling. "I just don't believe that my most trusted associates could have done this without consulting me. It's unfathomable. And now," he said, looking at her and squeezing her hand, "D.J.'s life may be in danger, too. I will never forgive myself, Claudia, never, if some harm should come to our son."

"Oh, Donald..." She wept in spite of herself. He held her close.

"Once I have refused the nomination, Carl has no reason to hold D.J. There will be no point and at least he will be safe. If for no other reason, I must do it for his sake. If anything happens to him, Claudia," he said, taking her by the shoulders and looking deep into her eyes, fear and anger boiling over in him, "I will kill Carl Stone."

"Donald!" she admonished. "Don't say such a thing."

"I swear to you I will kill him."

They embraced, Claudia realizing for the first time exactly how tormented her husband was over D.J.'s being held captive. She patted his head comfortingly, her eyes fixed on the little nightstand beside the bed.

The Sierra Nevada

D.J. lay on the rustic sofa watching Rodney move about in the kitchen. He was trying his best to be domestic for the two of them, but it was not coming easily. Now he was looking frustratedly into a skillet of burned butter, the smoke billowing up into his face and escaping through the small window above the sink. He held a trout in one hand, the skillet in the other. "Tell you what," D.J. said, getting up, "I'll cook dinner if you'll do the dishes."

"That's a deal," Rodney said with enthusiasm. He set the skillet down and laid the fish back in the sink. "I never was any good at this kitchen stuff," he said, moving aside and wiping his hands on the dishtowel that was looped through the handle of the refrigerator. He watched D.J. wipe out the frying pan and melt some more butter in it, adding just a few drops of peanut oil to keep it from burning. Rodney shook his head as he moved into the living room with the silverware. After he set the table, he settled down on one end of the sofa with a magazine.

"You know something, Rodney," D.J. said from the far end of the cabin, where he was dusting the fish with flour, "I could easily stay here for the next four years."

Rodney grunted his agreement.

"I'm serious," D.J. continued. "Things are so much more sensible here. Even you and I have been getting along better."

"Well, I have to admit that's true," Rodney conceded.

D.J. came into the living room and handed Rodney a beer. "Let's celebrate with a brew," he said, raising his own beer can in a toast.

"I really shouldn't with my medication...," Rodney said.

"Oh, c'mon," D.J. urged, "one can of beer isn't going to hurt you. By the way, isn't it time for your pill? Sit still, I'll get it."

He went to one of the cupboards above the kitchen counter and retrieved a pill from a large prescription bottle. "Here," he said, returning with the medication. Rodney swallowed the capsule with a swig of beer.

"That's more like it," D.J. said. "Here's to us and the mountains ... wherever we are." He clinked cans with Rodney and they both drank.

"I told you where we are," Rodney said, going back to his magazine.

"Somewhere in the Sierras isn't exactly telling me where we are, Rodney."

"Somewhere in the Sierras is close enough," he said, turning the page. He was engrossed in a detailed account of the hunting and shooting of a Kodiak bear, never noticing the three Valiums that D.J. had dropped into his beer.

From his bed next to the window, D.J. could see moonlight glancing off the metal wind chimes on the porch, yet it seemed, when he raised himself up to look out, that no moonlight fell on the ground. The trees kept the forest as dark as a closet. He turned and looked at Rodney, who was lying perfectly still on the twin bed in front of the open door that led to the living room. Rodney had blocked the door with his bed so that D.J. couldn't leave the room without waking him — or so he thought. Now, however, D.J. wasn't worried about Rodney waking up. The drugs he had slipped him had seemingly done their job well, although not as quickly as he had imagined they would.

After dinner, Rodney washed the dishes and the two of them sat in the living room reading. D.J. soon began yawning and saying he was tired. He asked if Rodney minded if he went to bed and Rodney, always suspicious, said that it was all right with him and that he thought he might turn in early, too. By the time Rodney had moved the bed in front of the door and stripped to his shorts, he could hardly keep his eyes open. D.J. pretended to have already dozed off, and Rodney lay reading for a few minutes, then dropped off to sleep himself. D.J. waited for over an hour, watching to see if Rodney stirred at all. He moved a couple times and then slept in the same position for almost an hour. When D.J. thought it was safe, he made his move.

He dressed quietly, putting on Levi's, work boots, and two flannel shirts to protect himself against the cold mountain air. Then he went to Rodney's bed and proceeded to slide under it and out the door on the other side, which had been left open to let the heat from the fireplace warm the bedroom.

For over thirty minutes, D.J. searched for the keys to the Jeep, but it was no use. He had never been able to find where Rodney put them after they arrived. He would just have to do this on foot.

He went to the kitchen cabinet and retrieved a bottle opener, then slowly, carefully, opened the front door of the cabin and stole into the night, pausing only long enough to press the bottle opener's pointed end into the air valve of the Jeep's right rear tire until all the air was out of it.

For a long while, he followed the road, but then he began to fear that Rodney would somehow sense his absence, wake up, and follow him, so he moved off the road, trying to keep parallel with it, but hidden by the darkness among the trees. The forest was a mass of yellow and Jeffrey pines and red fir, and he had to move slowly to keep from walking into them. Several times, he bumped his shoulder against the large trees, and once, he walked smack into a giant evergreen, striking his head and cutting himself so that blood ran down the right side of his face, blinding him in one eye temporarily. He moved more slowly, straining to see what lay in front of him and hoping he was keeping alongside the road. Every once in a while, he moved several yards to his right to make sure the road was still there.

He walked along in this fashion, worrying about how much distance he was putting between him and the cabin and checking for the road less and less as he tried to make better time. At one point, he came to a meadow. There before him lay a large natural pasture filled with moonlight, the dirt road he had been following nowhere to be found. He backtracked several yards, a quarter mile, a half mile before he found where the road had veered off. He was losing precious time. He decided to stay on the road and walk quickly, listening for the sound of a motor behind him so he could jump into the darkness should Rodney come after him. He walked for three hours before the sound came. Somewhere behind him, probably half a mile or so, an engine roared angrily down the trail. D.J. jumped off the road and ran for about twenty yards, until he was sure he couldn't be seen. He hid behind a fallen pine tree and waited for the headlights to illuminate the road.

The vehicle came around a curve slowly, then picked up speed. He could hear the gears shift as it approached. He lifted his head just as the headlights were even with him and watched in desperation as a light-colored pickup sped into the night. By the time he scrambled to the road waving his arms, the truck was gone. He trudged on, his heart pounding wildly.

The air was thin and cold, colder than he had imagined. We must be up at least five or six thousand feet, maybe higher, he thought, buttoning the collar of his outer shirt and thrusting his hands as far into his Levi's as he could force them. He wished he had a cap. He tried to concentrate on the smells around him: the fresh pine scent of the sap that oozed from the trees, the smell of the decaying needles on the ground. If he thought about those things, perhaps the disorienting darkness and the eerie sounds of animals moving about among the trees would seem less ominous. He wished he had a gun.

When he reached what appeared to be a state-maintained road, he calculated it to be about five a.m. The trees prevented him from seeing any unmistakable signs of sunrise, but he thought the ground was growing lighter, more visible. The sky looked more purple than black. Soon, he thought, the sun will be up and I will be able to see where I am. And so will Rodney.

He couldn't tell which way the road led down the mountain, so he took a guess and turned right. Soon, he found himself climbing a slight incline. He considered turning around, but that was too dangerous. Even if it were leading him up the mountain, there might be a ranger station or a lodge or store of some kind on the road. He continued, trying to walk faster and now feeling himself perspiring beneath the two layers of flannel.

By the time the sun was fully up, he had to remove one of the shirts. He thought of tossing it away, but then decided that Rodney might somehow come across it or, worse, that if by nightfall he hadn't come upon anyone yet, he would need it to keep warm. For two hours he walked along the side of the road, not once seeing or hearing any sign of another human being. Then, out of nowhere, a huge logging truck came barreling down the hill behind him. He turned and waved his arms frantically, stepping out into the road to block the truck's passage. But the driver sounded his horn and kept coming, down the hill and up again, the chrome horns atop the cab blasting, lights blinking, until it was clear that he would run D.J. over rather than lose his momentum for the climb up the next grade. D.J. threw himself onto the grassy shoulder, rolling over twice and tearing his left leg open on the sharp limbs of a dead fir tree lying a few feet from the pavement. He watched the truck climb and disappear over the crest of the hill, red flags fluttering in the wind from the ends of the giant trees protruding from the truck's flat bed.

He looked down at his torn jeans. Blood was beginning to soak through. It wasn't a deep cut, but it stung badly. He got up and continued walking, limping and cursing the truck driver. He felt like crying, but knew if he allowed himself that luxury, it would drain too much of what little energy he had left. He was beginning to feel the fatigue of having not slept, his limbs growing sore, his joints aching. A large bird circled in the sky overhead. Was it a hawk or an eagle? Or was it a vulture, waiting for him to drop?

He made it to the top of the hill and felt his eyes flood with tears at what he saw. There, about three hundred feet on the other side, was a small roadside stop with a trash barrel, a wooden billboard protected by what appeared to be a glass case, perhaps with a map in it, and, most important, a telephone.

He ran, stumbling, falling twice, until he reached the phone. He picked up the receiver, then let it drop as he went around to inspect the front of the bulletin board. The glass was broken, and whatever map had been there was gone. The only thing left was a sun-bleached poster of Smokey the Bear, pointing a menacing finger at D.J. and warning him to "Crush them dead."

He looked all around for some sign of where he might be. About a hundred yards up the road, he saw a sign. He ran along the shoulder until he could make out the numbers on it: 108. He went back to the phone, his leg throbbing now and bleeding profusely again. He dialed "0" and waited, but nothing happened. He hung up and tried again, reading the card on the phone while he waited for the sound of ringing on the other end. As he read, his heart sank. It was an old phone that required a dime before ringing through to the operator. He searched his pockets, knowing he had no money at all. He banged the receiver against the hook furiously, then collapsed on the ground, sobbing and rocking back and forth on his knees. It was useless. He was doomed. He fell forward, pounding the earth in anger, and, as he opened his eyes, saw dangling before him on the silver chain the tiny washer that Terry had taken from their bed in France. It was just about the size of a dime.

He ripped it from around his neck and removed it from the chain, holding his breath as he dropped it into the coin slot. It fell into the phone. Silence. He banged his fist against the coin box and a second later heard the dull drone of the dial tone. He laughed aloud. "Terry, Terry, Terry...," he chanted. "My God, you're saving my life, little one."

He didn't even try to explain to the operator what was happening or who he was. He knew he would sound like a madman and was taking no chances that she would dismiss him and disconnect. He placed a long-distance call to Phil's office, charging the call to his phone in New York as evidence later that it was really him, for very few people knew that unlisted number. As luck would have it, Phil was not in yet, but was on his way and expected shortly. He tried to leave the number of the pay phone, but when he looked on the dial there was no number written on the white card beneath the plastic insert. Besides, he knew he couldn't just stand there in the open now waiting for the phone to ring. Soon, Rodney would wake up and come looking for him like a groggy bear. "Please give him this message. Do you have a pencil?"

"Yes, go ahead," the female voice on the other end said, somewhat annoyed.

"Tell him D.J. called…"

"B.J.?"

"No, D.J. 'D' as in dog, 'J' as in Jack."

"I got the 'J,'" the woman said sarcastically.

"I'm calling from a pay phone on Route 108 somewhere in the Sierras, I think. No, just say from a pay phone on Route 108. I'm not exactly sure where it is. Got that?"

"Yes, Route 108. I'll give him the message as soon as he arrives."

"It's very urgent," D.J. said, now unsure whether this person on the other end would really deliver a message from someone who wasn't quite sure where he was.

"Yes, well, I'll tell him."

"Do you know who this is?" D.J. asked, trying to impress upon her now just how urgent it actually was. He didn't want to take any chances that the message didn't get delivered to Phil.

"No, sir, I'm sure I don't," the woman answered, patronizing D.J. as though he were some crank with a "hot tip" for the network.

"This is D.J. Marshall," he said.

"Who?" she answered, now aware that perhaps she should recognize the name.

"D.J. Marshall," D.J. repeated. "This is the President's son. I'm—" He felt a powerful blow at the crown of his skull, and the next thing he was conscious of was being dragged into the bushes, his feet scraping pine needles, manzanita bushes reaching out their spindly arms to catch at his face and shoulders.

There had been no sign of the Jeep or any other vehicle, and he hadn't heard anything before he was struck down. He dropped now with a dull thud against a rough-barked tree. He heard Rodney's voice before he saw him towering above, his face red with rage, his eyes bloodshot and menacing.

D.J. began to black out, falling over onto the earth. The smell of pine was pungent and sweet. He liked it and gave himself up to it, sinking deeper and deeper into unconsciousness, smiling at the clean scent of sap.

New York City

"All right," said Fred DeLeach, vice president in charge of network news, "let's summarize what we've said and agreed to here, so it is clearly understood and documented for the record." He looked around at the three network lawyers to make sure he had their attention in case he misstated anything. Each man had been taking notes, whispering to his colleagues, and making legal points during the conversation, which had occupied the previous hour and a half. One of the men nodded at DeLeach, indicating he could proceed at any time.

Phil watched nervously as the secretary turned to a fresh page on her steno pad. DeLeach continued. "First, Phil Kramer states that the diary we have been given and which we now have in our possession is one kept by Richard Billings, son of Thaddeus Billings, the current White House chief of staff. In it is written an entry which claims that stock in Fairbanks Aviation has been purchased on more than one occasion within the past six to twelve months for Claudia Marshall, wife of the President of the United States, through Carl Stone, former head of the CIA and present chairman of the Committee to Re-elect the President, and Thaddeus Billings, in the name of Billy Dailey, stepson of Carl Stone.

"Billy Dailey has signed the legal documents of those sales in such a way as to identify the approximate time and place when those stocks were purchased, thereby verifying that they were purchased immediately before, during, and after the awarding of a contract to Fairbanks Aviation to build new APANS aircraft to replace those being sold to the Sudan as a direct result of a bill introduced into the Congress by the Marshall administration.

"Second, that an eyewitness will give a sworn statement within the next twenty-four hours that he saw both Terry Guidi and Richard Billings murdered in a house on Fire Island, New York, and that the murderer is a member of the Secret Service team assigned to guard Donald Marshall, Jr., the President's son.

"And, finally, that at approximately 10:35 a.m. Eastern Daylight Time, a call was received by Betty Neal of the

CBS news department, in which a man claiming to be Donald Marshall, Jr., left what he described as an urgent message for Phil Kramer of the news department, stating that he was on Route 108, which we now believe to be a state road somewhere in the Sierra Nevada of eastern California.

"The cumulative effect of these facts is that it is believed that the President's son is being held against his will and that his life may be in danger. Is that complete?" he asked, looking again at the row of lawyers. They all nodded in agreement.

"Phil," DeLeach said, turning to him, "is there anything we've left out?"

"No, sir, I don't believe so," Phil said, wiping his damp palms on his trousers.

"Very well, let's continue, then," DeLeach said, pouring himself a tumbler of orange juice from a crystal pitcher on the conference table and lighting a cigarette. "As arranged with the White House several weeks ago, and agreed to by CBS management, Phil Kramer, along with Barbara Jackson, is to interview Elaine Marshall, wife of Donald Marshall, Jr., at the Democratic national convention in New York City on Tuesday, June 22, the evening of the acceptance speech by the President, assuming he is nominated by the convention on the first ballot.

"It is to be clearly understood that none of the aforementioned topics will be discussed in any manner if corroboration of the President's son's whereabouts and verification of his being in a life-threatening situation is not received and accepted as fact by myself or the president of the network. This last point is crucial and irrevocable, is that understood?" he asked, looking now at both Phil and co-anchor Barbara Jackson. They nodded.

DeLeach went on. "I am authorizing a team of reporters and a camera crew to fly in a network jet to California this evening, where they will be joined by members of our affiliate in San Francisco, and sent into the Sierra Nevada to search for the President's son. They will be joined by members of the California Highway Patrol and the FBI..."

At this point, Phil lurched forward in his seat. "But...," he exclaimed.

"I'm sorry Phil, but we cannot withhold this kind of information from the authorities without opening ourselves to serious legal problems," one of the lawyers said, toying with a pipe he had been smoking. "Surely you know that."

"But you don't know who to trust," Phil protested. "What if..."

"I hardly think," DeLeach broke in, "that once we have a camera crew and news team on the scene, anyone is going to be able to hide anything, let alone harm anyone. It will be perfectly safe, I assure you."

Phil sank back in his chair, as DeLeach continued. "Once we have located the President's son — if indeed we do locate him — word will be transmitted immediately back to news central here in New York and relayed to Barbara and Phil, authorizing them to conduct the interview according to what we discover. If the young man is not found by airtime, the interview will cover the topics already approved by the White House. If he is discovered and he indeed has been held against his will, then we will allow the interview to cover anything the young woman has to say regarding anything at all she might know about the topics mentioned here previously."

"Including the stock sale?" Barbara Jackson asked.

"Including the stock sale," DeLeach answered.

"Including the fact that he and Terry Guidi were homosexual lovers?" she asked.

"Yes, including their personal relationship. Being gay does not give anyone the right to kill you, Miss Jackson," DeLeach said, smiling sarcastically. "If it did, and all gay people were murdered tonight, we wouldn't have enough people around here to see to it that your nightly news broadcast got on the air." DeLeach surveyed the rest of the group. "Is there anything I've left out? No? Very well, then, let's all get back to work." He stood and gathered up some notes as the others filed out of the room.

"Mr. DeLeach?" Phil said, once the others had left. The corporate vice president turned from his desk. "Yes, Phil?"

"I would very much like to go to California."

"I don't think that's necessary, Phil. We have plenty of qualified staff to handle this. Besides, we've agreed to let you interview the Marshall girl..."

"I would rather let Barbara do it and go to California to look for D.J.," he said.

"I know he's a friend of yours, but in a situation like this, the fewer people..."

"Mr. DeLeach, it's not just that D.J. and I are friends. When Terry Guidi was on the island and his life was in danger, he placed a call to me, asking me to contact D.J. for him because he knew he was in trouble. I attributed it to drugs or drinking and never made that call. Now, after D.J.'s call to me, I have to go. I have to do something to make up for my inaction the first time. Besides, I'm not asking to be on camera, or even file the story. I just want to help look for him, to be there if and when they find him."

DeLeach studied Phil's face for a moment, then walked around his desk and sat in the huge black leather-and-chrome chair. "Very well, Phil. I'll see to it that you're on board that plane."

"Thank you, Mr. DeLeach. I'll never forget this," Phil said.

"Phil," DeLeach called as Phil was about to close the door.

"Yes?" Phil answered, sticking his head back inside the sumptuous penthouse office.

"You will also be authorized to file the wire story and to appear on the syndicated tape. I can't let you on camera for the network report. Network politics, you understand. Contracts and all that. But I'll see that you're involved in the heart of this one."

A chill went through Phil's body and he could feel the goose bumps forming on his arms. "Thank you, sir. You won't be sorry. I won't let you down."

"I'm sure you won't," he said, reaching for his telephone. "You'd better pack, you've got a plane to catch in less than two hours."

New York City

Elaine's stomach had been in knots since Phil told her about the message from D.J., but this evening, it was even worse. The family had been gathered together in the presidential suite on the eighth floor watching the delegates cast their first ballots. Marshall had won easily, but a sizeable number of delegates had refused to abandon Bif Tucker. The entire Oregon delegation and most of Massachusetts voted for him, as did small pockets of delegates in most of the eastern and western states, but by the time the entire convention had voted, it wasn't even close.

Elaine, the Marshalls, Fran Altman, and Billings had been served a light supper in the Marshalls' suite and sat around sipping cocktails and commenting on the voting. The President and Claudia appeared distracted during most of the balloting, sitting together on the large sofa the entire time. Twice, Elaine had noticed Claudia staring at her husband as he fixed his gaze on the television screen, his face blank, as though he were looking right through it. Billings spent most of his time making notes and tallying votes as they were cast.

White House staff members came and went in the suite of rooms, and campaign workers reported on information they were receiving from their floor captains back across the hall, where they were all plotting votes and trends and still working delegates by telephone. The President seemed to participate only marginally in what was going on, and even Billings didn't seem as enthusiastic as Elaine thought he should be at a moment like this.

Several times, Elaine caught a glimpse of Parker milling about in the hall, checking credentials of people coming in from the outside or leaning against the wall talking to fellow pinschers. Their eyes met once, and he gave a nervous, tenuous smile and nodded. She knew he was weighted down with the knowledge that she was watching and waiting for someone to make a wrong move or say the wrong thing, hoping someone would give away the fact of being aware of D.J.'s situation. That never happened.

Shortly after the balloting was over, the President and Claudia excused themselves for the evening, saying they were tired and that he had more work to do on his speech for the following evening. The room cleared, staff members packing up their folders and notes and going across the hall to celebrate and unwind and find out where the parties were going to be held. Parker and Elaine walked down the hall toward her suite at the other end of the floor.

"I've been trying to get your attention all night," Elaine said as they approached her door.

"And I've been trying to avoid you. They don't like it when there's a lot of personal conversation between us," Parker said. He unlocked her door and went in ahead to secure the suite. When he had checked each room, he announced it was okay, but she had already plopped herself on the sofa.

"Phil got a call from D.J.," she said.

"He's been found?" Parker exclaimed, after closing the door. His face reflected the relief he was feeling as a result of Elaine's news. It furrowed again just as quickly with her answer.

"No, that's just it. He called from somewhere in the Sierras, trying to tell Phil where he was, but Phil wasn't there yet and evidently he was afraid to say too much. He just gave a general location and then hung up or was cut off. The woman who took the message wasn't exactly sure. At the time, she didn't realize who she was speaking to."

"Is he all right?" Parker asked, stepping closer to Elaine.

"Well, he was all right enough to call, but that doesn't tell us much, I'm afraid. He's obviously in trouble or he would have either called the police to pick him up or called back by now to talk to me. I'm worried."

She explained the arrangement with the television network and how she would have to wait for a report from Phil before they would let her tell her story. Parker told her that he had nothing to report from his end.

"What if you don't hear from Phil?" he asked. "What then?"

"Then I give them the 'obedient Mrs. Marshall' interview that the White House has planned. They won't let me say anything on the air without some sort of concrete proof."

"Well, I can understand that," Parker said. "What do we do between now and tomorrow evening?"

"We wait," Elaine said. "We keep our wits about us and wait — and if you know how to pray, you can do some of that, too. I have a bad feeling about how all of this is going to turn out, Parker. I'm scared."

"What time are you supposed to be interviewed?"

"Tomorrow evening we all drive to the Garden for the President's acceptance speech. They take us into that room..."

"Right, the holding room behind where the stage is set up."

"Yes, then you and I take the elevator up to the top of the Garden and walk around to the anchor booth while the President waits for his introduction to the convention. After he finishes his speech, I go on live with the interview."

"You know which elevator it is, don't you?" Parker asked.

"No, I thought I'd just follow you," Elaine said, taking off her shoes and putting her feet up.

"Okay. It's a real secure area, so we shouldn't have any problems getting out of there and up to the top floor. You'd better get a good night's sleep. We're going to need all our strength tomorrow." He smiled and said good night.

Elaine fell asleep on the sofa and slept fitfully until ten the next morning, waking every few minutes to find herself alone in the dark hotel suite with nothing changed and feeling danger everywhere.

Sonora Pass, California

Route 108 begins at Oakdale in Stanislaus County and winds up the Sierras through the Stanislaus National Forest and the Emigrant Basin Wilderness, over the crest of the mountains just north of Yosemite, and ends at Devil's Gate, a treacherous stretch of wilderness penetrated only by the

single highway that links Reno, Nevada, and the southern
portion of the Sierras to the more populated regions of
California. Phil and the search party had covered the
stretch of highway from Oakdale to the Sonora Pass, stopping at every gas station, country store, lodge, and telephone booth, asking questions, but trying to be as discreet
as possible, lest they tip off whoever it was who was holding
D.J. captive.

After meeting with the state highway patrol and a rep-
resentative from the governor's office at sunrise, it had been
decided that only seven people would form the party itself,
while scores of backup men would follow. They would try
to pass themselves off as a group of campers and hikers
looking for the most remote place to explore. They traveled
in two campers, the television equipment stored in the back
beneath blankets and sleeping bags.

The group consisted of Phil, two cameramen from
KPIX in San Francisco, two women reporters — one of
whom was the local anchor person for the San Francisco
affiliate — and two highway patrolmen. They started out
from San Francisco early in the morning and began stopping and inquiring of people just outside Oakdale. One of
the women reporters had suggested they not bother looking west of Knight's Ferry, since there really wasn't any
mountainous terrain on that part of the highway, but the
troopers said they should be as thorough as possible right
from the start to eliminate any unnecessary backtracking.
It had taken them longer than they expected to get up the
mountain, as they found more places to stop than they had
anticipated.

Every time they found a side road, the group would
follow it, checking out any cabins or camps. Phil was attempting to be as discreet as possible, trying not to appear
as though they were looking for someone, but by nightfall,
he had changed his mind about their tactics and suggested
to one of the highway patrolmen that perhaps they should
just begin asking people if they had seen two men. The
patrolman confided to Phil that less than an hour behind
them was a full-fledged search party of police and federal

agents combing the area with dogs and photos of D.J. and Rodney, making certain that they didn't slip out once the news crew had passed through. Also, on the other side of Devil's Gate was another party of state police working their way up from the south. They would meet at Devil's Gate where Highway 108 intersected with Interstate 396.

That night Phil crawled into his sleeping bag more assured, but unable to sleep. So far there hadn't been even a trace of D.J. and Rodney, and they had only a few miles left to cover in the morning between Sonora Pass and Devil's Gate. What if they were already gone? What if Rodney had found D.J. at the phone booth or caught up with him later and taken him someplace else? Or perhaps D.J. had panicked and gone deeper into the forest and was lost in the wilderness. A lone man inexperienced in wilderness survival, without the proper supplies and equipment, couldn't survive long in this terrain.

He thought of Elaine waiting in New York for some word about D.J. He pictured her tossing and turning in her bed the way he was thrashing about in his, waiting out the night, hoping the dawn would bring answers to their terrible questions. He missed Jessica now more than he remembered ever missing her in the past. He wished she were with him and thought of their lovemaking just a day earlier. He longed to feel her body beneath his, her lips kissing his shoulder and the back of his neck as, wound about each other, they drifted into a secure sleep. He pulled the sleeping bag up over his head to escape the penetrating cold of the mountain air at almost ten thousand feet. *Please, D.J.*, he prayed, *stick in there. Wherever you are, whatever you're going through, hang on for just a few more hours.*

New York City

Elaine had just poured her first cup of coffee and opened the *New York Times* when the phone rang, causing her to freeze momentarily and stare at the receiver. She had waited anxiously for it to ring all day the day before, hoping it would be Phil with some word about D.J., but now she was afraid. For the first time since Phil had left, she realized that the message coming over the wires could actually be one she didn't want to hear. She set down her cup and grabbed the receiver.

"Yes?" she answered with no emotion in her voice.

"Elaine?"

Elaine relaxed. The voice on the other end belonged to a woman.

"Yes, this is Elaine."

"Elaine, this is Rachael Billings. Can you call me back?"

"Call you back?" she asked.

"Yes, from another phone. Is that possible?"

"Yes, I suppose."

"Please do," she said and gave a number. She said she would be waiting.

Elaine dressed, not bothering to finish her coffee, and went to the lobby, Parker on her heels, along with two other pinschers. Much to the agents' consternation, she went directly to the women's lounge, where she could have privacy, and returned the call.

"Thank you," Rachael said. "I'm sorry to inconvenience you this way, but I have something to tell you and I don't trust those phones in your room for a second. Are you sure this phone is secure?"

"No, frankly, I'm not sure any of the phones are secure, but it's the best I can do at present. They're not going to let me out of the hotel without a full escort, especially to make a phone call. I think we can talk. What is it?"

"You told me in Syosset at Richard's funeral that you'd get to the bottom of all this even if you had to do it alone. Well, how would you like some help?"

"Help? What kind of help?" Elaine asked, trying to shift mental and emotional gears now from the predicament D.J. was in to Terry's murder.

"My sister and I will help you in any way we can, Elaine," Rachael said.

"I appreciate that, Mrs. Billings, but I don't see how..."

"Between the two of us, we have some very incriminating information. We have just come from seeing my nephew in the Nevada state prison and what we found there was not very pretty. Also, it turns out that Rebecca has some documents that could be useful to you."

"What kind of documents?" Elaine asked, looking around to make sure no one was within earshot. Only a couple of delegates' wives were primping at a mirror across the room.

"Well, I can't go into it now, but they have to do with that Mideast business I told you about."

"That would probably be very helpful, all right," Elaine said.

"Yes, we think so too," Rachael said bitterly.

"Are these papers in a safe place?" Elaine asked, worried that if their conversation was tapped, Rachael's life might be in danger.

"Don't worry, honey, not only are they in a safe place, but there are so many copies of them now, if anything happens to either one of us, there's no way they could be kept secret for long."

"And your sister is willing to come forward with all of this?" Elaine asked, incredulous.

"Yes, she is willing and anxious. We've both been pushed beyond our limits with all of this and feel it's our duty to help you. I would be lying if I said there wasn't some tinge of vengeance as well. They have to be stopped. It's really as simple as that. They've hurt too many people."

"I agree," Elaine said, thinking now of D.J., as well as Terry and Richard.

"You know," Rachael said, "what you're doing is very brave — and dangerous. You realize that, don't you?"

"I have to do it. Now D.J. is also involved. I guess you know all about that."

"Yes, we heard. You're a good woman, Elaine. I respect you deeply. We both do. I'd better let you go now."

"Thank you, Mrs. Billings. You'll be hearing from me," Elaine said.

"My prayers are with you, darling. Oh, and one last thing. If something should happen to me or to the both of us, you must contact an attorney in Los Angeles. His name is Paggioli, Steven Paggioli. He will give you what you need. God bless you, dear, and ... good luck."

Elaine sat for a few moments after hanging up, reeling with the implications of the phone call she had just concluded. This was getting completely out of hand. If anyone found out what was going on now, she would be dead meat.

Parker was waiting right outside the entrance to the women's lounge when she emerged. "Are you all right?" he asked. "What the hell is going on? What were you doing in there?"

"Parker, how long do we have until the interview?" she asked, looking suspiciously at the two pinschers who were standing several feet away, watching the crowd in the lobby.

"About eight hours, why?" he answered.

"Don't let me out of your sight, do you understand? Not for a second."

"Don't worry, I'm not about to," he reassured her.

"Parker?" she said, grasping his arm.

"What?"

"Is your gun loaded?"

"Well, of course it is. What good would it be to me if it weren't? What the hell is going on?"

"We have to be extremely careful now, Parker. This thing is getting bigger by the minute. I'm scared."

"Frankly, you're beginning to frighten *me* a little," he said.

"I trust you, Parker," she said. "I trust you because D.J. trusts you."

"Don't worry, we'll make it."

"We just have to get into that booth tonight and we're home free," she said.

"You leave that to me," he said, and smiled reassuringly. "And don't worry, they're going to find D.J."

"I hope so, Parker. God, do I hope so."

Devil's Gate, California

The hounds were barking and crying insanely as the men tried to restrain them, pulling back on their leads so tightly that some of the dogs were choking. Already, there was a chill in the late-afternoon air. Phil folded his arms, tucking his hands into his armpits to warm them as he watched the man dig. First there was a hand, bloodlessly white, almost blue in the dark shadows of the pines, its fingers stiff and slightly curled. The index finger pointed toward the sky, as though to direct their attention somewhere other than to what they were about to uncover.

The men dug now with their hands so as not to damage the body. Slowly, handful by handful, the loose earth came away, revealing the blue jeans, the plaid flannel shirt, and finally the pale, expressionless face, its blue lips and closed eyes caked with dirt. "It's him," one of the men said, turning to the highway patrol officials who had arrived on the scene just a few moments earlier. The Tuolumne County coroner pronounced him dead and the county sheriff turned to Phil. "You're the only one here who knew him personally," he said. "Can you positively identify the body?"

Phil nodded his head.

"This is Donald Marshall, Jr., then?"

"Yes," Phil said. He walked back to one of the trucks and sat on its front bumper. The sun was just below the tops of the trees, bathing the road and the hillside in a golden light. He sighed, but he did not cry. That, he knew, would come later, in private, once he had the leisure to think about what had happened.

One of the cameramen handed him a pint of whiskey. Phil stared at it and took a swig. The booze burned in his mouth and warmed him inside as he swallowed it. "Do you have a dime?" he asked. The man dug in his pocket and handed him the coin. "Are you going to file the wire story?" the man with the dime asked Phil, who was on his feet again.

"No, not yet. I have a call to make first," he answered, walking slowly toward the same phone that he knew D.J. had used to place his last call trying to reach Phil, trying to get help — just as Terry had done.

New York City

There were four holding rooms, or VIP lounges, set up just below the stage where the President and Mrs. Marshall would greet the convention. These rooms were used to apply makeup and as a place for those going onstage to group and prepare for their entrances. Elaine had arrived at eight o'clock sharp, as planned, and was already in full makeup by the time the President and Claudia came in at twenty past eight. The convention proceedings were behind schedule, and those who were to appear onstage with the President and First Lady were waiting in the largest of the four rooms, congratulating one another and finishing last-minute cocktails, "bolsterers" Carl Stone called them, laughing with the bartender. Billings sat solemnly on a sofa, watching the group, trying to psych himself up for what should have been a glorious moment in his career. But he knew Marshall was disturbed, and it galled him to see Carl Stone now joking and carrying on with high-ranking party officials and key senators, who had been invited to be present on the platform when Marshall gave his acceptance speech.

The President came out of the room where he had been having his makeup applied and greeted the assembled group of men, receiving their congratulations and good wishes. He smiled and thanked each of them, but Billings could see the troubled look in his eyes. Across the room, waiting for the call that they were ready for her in the CBS anchor booth, Elaine stood next to Parker, holding a cocktail that she hadn't touched. Parker's eyes never stopped darting around the room, like those of a leopard waiting to pounce as soon as someone made a false move.

The door to the second makeup room opened and a woman in a white smock came out, looked around for a moment, then went up to Carl Stone and whispered in his ear. He nodded and disappeared into the room where Claudia was waiting.

"All right, gentlemen," a woman with a headset announced, "take your places, we're just about ready. Mr. Billings, you stand here," she said, motioning for Thaddeus to come forward and get in place. "Mr. President, you and Mrs. Marshall will be last, followed by two Secret Service agents."

Inside the makeup booth, Carl Stone bent down and kissed Claudia on the cheek. "Congratulations," he said. "It's clear sailing from here on out."

"Carl, I want to know where D.J. is," Claudia said, feeling soiled on her cheek where Carl had kissed her.

"He's perfectly safe, Claudia, I told you. He's comfortable and having a good time." He took a sip from his glass and smiled at her.

"You said he would be able to come back once the nomination was won. Are you going to keep your word?" Her hands were clasped in her lap. She was wearing a pink tailored suit and white blouse that buttoned at the neck. A long double strand of pearls rested against her breast.

"I've always kept my word to you, haven't I?" he asked, trying to sound hurt that she would doubt him.

"Then he's on his way back here now?"

"I thought we'd talk about that tomorrow," he said. "When we're all a little more rested."

"Carl, are you letting D.J. come back, or aren't you?" she snapped.

"I said we would discuss it tomorrow, Claudia," Stone said and headed for the door.

"You're not going to be in a very good bargaining position tomorrow, Carl, if you're thinking of keeping D.J. where he is any longer. I want to know where he is, and I want to know now," Claudia said fiercely, all her maternal instincts rising to the fore.

Carl turned, a mean look in his eyes. "I'm not bargaining at all, Claudia. I'm calling the shots, remember? It may be wiser to keep your son where he is for a while. We're getting a lot of good press from that brainstorm of mine."

"Your days of calling the shots are about to come to an end, Carl."

"Oh, are they?" he said, curling his lip in a snarl.

"Yes, they are. In just about ten minutes, as a matter of fact, when Donald climbs up on that platform and refuses the nomination. So you might as well tell me now where my son is."

"What are you saying?" Stone spit, moving to Claudia and lifting her to her feet by her arms. She looked into his face with great satisfaction at having been the one to snatch his power away. She hated him more than she had ever hated anyone in her life.

"Donald is refusing the nomination, Carl. He's not going to run for president, and you're not going to have a job tomorrow morning."

"We'll see about that," Stone said, heading for the door again.

"There's nothing you can do about it, Carl," Claudia shouted. "Nothing!"

"Oh, isn't there? Does he know all our little secrets, my dear?" Carl asked, the words grinding out of his mouth. "Does he know how instrumental you were in the Altman case? Does he know just how close you and I have been in the past?"

Claudia's body shook with fear. Carl had hit upon the one and only indiscretion that would turn Donald away from her. She remembered vividly the fastidious penmanship of his words in the diary. "Carl," she began to plead, then decided to call his bluff. "Yes, he knows everything, and it doesn't matter. He loves me, and he knows what he has to do. You can't stop him now, no matter what you say."

"Well, then," he said as the door opened from the outside, "I have nothing to lose by trying."

"We're ready for you now, Mrs. Marshall," the woman with the headset announced. "The party has already started up the steps to the stage. Mr. Stone, you have to hurry." She ushered Carl out of the room to the stairs. Claudia, feeling light-headed, steadied herself by grabbing on to the dressing table, then picked up her small white clutch and went through the door. She was swept up in a wave of emotion that she hadn't felt since she was a child. She felt completely alone, abandoned.

She looked around the room, which was a hive of activity now, people moving in every direction, convention marshalls herding people to and fro. Donald was waiting at the end of a long line of men slowly ascending the stairs.

Near the door, Elaine was talking on the telephone, Parker standing by her side. Claudia started toward her husband. She had taken only a few steps when she felt someone grab her arm. She turned to find Elaine, whose face was distorted as though she were in pain, tears flowing down her cheeks. "They've found D.J.," she said to Claudia.

"What?" Claudia said. "They've found D.J.? Oh, thank God," she said, feeling a tremendous burden lifting. She moved to embrace Elaine, but Elaine held her back.

"They found him in the Sierras. In a shallow grave. Those sons of bitches killed him. They killed him! Be sure the President mentions that in his acceptance speech."

Parker grabbed her before she could get any more worked up, and the two of them disappeared into the elevator that would take them to the top of Madison Square Garden. The next thing Claudia was aware of was the President pulling her along up the stairs, asking, "Are you all right, honey? Are you sick? Is anything the matter?"

The elevator doors opened, and there to meet them was Jessica. Coming toward them up the long catwalk that overlooked the Garden floor were two huge men in slacks and sport coats. Parker could detect the guns bulging in their jackets and stepped in front of Elaine. He looked quickly around and saw that there was no place to run. He would have to take his chances and shoot it out with these two thugs if he couldn't take them down with karate. They stopped a few steps away and one of them looked past Parker to where Elaine and Jessica stood holding on to each other.

"Mrs. Marshall?" he inquired.

"Yes," Elaine answered nervously.

"Come with us, please, they're waiting for you in the anchor booth."

All three of them breathed a sigh of relief as the two network security men turned and led the way to the glass-enclosed booth high above the convention floor. They stepped inside, surprised to find it much smaller than it appears on television, and Barbara Jackson came around from where she was stretching during a commercial break to greet them. She shook Elaine's hand. "It's a real honor for me to meet you," she said. "I'm terribly sorry it has to be under these circumstances. We've just spoken to Phil Kramer, and on behalf of everyone at the network, I want to express our deepest sympathy. You are an incredibly brave woman."

Jackson was a tall, slender woman with dark, closely cropped hair. She wore a navy suit with a light blue cotton blouse open at the neck. She gestured Parker to a folding chair, which had been placed off to the side of the main camera and out of the way. "Elaine, you'll sit next to me behind the console. We have about two minutes before we're back on."

The two women took their places, Barbara Jackson placing the wireless receiver in her ear and smoothing her jacket. "The network has decided to preempt the President's speech with this interview. We're afraid that the news has already leaked to local stations in California, and we want to get on the air before any of them do. I hope you understand."

"I understand," Elaine said nervously. "I'm not sure exactly what I'm going to say, though."

"Just let me do the lead-in and then tell your story any way you like. I'll interrupt with questions if I think you need help. I'm going to start by announcing that D.J.'s body has been found in the Sierras and that a full report from our reporter on the scene in California will follow this broadcast. They're almost ready with it in San Francisco."

Elaine put her hand to her forehead, feeling the tears starting up again.

"Mrs. Marshall," Jackson said, gripping her forearm, "you must get hold of yourself. Remember, you're doing this not only for the country, but for your husband, as well."

Elaine brushed the tears aside, and a makeup man moved in immediately to powder her face. She was feeling more and more numb. She took a deep breath and let it out slowly. Barbara Jackson sighed deeply. There was a moment of silence.

"One minute, Ms. Jackson," a technician announced.

Down on the convention floor, the assembled delegates were celebrating wildly. Thousands of balloons had been released just moments earlier, as the President and First Lady appeared onstage, surrounded by the formal entourage of party and political dignitaries. A hundred-piece marching band was snaking through the crowd playing "Stars and Stripes Forever," and the President was waving warmly at the crowd and reticently receiving handshakes and pats on the back from the fellow politicians surrounding him. Claudia stood a few feet away, a smile that looked more like a grin fixed on her lips. She was staring at a bouquet of two dozen red roses that someone had placed in her arms as she reached the top step of the platform.

Carl Stone made his way through the men around him and took the President by his arm, turning him so he could speak into his ear. He said something, and the President leaned back and looked Stone in the eye, then looked around to where Fran Altman stood applauding near the back of the stage. Stone leaned forward again to speak into the President's ear. Claudia, the grin still on her lips, her eyes glazed, fumbled with her little white bag beneath the bouquet of roses as she stepped across the stage and forced herself between the two men, shoving her husband so hard that he fell backward a couple steps. Then she leaned forward as though she might be about to kiss Carl Stone on the cheek or perhaps whisper something to him. Below them on the crowded floor, placards danced amid the delegates and the band blared out "Hail to the Chief."

"Three ... two ... one," the technician said and pointed to Barbara Jackson, cueing her. They were now on live and nationwide.

"Ladies and gentlemen, this is Barbara Jackson back at Madison Square Garden in New York City. CBS News has just received word that Donald Marshall, Jr., President Marshall's son, who was reported missing in a freak airplane accident last week, has been found dead in the Sierra Nevada in eastern California. His body was discovered late this afternoon in a shallow grave near Devil's Gate, just

north of Yosemite National Park. We have with us in the
anchor booth Mrs. Donald Marshall, who has a most terri-
fying and incredible story to tell. Mrs. Marshall..."

Elaine stared into the huge color camera, the lens re-
flecting a distorted image of her face. She spoke haltingly.
"Within the past month, three innocent young men have
been murdered. My husband was one of them..."

Behind Elaine, and several stories below her, the delegates continued to whoop and shout as the band, now
immobilized by the press of bodies jammed onto the convention floor, blasted out "Happy Days Are Here Again."
Up on the platform, only the President heard the four loud
cracks above the cacophonous music. It took him a moment
to realize what they were, and then he saw Carl Stone
slumping to the floor, a large red stain spreading across the
front of his shirt. Claudia turned, the grin now seemingly
permanent on her lips, and waved broadly at the convention, blowing kisses to the balconies, as even louder waves
of cheering greeted her back.